Kissing the Sky

OTHER TITLES BY LISA PATTON

Rush

Southern as a Second Language

Yankee Doodle Dixie

Whistlin' Dixie in a Nor'easter

Kissing the Sky

a novel

LISA PATTON

LAKE UNION
PUBLISHING

Published by Lake Union Publishing, Seattle

www.apub.com

EU product safety contact:
Amazon Media EU S. à r.l.
38, avenue John F. Kennedy, L-1855 Luxembourg
amazonpublishing-gpsr@amazon.com

ISBN-13: 9781662535376 (paperback)
ISBN-13: 9781662537776 (hardcover)
ISBN-13: 9781662535383 (digital)

Cover illustration and design by Jarrod Taylor

Printed in the United States of America

First edition

For Holly, in whom grace abounds

I'm going on down to Yasgur's farm
I'm going to join in a rock 'n' roll band
I'm going to camp out on the land
I'm going to try an' get my soul free
—Joni Mitchell

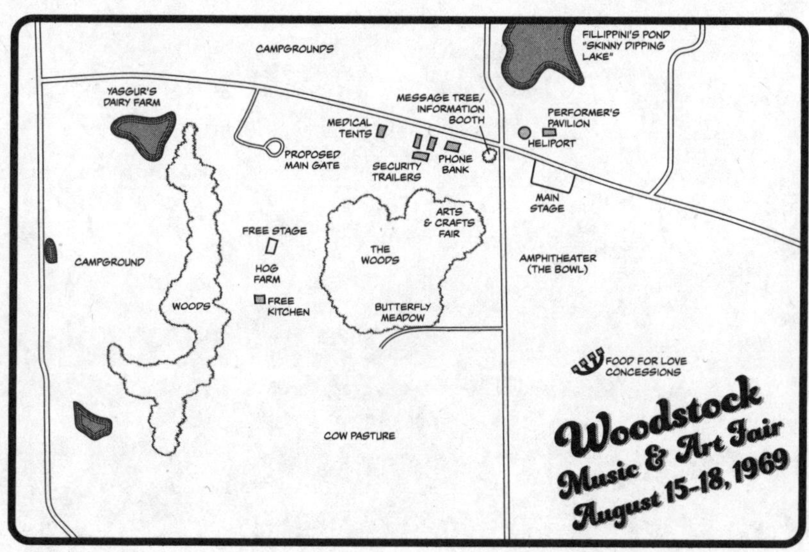
CAMPGROUNDS
FILLIPPINI'S POND "SKINNY DIPPING LAKE"
YASGUR'S DAIRY FARM
MESSAGE TREE/ INFORMATION BOOTH
PERFORMER'S PAVILION
MEDICAL TENTS
HELIPORT
PROPOSED MAIN GATE
SECURITY TRAILERS
PHONE BANK
MAIN STAGE
ARTS & CRAFTS FAIR
FREE STAGE
THE WOODS
CAMPGROUND
AMPHITHEATER (THE BOWL)
HOG FARM
WOODS
FREE KITCHEN
BUTTERFLY MEADOW
FOOD FOR LOVE CONCESSIONS
COW PASTURE
Woodstock
Music & Art Fair
August 15-18, 1969

Woodstock 50th Anniversary Celebration

Bethel, New York

Thursday Morning, August 15, 2019

They say if you remember Woodstock, you weren't really there. That may have been true for all the thousands of drugged-out hippies in attendance, but not for me. I spent all four days at Yasgur's dairy farm and can still remember almost every detail.

My eighteen-year-old granddaughter is sifting through a bowl of vintage buttons in the gift shop. She picks one up and reads the slogan out loud. "'Make love, not war.' Did John Lennon say that?"

I hear her question, but my gaze has shifted to a replica of the Message Tree. Fifty years ago, it bordered the information booth, the place where thousands of lonely Woodstockers gathered in hopes of finding their lost companions. The sight of it now causes the hair on the back of my neck to rise. Far too many anguished moments spent at that booth.

Adelaide tugs on my sleeve. "*Hello.* Earth to Grammy. Was it John Lennon?"

I whirl around to find her pinning the button on her T-shirt. "I don't think so," I say. "But John and Yoko certainly did their part. You've heard about their bed-ins, haven't you?"

"Duh. They wanted to promote world peace. I know everything about the Beatles, thanks to you." She tosses me an airy smile, then pays for her button.

"I'm glad I could pass something worthwhile along to you, my love." With a tap on her cute little nose, I smile back.

"Stop. I got your voice, didn't I? I'd have never gotten into NYU if it weren't for you."

"That's not true. You did that all on your own. Your voice is richer than mine ever will be."

She dismisses my comment with a slight shake of her head, then hooks an arm through mine as we stroll through the Bethel Woods Center for the Arts museum, gazing at memorabilia. Adelaide loves all things Woodstock. She's watched all the documentaries and read countless books and internet articles. The 50th anniversary has prompted her to dig deeper.

The second we stepped out of my '66 Mustang an hour ago, I entered a time capsule. I could feel the mud squishing between my toes, smell the musky scent of marijuana, and breathe the stench of cow pies. I saw the nudies, heard the magic of Crosby, Stills, Nash & Young; Janis Joplin; Sly Stone; Joe Cocker; the Who; and the one and only Jimi Hendrix.

Our tour of the festival grounds starts at one. Later we'll come back for the museum party at six, followed by an Arlo Guthrie concert in the new Bethel Woods amphitheater. He's one of the Woodstock originals who'll be performing throughout the weekend. It's the kickoff to the 50th anniversary weekend, where hundreds of festival attendees have come with their children and grandchildren. The official anniversary concert in Watkins Glen, New York, was canceled a few weeks ago for a plethora of reasons. I'm not sorry at all. This low-key celebration on the original grounds is much more my speed.

I've been looking forward to my time with Adelaide for months, hoping to snag the chance to impart a little grandmotherly wisdom. We've always been close. I tell her things I'd never tell her father. Why that is, I don't know. Perhaps it's because the pressure to succeed as a parent isn't there. Or, if I'm being honest, maybe I'm hoping she'll learn more from my mistakes than from my accomplishments.

I catch sight of a life-size poster hanging on the wall. It's Country Joe McDonald, clad in his army green Vietnam uniform, wearing sunglasses and a bandanna tied around his forehead. I can still hear him singing his protest song, "I-Feel-Like-I'm-Fixin'-to-Die," and, just like it did fifty years ago, my blood freezes. Anytime I'm reminded of Vietnam, my brother's face sears a hole in my heart. He spent far too long on the front line . . . because of me.

An aerial photograph showcasing the half a million people who were here in '69 catches Adelaide's eye. As does the one next to it with five naked guys in a canoe. Darting her eyes between the two, she nudges my elbow. "When you decided to come here, did you ever think it would become this massive legendary event?"

"Heck no. I had no clue what I was getting myself into." Even at twenty years old, I was as pure as a baby lamb, a virtue that embarrassed me from the moment I left home.

"What did your dorky parents say when you told them you were going?"

"I never told my parents, darling."

Adelaide's eyes grow wide in disbelief.

I pat her on the shoulder. "They wouldn't have allowed it."

She knits her eyebrows. "You were already eighteen."

"In those days, you weren't considered a legal adult until you turned twenty-one. Your parents still had the right to decide everything for you. How you spent your time, where you lived, how late you stayed out."

The sound of her gasp makes me laugh.

"I'd hate that," she says.

"I did hate it. Like I've told you, your great-grandfather was impossible."

"So where did you say you were going?"

I hesitate just long enough for her to suck in another deep breath.

"OMG, Grammy. You snuck out!"

Bobbing my head from side to side, I give her a wry grin. "You could say that."

Her smile explodes. "You were a badass!"

"I guess maybe I was," I say, flashing back to the heinous confrontation I'd had with Dad.

Adelaide whirls around, steps in front of me. "Details. I need details. Starting with how you snuck away."

I lean in, pressing my cheek against hers. "It's a long story, with twists that turn into plenty of agonizing knots."

She checks her phone for the time. "We've got an hour and a half till our tour. Is that long enough?"

"Not even close." I chuckle, then guide her toward the psychedelic-painted school bus in the middle of the museum. Fifty years ago, I would have killed for a peek inside.

"You can't leave out one single detail. I want to know it all."

I'm sure she does want to know it all; there's quite a bit I want to tell her. But there's even more I'll have to keep to myself.

Fifty Years Earlier

On the Road to Woodstock

Somewhere in West Virginia

Friday, August 15, 1969
6:00 a.m.

My bare feet rested on the dash. The wind blew the hair around my face. And our road trip was getting long. "Ugh," I moaned, leaning my head back. "How many more hours do we have left?"

"An hour less than last time you asked me. Jeez. You sound like a little kid," my no-longer-ex-best friend said, using her middle finger to flick her cigarette out the window. "Look at the map."

Never in my wildest dreams could I have imagined Livy Foster and I parting ways. She was the sun, and I a planet desperate for her warmth. But Dad forbade me to ever see her again. She'd embraced the free love movement with gusto, Jesus was not her Lord, and Dad believed I'd end up just like her. He was dead wrong. I never wanted to be just like her; I simply longed for her beauty. And her confidence. And her ability to have any boy she wanted.

We had been friends again only three weeks and had already fallen back into our old patterns. She could say jump, and I'd ask how high.

That may have been because she was nine months older and inherently cooler, but I'd idolized her for as long as I could remember. She'd taught me everything I needed to know about becoming a woman, and I felt older whenever she was near.

Livy had betrayed me, *twice*, both times crushing me to the bone. Even still, having her back in my life was almost as good as having the Beatles back. Dad had banished them too.

I reached for the *Sgt. Pepper's* eight-track, shoved it inside the player, and turned up the volume. So loud there's no way we could have heard a siren. I sang the whole chorus of "Lucy in the Sky with Diamonds" at the top of my lungs.

"That's a reference to LSD," Livy shouted.

With haste, I reached over and turned off the music. "What did you just say?"

"I said 'Lucy in the Sky with Diamonds' is about LSD."

I sat up straight, shooting her an incredulous stare. "Do you think the Beatles do that?"

"Drop acid? Of course they do that."

I nearly passed out. The thought of my Beatles doing *LSD* made me choke on my own breath. As I sat with the awareness, shame crawled up my sternum. It was yet another reminder of my sheltered upbringing. I wished I could take my question back.

Livy brushed back the hair flying around her face. "They aren't the only ones singing about it. Jimi Hendrix wrote 'Purple Haze' about LSD. Guarantee you there'll be tons of it at the festival."

As ridiculous as it sounds, the idea of drugs had never crossed my mind when I'd decided to go with her to Woodstock.

She stole a quick glance at my face. "Uh-oh. Does acid scare you?"

I swallowed. "Kind of."

"Does pot scare you?"

I didn't want her to think of me as an even bigger Goody Two-shoes, so I didn't *quite* admit it. "Does it scare you?"

"Not a bit."

"Have you tried pot?" I asked hesitantly, afraid to learn the truth.

Livy answered with a simple nod, then smiled like a child digging into her trick or treat bag.

Without realizing it, I gnawed on my thumbnail, pondering the revelation that Livy smoked dope. "What does it feel like . . . when you're high?"

"It depends. On your mood. Sometimes it makes you laugh. Other times it makes you mellow. Every now and then it can make you paranoid, like somebody's out to get ya." She grabbed me by the arm, made a scary face.

I gaped at her. "That doesn't sound fun at all."

"Relax." She patted my knee. "It doesn't happen that often. Bob Dylan got the Beatles into grass."

"No surprise there," I said in a mocking tone. Everybody knew Bob Dylan smoked grass.

"You'd *love* it, Suzannah. You feel so damn good. So uninhibited, so *alive*! When it makes you laugh, it's the most fun you'll ever have. You have to grip your stomach with all your might because you cannot stop laughing."

"That does sound fun," I said, warming *slightly* to the idea. I gave her a sidelong glance. "You haven't done LSD, have you?"

"No. But I'm not saying it's out of the question." She tried to tuck another lock of loose hair behind her ear, but the wind wouldn't let her. "My boyfriend has. He says it's euphoria. And it makes you think you can . . . I don't know . . . you might think you're Michelangelo and can paint another Sistine Chapel."

This surprised me. It's not like I'd ever thought about what happens while using LSD, but as cool as that sounded, I'd never do anything that stupid. It was a drug. A powerful drug.

"He says it makes you grasp the deeper meaning of life." She poked my knee. "You might even see God."

"That's a *lie*."

"That's what he says."

I'd set her boyfriend straight if he ever tried telling me that. "What does *LSD* stand for?" I asked.

"No clue." Livy paused. "I'm sure Ronny's doing it. To cope with what he's seen in Vietnam."

The thought of my only brother "dropping acid" in Vietnam freaked me out. "No way. He'd never do drugs."

Livy shrugged. "Lots of soldiers do it. They've gotta get the images out of their head somehow."

That wave of panic I often got when thinking about causing Ron's enlistment erupted like a geyser. My heart pounded against my chest. My palms dampened. I felt dizzy. Nauseous. With a lock of hair coiled around my index finger, I tugged at my scalp, whispering, "I had no idea."

Livy shifted in her seat, then glanced over at me. "I'm not trying to be mean. But it seems like you've been living under a rock since the last time I saw you."

Instead of answering, I stared out the window. Fields, cows, barns, and billboards flew by while I pondered a response. She was right. I had been living under a rock. And I'd been forced to bury my singing dream underneath it with me. Part of me wanted to scream *How would you know, Livy Foster? You didn't even call me for three years.*

But I did not want to get into a fight this early in our epic escapade.

Three Weeks Earlier

Goldsmith's Department Store

Memphis, Tennessee

Friday, July 25, 1969

"Just make it through the summer. You can do it. It's only three months of hell."

Chanting my mantra over and over, I drove ten miles over the speed limit toward work. Union Avenue was my best route—it had three lanes going east—so I wove in and out of traffic like a madwoman, keeping my eye out for cops. I'd overslept. Stayed up till three in the morning savoring my new library book. *The Godfather* was the most titillating novel I'd ever read. It lived under my mattress whenever I left the house. No possible way I could take a chance on my parents finding it.

As usual, the mantra quickly dissolved into a rumination on why I hated my life. Why I wanted to scream *Get me out of here!* at the top of my lungs, ten times a day. I had just completed my sophomore year of college, yet my austere, old-as-Methuselah dad still believed he had the right to manage my every move.

With a glance at the Hole of Horror in my Mustang's dashboard, I yelled, "You were right, Ron! Our father is a *royal* asshole!"

Not only was Dad a Korean War army colonel, but he used every rigid core tenet from our church as our family's guidebook. No drinking. No smoking. No cussing. No dice. No premarital sex. But the worst church statutes for me were no rock and roll—especially the Beatles—and no dancing.

Music nourished my soul. It kept me breathing. Yet Dad took it away. "Rock and roll is devil music," he often lectured. "Immoral and harmful to the spirit. You'll go to hell if you give way." Going to hell scared the daylights out of me. The Bible called it a place of everlasting punishment.

"Home is a place of everlasting punishment!" I yelled.

The employee parking garage was nearly full by the time I arrived. I whipped into one of the last spots, jumped from the car, and then flew lickety-split to the entrance. With only two minutes to spare, I raced through the front door and up the escalator, skipping steps past coworkers. After hustling between the nightgown rounders, I made it to the stockroom and punched my time card. Safe.

As embarrassing as it was to admit, I worked that summer as a bra clerk. *A. Bra. Clerk.* At Goldsmith's—Memphis's fine department store. There are not enough words in the English language to sufficiently explain my embarrassment. By the time I'd applied, both Juniors and Ladies' Dresses were full, so they stuck me in Lingerie.

I'd seen and touched more old-lady bosoms in two months than if I'd worked three years at a nursing home. "Lean over and drop," I'd tell the ladies before hooking their bras, but some never got it. The first time I had to lift a boob and gently place it inside a brassiere, I broke out into a cold sweat.

No other young girls worked in Lingerie, so my only friend was a sixty-two-year-old lady named Gertie, short for Gertrude. Despite our age difference, we actually had a little fun together. She was already on the floor hanging nightgowns when I yanked back the curtains to the stockroom. "Good morning, Gertie," I said. She'd insisted I call her by her first name. She said it made her feel young.

"I declare. Those liberal bra burners are liable to burn me out of a job."

This was the tenth time I'd heard her rag about girls tossing their bras into a burning trash can at last year's Miss America pageant. "That's a myth," I told her, for the tenth time. "The cops wouldn't allow it. They were scared the boardwalk would catch fire. Remember? I told you I read about it in *Life* magazine."

Gertie pretended not to hear. Perspiration beads dotted her hairline. Her face flushed as red as a tulip. She scurried over to her purse and opened her Japanese hand fan. "Hot flash," she announced, then proceeded to fan herself like she was sitting next to a bonfire in the summer.

"How was your evening?" she asked, fanning harder.

"Uneventful. As usual."

"I declare. When are you gonna have a little fun? You're in the prime of your life, Miss Suzannah."

"Fun is not allowed in my family. Unless you consider Parcheesi a good time."

She pressed her lips together, holding her tongue, but I knew what she was thinking: *What the heck is wrong with your family?* "Any word from your brother?" she said at last.

My shoulders clenched as her words burned a hole in my heart. I lowered my eyelids. "No ma'am."

She sidled up next to me, wrapped an arm around my shoulders, and gave me a squeeze. "Overseas mail is as slow as a caterpillar. You'll hear from him soon."

A forced smile was all I could muster. Ron hadn't written me, or our parents, in months. Not that I could blame him. Even still, I missed him with every fiber of my being. We were Irish twins, only eleven months apart, and had never known life without the other. Until Vietnam. Until my mistake.

"Say, would you mind taking your lunch break early?" Gertie asked.

An odd question. She always lunched first. "Sure. Is everything okay?"

"Lazy Wayne forgot to pay the utility bill," she said with a loud groan, the way she did when her bunions were bothering her. "Now *I* have to drive way downtown to MLGW when the lunch rush is over."

"Why can't he do it? I thought he retired."

"He claims his sciatica is acting up. Don't even get me started. He makes me madder than a wet hen."

~

At eleven thirty on the nose, I grabbed my brand-new macramé purse, bought with my store discount, and tossed it over my shoulder.

Gertie's plump face lit up like a jack-o'-lantern. "Where ya dining?" She asked the same question every day. Food was her favorite subject.

"Not hungry. I'm going over to Kress for a bottle of Love cologne. I wish they carried it—"

"Only high-dollar brands sold at Goldsmith's." Gertie pressed an elbow into mine, raising her eyebrows sky-high. "Say, would you mind picking me up a can of Aqua Net Super Hold while you're there?"

"No ma'am. Need anything else?"

"I don't suppose." She moved over to her purse, hidden under the checkout counter. Gertie made a swishing sound when she walked. I didn't know if it was her thick-as-mud hose or her thick-as-mud girdle, but I'd know her anywhere, even with my eyes closed.

When she bent down to riffle through her wallet, I held my breath, afraid her skirt might split.

As soon as she stood up, two quarters in hand, her gaze dropped to my legs. It wasn't the first time.

Before she started the lecture, I cut her off at the pass. "I know what you're thinking, and I appreciate your concern. Truly I do. But I don't wanna wear support hose. They're hot." I stopped short of saying *They're ugly.* After all, Gertie wore them. Suntan was her shade, sold right there in the lingerie department. You couldn't even see your hand while tucked inside the tester.

Gertie lifted a finger to punctuate her words, then singsonged, "You'll be *sor*-ry when varicose *ve*-ins pop out all over those pretty little *le*-gs." The way her voice rose and fell sounded like she was performing a recitative in an opera.

I sang back. "Varicose *ve*-ins aren't high on my *wor*-ry list." I plucked the quarters from her palm. "See you in an *hou*-r."

"My, you have a nice voice," she said, hands pressed against hips. "Have you considered a major in musical theater?"

Of course I'd considered a major in musical theater. I thought about music almost every hour of the day. My senior year in high school I'd played Amaryllis in *The Music Man*, and the year before, I'd played Aunt Eller in *Oklahoma!* Not lead roles, but I'd enjoyed them. Immensely. Nonetheless, a major in musical theater would have been impossible. Dad would have never allowed me to major in anything that might take me to a lewd place like New York City, full of sinners bound for hell. I settled on liberal arts.

"No ma'am, I have not." I spun around hastily, hoping Gertie would take the hint and drop the subject.

As I wove through the bra racks toward the escalator, the sound of her heavy Southern drawl rang out through the department. "If you reconsi-dah, you could become a star on Broadway."

I ignored her. Although I had to admit hearing Gertie mention the word *star* struck a major chord. My true life's calling—the passionate one Dad forced me to bury—was to become a folk-rocker like Mary Travers from Peter, Paul and Mary. Or a pop rock singer like Dusty Springfield.

But that was before my Beatles disaster. The worst, most shameful day of my life, inflicted upon me by my very own father.

"Why don't you go somewhere fun this weekend so you can wear that new cologne?" Gertie called loudly, even though customers in the next department could hear. That's another thing. Gertie considered it her job to construct a social life for me. And find me a boyfriend. She'd been shocked when I told her I'd never had one.

I tossed her a wave without turning around and headed straight for the escalator.

Kress Department Store

Memphis, Tennessee

Friday, July 25, 1969

A front parking spot was waiting on me as soon as I drove up. Even though Dad told me to park as far away from other cars as I could, I didn't. Have no doubt, I adored my Mustang, but Dad was out there about cars. He demanded that mine be kept pristine, just like everything else in our military household.

After my Beatles disaster, Dad bought me a brand-new, pastel yellow '66 Mustang for Christmas. Although he never admitted it, nor asked for my forgiveness, Mama claimed he felt terrible about pushing me to my breaking point that fateful day in front of the Mid-South Coliseum. The doctor said it was probably a heatstroke or maybe even an anxious episode. *Baloney.* It didn't take a medical degree to know it was, in fact, a consequence of Dad publicly humiliating me like I was Hester in *The Scarlet Letter*.

Buying me the Mustang was his way of apologizing. Apology gifts were nothing new. Ron and I had several of them. Ron's '63 Plymouth Barracuda, affectionately called "Cuda," was one of his I'm-sorry presents. It came after Dad humiliated him in front of the Central High football team by calling him a "gutless chicken liver" during practice.

Ron's Martin guitar showed up two days after our father shamed him into believing—Dad's words, not mine—"your late arrival to puberty, and lack of facial hair, is in truth a lack of masculinity. You need to man up, boy."

My bright-red Schwinn bicycle with the white banana seat showed up the day after he called me *plump* in the seventh grade and questioned who would want to marry me if I didn't get a hold of my weight problem. I was thirteen. A little chubby. A husband was the last thing on my mind. But his comment stuck.

Just once I would have loved to hear Dad come out and say "I'm sorry for hurting you" and forgo the present.

Once inside the store, I headed straight to the cosmetics aisle. Donovan's voice rang inside my head, "Wear Your Love Like Heaven." When Love had come out with that ad, every teen in America who loved Donovan's music bought a Lovestick. Love had the prettiest lipsticks I'd ever seen. Sunlit was my shade. Their fragrance was just as luscious. The second I smelled it on a girl in the Goldsmith's break room, I knew I had to own it.

Scanning the shelves up and down, side to side, I found everything *but* Love cologne. *Where the heck is it? It must be right in front of my face.* Sensing a salesclerk behind me, I whipped around for help. "Excuse me. Where can I find . . . Oh, sorry. I thought you worked here."

Hardly an old-lady Kress clerk, the girl was young and pretty. *So pretty.* She wore cool aqua-tinted round sunglasses, even inside the store. Her waist-length, straight blond hair and bangs were parted in the middle. Freckles sprinkled her nose. A pale shade of frosty lipstick colored her lips.

"Suzannah!" the girl exclaimed, pushing her sunglasses atop her head. "It's me."

My mouth dropped open.

"It's been so long," said my *ex*–best friend.

I'll say. Three years without a single word. When Dad banned me from going with Livy to the Beatles concert, she turned around and invited that liar Marianne Gentry to use *my* concert ticket, even after learning Marianne was the one who had passed around the nasty rumor about her and blamed it on me.

Mad and hurt by her betrayal, I could hardly function. I kept waiting for an apology, but the phone never rang. It didn't help that Livy's parents transferred her from Central High to an all-girls college prep school way out on Ridgeway. I'd heard she had all-new high-society friends.

She stepped forward to hug me, but I kept my arms by my side. I was still hurt. And mad. "How are you?" I forced myself to ask, resisting the urge to yell, *You're damn straight it's been so long. Three years!*

Livy seemed fine, unfazed by the past. "Groovy," she said. "Working at Dinstuhl's for the summer. Can't believe I'm running into you. I've been thinking about you a lot lately."

Is that so? Are you finally sorry for what you did to me? I wanted to say. Instead, I said nothing.

"What are you doing these days?" she asked.

It felt strange and awkward, but somehow, I pushed through the uneasiness. And my anger. "Working at Goldsmith's for the summer." I stopped short of telling her which department I worked in. "I get a great discount," I said, pinching the fold on my favorite skirt. "But I end up spending too much of my paycheck."

Livy's gaze traveled the length of my body, but she never said anything about liking my outfit. She was dressed differently. Hip-hugger bell-bottom jeans and a wide leather belt with a peace sign buckle. A sleeveless yellow peasant top grazed her belly button. She'd gone hippie.

"Can you wear that to work?" I asked.

"No way, man. Mrs. Dinstuhl would never allow us to wear jeans. I'm off today." Dinstuhl's was Memphis's fine candy store, around the corner from Kress. I couldn't help wondering why she had a job in the first place. Her parents gave her all the money she needed.

"Goldsmith's has a lot of neato things right now," I told her, for lack of something better. And to ease the tension. The old Livy would have loved everything Goldsmith's had.

"Cool. I'll have to check it out." Not a single note of sincerity threaded her voice. I was just about to walk away when she asked, "Where are you going to college?"

After an awkward pause, I answered. "Union University." Just hearing my own words made my muscles stiffen. Livy wouldn't even know Union U existed.

Just like I thought, she tilted her head to the side. "Huh. Where's that?"

"Jackson. It's a small church school. You know my parents. I didn't have a choice. Where'd you go?"

"I'm at Radcliffe."

"*Radcliffe?* Wow." Livy had always been smart. I couldn't remember her ever making less than a B-plus on anything, and that was rare. Even so, Boston sure was a long way to go for college. Vanderbilt was much closer. "How did you end up way up there?"

"Don't you remember? Daddy went to Harvard. Just following in his footsteps," she answered with a confident glow. "Regardless, it was time for a change. With all the racial injustice here, I didn't wanna go to college in the South."

I knew what she meant, but leaving would not have been an option in my family. I cleared my throat, feeling even more humiliated.

"After Dr. King's assassination last year, I'm glad I'm in Boston. It was awful seeing all the tanks on Poplar Avenue, and our city under *martial law*. Damn."

"Yeah. It was bad."

"Daddy talked about moving our family to Boston, but he didn't want to relocate his law practice. He's doing too well here." After a loud gasp, she changed the subject. "This cool movie's filming on our campus called *Love Story*. The lead is so dreamy. Remember Ryan O'Neal? From *Peyton Place*?"

"Of course I do." I was forbidden to watch *Peyton Place*. I had watched it at Livy's.

"I got to meet him!" Her voice lifted the way it once did when she was talking about a new crush.

"Cool," I said, tingling with envy.

She threw her head back. "It was *so* cool. Hey, wanna grab a bite? I'm starving."

I glanced at my watch, then over at the lunch counter. A few stools were open and two booths. "I . . . guess I could," I stammered. "I don't have much ti—"

"You've got to eat. They're quick here." Livy peered at me with that same old bossy stare, which, of course, made me relent right away.

We strolled over and sat down at the back of the Whirly-Q Luncheonette. As we scooted into the booth, I mused back to the last time we lunched at the Whirly together. All was well. Still best friends.

Livy grabbed the menu out of the holder, then put it back as quickly as she had picked it up. "I don't know why I look at this. I get the same thing every time."

"Grilled cheese?" I asked, even though I knew the answer.

"That's it."

"With a cup of tomato soup," we said in unison. Then laughed. It chipped at the ice block inside my heart. I had to admit it was kind of nice hanging out with Livy again. She was a fun person. Everybody wanted to be her friend.

After the waitress took our order, Livy removed a Yardley frosted lipstick from her purse and spread it over her full, naturally pink lips. She pointed it toward me. "Wanna try it? It's Pink a Pale."

"Sure." I took the lipstick, spread it across my not-so-full lips.

"Looks good on you," she said.

"Thanks." Mashing my lips together, I handed it back.

A stretch of awkwardness followed before she leaned forward. "How's Ron?" The tentative way in which she asked seemed as though she wondered if he was dead.

Imagining that scenario made my stomach clench. I zipped my cross to and fro on the chain. "Still in 'Nam. Halfway through his final tour."

"How many did he do?"

"Three."

"*Three* tours? Why so many?" Livy asked, with genuine concern.

"Dad made him. He said it was the only way he'd ever grow up."

"Okaaay." She drew out the word, showing her disapproval. "But that's cruel."

"At least he gets the GI Bill. And a pension."

Livy rolled her eyes. "Screw the GI Bill. *And* the pension. That's way too long to be in 'Nam. Don't you agree?"

Of course I agreed. But somehow knowing he would receive added money for his service eased my guilt. "I'm counting down the minutes till he gets home."

Like all my girlfriends, Livy thought Ron was cool. He may have been shy, but he was known as one of the cutest boys at Central High. After school he'd give me and Livy rides home, and they'd smoke cigarettes together. She'd said he was the brother she never had.

Remembering the better days gave me comfort. My muscles started to relax. "The only good thing that's happened is he got to take his last R & R in Hawaii. The army usually reserves Honolulu for married guys, but Mama insisted Dad pull strings so she could go see him."

"When was that?"

"Over New Year's." I lowered my eyes. "I wish they'd have let me go."

"Is your dad still a psycho?" Livy's hands shot up to her cheeks. "Sorry, I shouldn't have said that."

I threw my palms up in a show of solidarity. "I don't care. The answer is yes. And he's gotten worse since Mama got back from Hawaii. I think he's finally wrestling with the truth that his own son hates him."

"Your dad was so *mean*."

"Tell me about it. What father makes his only son enlist before college?" Leaning back in the booth, I squeezed my eyes shut. The very thought of it made me nauseous. I was the one to blame.

"Your dad really believes in this war, huh?"

"Of course he does. He's a colonel!"

The look of despair in Ron's eyes had nearly killed me the day Dad marched him down to the army recruiting office. It was a Saturday in April, Ron's senior year in high school. He was not quite eighteen, and the mere thought of war filled him with terror.

"I'm not a soldier, Dad," Ron said, an hour before they left. "Not all boys are meant to fight wars." Ron and I had been sitting on his bed listening to his transistor radio when Dad sauntered into the room. Ron's guitar was in his hands. It lived in his hands.

I met Dad's gaze. "He's a boy who believes in peace, not war. He wants to make music, not gunfire." I shouldn't have said it. The US military was tradition in our family. But I had to say something, didn't I? Even if it meant I'd get in trouble. The whole thing was my fault.

Dad peered angrily at me over his glasses, the ones he wore low on his nose. "That's precisely why he must go. War has a way of turning a boy into a man."

Ron pleaded with him. "Please let me go to college with my friends. None of their parents are making them go to 'Nam. They're finding ways to get their boys *out* of it."

"I don't care about them," Dad answered. "I only care about you."

Ron and I cut our eyes at one another. That was bull crap. Our dad only cared about the military.

"If you care about me, then let me go to college," Ron begged. "I'm sorry for what I did."

"This is best," Dad said. "One day you'll understand."

"I'm not like you, Daddy," Ron had said with tears in his eyes. He never called our father Daddy anymore. "I know you wish I was, but I'm not."

"And you never will be," I had muttered under my breath.

Livy nudged my foot under the table. "Suzannah?"

I blinked. "Sorry, I zoned out. Thinking about Ron."

"At Harvard kids think differently about the war. I belong to two campus antiwar groups. I've been to several demonstrations at—"

I had to interrupt. "Aren't you afraid of getting arrested?"

"No." Livy shook her head, wide eyed. "I hate what's going on in our country. Don't you?"

That was rhetorical. She already knew the answer. Still, I offered a nod.

"I'm sure plenty of protests are going on at your college," she said in earnest.

That made me belly laugh. "No. They're not."

She knitted her brows. "Huh. Well, I guarantee you the kids are listening to the cool protest music. You're listening, aren't you?"

After a long pause, I lowered my eyelids. "I'm not all that familiar with protest music."

"How can you miss it? It's everywhere."

Livy poured a bucket of shame on my head. It's not like I didn't want to listen to the cool protest music. I did. But after John Lennon made his stupid proclamation, Dad banned me from all forms of rock music. He took away my transistor radio, all my forty-fives, and all my albums.

Truth be told, I had cheated while driving the Mustang but, like a moron, left the volume turned up after parking in the driveway. It happened to be the very day Dad decided to take my car for an oil change. Afterward he marched into my room, told me I had disobeyed his command—like I was one of his soldiers—and then had my radio yanked from the car, leaving me with the Hole of Horror.

As I eyeballed the haughty look on Livy's face, it crossed my mind to say, *Does that liar Marianne Gentry like the cool protest music?* But I restrained myself. No sense in digging up the past. Not here anyway.

She crossed her arms on the table and leaned toward me. "You know Bob Dylan's songs 'The Times They Are a-Changin,' 'Blowin' in the Wind.'"

"Sure."

"That's protest music. You've heard of Joan Baez, haven't you?"

"I've heard of her, but I don't know her music."

"You would love Joan. Her voice gives me chills. Like yours."

Did Livy just say my voice gives her chills?

"Joan's outta sight, man. She's extremely outspoken about the war."

"Cool," I said, though I was sure Livy could tell by the tone of my voice I wasn't all that interested. What was the point? I had no radio, no record player. How could I possibly listen to Joan Baez?

"*SuSu.* There's so much great music out there. It's about peace and love. You would dig it all." Hearing her call me SuSu brought back memories of a sweeter time. Besides Ron, Livy was the only one who ever called me that.

I shifted in my seat. No other way around it. I had to confess why I didn't know about Joan Baez or any of the other protest music. Our friendship had ended before she would have known. "To be perfectly honest, Dad forced me to give up all rock music after what John Lennon said."

She rolled her eyes. "Your dad is *out-there.*" With a soup spoon to her lips, she paused. "But you're still gonna be a singer."

My heart dropped as I slowly shook my head from side to side.

"Why not? You're so good!"

I dipped my chin. It pained me to talk about it. "I just told you. Dad made me give up rock music." As tempted as I was to tell her more, I didn't. As far as I was concerned, she had lost the right to ask. I didn't trust her anymore.

"You're in college now. Can't you just do it behind his back?"

"No way. This is my new life, Livy."

With her lips pressed together, Livy squeezed her eyes shut. I knew she was probably holding her tongue; she knew all about Dad. But it made me wonder if she could be considering an apology for giving that liar Marianne Gentry my Beatles ticket. I was hoping she might finally admit what she'd done and say she was sorry for not calling for three years. "I have a record I want you to hear," she said instead, completely ignoring what I'd just told her about Dad. "Let's go to the music section when we finish lunch."

~

With only fifteen minutes left in my break, we hurried over to the music department. It was a big waste of time, but I didn't know how to stop Livy. She had always been headstrong.

She sprinted over to the B's, then hurriedly flipped through the stack until she found a white album with a sunshine on the cover. Holding it up in front of her, she said, "This is Joan Baez. Oh, SuSu, you'll *love* this record. Joan's a little edgier than Peter, Paul and Mary, but her voice is angelic. Like yours."

Livy's compliments made me curious. Compliments weren't her style.

"All the songs were written by Bob Dylan—those two were in love—and it was recorded *in Nashville*." She pointed to the cover. "That's Joan's artwork. How cool is that?"

I just stood there with an aching spirit as she shoved the album into the crook of my arm. The mere feel of it against my skin flooded my heart with a yearning I hadn't felt in ages.

The next thing I knew, she was holding up an album with a hand-drawn painting of a pretty blonde on the cover. "This is Joni Mitchell. Wait till you hear her voice. Your whole life is gonna change. That's her self-portrait, by the way." She added the album, *Clouds*, to my growing pile, then, as an afterthought, said, "Y'all's voices are similar."

Before I could comment on her third compliment of the day, she scurried back to the C's. "Hang on. You've got to hear this one first. It just came out in May." She retrieved an album with three longhairs sitting on a dilapidated maroon velvet sofa and held it in front of her chest. "You will love Crosby, Stills & Nash. They harmonize like celestial beings."

"Seriously?"

"Seriously. Crosby was with the Byrds. You know, 'Turn! Turn! Turn!'" She *tried* to sing it.

Knowing that song well, from *before* my rock and roll ban, I said, "The lyrics are straight out of Ecclesiastes."

"No way."

I jerked my head back. "You mean I know music trivia you don't?"

Livy laughed. "I'd have never known that. Anyway, Stills was in Buffalo Springfield, and Nash was in the Hollies." She sang the first line of a Hollies song we used to love. "'Hey, Carrie Anne.'" She pointed to me.

"'What's your game now?'" I sang back.

In unison we crooned, "'Can anybody play?'" It was so much fun it made me long to reverse time and never beg my parents for Beatles tickets.

"You'll love them, man," she said.

As much as I wanted to listen to the records, I handed them back, wondering if she'd paid attention to a word I'd said. "Rock and roll is a part of my past."

Livy looked me dead in the eye. "I find that tragic."

"That makes two of us." I glanced at my watch. "Gotta go. I'll get in trouble if I'm late."

She put the records down and reached out for a hug.

At first, I resisted. But upon remembering all the good times, and the safe feeling I'd once had around her and her family, I hugged back. With vigor. In truth, I didn't want to let her go. "I had fun today," I said, wishing we could do it again soon.

"So fun," she answered.

I threw my hand up in a quick wave and bolted out the front door.

I peeled out of the Laurelwood Shopping Center, only to catch the red light at Poplar Avenue. While drumming my fingers impatiently on the steering wheel, I read the sign in front of Christ United Methodist Church: "Forgiveness opens the door to trust and freedom." *Just one more church telling people how to live their lives,* I thought but stared at it anyway. I didn't trust anyone, except Ron. And I damn sure didn't have any freedom.

"What am I going to do with you, young lady?" Gertie asked—hands on hips—when I returned without my cologne. She didn't care about the hairspray. "If you don't start taking care of yourself, I'm likely to have a fit. Men love perfume. Don't you even want a boyfriend?"

I stashed my purse under the checkout counter, then slowly turned to face her. "I haven't met one single boy who interests me except Paul McCartney. And we broke up."

~

As my final customer of the day stepped away from the counter, I did a double take at the sight of someone heading swiftly toward me, a large brown paper tote dangling from her grip.

Plopping the bag on the counter, Livy sighed. She combed her fingers through her hair. "It took me forever to find you. You didn't tell me you worked"—she glanced around—"in the brassiere department."

I leaned in toward her, shutting the money drawer with my belly. "Cupping ladies' breasts is not something I brag about."

She chuckled, then handed over the heavy sack.

A quick peek inside revealed a bushel of albums. "You didn't have—"

"Oh yes, I did. The thought of you giving up rock and roll won't leave my brain."

I noticed Gertie eyeing us from a few feet away, eavesdropping.

"After you left, I remembered more of my favorites. There's a surprise in there too."

"A surprise?" I loved surprises.

"You'll see," said Livy.

Like Dad's many apology gifts, this was Livy's nonverbal olive branch, her I'm-sorry-I-betrayed-you present. Even so, she had spent an exorbitant amount of money. Twenty dollars. Maybe more.

"Gosh, Livy, you spent way too much. I'll pay you back."

She shook her head. "Oh no you won't. It's the least I can do. These albums will change your life. I swear."

"Change my life? That's a big swear." Truthfully, butterflies swarmed in my stomach as I eyed the stack of records. I was dying to listen to them. But how? Where? When?

Gertie butted in. "Why don't you girls paint the town tonight? I hear the Bitter Lemon is a hot spot for all you young folk."

"No ma'am. Not tonight," Livy told her. "My boyfriend's calling me long distance at six thirty. I promised him I'd be waiting by the phone."

"Perhaps he has a friend for little Suzannah here," Gertie said, rubbing a gentle hand across my back.

"She'd have to move up north for that to happen." Livy tapped the counter. "Gotta split. Hope you love the records."

While I watched Livy move toward the escalator, it occurred to me that I'd forgotten to thank her. "Thank you," I yelled as she was stepping on.

She looked my way, then flashed me the peace sign.

Hope clung to my heart. *Maybe life holds a second verse for us,* I thought as Livy's head slowly disappeared from sight.

I turned to Gertie. "Livy's an old friend. I guess she's a hippie now."

"I'll say." She pursed her lips in disapproval.

I had no desire to be a hippie or become part of the counterculture. The laid-back, hippie-dippie scene flat out annoyed me. *Hippies are too wild,* I often thought. Though I had to admit eating lunch with hippie Livy had given me a lift. A big lift. As mad as I'd been at her, spending time with my ex–best friend had boosted my spirts and given me a reason to hope again.

After quickly tidying up the checkout area, Gertie and I reached for our purses at the same time.

"That young *la*-dy looks awfully fa-*mil*-iar," she singsonged, slipping her purse strap onto the crook of her arm. "I've *seen* her be-*fore*."

"You're thinking of Ursula Andress. Livy looks just like her. Only prettier."

"Oh, I know Ursula. She's that sexpot in *Dr. No*. Wayne's dragged me to see it three times now, and it's *not* because of Sean Connery."

I had no idea what to say to that.

As we weaved our way through the robe racks, I yanked Gertie's sleeve. "I know! You saw Livy at the last protest rally you attended."

"Why, Miss Withers, you caught me." Gertie's eyebrows lifted as she gave me the peace sign, and we headed toward the escalator.

Gridiron Restaurant

Memphis, Tennessee

Monday, July 28, 1969

Three days later Livy showed up at Goldsmith's again wearing a darling miniskirt, asking me to go to lunch. She claimed she had this great idea she wanted to run past me. The one time I'd dared to wear a miniskirt, Dad ordered me back to my room to change, telling me I looked like a streetwalker.

We walked over to the Gridiron and had to wait ten minutes for a booth. I felt giddy having Livy back in my life. Sure, there was a ten-ton elephant in the restaurant with a sign on his back reading: **LIVY WALKED OUT ON YOUR FRIENDSHIP THREE YEARS AGO, AND NOW SHE WANTS BACK IN. WITHOUT A VERBAL APOLOGY.** But I did not care. She had a gravitational pull, tugging me inside her orbit. Always had.

"Have you listened to the records?" she asked as soon as the waitress took our order.

"Three of them."

"That's *all*?"

"It was hard enough listening to three. I told you I'd have to sneak. It was incredibly risky."

"And? What'd you think?"

"You were right. Joni Mitchell's voice is life changing. Same with Joan Baez. But the Crosby, Stills & Nash record is from another galaxy."

"I knew it!" She bounced in her seat. "Tell me all about it. Where did you listen?"

"It was the biggest high-risk gambit of my life."

~

Sometime around one in the morning—once I knew my parents were long asleep—I had picked up my desk chair and set it down inside my walk-in closet. Even though my better sense told me not to, I stood on the chair and reached for my old record player high atop the shelf. I couldn't battle the temptation another second. The records were burning a hole in my soul.

Before stepping down, my eye caught sight of something else covered in dust. Ron's guitar case, with his Martin tucked inside. Just the sight of it made my heart leap. I considered it half mine.

Without an electrical outlet in the closet, I had to plug in the record player outside the door and stretch the power cord underneath. My heart felt like a hammer pounding inside my chest, elation intensifying with every beat. One by one, I pulled the albums out of Livy's shopping bag and studied their covers. The mere feel of them in my hands sparked that flame I'd once felt while holding a brand-new Beatles record.

Livy had affixed numbers on the covers indicating the order in which she wanted me to listen. That made me snicker. *Bossy Livy rides again.*

My surprise lay on the bottom with a note taped to the cellophane: *Save the best for last!* The Beatles, the White Album. I clutched it to my chest, tempted to listen to it first.

But the three guys sitting on a tattered velvet sofa were calling my name. *Crosby, Stills & Nash*. I ripped off the cellophane, then reveled in the sound of the album cover cracking open. Pressing my nose inside the fold, I lingered, savoring the new-album scent, then studied the inside photo. Three handsome faces, all wearing fur parkas, stared back at me, inviting me to take a listen.

I pulled the vinyl from the cover, then removed it from the sleeve. Shiny and unblemished, I held the record on the insides of my palms—careful not to smudge it—then gently placed it on the turntable. I lowered the needle. And the volume.

As soon as I heard the opening guitar chords of the first song, "Suite: Judy Blue Eyes," I lay down on my back. Seconds later all three guys sang together in flawless harmony. "It's getting to the point, where I'm no fun anymore."

Holy crap! What the heck is coming out of my record player? The music was so melodic, so pretty, so outta sight, for a moment I forgot where I was. Instead of a closet full of hanging clothes, I was surrounded by palm trees, stranded on a desert island, listening to my own personal Crosby, Stills & Nash concert.

By the end of the first verse, I had left planet earth. If I hadn't known better, I would have sworn a supernatural power had lifted me to the ceiling, high above my record player.

I scrambled up from the floor, picked up the insert with the lyrics, and sang along with the guys, remembering what happiness felt like. "Chestnut brown canary, ruby-throated sparrow. Sing the song. Don't be long. Thrill me to the marrow." As the song went on, I imagined picking it out on guitar. I almost reached for the Martin but decided not to. For now, I would simply sing along.

Once it was over, I played it again. Felt all the same emotions. Then played it a third time, and a fourth. The only thing I could compare that moment to was the euphoria I had felt the first time I sat behind the wheel of my Mustang, no one else in the car. With the windows rolled down and the wind in my hair, I feasted on my first taste of freedom.

After flipping the album over and hearing "Helplessly Hoping," I knew for sure I was levitating. When Crosby, Stills & Nash harmonized, it was impossible to tell whose voice was prettier. They sounded like the same person. One voice. One sound. An intricately woven mosaic fused with multicolored glass.

A glance at the cover, with Stephen Stills holding his guitar, reminded me of Ron and convinced me to scramble back up the chair for his Martin. The second it was in my hands, adrenaline flooded through my veins as if it was a drug. I felt a rush, even while strumming the C chord. But the Martin sounded way out of tune, so I tightened the strings. I replayed "Helplessly Hoping" three more times, harmonizing along with the guys and picking out the chords. Crosby, Stills & Nash seemed to have written the song for me. I was helplessly hoping my life could change.

~

Livy clapped her hands as fast as a hummingbird's wings. "I knew you'd love that band."

"I love them almost as much as I love the Beatles." Heat spread through my chest. "Joan Baez and Joni Mitchell are right up there. I stayed up till four in the morning singing along with them in my closet."

"I can't wait for you to hear Hendrix. You've got to do it again tonight."

"No way. I have to play this game with extreme caution." Imagining Dad's wrath if he caught me was terrifying.

The waitress delivered our lunch. Like many times before, when we had eaten at the Gridiron, we both ordered the same thing: yummy chargrilled cheeseburgers, french fries, and large Cokes. "So what's your great idea?" I asked, dropping a dime in the booth's jukebox. I chose one of my favorite Beatles songs, "Can't Buy Me Love." Crosby, Stills & Nash wasn't an option.

Livy shifted in her seat and tucked her long silky Breck Girl hair behind her ears, raking her fingers through to the ends. Jealousy threatened to rear its ugly head. Her beauty slayed me.

"Promise to hear me out before you say no?" she asked.

"I don't make promises anymore."

She rolled her eyes, dismissing my comment. "I didn't get a chance to tell you about my boyfriend the other day. He's gorgeous, funny, and so much fun. You'd love him."

"Cool," I said, fighting the urge to say, *Of course he's all those things, Livy. You can have any boy you want.*

"He's *so* cool." She looked up with yearning in her eyes. "Last night on the phone we talked about this outdoor music festival in New York. They're billing it as an Aquarian Exposition with three days of peace and music. Kinda like last year's Monterey Pop Festival. You heard about that, right?"

I nodded, even though I hadn't.

"Lots of the musicians who played Monterey will be there. It starts in three weeks."

"Is your boyfriend going?"

"Definitely. Some of the best bands in the world are on the bill." Using her fingers, she counted them off. "Joan Baez; Jimi Hendrix; Janis Joplin; Creedence Clearwater Revival; Blood, Sweat & Tears. You know them: 'Spinning Wheel.'" She sang the title and gestured toward me like I was supposed to sing the next line.

I shook my head. "I've heard it, but I don't know the words." That was a lie. I'd never heard it before.

"Wanna know what else is cool?"

Anything was possible with Livy.

She bounced in the booth, throwing her arms up like a cheerleader. "Crosby, Stills & Nash will be there!"

Just the mere mention of that band made my body twitch.

"I can't wait!"

"*You're* going?" I asked, the green-eyed monster nipping at my heels.

"Of course I'm going. But my last day at Dinstuhl's is August thirteenth, and it starts the fifteenth. My boyfriend's going early to get us a good camping spot."

"Will Joni Mitchell be there?"

"She's not on the roster, but she and Graham Nash are lovers. I bet she makes a surprise appearance."

"Wow," I muttered, even more jealous. If that was possible. "Promise you'll write me all about it when you get back to school?" I took a sip of my Coke.

"I don't make promises anymore." Livy smiled. "Besides, I won't have to. You're coming with me."

Guttural laughter—and Coca-Cola—spewed from my lips. "Obviously you've forgotten who my father is."

Livy didn't laugh. Crestfallen, she gripped the table ledge. "I have *not* forgotten who your father is, trust me. But, SuSu, you're twenty years old. You should be making your own decisions."

"Maybe you can do stuff like that in your house, but I sure can't in mine. As Dad often reminds me, I won't be a legal adult until I'm twenty-one."

"Yeah," she said sarcastically. "We can't drink, we can't vote, we can't gamble, but we can damn sure put automatic weapons in the hands of our eighteen-year-old *underage* boys and send them off to Vietnam to be shot to hell."

"Livy!"

She gasped, thrust a palm over her mouth. "Oh, SuSu, I'm sorry. I shouldn't have said that." She reached over to squeeze my hand. "Vietnam just gets me so angry."

With a loud sigh, I squeezed back but quickly let go.

"Technically we're still minors, but who's following that rule these days?" she said.

"*Me!* My parents made it very clear. If I'm on their payroll, I abide by their rules. They pay for everything. Except my clothes."

"Ugh," Livy moaned, throwing her head back.

"Would you rather I not go to college? Work here the rest of my life?" I gestured toward the cooks in front of the griddle.

"Of course not. I just think there's a way around it. It's *your* life! You should be living it the way *you* want to."

"Believe me. I fully intend to live my life on my own terms, the second I turn twenty-one."

Livy's eyes widened. "You're gonna let your parents police you for another solid *year*?"

I crossed my arms over my chest. "You're lucky, Livy. Most parents aren't as lenient as yours."

"I think they've figured out I'm gonna do what I want, so they might as well support me." She grinned. "Within reason."

"Can you imagine my dad if I came to him and said, 'Hey, Dad, Livy wants me to go to an outdoor music festival with her. I need you to support me on this.'" Lifting in my seat, I leaned halfway across the table. "'Oh, and by the way, it's in New York. I'll need seventy dollars to cover my expenses.'" I sat back down, took a bite of my burger.

"Oh gosh. Don't do that." Livy sliced her hands through the air like an umpire. "Listen, you're wrong about the money. The tickets are only eighteen dollars for all three days."

I covered my full-of-cheeseburger mouth, speaking through slits in my fingers. "I only make a dollar thirty-five an hour."

"If you consider we'll be seeing the best bands in the world, *and* camping for free, it's a bargain." With palms in the air, she gave me a fixed stare.

"Maybe a bargain for you." I glared back like she was crazy. "Are you *lost in space*? You know I can't go. Besides, you're talking about driving all the way to New York. How many hours is that?"

"What happened to your sense of adventure? There was a time when you would have jumped on the stage with the Beatles."

Sadness pricked an old wound. "Not anymore." As quickly as the sorrow arrived, hearing her mention the Fab Four kindled a thrill I hadn't felt in a very long time. So I reconsidered. "Will they be there?"

"Maybe. The only live show they've played in three years was that rooftop show in London. But even if they aren't there, the festival will still be outta sight."

I fingered the gold cross around my neck, zipping it back and forth on the chain.

"Come on, SuSu. You need this," Livy begged. "Please come with me. I'd love for you to meet my boyfriend."

More than anything I wanted to go. But I'd have to run away to do it. After an extra-long pause filled with mental turmoil, I zeroed in on my oldest friend's face. "I appreciate what you're doing. I swear. But there'd be hell to pay." Leaning back in the booth, I gave her my final answer. "No way, José."

Livy rested her chin on the table, then lifted her eyes. "Are you one hundred percent sure?"

Even though deep down inside I was torn—so torn—I said, "Maybe after I turn twenty-one there'll be another Aquarian something or other in New York. We can go to that one."

"Look," Livy said, in her signature bossy voice. "Don't make your decision right now. Just take a couple weeks and think about it. *Please.*"

I would have killed to go, but there was no way in heck I could risk it. Even still, I could read the writing on her forehead in all caps: **I WILL NOT STOP BUGGING YOU UNTIL YOU SAY YES.** "I'll think about it," I said. "But please do not count on me."

"You'd be making a giant mistake. The festival is gonna set your soul free. And that's *exactly* what you need." She pressed her lips together and gave me an oversize shrug.

Anger flared. *How do you know what I need, Livy Foster? And what the hell gives you the right to decide it for me?* "I can make my own decisions about my life, thank you." I leaned back in my seat, crossing my arms over my chest.

Livy shut her eyes for an extra-long moment, then dived down to her Coke for a sip. With lips inches from the straw, she looked me square in the eye. "I bet Ronny would give anything to be there. If nothing else, you should go for his sake."

Goldsmith's Department Store

Memphis, Tennessee

Monday, August 11, 1969

Two weeks went by without so much as a phone call.

I was sure Livy would be on me like a rat on a Cheeto, persuading me to go to Woodstock. Boy was I wrong. Not only was there no persuading, but there was no Livy.

The loss of her a second time made me want to break down and weep. Having her back had been like finding that special something you thought you'd lost forever. We'd picked up right where we left off, as if a single day hadn't passed without best friendship.

It must have been my comment about making my own decisions, but considering we'd just reconnected after three years, you'd think she would have at least called to see how I was doing. Sure, I could have called her, but it was a matter of principle. *She* walked out on *me* in the first place. And that comment about going to Woodstock for Ron's sake? What a low blow.

That was Livy. She could be ruthless if it meant getting her own way.

The whole way to work, I kept thinking about it. My big regret in our short-lived reacquaintance was not finding out why she had lied about giving Marianne Gentry my Beatles ticket and going AWOL the first time.

For the past two weeks, I'd been obsessing over that backstabber, wondering if she and Livy were still friends.

All those years ago Livy had told me what Marianne said behind my back, and her words still echoed as loudly today as they had three years ago. "She said you were the one that told everyone I went all the way with John Dearing." What a lie. Marianne was the one who had said it. I'd have never betrayed Livy like that. Never in a million years.

Yet she had betrayed me.

~

I spent the first fifteen minutes of my workday tidying up the stockroom. When I made it out to the floor, Gertie glanced up from counting money in the register. Using her left palm as a shield while pointing her right index finger to the far end of the department, she softly singsonged, "You have *com*-pany."

Well, what do you know? There stood Livy, studying a display of expensive lacy silk panties.

"Hi, Livy!" I called from the counter, my insides vibrating with relief.

She turned around with an excited glow. "Morning. I need some new lingerie." With hands on her hips, she walked toward the register. "The sexier the better."

"Oh my," Gertie whispered, pressing a hand to her neck, then pointed to the wall display behind the counter. "Why don't you try the Sea Dream Collection. It's Maidenform."

Livy glanced at the display. "I don't think so, but thank you anyway." She then roamed around the department, stopping to finger every pure-silk garment she could spy. At the sight of the Christian

Dior display, she sucked in a breath, then held up a dainty pair of lace panties. "Now *this* is what I call *sexy*."

"Mighty *pri*-cey," Gertie singsonged under her breath. "May we interest you in a Dior brassiere to go with it?"

"No ma'am. Not today." Livy grabbed three pairs of pastel-colored panties before her eye caught on something sexier. "Ooh la la, I love this baby doll nightie." She pulled it from the rack, waving me over. "Help me decide."

She headed straight for the largest dressing room, which was at the end of the hall. Once we were inside, she snapped the curtains shut. In seconds flat she had stripped down naked. The yellow panties were at her knees before I could stop her.

"Wait. You can't try them on without these." I handed her a pair of disposable paper panties from a stack on the table next to a bench.

Outraged, she snatched the paper panties from my hand, like I had asked her to clean my toilet. "How am I supposed to know how I look wearing these awful things?"

"Just do it. It's the rule."

"You're such a rule follower these days."

"I've been forced to be a rule follower," I said.

Pulling them on reluctantly, she sighed, then stepped into the yellow silk panties and tugged them over the paper ones. She slipped the baby doll nightie over her head, sliding it down to cover her voluptuous breasts. Goose bumps had risen on her flesh. No wonder—Goldsmith's felt like a meat locker.

Watching Livy pose in the mirror, turning this way and that, left me flabbergasted. She was pretty three years ago, but now she had blossomed into a full-fledged model. Perfect face. Perfect body. Tanned long legs that wouldn't quit. With her ankles touching, her legs passed the three-diamonds test with flying colors: one diamond between her thighs, one below her knees, and another above her ankles.

She cocked her head to the side, speaking to me in the mirror. "I wanna look sexy for my boyfriend."

"Will you wear that inside the tent or out?"

Her face drooped. She peered at me with an annoyed glare.

"It just seems kind of dressy for an outdoor music festival."

"Not when it's been three months since you've seen your boyfriend." Livy adjusted the side mirrors to see her backside, her tan lines a dead giveaway of how she'd spent her summer. The Fosters had a pool in their backyard. "Speaking of the festival, have you given any more thought about going with me?" she asked. "I leave Thursday."

Sliding down onto the white leather bench, I twisted my hair into a bun, securing it with a pencil I'd spied on the table. "I have."

"And?"

I shook my head.

With hands on her hips, she sighed. "Why not? I really want you to meet my boyfriend."

"I'd love to meet your boyfriend. But the only way I could do it is to lie. If Dad caught me, and he *would* . . ." I shook my head, the consequences too horrible to imagine. "Not worth it."

Livy sat down next to me on the bench. With her perky nipples smashed inside the see-through pale-yellow negligee, she looked like a *Playboy* centerfold. "What I don't understand is why he thought it was okay to send his young, eighteen-year-old son to the battlefields of Vietnam yet now requires his twenty-year-old daughter to live in a cloister. *Psycho.*"

She was right. But what could I do about it? I took a deep breath, exhaling loudly.

Livy stood back up and gazed at me in the mirror's reflection. "I know you, SuSu. The festival is *you*. The *true* you. If you go, you'll discover the real Suzannah."

My shoulders fell. "Believe me. I plan to discover that girl as soon as I turn twenty-one. Not a day later."

"Have you thought about moving across the river to Arkansas? People are legal adults at eighteen. Same with Kentucky."

"I don't know anyone in Arkansas or Kentucky," I said with a sigh.

"Just trying to help." Flipping her long hair behind her shoulders, she added, "At least you have cool new records. Have you heard the rest?"

"I can't take another chance. Too risky."

Livy's face beamed with a sudden sunshine. "Bring them to my house tonight. You can have dinner with us, and we can listen together."

"I wish I could. Mama's been talking about making her lasagna all week. We're having it tonight." Mama's lasagna tasted better than fudge. Even Livy couldn't make me miss it.

She whipped around to face me. "You're acting paranoid. Your dad is not going to catch you. When he goes to sleep, just listen in your closet like last time. Once you hear the records, you'll change your mind about the festival." Livy knew how hard it was, yet she wouldn't stop.

I sighed. Loudly. "This is hard enough. Please try to understand."

"I know it's hard, but I'm telling you, the best bands in the world will be there." She refused to take no for an answer. Always had.

I collapsed flat back onto the bench and kicked my legs in the air.

"Crosby, Stills & Naaaaash!" She turned back to the mirror with a hand on her hip and a tilt of her head. "Do you like?"

All I could muster was a nod.

"Do you think my boyfriend will like?"

"How could he not?" *Geez, Livy. Could you be any more perfect?*

"You're right. I'll take it. And the panties too." She lifted the nightie over her head and stepped back into her street clothes.

I would have loved the chance to spend more time convincing her of the reasons why I couldn't go to the festival. Why it wasn't worth the risk. Why my father's dominating power still ruled my life. But it wouldn't have made any difference. Livy would never understand. She came from an open-minded cool family with parents who trusted her to make her own decisions.

A truth about my family dawned on me right then. *Oppression is just something you get used to.*

I stood up. "Sure you don't need a new bra?" I asked, gathering the merchandise she'd left on the floor.

Livy shook her head. "The only time I wear one is when I'm home." She popped her home bra strap against her shoulder.

Once I'd written up the sales ticket and shown her the total, I was surprised she didn't balk. It was an exorbitant sale—for a twenty-year-old, anyway. I was dying to ask how she could afford such a luxury, despite her parents' money, but decided it was none of my business and certainly none of Gertie's, who had been hovering around us like a dragonfly.

After folding the lingerie in tissue paper and placing it neatly inside a shopping bag, I walked around the counter to hand it to her. "Sorry it's not working out for us to go to the festival. But we should still get together."

"Call me," she said. "We have the same number."

"So do we," I answered, my voice barely audible. Despite everything that had happened in our past, I groaned at the thought of losing her again. I'd been devastated by her betrayal three years ago. So much so that I had never allowed myself to imagine her reentering my life.

Livy took one step toward the escalator, then turned back around, lowering her voice for my ears only. "Take a walk on the wild side, Suzannah Jean Withers." She was referring to a book on the Central High summer reading list. I hadn't been allowed to read it. She had. "If you go to the festival, you'll be the talk of Union U when you get there in the fall."

I laughed. "You're so right about that."

"At the very least, listen to the rest of the records." With a hand on my shoulder, she gave me a gentle squeeze. "Today's music is a reflection of what's going on in our country. Society is changing. You need to be a part of the resistance. Ron's life depends on it."

Fifty Years Later

Woodstock 50th Anniversary Celebration

Bethel, New York

Friday Afternoon, August 16, 2019

The *whomp-whomp-whomp* of the helicopter blades and the *pop-pop-pop* of the machine guns echo inside our eardrums. The deafening roar burns into my flesh and takes me back to *Evening News* with Walter Cronkite, Dad planted in his chair in front of the TV, a finger to his lips if I dared to speak. Dead bodies on stretchers. Teenage boys on stretchers. Always wondering if one of them was Ron.

The Vietnam War video at the Bethel Woods museum runs on a loop. We've just walked up in the middle of the program.

Adelaide looks at me, one eye squinted. Her head is tilted at an angle. "Are you okay to watch this?"

Truth is, I'm not sure I am. I left in the middle of *Platoon*, the film based on Oliver Stone's experience as a US infantryman in Vietnam. I couldn't handle that movie in 1986, and I'm pretty sure I can't handle this short film now.

Perhaps the blood has drained from my face. Adelaide changes her mind. "Let's skip it."

I manage a weak smile.

Life-size photos of bloody war scenes line the walls of the exhibit, along with pictures of helmeted police officers holding billy clubs and tear gas cans while dragging away bodies of peaceful protestors at the 1968 Democratic National Convention.

Adelaide covers her ears and squeezes her head. "I can't imagine my brother being *forced* to fight in a war, in a hot jungle, at *my* age! Your dad was so mean."

I nod with my eyes shut. "Roughest time of my life. No doubt about it."

"You shouldn't have blamed yourself, Grammy. It was his fault. Not yours."

After a long sigh I say, "I know that now, lovey. But at your age, I was hard to convince."

Adelaide hooks her arm inside mine and leads me away from the Vietnam exhibit over to a bench next to an old VW Bug painted in swirls of retro colors, flowers, and peace symbols. We sit down, right next to each other. It feels good to have her warm body close to mine. It's chilly in here.

"I still have all his letters," I say, thinking back to the worst period of my life.

Adelaide's eyes widen. "Did you bring them with you?"

I chuckle. "I don't travel with Ron's letters."

Her shoulders slump. "I wanna read them."

"Next time you're at my house, they're all yours." I stretch an arm across her shoulders, give her a gentle squeeze.

She sits up straight as an arrow, indignance lacing her tone. "Why did America get involved in Vietnam in the first place?"

It's hard to imagine how little my eighteen-year-old granddaughter knows about the very thing that defined my life when I was her age. Even harder to comprehend that I'm seventy and can still remember it all. "It's complicated," I say. "The men in Washington thought if

South Vietnam fell to communism, the other countries in Southeast Asia would follow. They called it the domino theory."

She knits her eyebrows together. "Why was that America's problem?"

"That's what everyone wanted to know by the end of the war. Don't they teach about Vietnam in school?"

"A little. Mostly noncontroversial stuff like Ho Chi Minh and the French occupation. Not much about the actual war. Maybe I'll learn more while I'm at NYU."

"You're better off watching the Ken Burns documentary. It tells you everything you want to know and even more you don't." My heart speeds up at just the thought of it. "Watching it made me so angry. Johnson knew exactly what he was getting us into. He lied to the American public. And the worst of it was the way the public treated our vets when they got home. Like *they* were the problem." I squeeze my eyes shut. "Atrocious."

"What was Uncle Ron's draft number?"

"He didn't have one, lovey. He enlisted before conscription started."

A look of horror crosses her face. "Do you think they'll bring that back?"

"I certainly hope not." I place two fingers under her chin. "Don't misunderstand me. The men and women in our military are *heroes*, every one of them. But not all people are meant to be soldiers. Your great-uncle Ron was one of those people. He was born with a peace symbol sewn into his beautiful heart."

A beat passes before Adelaide speaks again. "Some girls might be, but I'm definitely not born to be a soldier."

"You don't think so?"

"No ma'am."

"What do you think you were born to be?" I ask with a gleam in my eye.

"An actor. Broadway first. Then Hollywood." She says it like it's the most natural thing in the world.

My smile fades. A picture of her on a casting couch with some asshole hovering over her, fumbling with his zipper, flashes across my brain. *In living color.* The good Lord knew what he was doing by not giving me a daughter. I'd have never survived her teenage years. I'm barely surviving Adelaide's. "You should be whatever you want," I force myself to say.

"I think I've got what it takes."

"That you do!" I've flown to Arizona to sit in the front row at every one of her high school musicals, whether she's been the lead or had a supporting role. "Can I tell you something honest?" I ask. The last thing I need to do is preach. But I can't help myself. I don't want her to get hurt.

"You can tell me anything, Grammy. As long as it's not something bad about my tattoo." She chuckles, then touches her sleeve, under which that tattoo is hiding.

My tattoo. Oh, for goodness' sake. And to think I consider myself somewhat liberal. I turn to face her. "The competition gets much tougher once you start college. Even worse outside of college. I hate to say it, but you'll hear plenty of nos."

"That won't stop me."

She says it so fast I chuckle to myself. My girl cries at the drop of a hat. I can't imagine what it will do to her when she's told no over and over again. Very few overnight success stories out there.

I know exactly what that's like, the power of no. It cuts deeply into our psyche and strips us of our self-worth. It destroys our confidence and has the power to make us question whether our talent is even real. I've been told no more times than I can count.

It's a great irony. We creative people tend to be highly sensitive. Yet we are drawn to the jobs that dish out the most criticism. Nowadays anyone can sit behind a computer screen wearing a judgment hat and place a snarky review on a record, a book, or a movie, just because they didn't connect with the art. Just because someone believes their taste to be superior.

It kills me to think of anyone judging Adelaide.

"We should sing a duet together," she says. "How fun would that be?"

"Now you're talking!"

"Let's make it a Beatles song!"

"Now you're really talking. Or . . . what do you say we write one ourselves?"

"Yeeees!" Adelaide lets out a little squeal and stands. She extends her hand to pull me up—not that I need it or anything. "Let's go back to the hotel and get started."

When I feel her hand slip into mine, my heart explodes.

On the Road to Woodstock

Somewhere in Maryland

Friday, August 15, 1969
7:30 a.m.

Our "epic escapade," as we had dubbed it, was a nineteen-hour car ride, eleven hundred miles from Memphis, Tennessee, to Bethel, New York. Originally the festival was to be held in Wallkill, New York, but they moved it at the last minute. Thank God Livy had heard the news. Otherwise we would have driven another hour.

Yesterday we drove all the way to Roanoke, Virginia, and spent the night at a Holiday Inn—compliments of Livy's dad. He'd also given her the car we were driving, a groovy green '67 Chevy Impala with a white interior and a matching vinyl top. Livy had decorated the back end with peace sign stickers and painted massive flowers all over the doors and hood. We looked like a daisy patch on wheels.

The coolest part of "Pally," as Livy called her, was the sound system. For her birthday, Livy's dad had hired RadioShack to install an eight-track player under the dash with an AM/FM deluxe radio *and* a rear speaker. At my feet lay a box of eight-tracks we'd been playing nonstop.

"Looks like we've got . . . four and a half more hours," I said, studying our route. As soon as I spotted the city of Hershey, Pennsylvania, I pressed a hand to my heart. "Let's tour the chocolate factory. I've always wanted to do it."

Livy's face said no, but she still said, "Maybe. We'll see when we get closer. My boyfriend does not want us to be late."

Nick, her new Harvard boyfriend, had made plans to meet us at the front gate of Woodstock at one o'clock. It was eight in the morning now, and we were somewhere in Maryland with a groovy song called "Put a Little Love in Your Heart" blasting from the radio. Livy knew every word. I didn't know one.

"Do you ever sing anymore?" she asked.

With a long low sigh, I dug into the bag of Seessel's cookies we'd brought from home. "To myself."

Her face fell. I could tell she felt bad for me. "Do you play guitar?"

"Nope."

"Piano?"

"Sometimes. Only classical music."

Genuine sorrow seeped across her face. "That's so sad."

Shrugging it off, I popped a turtle cookie into my mouth. The way the chocolate melted on my tongue gave me momentary pleasure. Seessel's cookies were the best in town. On the way out of Memphis, we had bought a three-dozen variety for the trip.

I'd moved on, but Livy had not. "I really hope this weekend frees you to sing again. You have the prettiest voice of anyone I know."

"You're blitzed."

"No, I'm not. It's true." The adoration in her eyes made it seem like she meant it.

For that one moment, I considered confiding in her about my wildest dream, the one I'd buried underneath a rock three years ago. I even let my mind drift to truly making it as a singer one day. But it didn't take long to come to my senses. If I kept my dream buried and never talked about it, I didn't risk my heart shattering into a million new pieces. It was much safer under the rock.

"When you get back to college this fall, you should sing at an open mic night at a coffee shop. Lots of people get their start at coffee shops."

I whipped around, stupefied. She had to be a mind reader. "There are no coffee shops with open mic nights around Union University."

"Sure there are. They're all over Cambridge."

I stretched across the middle seat, making sure she saw the serious look on my face. "Hear me when I say this. The college I go to is *very* conservative. Less than a thousand students. There are no coffee shops on campus, much less doves like you."

"There's got to be a few kids at Union who think like we do."

I threw my head back in a burst of laughter.

"What's so funny?"

"Union kids have curfews. We have to be back in our dorm rooms by eleven o'clock sharp."

"In *college*? I'd quit."

"We have a dress code too."

Livy's mouth dropped open. "No way."

"Below-the-knee skirts and dresses only. The dorm mothers measure them."

"I'd whip the dorm mother with my skirt if she tried to measure mine," Livy said.

"Oh no you wouldn't. Speaking of school, how am I getting home?" The only plan we'd discussed was me taking a bus back to Memphis and hiding at my friend Penny's house until college started.

"I told you. The bus." Livy lit another cig and turned the music back on, leaving it at a level where we could talk without yelling. "Or maybe you'll want to hang out in Bethel a few days. Just play it by ear."

"You know I'm not a play-it-by-ear kind of person."

"Stop worrying. My boyfriend and I will make sure you get back to Memphis, or Union U, or wherever you want to go. Okay?"

"Okay."

"Why didn't your parents want Ronny to go to Union?" Livy asked, in an abrupt change of subject. Ronny was what everyone had called my brother when he was young.

"Union didn't have an ROTC program. UT did."

"I'm surprised your dad didn't make him go to West Point. Didn't he go there?"

"Dad, my grandfather, my great-grandfather. All the way back to the Civil War. It's our family legacy."

Livy sneered. "I'm glad it's not mine."

I ignored her comment. Despite what Dad had done to Ron, I was proud of our heritage. "Ron couldn't have gotten into West Point," I said. "Don't you remember how much he hated school? All he wanted to do was play guitar. Not do homework."

In the Withers family, military service was a rite of passage from adolescence to adulthood. Dad's words reverberated through my brain: *War has a way of turning a boy into a man.*

Mama's pleading with him to change his mind echoed even louder. She'd never wanted her son to go to Vietnam—her *only* son, who abhorred guns and loved peace. Even though serving his country was the most honorable duty of all, she recognized Ron was not a soldier. On the deer-hunting trips to Arkansas Dad had insisted he go on, Ron would avoid killing the deer by "accidentally" missing his target. Then he'd hide his tears when Dad hit his.

With my own tears threatening to fall, I leaned my head back. "Dad blamed it on Ron's poor grades, but the real reason he made him enlist was that girl."

Livy hit the steering wheel in anger. "Why didn't Ron just leave? How could your dad *make* him go to Vietnam?"

"Dad said he'd *disown* him if he didn't go. You know my dad. Could you have told him no?"

"I guess not. He scares me."

"My point exactly. Besides, where was Ron gonna go?"

"Canada."

I looked at Livy with a sarcastic stare. "Right. And humiliate our father? A decorated army colonel?"

"Plenty of fathers are wrangling 4-Fs for their sons. My friend's dad helped him falsify his medical records."

"Not ours! I'm convinced Dad wanted to make an example out of Ron. He didn't want anyone thinking his son would get favoritism."

My first thought every morning as soon as I opened my eyes was whether I'd see my brother again. If he died, I'd be an only child. I'd have no one with whom to commiserate about growing up with all the ridiculous rules in our house. "I swear, Livy. Sometimes I can't sleep worrying about my mother and what will happen to her if Ron dies. I'm not sure she could live through it." News of American soldiers dying on the front lines dominated the headlines. Especially after the Tet Offensive. The tears I'd been holding back crept down my cheeks.

With flared nostrils, Livy shook her head in disgust.

"Other nights I stay up for hours worrying about how scared he must be over there," I said, swiping my tears away.

Livy checked her mirror and mashed the accelerator to pass someone at ninety miles an hour. Once we were safely back into the right lane, she yelled, "Of course he's scared. This war is frightening! Horrific! Senseless!" She punched the steering wheel with each word. "Washington bastards. I blame them for the massacre in My Lai." She glanced at me. "Ronny wasn't there, was he?"

"I don't know, and I don't want to. What I do know is that he's not a killer." I wrung my hands, kneading my palms with my thumbs. "He could at least write. We never hear from him anymore."

Livy readjusted her sunglasses. "That's weird. When was the last time you got a letter?"

Staring out the window, I answered, "Last November. Things at our house have been at a fever pitch since Mama met Ron in Hawaii. Dad has become impossible." I turned to face her. "I guess I can't blame Ron for not writing. Dad insists on being the first one to read all his letters. He won't even let Mama check the mailbox. Can you believe that?"

"Psycho."

"Thank goodness we worked out a plan before he left. He sends my letters to Penny's house or my PO box at Union. I have them all right here." I patted my purse. "I don't know how he's made it through. Boys in his platoon have died. Others have had their limbs blown off. Vietnam is a living, breathing nightmare."

"It's worse than a nightmare. It's an abomination." Livy hesitated a few seconds, then asked, "Will you read me one of his letters?"

Dammit to hell. I should have anticipated that. I didn't want to read her one of Ron's letters. They were all I had left of him. A private moment. Just between the two of us.

On the Road to Woodstock

Somewhere in Maryland

Friday, August 15, 1969
8:00 a.m.

Whether *I* wanted to read Livy one of Ron's letters wasn't the issue. As the awkward silence between us grew, the situation became clear. I was in checkmate. Livy had put my king into an inextricable check from which I had no escape. Reluctantly I dug a hand inside my purse, plucked one of the letters out at random, and read aloud.

> November 4, 1967
> Long Binh, South Vietnam
>
> Dear SuSu,
> How are you, little sis? I hope you're enjoying your freshman year! I'm happy I can write to you at your PO box without Dad reading every word.
>
> I'm pretty good. To answer your question, yes, it's still miserable here but I'm trying to improve my

attitude. It's best for me to think about the future instead of the now. The irony is the beauty of this place. Despite the death and destruction, the landscape is gorgeous. The sunsets are from another universe. When our chopper flew into this one beach all I could think about was how, under different circumstances, I'd love to vacation here. The Vietnamese girls are pretty, too. Ha ha!

I glanced at Livy with a tight-lipped smile.

So far, I'm the only guy in my company whose dad insisted I enlist. I'll probably meet more before I go home. My CO told me there are plenty of men Dad's age who think their sons ought to serve their country like they did. If I hadn't enlisted, it would have been a reflection on him. He doesn't care that the US shouldn't be here in the first place. I love my country, and I used to think it was an honor to serve in the military, but that was before Vietnam. I'd give anything to be holding a protest sign instead of an M16. I don't believe in this war.

I have something gross to report today. I never gave getting leeches much thought until I got here, but during our mission we had to cross several streams with marsh and reed grass. The streams had waist-high water. Even with our pant legs tied, fitted tight over our ankles, we still got leeches. The only thing that helped to remove those blood suckers was our lit cigarettes. Our CO told us not to remove them with a knife because that would only remove their bodies.

Remember in my last letter I told you we stayed wet for days? Well, jungle rot happens if you can't

> change into dry clothes and socks. We get skin ulcers that resemble moon craters all over our legs and groin. They're pus-filled lesions that look like giant chicken pox sores.

I looked over at Livy in horror. "Gross!" we both yelled at the same time.

> One of the saddest things about this war is the thousands of innocent Vietnamese women and children who are dying. I won't even go into detail about those horror stories. It would make you wretch. I've witnessed things no person should ever see. It's hard to sleep because I can't get the images out of my head. Johnson is lying to everyone over there. Don't believe him.

"See, I told you," Livy interrupted. "Keep going."

I cleared my throat—to banish my own ghastly images—then went back to the letter.

> My friend, Freddy C (we call him that because there are two Freds in my platoon), is better than a brother. We look out for each other. He saved me from a venomous snake bite the other day. The rascal had curled up inside my boot looking for a dark warm smelly spot, ha ha! Freddy C reminded me to shake it out before I put it on. Otherwise, I'd have met my Maker from a snake bite. That sounds like a better way to go than having my head blown off, if you want to know the truth.
>
> In your last letter, you told me you stay up at night worrying about me. Please try not to. Maybe I'll

come out better for being here. I have a lot I want to do for mankind when I'm free again.

Gotta go. They're coming for the mail now. I'll write more later. As always, thanks for your prayers.

Peace and Love,

Ron

Livy's knuckles had turned white from gripping the steering wheel. "None of that surprises me. But hearing it straight from Ronny makes it so much worse." She glanced over, thrusting her cigarette toward me. "By the way, you are *not* responsible for him being there."

I *was* responsible. And she knew it.

Returning my gaze to the window, I happened to catch the sign welcoming us to Pennsylvania. Several seconds passed before I answered. "I was such an idiot. I can't believe I left my diary on my bed. With the key in the lock. I knew better." Biting my bottom lip until it hurt, I grew disgusted with myself all over again. "I still don't know if it was Dad who read it or Mama. I thought diaries were supposed to be sacred."

"They are sacred. My parents would never read mine." Livy stubbed her cig in the ashtray. "Did you ever learn who the girl was?"

"He refused to tell me."

"Would it make any difference now?"

With a long sigh, I pressed my fingers into my temples. "I think I'm just looking for someone else to share the blame."

Livy reached over and squeezed my knee. "It's not your fault. You have to forgive yourself."

A small shrug was my response to that. "We're supposed to wait for marriage to have *relations*." I overemphasized the word *relations*. "The Bible says it's a sin to have sex before marriage. That's why Dad got so mad. He told Ron he'd burn in hell for what he did."

"The Bible was written a loooong time ago. Times have changed."

Her comment made me think of Mama's tattered Bible, which made me think of something else. I blurted it out without thinking. "I could have sworn I smelled alcohol on Mama's breath the night I left."

"Duh. She has to cope somehow. Between her son in Vietnam and her psycho husband? I'd be a lush too."

"She's not a lush, Livy!" I said, fury rising. "I've never seen my mother take a single drink. Not once in my entire life."

"With all the church rules in your house? She's forced to hide it. I bet it's vodka. Not as noticeable."

Could Livy be right? Had Mama been drinking vodka to cope with how much meaner Dad had become? And with the pain of missing Ron? "If the church ever found out, or if Dad ever found—"

"Our family goes to church, but they don't tell us we can't drink. It was Jesus who turned water into wine." She gaped at me with *What the hell?* written all over her face.

I didn't respond.

"Where in the Bible does it say you can't drink? Or listen to rock music, or dance to your favorite song?"

This time I gave her a big shrug.

"Why is your church like that?"

Now I was defensive. There were plenty of good things about my church. "I don't know, Livy. It's the only church I've ever been to." She was flat getting on my nerves. I decided to block out her know-it-all voice by humming "Lucy in the Sky with Diamonds." *Loudly.*

But Dad's vicious voice boomed even louder in my mind. I started obsessing over what he'd done the night I ran away. I hated him now more than ever. Part of me wanted to tell Livy what had happened, but I knew it would just lead to another lecture I didn't want to hear. "I don't think you understand how hard it was for me and Ron to grow up the way we did. It's the reason I'm . . . me. I can't help it, Livy." I couldn't meet her eyes; the shame about Dad and my unworldliness was too much to bear.

"I do understand," she said in a much sweeter voice. "I was there."

"No, you weren't! Dad's gotten much worse since you and Ron left. I'm only allowed to spend the night at Penny's house because her family goes to our church. Even when I'm home *from college*! I'm required to be in the front door by eleven o'clock, and music is a thing of the past. Never mind that I'm twenty years old! I. Have. No. Life!"

"You do now. Your old life left the minute you decided to come with me. So long, psycho dad. Hello, happiness!"

Livy's voice sounded scratchy when she said *dad*. For as long as I could remember, her voice had a raspy quality, like it had to pass through a grater to get out of her mouth. I couldn't wait to change the subject. "Do you remember how Ron used to call you Flea Bit? Because of your scratchy voice."

"I'd get so mad at him," she said with a grin.

"He flirted with all my friends." As soon as the words left my lips, my anger returned. "Forget Ron. I'm getting mad at him for not writing. Let's just focus on our fun weekend." Leaning back in the seat, I pictured us in a sunny meadow with a cool breeze, listening to Crosby, Stills & Nash—live.

"Okay, but I want to say one more thing." Tenderness laced her tone. "This is not meant to scare you."

I whipped my head around to find her lips mashed together. *"What?"*

"Do you think there's a possibility Ronny's been . . . wounded?" She glanced at me briefly, then back at the road. "And that's why he's not writing? Maybe your dad's keeping it from you and your mom, so y'all won't worry."

"I don't want to think like that, Livy," I said, with renewed fury in my voice.

She backed down immediately. "Okay. Fine. It was just a thought."

"My father doesn't protect us from anything. He used to sometimes, before he made Ron enlist, but not anymore."

I closed my eyes, daydreaming about the good ole days, long before the Vietnam War, when it still seemed like Dad loved me.

At least some of the time.

On the Road to Woodstock

Somewhere in New York

Friday, August 15, 1969
10:30 a.m.

"Suzannah. Are you asleep?"

Seconds slipped by before I answered. "No. Just thinking."

"About what?"

"How hungry I am," I lied. I was sick of listening to her snide comments about my church and about Dad. I could hate him all I wanted, but she couldn't.

"Me too. Let's stop. We need gas anyway."

Right before the New York border, we filled up at a 7-Eleven and stocked up on Milky Ways, peanut butter crackers, and Juicy Fruit gum. We even bought suicide Slurpees, mixing together a little bit of each flavor. After thrusting cash at the clerk, Livy dashed out the door, scurrying back to the car with both hands full. Getting to her boyfriend was all she could think about. I was barely inside the car when she peeled off and my door slammed shut. I nearly lost a foot.

Back on the road—a scenic two-lane highway dotted with cows, silos, and old farmhouses—my mind drifted, once again, to Mama. I had wanted to call her from the pay phone at the 7-Eleven, but Livy was in a mad rush. Besides, I was afraid *he'd* pick up. She was probably worried sick about me, though. I'd call her from Bethel.

After a big sip of my Slurpee, my mind switched to Gertie. At first, I'd been scared to call her. I didn't want to let her down. She'd been a friend to me, and I was afraid she might disapprove of my quitting. Boy, was I wrong.

"Why, Suzannah, I declare. It's about time you did something fun for yourself," she had said when I called her the morning we left. "I heard Dick Cavett talking about that thing on the TV Tuesday night. Hippiefest, they're calling it. Go enjoy yourself!"

She urged me to be mindful of the Hong Kong flu pandemic and reminded me that even President Johnson had contracted it the year before. "It's killed over a million people worldwide," Gertie had said. "Don't share your drink." Right before hanging up, she'd shocked the life out of me with one final admonition. "You need to cut loose for a change. Strike a match when you get up there and burn your bra."

I still had on my bra. But I had to admit I loved my new clothes. Livy had given me a pair of hip-hugger bell-bottoms and a cute pink baby doll top with puff sleeves. I'd almost made us late making sure the top was pressed.

As for Livy's festival outfit: blue jean cutoffs, a suede V-neck top with fringe hanging from the sleeves, several strands of love beads draping her neck—even more on her wrists—leather sandals that crisscrossed and tied under her knees, and no bra. She looked like a hippie goddess.

"I can't believe we've been together two days and you haven't told me a thing about the boys at Union U," she said. "Do you have a boyfriend?"

"No way."

"Why do you say it like that?"

"I don't know."

"Don't you want a boyfriend?"

More than anything in the world, I wanted a boyfriend, but none of the boys I was interested in seemed interested in me. "Boys are untrustworthy," I told her, propping my feet on the dash. I'd just leave it at that.

"I trust my boyfriend."

Crossing my arms, I turned toward her. "How do you know you can trust him?"

As often as she had answers for everything, I could tell I'd stumped her. After thinking about it a few moments, she said, "Well, we think alike. We have the same ideology."

"Cool. But give me one good reason you trust him."

With her eyes pinned on the road, she gave my question more thought but got distracted upon noticing two guys ahead with their thumbs out. She slowed down to fifty. "Wanna pick them up?" she asked, with a thrill in her raspy voice. I hesitated just long enough for her to pass them by. "Maybe the next ones," she said.

Ron picked up hitchhikers, but I never did. Too risky.

Before Livy decided to discuss the joys of hitchhiking, I turned the conversation back to trust. "You still haven't answered my question."

Livy gnawed on her bottom lip, like she was pondering another chess move. "He's a Leo," she actually said, like there was no more room for discussion. "Fiercely loyal. Brave. Sometimes stubborn, but *always* passionate." She shimmied in her seat at the word *passionate*. "It's my favorite sign."

I rolled my eyes.

"Don't tell me you don't believe in astrology." She gave me an incredulous stare.

"Okay, I won't tell you." I threw my palms up. "Come on, give me a real reason."

A slight squint in her eyes told me she was wondering the same thing. "He's never cheated on me." She tapped the dashboard, as if that was her final answer.

"How do you know he's never cheated on you?"

"I just know."

I shrugged with a whatever-you-say look.

"Okay, I don't know. But he sure knows how to please me, if you know what I mean." She giggled and playfully honked the horn. "I've got all kinds of trust in him for that." With a glance in my direction she added, "When he licks—"

I thrust my hand toward her. "I get the picture."

Livy slid her fingers back and forth along the slick curve of the steering wheel. "So you may not want a boyfriend, but you're on the pill, right?"

"Nope."

She tilted her head. "Is that because you use another kind of birth control, or you're not having sex?"

Should I lie? Or come clean? Surely she knew the truth. "Not having sex."

The furrow between her brows deepened. "But you've had sex before . . ."

Despite the anxiety I felt about fessing up, I still shook my head no.

The shock, both in Livy's voice and in her eyes, was thinly disguised when she dived in for her next question. "Maybe you haven't gone all the way, but you've done other stuff. Surely, you've had an orgasm."

Okay, now I had to lie. It was Livy asking the question. She'd never understand my chaste existence. And she'd scream if she knew I'd never even been French-kissed. The only kisses I'd ever gotten were a few pecks at Emily Freeburg's spin the bottle party in eighth grade. "Of course I have," I said.

"But you're a virgin." She put a finger to her chin. "That's interesting. Are you following your family rule about no sex before marriage? Or are you afraid of getting pregnant? The pill has changed that, you know."

How on earth have we landed on this subject, and what can I do to get off it? I would rather have poked a fork in my eye than keep this sex talk up. "I'm . . . not sure," I said. Of course I wanted to have sex. I fantasized about it all the time. But staying out of hell seemed like the better choice.

Livy sat up straight, with a serious tone to her voice. "I don't think the church, or the state, has the right to tell a woman what she can or can't do with her own body. The pill gives us the freedom to have sex without worrying about pregnancy. Even that liar President Johnson gave the pill the thumbs-up before he left office. You heard about that, didn't you?"

"I think I heard it somewhere." Another fib. I hadn't heard.

"Can you believe the pill didn't exist ten years ago?"

"Not really." Truthfully, I couldn't have cared less.

"Free love is beautiful, man."

My mind swirled with questions. When did Livy adopt this free-thinking mindset? Going all the way with John Dearing our junior year was a wild thing to do, but nothing to this degree. She talked like she had sex *often*. "When did you . . . get like this?" I flat out asked her.

"When did I become a freak?"

"You're not a freak, Livy. I'm asking when you turned into such a free love person?"

"Hey, I'm proud to be a freak. It's not a bad thing. But to answer your question, I guess going to Radcliffe has helped me see things differently." She narrowed her eyes. "Dammit. It's the fuzz."

The blinking blue lights at the roadblock ahead, with policemen positioned outside their cars, sent a stress signal to my heart too. I leaned into the dash. "Wonder what's going on?"

Quite honestly, danger or not, I was thankful for the distraction. All the sex talk had me unnerved.

"Probably looking for drugs." She mashed her foot on the brake, stopping behind several others who were waiting to pass through.

I grabbed her arm. "Tell me you don't have pot in this car."

"Not where they can find it."

"Livy!" My body temperature dropped fifteen degrees.

"Chill out. They won't stop me, man. Hand me my lipstick, please. It's in my purse."

Once we got up to the squad car, Pink a Pale Livy confidently poked her head out the window, resting her chin on the back of her hand. "Good morning, officer."

From the way the cop beamed at her, I knew she was right. Between her scratchy Southern accent and her inordinate beauty, he'd clearly rather search her than the car. Without further ado, he waved us through but stopped the VW bus behind us. I whipped around, and Livy watched through her rearview to see eight longhairs pouring out of the vehicle.

As Pally's engine roared, picking up speed, Livy gave the fuzz a middle finger salute.

I was beginning to wonder what in the heck I'd gotten myself into. Pied Piper Liv had a way of convincing people to follow her to the ends of the earth. Especially me. She could convince me to do just about anything, even if it meant I'd get in big trouble.

On the Road to Woodstock

Almost to Bethel

Friday, August 15, 1969
11:00 a.m.

You'd think we'd have been tired after all the driving. Nothing could have been further from the truth. We were energized.

As we closed in on Bethel, Livy and I grooved to the music, crooning along with Jim Morrison to "Light My Fire." I tapped out the beat on the dashboard. She used her steering wheel as a conga drum, her cigarette pinched between two fingers. After listening to the Doors' self-titled album all the way through, we both agreed Jim Morrison had the sexiest voice on earth.

"He's the most gorgeous hunk I've ever seen," Livy said. "It's a crying shame he won't be at the festival."

"Wonder why?"

"Probably booked elsewhere. What other reason would they have for not playing?"

The closer we got, the more traffic slowed. We crept along for several miles, at no more than fifteen miles an hour. Once we were on the other side of Eldred, New York, past a cemetery, all movement stopped. Our road, a lazy two-lane stretch with a hill in the distance, kept us from seeing all that far, but what we could see was a long line of cars stuck together like a freight train.

"*Crap*. There's a wreck," Livy said, gripping the sides of her head. She glanced at me with a clenched jaw. "Look and see how far away we are. We can't miss Nick, SuSu. We can't."

I had my doubts. We were supposed to meet him in two hours. Good thing we hadn't stopped at the chocolate factory.

After another map check, I learned Bethel was still eleven miles away. Not wanting to alarm Livy, all I said was, "Even if we're a little late, you'll find him. You're the most persistent person I know."

An hour later we had not budged an inch.

Pretty soon people grew impatient. Cars passed us on both sides of the road with folks standing in the back seats of convertibles, others riding on the tops of hoods and trunks, all holding on somehow. Kids waved and flashed peace signs as they passed.

Like an ambulance driver in a mad rush, Livy whipped Pally over to the right shoulder to tail behind a '67 GTO convertible with a Pennsylvania license plate overflowing with hippies. Only that didn't get us very far. Once we crested the hill, all traffic stopped again. Hundreds more had had the same idea. Clearly, a wreck had not caused the colossal traffic jam. It was the festival. Had to be.

Highway 55 was no longer two lanes; it was four. All headed in the same direction, to the same place. Woodstock. As far as the eye could see, it was one gargantuan parking lot. The only vehicles moving forward were motorcycles, weaving in and out of the lanes and shoulders. The car next to us had steam pouring out of the hood.

Livy drummed her fingers impatiently on the steering wheel. "I can't believe this is happening," she murmured through gritted teeth.

"Try to calm down," I told her. "It's gonna be okay."

"How am I supposed to calm down?" She looked at her watch. "My boyfriend will be frantic if we aren't there."

Before long people gave up. They turned off their engines and spilled out of their vehicles. Some propped up on trunks, others sat down on the road, and more settled in the fields. A few yards in front of us, we spied a dude playing his guitar on the roof of a VW bus. Despite the gridlock, no one seemed upset.

No one except Livy.

It was one giant street party, and I, for one, ached to be a part of it. "Look behind you," I said, turning around in my seat. Hundreds of people laden with suitcases, tents, coolers, and sleeping bags were headed our way.

Livy stuck her head out the window, then waved down a boy as he passed. "Excuse me! Where did you park?"

He stopped, then squatted so his head was level with hers. Laughter filled his voice. "On the road."

"You left your car in the middle of the road?" she asked, wide eyed.

Another chuckle, then a silly face. "Yeah, man. I figure no one's going anywhere around here till Sunday." He handed Livy a wildflower. "For you, Sunshine."

"Aw. Thanks, man!" She tucked it behind her ear, shooting him one of her flirty smiles.

After a lustful grin of his own, he flashed us the peace sign and continued on his journey.

She turned off the engine, snatched the keys from the ignition. "Get your stuff, SuSu. Hurry."

"Are you serious?"

"Dead serious." Cranking up her window at rocket speed, Livy motioned for me to do the same. "There's no telling how much longer we'll be stuck here." She adjusted the rearview mirror, glanced at her flawless face, and then slipped her purse strap over her shoulder. "Dear God, I hope we don't have to walk far."

I kept my mouth shut. According to the map, we still had ten miles to go.

Livy was out of the car by the time I'd stuffed the last of our snacks inside my purse. I shoved the passenger door open with my foot, as wide as it would go.

"Ow!" a male voice bellowed out of nowhere, followed by a long moan.

What the heck? With a glance outside, I noticed there was a boy right next to my door, stooped over, rubbing his knee. I stumbled out, gripping the sides of my cheeks. "I'm so sorry. I didn't see you."

"It's okay. I have another knee." When he straightened up and smiled, I did an unexpected double take.

"Two knees are . . . much better than one," I managed to say, surprised I could even speak. I was so taken with his beauty. Without thinking, I reached out my hand to caress his kneecap but drew it back in a hurry, embarrassed.

His second smile let me know he didn't mind. "You guys headed to the festival?"

Duh. Where else would we be headed? A funny look was all I could muster.

"Hey, maybe you dig traffic jams. I don't know." When he cracked up at himself, I was equally taken with the sound of his laughter, a playful yet manly giggle. Like so many of the boys walking past, he was shirtless, so I zeroed in on his chest, sculpted to perfection. Strands of dark-blond hair poked through like the sprouts of an early garden. A beefy silver-and-turquoise cross hung smack-dab between his nipples. Other than Paul McCartney, he was the cutest boy I'd ever seen.

His dishwater-blond hair was parted in the middle. It hung to the middle of his neck, but he kept it tucked behind his ears. He had muttonchop sideburns, and a cute dimple indented his chin. He wore cutoffs and high-top white Converse tennis shoes. There was a large pack on his back, a cigarette between his fingers, and another cute boy next to him.

By this time Livy had opened the trunk to retrieve our canvas overnight bag. We heard her slam it shut before walking up to join us. A suede floppy hat dipped over one eye, but you could still see her gorgeous face, freckled and tanned. There was a fresh coat of Pink a Pale on her lips. Even I found her irresistible.

She sidled up next to me and peered at the two boys. "Hey. I'm Livy," she said in her trademark raspy voice.

"Leon," Boy Beautiful said, then pointed a thumb toward the other. "My cousin, Handsome Johnny."

They both smiled, then shifted their gazes to me.

"Oh, hi! I'm Suzannah," I said with a nervous giggle, still flustered at what I'd done and to whom I'd done it.

"Where are y'all from?" Livy asked, confident and *un*flustered as usual.

Leon answered for both of them. "Tar City, Pennsylvania."

"Hm. Never heard of it," she said, looking at her watch—not them.

"Is there a lot of tar there?" I asked, desperate to add something, anything, to the conversation.

After glancing at each other, the boys busted a gut. Both roared with laughter.

I felt heat burning my cheeks. "What's so funny? That was a fair question."

"It's actually *Tower* City. We pronounce it weird. It's a PA thing," said Handsome Johnny. That may have been his name—and he was indeed handsome—but he didn't hold a candle to Leon. In my opinion, anyway.

"*Y'all* aren't from around here." Leon took a giant step backward to glance at Pally's license plate. "Where do you guys live in Tennessee?"

Both Livy and I answered at the same time. "Memphis."

"Helluva drive," said Handsome Johnny.

Livy put her free hand on her hip. "No shit, Sherlock."

Propping an elbow on his cousin's shoulder, Leon winked. An emerald sparkle glistened in his eye. "How's Elvis?"

"I wouldn't know," answered Livy. "Not a fan." After another check of her watch, she took two steps forward, then turned back around. "Wanna walk with us? I'm supposed to meet my boyfriend at one."

Leon flashed her a beaming smile. "Did you bring your helicopter?"

Snapping her fingers, she smiled back. "Darn. Left it at home."

"Then we better get a move on. We've got a long walk ahead."

Livy never asked *How long?* And she no longer appeared frantic. The cute boys must have calmed her nerves.

Leon stretched out a hand to guide our path. "After you, ladies."

Wonder if he's disappointed Livy has a boyfriend?

As the four of us began our trek toward Bethel, with what had to have been five thousand other young people, maneuvering in and out of erroneously parked cars, I couldn't get over the New York August temperature. It wasn't all that hot. On the contrary, it was delightful. Good thing because the road was not exactly flat. We were in the Catskills, after all. With the scent of pine in the air, it reminded me of my days at Young Life camp in North Carolina.

Darling little barns dotted the landscape—one with a weather vane. Dense evergreens filled in the sides of the road. Every now and then, at a clearing, we could see lush green fields spotted with black-and-white dairy cows. Handsome Johnny wanted to stop and milk one, but Livy wouldn't let him.

The landscape thrilled me, but my eyes were having a field day over something else. All the people around me—what they were wearing and the abundance of items they were lugging to Woodstock. All Livy and I had packed were essentials. Her boyfriend was in charge of the rest.

One girl, dressed in a full-length tie-dyed muumuu, was carrying a suitcase—a *big* suitcase—and a sleeping bag underneath her arm. Another girl, wearing a feathered headdress, carried a round makeup case in one hand and a thin rolled-up mat in the other. A camera bag hung from her neck.

The scene reminded me of the exodus when the Israelites departed Egypt, heading for the Promised Land. Only these women weren't wearing robes. It was quite the opposite. I found myself staring. From the looks of the other girls, I wondered if I'd ever fit in.

One girl, around sixteen I'd say, wore a bikini top and jeans that hit even farther below her belly button than mine. But that's not what made me gawk. The black bush poking from each of her underarms had me bug eyed. My jaw dropped like a codfish's when I saw a redheaded girl's barely tied halter top, so loose you could see her boobs bouncing with each step she took. She may as well have been topless. Johnny couldn't take his eyes off her. Leon watched too. On one hand, it made me grateful for my new bra. On the other, I felt like a wallflower at a hippie sock hop.

An hour later, we were still walking, I was still rubbernecking, and Livy was freaking out. Her excitement about Woodstock had been eclipsed by panic. We were supposed to have met Nick at the main entrance an hour ago. And the truth of the matter was none of us knew how much longer it would take to reach Bethel.

As for the good news, the long walk gave me an opportunity to learn more about Leon. He was "almost a senior" at Penn State, in no hurry to graduate for fear Uncle Sam would call him up as soon as he did. He'd been born in Tar City, but his family had moved to Harrisburg when he was twelve.

Aside from discovering his great sense of humor, I learned he came from a large, tight-knit Catholic family. He was the eldest, with five little sisters and one younger brother. Leon bragged on his family, especially his sisters. He talked about how they sometimes drove him crazy, but his life would be miserable and incomplete without them.

Would Ron ever say something that nice about me?

Like mine, his mother was a homemaker. His dad worked in the steel industry, which Leon claimed was in a terrible slump. By the way he talked, I could tell he was concerned with how his family would make ends meet. He explained it was a good thing he was on scholarship, otherwise his parents wouldn't have been able to send him to college at all. He'd just turned twenty-one in June. I asked him what it felt like to be a legal adult. He just laughed and said, "Nothing's changed."

During our stroll, we learned that he and Handsome Johnny were in deep opposition to the war. Both claimed they would never go to Vietnam, even if it meant moving to Canada.

Livy loved that idea. "I have contacts there who could help y'all if you have to go."

Handsome Johnny jerked his head back in surprise. "That would be rad, man! I'm headed there after the festival. Time's up. Burned my draft card at a New York rally."

"Good for you," said Livy.

"If you've got the dough, you won't have to go," Leon chanted.

Livy threw her head back in disgust. "Plenty of rich fathers are getting their sons out of service." She glanced at me to add more, but I shook my head. I didn't want to tell our new friends anything about Dad.

Leon went on to explain that his little brother had been drafted the year before, simply because he didn't have the grades for a scholarship and his parents didn't have the money to pay for his tuition. I told him my brother was in 'Nam, too, but refrained from saying why. We discussed how much we missed our brothers and feared for their safety. Both of us having brothers in Vietnam gave us a special connection.

At least I thought so.

A mile later, while babbling on and on to the group about my brother and what it was like growing up in Memphis, I noticed Leon staring at me. While it gave me a thrill, the longer he stared, the more it jangled my nerves. Not able to take it much longer, I blurted out, "Why are you staring at me?"

With a finger to his lips, he held up his other palm so I'd stop walking. Slowly he reached toward me with both hands, then cupped my shoulder. "Look who landed on you." He opened his palms slightly, just enough for me to peek at a beautiful monarch butterfly slowly flapping her delicate wings.

"She was on my shoulder?"

"Yup. She mistook your pink top for a flower." Ever so slowly, he parted his thumbs so we could study her loveliness. Two vibrant shades of orange, veined in black, with careless white dots sprinkled across her wings and torso. This close, we could see her bulging onyx eyes, her willowy legs, and her erect antennae readying her for flight.

Once we'd both gotten a good look at her, Leon lifted his palms skyward. At first, the butterfly hesitated, perhaps wanting to linger. Within moments, though, aware of her loose chains, the graceful monarch gained the courage she needed and soared away to freedom.

Leon pressed his elbow into mine. "She wanted your nectar. Proves you're sweet."

It was his words that were sweet. Without knowing how to respond, I just smiled in gratitude.

Livy didn't take notice of, or care about, the butterfly. The butterfly was not her concern. She was engaging Handsome Johnny in a conversation of her own. And if I knew Livy, that girl was wearing him out with fear over missing her boyfriend at the front gate.

Leon took a second to light another cigarette. With a flick of his wrist, he expertly shook a single from the pack, then pointed it toward me. "Want one?" he asked, a Marlboro dangling from his pretty lips.

"I don't smoke."

"I'm quitting," he said with a wink. "After this weekend."

That wink of his set me on fire.

Woodstock

Day One

Friday, August 15, 1969
2:00 p.m.

We finally made it to White Lake—a hamlet of Bethel—two full hours after abandoning Pally. My mouth felt like a piece of dry toast. My feet ached, and I longed to sit down, even for five minutes. But Livy was in a mad rush. She didn't pause when we passed a man offering Cokes for sale. Or even look at the truck selling yummy-looking watermelon, with a long line of folks wrapped around twice.

So I kept walking. For her sake.

White Lake was a quaint little place with charming houses and motels encircling a crystal-blue lake. The number of cars that had invaded it was mind boggling. It looked like thousands of Hot Wheels had been dropped from the sky, landing haphazardly. It was one thing to see them abandoned on the highway—another to see them overrunning the town. With the multitude of tents pitched on either side of the road, it made it hard to know if grass actually grew underneath.

Homeowners sat in lawn chairs, waving as the sojourners passed. By their widened eyes and straight-lined lips, it seemed they were waving at freaks in a circus parade. Nevertheless, many of the townsfolk offered refreshments for sale, including *water*. Hard to imagine paying money for the most natural resource in America, but I couldn't stand it any longer. I marched right up to an old man selling water and bologna sandwiches. I didn't care how late we were; Livy could just be mad.

As soon as I opened my mouth to order, I heard her behind me. "Excuse me, sir. Where is the festival?"

"You've come a long way, little lady," the man said. "Can tell by that pretty drawl of yours." Even this old geezer wanted to flirt with our beauty queen.

But I needed water. And I needed it now. "May I please have—"

Another Livy interruption. "Yes sir, we have come a long way. Where is the festival? Please."

"Yasgur's dairy farm. No one else 'round here would have had it," he muttered under his breath.

Johnny, who was standing next to me, asked, "Why's that, sir?"

Livy interrupted a third time before the old man could explain. "Is Yasgur's dairy farm far?"

"Three miles. Maybe a little less." He pointed to his right. "You're almost th—"

"Three miles!" She sighed loudly. "We've just walked fifteen."

"More like six," said Johnny. "We'll take four sandwiches and four . . ." He hesitated. "How much for the water?"

The old man wouldn't look him in the eye. "Twenty-five cents. It's a large cup full."

Johnny glanced back at Leon, whispering, "We could buy a loaf of bread for twenty."

Leon just shrugged.

"Free refills," the old man added.

"Okay, four sandwiches and four waters, please," said Johnny. He handed the man a five-dollar bill.

"Thank you," I said, anticipating the cool water bathing my tongue.

Once the man handed over the water, you'd have thought all four of us had spent three days in a desert by the way we downed the cups and asked for more. Even Livy.

"That Max Yasgur is a hippie lover," the man said while stuffing our sandwiches inside a paper bag.

Johnny winked at Leon. "Is that right?"

"People 'round here been boycotting his milk 'cause of it." The sound of Livy's foot tapping against the pavement caused the man's gaze to travel from her face to her feet. "What's your hurry, little lady?"

Livy let out a loud "Ugh," throwing her hands up in exasperation. She turned on her heel and stormed off.

Johnny was still collecting his change. I didn't know whether to wait with the boys or rush to catch up with her. All I knew was that I wasn't ready to tell them goodbye. Or let go of the hope that we'd all sit together once we got to the festival.

Johnny yelled after her, "Don't wig out, love. You'll find your man."

Livy stopped, then turned to face us—forced smile, arms crossed, foot tapping.

As the street sign behind her came into focus, my lips split into a grin. Happy Avenue. Livy may have been mad, but I hadn't been that happy in my whole life.

~

Once we'd wolfed down our sandwiches, we took a roadside bathroom break, then started toward Yasgur's dairy farm. A mile later we came upon an overturned table with a message written in large letters: **LOCAL PEOPLE SPEAK OUT. STOP MAX'S HIPPIE MUSIC FESTIVAL. NO 150,000 HIPPIES HERE.**

Johnny made an about-face, but Livy turned him back around.

"Wow, that many hippies, huh?" Leon said. "No wonder the epic traffic jam."

"My boyfriend said they were expecting fifty thousand but sold over a hundred thousand tickets in advance," Livy explained, then let out a cry of relief as we passed another sign: **AQUARIAN PARKING.** "Thank you, God!" she shrieked, casting her gaze heavenward.

State troopers directed traffic with the help of a guy in a long-sleeved white jumpsuit. A red scarf hung loosely around his neck, and he wore a tattered straw hat with a hole in front that matched the hole in his smile where his front teeth should have been. He carried a walking stick in one hand and blew a kazoo with the other. "Welcome to Woodstock, folks!" he cried. "Glad you're here."

Fifteen minutes later, at three o'clock sharp, exactly fifty-five minutes after our water break, and thirty-two hours after leaving Memphis, our pilgrimage came to an end. Along with our two new friends and several thousand others, Livy and I crested a hill on West Shore Road, finally arriving at Yasgur's dairy farm. Agog with excitement, I looked around, taking it all in.

A panoramic view of a pop-up pasture city unfolded before our eyes. Instead of crops, people populated the fields, forming a human carpet that stretched from one side of the road, across the pasture, onto a hill, and through a surrounding forest. A continual flow of humankind descended on the land from all directions. It seemed like 150,000 people were already there, and thousands more trailed behind us.

A naturally sloped, bowl-shaped cow pasture had been converted into a mammoth amphitheater. A large wooden stage had been built at the base, with a white canvas roof. Two skyscraper-size cranes rested in a nearby field. A tall wooden fence of protection encircled the backstage area, while six three-story yellow scaffolds topped with giant spotlights and speakers stood like watchtowers near the stage. A jumble of folks clung to the metal poles underneath.

From where we were standing, we could see a good-sized lake behind the stage and smaller ones sprinkled throughout the farm. A campground scattered with hundreds of tents was off to the left. Dairy cows grazed freely among the people in the outlying pastures.

The concession stands looked like windjammers against a partly sunny sky, with multiple yellow canvas masts billowing in the wind. Temporary telephone and electricity poles had been constructed throughout the farm, and I noticed with relief a village of Porta Potties in the distance. A groovy, psychedelic-painted school bus was parked inside a chain-link fence that outlined a portion of the seating area. Only one thing seemed to be missing.

"Wonder where the ticket booth is," I asked, scouting the perimeter. No one was selling *or* checking tickets anywhere. What's more, hundreds of folks flooded into the amphitheater via a flattened section of fence—without presenting tickets.

Livy, pacing around in circles, stopped abruptly. She threw clenched fists in the air. "Forget the damn ticket booth! Where's the front gate? Nick told me to meet him at the front gate. There isn't one!" She was seconds away from tears. I heard them in her voice. But she was right. There was no front gate anywhere.

"You'll find him," Leon said tenderly. "Don't sweat it."

"You don't understand." Livy's voice cracked. "I haven't seen my boyfriend in three months. If we can't find each other, I'm going home. I did not drive eleven hundred miles to camp by myself."

I gave her a feeble wave.

"You know what I mean." She let our canvas bag slip from her shoulder and plopped down on top of it.

Johnny stooped down next to her, lit a cigarette, and handed it over. "You can't go anywhere till Sunday, love. Hang loose. Let him find you."

Livy put the cigarette to her lips, sucking in a long drag. "How's he gonna do that? Look at this mob," she said in a whiny voice.

The noise from a helicopter caused us all to look up. "See," Leon said. "Here he comes now. He waited on you to make his entrance." We all watched the baby-blue-and-white helicopter land on a heliport beside the stage. "Is your boyfriend Jimi Hendrix?"

"Very funny," Livy answered before taking another drag. She couldn't even muster a smile. Tears flooded her eyelids. "Y'all go on. You don't have to wait with us."

It was official. Olivia Foster was the dumbest person on planet earth. I wanted to mash my foot on top of hers until she screamed out in pain. That was the last thing I wanted her to say.

"You sure?" Johnny asked, seeming a bit disappointed.

"Y'all shouldn't have to miss out on a good spot because of us," she said.

Us? There's no us to it.

Johnny stood back up, turned to Leon. "All right, then. Let's go claim our spot. Before we have to see the show from back here."

I had feared the end was imminent, but when faced with it, I didn't know how to say goodbye. I'd just spent four wondrous hours with these boys and kicked myself for not suggesting to Livy earlier that we invite them to sit with us. But then again, shouldn't she have figured that out herself?

"Far out walking with you two Memphis belles," Johnny said, looking first at me, then down at Livy. "You'll find your boyfriend soon."

Yes, we will find her boyfriend soon. Please wait with us, I was dying to say. Instead, I patted his arm. "Yeah. Far out." With a switch of my gaze toward Leon, I felt my heart pound. "I hope things get better with your dad's business."

He tugged on his earlobe. "Thanks. I appreciate that."

"And your knee," I added.

He slid a hand down his leg and knocked on the good one. "I have two. Remember?" We both chuckled, and then he stretched an arm around me from the side, pulling me into his bare chest. My lips were kissing his turquoise cross, and I could smell his woodsy aroma.

Once he let go, I had a hard time looking at him. After a few seconds he said, "I hope your brother makes it home safely, Suzannah."

The sound of my name in his throaty, Pennsylvania accent caused the first throb of sadness I'd felt since leaving home. It washed over me unexpectedly. I had to bite the inside of my cheek to keep the tears away. I did not want him to leave.

"Harold, please go to the blue tent in the back for your diabetes medicine. Those of you hanging from the scaffolds, please come down," a man announced from the stage. He said something else, but between the whir of the helicopter and the chatter around us, his words were impossible to discern.

Handsome Johnny turned to Leon. "I think I can get us pretty close to the front."

The boys gave us one last look. I lifted my hand to wave goodbye. Watching them step over the flattened fence, soon to disappear into the monumental crowd, I memorized the back of Leon's dishwater-blond waves, hoping against hope I'd be lucky enough to spot them again.

That Livy Foster could make me go from loving her one minute to wanting to strangle her the next. Out of nowhere my mind drifted back three years. To the last weekend we had spent together. Two weeks before she betrayed me. For the second time.

Three Years Earlier

Home

Memphis, Tennessee

Thursday, August 4, 1966

Ron's first letter home lay face down on my chest. I'd devoured it ten times already, scrutinizing every word. It didn't seem like he was still mad at me for causing his enlistment, but he didn't sound mad at Dad either. Sarcastic maybe, but not mad. And that would have been impossible.

> August 1, 1966
> Fort Bragg, NC
>
> Dear Family,
> Well, Basic Training is over. Guess what, Dad? I'm a marksman now. I know how to shoot an M16. Not something I'm proud of but I know it makes you happy. Turns out I'm a pretty fast runner, too. My sergeant asked me if I was a sprinter or a running back. I told him I was a defensive end benchwarmer but thanked him for asking.

I got my induction cut. Y'all wouldn't recognize me. I look like Uncle Fester. (He's on The Addams Family, Dad.) No wonder they say a crewcut feels like a Brillo pad. It's a good thing you can't see me, SuSu. You'd be laughing your butt off.

I'm taking my four days leave in Myrtle Beach with three buddies in my unit. They've become my brothers. Most of them didn't attend college. (None of their families could afford it.) Only one of my brothers, Freddy C, got to go to college before Basic. He got drafted as soon as he graduated. He's the one good thing about the army. We've become as thick as the blood running through our veins in only two months.

After the leave we'll all report back for our flight to Vietnam. The sergeant says we better rest while we can. We won't have another break for a year, unless we get R & R sooner, which he said will never happen. I'll write again when we make it over there.

Peace,

Ron

P.S. SuSu, please don't scratch Cuda's hubcaps when you pull away from the curb.

P.P.S. Have so much fun at the Beatles concert. I would kill to be there with you. No pun intended.

Satisfied that he was not mad at me—at least not at the time he wrote the letter—I rolled off my bed, then grabbed both my suitcase and Ron's guitar. I turned out the bedroom light with my chin.

In no time I made it to the bottom of the stairs, a bit out of breath from the heavy load. The luscious smell of fresh-baked banana bread wafted from the kitchen. Poking my head inside the living room, I found Mama in her favorite chair, reading. Like every day, she was dressed as if she would be meeting Queen Elizabeth. Her husband expected it. His wife was a representation of him.

"I finished my book," I said, chewing my bottom lip in hopeful anticipation. "Can you please take me to Livy's now? She's waiting on me." Livy was my very best friend, and her home, my refuge. There were many reasons for that, but chief among them was the strict commandment in our household—*no dancing allowed*. That rule didn't exist in Livy's family. Dancing wasn't against their religion.

Mama turned off the lamp, gathered her purse. "I'm proud of you, honey. Is that your fifteenth or sixteenth book?"

"Eighteenth."

Elation spread across Mama's face as she clapped her hands together. "You're going to win that summer reading challenge. I just know it!"

"Impossible. Vicki Olson wins every year. Last year she read sixty. She has no life." Thinking about my eighteenth book, I moved toward the foyer, then placed my belongings down on the black-and-white marble floor. I'd spent the morning wrapped up in *The Catcher in the Rye*. Holden's troubles reminded me of mine. The way he missed his brother, how he struggled to discover his real self. Mama had no idea about all the *hell*s and *goddamn*s. Probably two hundred of them. If she'd known, the book would have been snatched away before I ever cracked the cover.

"That Mrs. Foster is a doozy," Mama said, high heels clacking against the marble. "Why, she invites you over every Friday night. You should return the favor more often, honey. I love having Livy here. She's a doll."

With a hand on the doorknob, I stopped, turned to face my mother. "Livy can't spend the night out anymore. Kim misses her too much."

That was a bold-faced lie. Livy and her little sister couldn't stand each other. She used to spend the night at my house all the time, but once Ron left and Dad turned into a first-class ogre, Livy grew fearful of him.

I picked up my stuff and rushed out the front door.

"It's the polite thing to do," Mama called from behind. "I wouldn't want the Fosters thinking poorly of us."

"They don't," I called back, walking swiftly toward the car. "I swear."

"Don't swear, Suzannah."

"Sorry, it was a slip."

"What game are you girls playing tonight?"

"Beats me," I muttered, almost to the car.

"Why don't you bring along our new Parcheesi board? Let's be generous."

Before I could object to such an embarrassing notion, Mama had already scurried back inside. I'd once told her that Livy's family, like ours, played a lot of board games. Lying had become one of my strong suits—born out of necessity—but in my mind, "Beats me" was not a lie.

While Mama was inside, my mind drifted. She was right. Mrs. Foster was indeed a doozy. Just not the way Mama thought. Aside from earning the title of Grooviest Mother in America, a moniker I had given her in the seventh grade, Mrs. Foster adored me, and, most important, she covered for me. Livy said it tore her mom up that I was growing up the same way she had, "in a strict religious family," so she felt it her duty to protect me from what she called "rebellion and other repercussions."

Not only did she approve of our dancing, but she danced with us. She let Livy smoke. Even bought her cigarettes. I'd never seen Livy's parents play a single board game, but I always saw them playing cards with their friends.

Cards were another sin in my family.

Moments later, Mama met me at the car with the Parcheesi board in one hand and the car keys in the other. "I'll take those," I said, slipping the key ring over my finger. I flew to the back and opened the trunk of my brother's prized possession—his '63 Plymouth Barracuda—and slung my suitcase, the guitar case, and the Parcheesi board inside.

I loved driving Cuda whenever I got the chance. According to Dad, it needed to be driven to keep the battery alive. He wouldn't let me take it overnight to Livy's, though. *Ridiculous.*

The Memphis heat made it impossible to sit down without airing out the car. After opening the doors and rolling down all the windows, Mama slid into the passenger seat, all the while exclaiming, "Oh dear, oh dear." She pulled down the vanity mirror and tied her car scarf under her chin. To protect her hairdo.

I jumped into the driver's seat and cranked the engine. Cuda roared to life. Struggling to turn the wheel—she had no power steering—I managed to inch away from the curb without scratching her hubcaps. With a glance in the rearview mirror, I watched our house, and my troubles, temporarily disappear.

Like always, I tuned the radio to my favorite station, WHBQ-AM. "Cherish" floated yearningly from the speaker. Just hearing the first stanza of the new song from the Association sent me straight into a fantasy about Paul: the soft melody, the unrequited love. *So apropos.* Knowing every word, I sang along. Singing made me feel good about myself. It gave me a reason to breathe. Especially with Ron gone.

Just as we came to a stop sign, "Cherish" ended. I noticed a smile on Mama's face. Good to see. Smiling was something she hadn't done much of since Ron left.

"You look happy," I said, careful to keep my eyes on the road. Mama was a stickler for that.

"Hearing you sing makes me happy." From the corner of my eye, I noticed her tenting her fingers, each one bouncing off the other. She shifted in her seat, then turned toward me. "Why don't you join the choir, honey? It would delight your father so."

If I had known she would bring that up again, I'd have never commented on her smile. "I already tried choir. It wasn't for me. You know that."

"God blessed you with a beautiful voice, Suzannah. It honors him when you share it with his church. Please give choir another chance."

Watching my mother's face fall, and the way she stared down at her hands, rubbing her thumbs together, made me reconsider joining the choir. Just to make her happy. Just to make her smile. But picturing those mean, gossipy biddies made me banish the thought, and I mashed the accelerator.

Singing in the youth choir was something I'd once loved. It had filled me with joy . . . until one evening after choir practice. I'd rehearsed "Holy, Holy, Holy" in front of the mirror all week long and belted it out during practice. The choir director even complimented my performance.

Once practice was over, I overheard two mothers saying terrible things about me. "Well, look at Little Miss Show-Off today. Doesn't she think she's something special," one mom said, in a mocking tone. "What gives her the right to drown out all the other children?"

"Shame on her," the other mom said, plenty loud enough for me to hear.

I bolted to the ladies' room, then hid inside a toilet stall for thirty minutes until I finally gained the courage to leave. It had never dawned on me that I was a show-off. I hadn't meant to be. I was just doing what I loved most. Singing.

Ron had saved me when I got home. "Forget those ugly biddies. They're just jealous their daughters don't sing as well as you do. We'll show them. One day we'll start our own singing group."

Livy's house was only eight minutes from mine. She lived in one of those groovy gargantuan mansions on Belvedere Boulevard, the kind with a carriage house in the rear and oversize rooms in the main. Playing hide-and-seek at Livy's as a ten-year-old was like getting lost in the fun house at the Mid-South Fair.

With a firm grip on the steering wheel, I inched up the Fosters' pencil-thin driveway and parked underneath their porte cochere. I leaped from the car, then flew to the trunk to grab my stuff.

"I love you, honey," Mama called, scooting over to the driver's seat. Normally she would have accompanied me to the door, even at seventeen, but this day decided not to. Relieved, I leaned in the window and kissed her cheek, dropping the keys inside her palm. I ran up the porch steps and watched her back down the driveway.

The Foster home was the one place I could forget about the rules in my life.

My finger had barely touched the doorbell when their housekeeper, Lorraine, opened the door. I greeted her with a friendly *hello*, then noticed Mrs. Foster heading my way.

"Suzannah!" she cried, stepping onto the porch to wave at Mama, who was waiting at the base of the driveway. She took the Parcheesi board from underneath my arm, and we walked inside the foyer. "What's this for?" she asked, shoving the door closed with her hip.

"Mama thought we could all play tonight," I said, my cheeks flushed with embarrassment.

With a tilt of her head, Mrs. Foster gave me a saucy smile. "We can do that. You girls just stay in."

"And miss Katy's party? No way." I hadn't told my parents about Katy Collier's party. They would have called her parents to make sure they would be home, which would have humiliated me to no end. It was yet another reason to lie. Livy's mom would cover for me, though. I knew that as well as I knew my own name.

She patted the guitar case. "I'd rather hear you sing than play Parcheesi, if you wanna know the truth."

The Friday night before, I'd played her two of my favorite Beatles songs, and she'd loved both. The whole Foster family knew singing was my life's calling. Whenever I sang for them, I felt good about myself. And dreamed about my future as a folk-rocker.

She pointed up the grand center staircase. "Livy's in her room. Need help toting your stuff up?"

"No ma'am. I'm okay."

"Dinner's at six. We're having spaghetti. And there's Ro-Tel cheese dip ready in the kitchen."

Ro-Tel and spaghetti were my favorites. "You're so good to me," I said, throwing my arms around her. The smell of her signature scent—Chanel No. 5 mixed with cigarette smoke—reminded me I was in a safe place.

Mr. and Mrs. Foster were much younger than my parents. He'd grown up in an Irish Catholic family in Massachusetts, but she'd been raised in the house where we were standing. Ten years earlier, when her parents had died in a tragic car crash, she'd inherited the home. Dad and Livy's grandfather had been dear church friends since they were boys. Fortunately for me, that was all it took to gain my parents' approval of Livy. They knew nothing about Mrs. Foster's new lifestyle, though. Or Livy's.

I bounded up the stairs, two at a time, then burst into Livy's room, where I found her on the phone, propped up on her bed. "Hey," I whispered, not wanting to interrupt. I dropped my stuff down in my corner.

After a finger wave, I thought I heard her say "I better go," like she was hiding something, but the hum from the window unit made it hard to know for sure. She placed the handset into the cradle of her pink princess telephone resting next to her on the bed. She was the only friend I had with a phone in her room.

"Who was that?" I asked, not to be nosy. We knew everything there was to know about one another.

Livy hesitated, then reached up to twirl her hair. "Marianne." I looked at the floor, instead of her, so she changed the subject. "Did you bring your money?"

"It's in my suitcase." We'd been saving for *Revolver*, the new Beatles album, due in record stores the next day. As thrilled as I'd been to get my hands on it, the mere mention of Marianne Gentry took away my joy. Livy knew how I felt about that hussy. It really teed me off that they were still friends after Marianne had spread the rumor about Livy and John Dearing going all the way and blaming it on me. The betrayal had nearly killed me.

In her usual authoritative manner, she sat up straight, swinging her legs off the bed. The trail of smoke from her cigarette circled underneath her bedside lampshade. "I called Pop Tunes. We need to get there by seven in the morning if we want a prayer of owning the record. The manager suspects a really long line."

"Then we should get there at six," I said, heading straight for Livy's closet, where my go-go boots were tucked safely inside. Last February, when Nancy Sinatra had introduced the world to her tall shiny white boots, Mrs. Foster had taken us out to buy pairs of our own. She'd even bought a pair for herself.

Livy was already wearing her go-go boots and a baby doll dress that flared at the hem. Her hair was cut into an adorable bob. She looked just like Twiggy. My father hated the new bob, so he commanded that I keep mine in a *Gidget* flip.

After zipping up my boots, I picked up her teasing comb and primped, all the while watching her drag on her cigarette through the mirror's reflection.

"I just hung up with David," she said, trying to mimic Twiggy's British accent. "He's meeting us at Katy's party." David was Livy's latest crush—captain of the football team. He'd never given me the time of day.

I put the comb down, then dived onto the bed next to her, propping myself up on my elbows. "David's such a hunk." I said it in my British accent, which sounded much more authentic than hers.

"So is his friend, Jack." She lifted her brows, like she wanted the two of us together.

But I wasn't interested. My heart belonged to someone else. "Both skuzzes compared to my *Paul*." I loved saying Paul's name like I was a Brit. It sounded sensual.

A stack of teen magazines lived on Livy's bedside table. I reached over and grabbed the whole lot, then plopped it down on the bed. I sorted through till I found the one I wanted—the June issue of *16 Magazine* with the headline: McCartney: His Hidden Life Top Secret Pix. Having read the article a hundred times, I flipped right to it.

My heart exploded at the sight of Paul's baby face. I held up his picture, pressing my lips against his. Almost every night after my parents had gone to bed, I had the same ritual with my own photos. Paul was my imaginary boyfriend. I wasn't allowed to date. From the magazines, I knew his real girlfriend was Jane Asher, so I pretended to be her. I even got bangs like hers.

Livy pulled another magazine from the stack, the February issue of *Tiger Beat* with giant color portraits of the Monkees and Davy Jones on the cover. She smashed her lips on Davy's face, then shifted a squinty-eyed gaze toward me. We both cracked up. Me kissing Paul, her kissing Davy. She vacillated between wanting to marry Davy and wanting to marry George. At first, she'd wanted to marry Paul, but she decided to let me have him. Only a best friend does that.

"Two. More. Weeks!" she squealed. "Will it ever get here?"

"I've never wanted time to pass so fast in all my life," I said, grasping her arm. "Don't be surprised if you look over during the concert and I'm gone."

Livy put the magazine down. "Gone where?"

"I'm thinking of jumping onstage with them."

"The police would never let you do that," she said.

"That doesn't mean I won't try."

Livy sat up straight, gaping at me. "We should go to the airport when they land!"

I scrambled up to face her. "Yes!" Why hadn't I thought of it first? Girls in other cities were doing it, walking away with autographs. The idea of Paul a foot away from me was enough to drive me wild. With a hand on my heart, I leaned in close to Livy. "Please don't let me scream in Paul's face. I must talk with him calmly."

"I wouldn't dare let you scream in his face." She pointed a finger at me, even though she knew it was rude. "And you better not wet your pants." We'd read all about the girls who'd left their seats wet at Beatles concerts.

"Ew, Livy. I'd never do that."

"Just making sure," she said, then went back to reading the magazine.

Memphis was the only Southern stop on the Beatles' USA tour. We had tickets to the four o'clock show. Good seats to the eight-thirty concert had gone in a flash. It had taken me forever to convince my parents. Anything normal people thought to be groovy, they were against. The Beatles were no exception. My parents were afraid I'd lose interest in the Bible and worship the Fab Four instead. Their hairstyles didn't help. Young men weren't supposed to have long hair.

But all the kids from school were going to the concert, even several from church. So I decided not to take no for an answer. My parents endured months of me leaving little notes in their drawers. Some in my mother's purse. More in my father's shoes. *"Please Please Me,"* I wrote. *Send Suzannah to the Beatles concert for her birthday, "She Loves You."* Or *"Help!" I need Beatles tickets for my seventeenth birthday. "P.S. I Love You."*

After begging and pleading for months, I won. Although Dad didn't approve of rock and roll, he made an exception. He bought good seats too. On the floor. One for me, and one for Livy. He even paid for a third ticket for Mrs. Foster, who had called Mama and volunteered to "chaperone."

"You'll sit through all that screaming?" I heard Mama say to her on the phone. "That's well worth the extra five fifty." What Mama didn't know was that Mrs. Foster wasn't offering to chaperone. She wanted to see the Beatles herself. With her daughter.

I scrambled off the bed and over to Livy's record player. Her albums were kept in a messy pile, so I shuffled through till I found *Meet the Beatles!*, then gently placed the needle down on the first song.

As soon as she heard the first chords of "I Want to Hold Your Hand," she yelled, "Turn it up," then joined me on the dance floor in front of the bed.

Using our fists as microphones, we sang along, knowing every Beatles song by heart. During the second verse, we shook our shoulders and leaned into one another. Smiling and laughing, we leaned back, shaking even harder. I held my nose and twisted to the floor. Livy held her nose and crawled across the room.

We were masters of every dance move, having learned everything we knew from watching *American Bandstand* and *Shindig!*—at Livy's, of course. But it was *Talent Party*, the local Saturday-afternoon dance show, that had turned us into pros. Our fondest dream—besides marrying a Beatle—was to become a WHBQutie on *Talent Party*. The Quties wore go-go boots and miniskirts and darling hairstyles. They were the envy of every Memphis teenager.

When "I Saw Her Standing There" played, we ponied all over the second floor and into Livy's little sister Kim's room. During the slow song, "This Boy," we rested. But as soon as I heard the opening chord of "All My Loving," I fell back onto Livy's bed, slipping into my fantasy world. Paul was singing about me.

Through slits in my eyelids, I happened to notice Livy's mom in the doorway, holding the evening newspaper. Normally she would have bopped in and danced along with us, but she moved over to Livy's record player with an odd look on her face. She turned down the volume and sat on the edge of the bed. "I think you girls should read this," she said, holding up the paper.

Livy yanked it out of her mom's hands. "Read what?"

Mrs. Foster pointed to the front-page headline, and Livy read aloud. "'DJs ban the Beatles for Lennon remarks.'"

A strong sense of foreboding flooded my veins.

"'Dozens of rock 'n' roll disc jockeys have banned the Beatles from their turntables because of John Lennon's comment in a teenage magazine that the mop-haired foursome is more popular than Jesus.'"

I gasped. My heart slipped down into the cavern of my belly.

Livy continued. "'The Beatle Boycott was begun last week in Birmingham, Alabama, by two disc jockeys who took umbrage with quotes attributed to Lennon in a *Datebook* magazine article.'" She pointed behind me. "Hurry, Suzannah. Find my *Datebook*. We must have missed it."

"It just came out, honey," her mother said. "Keep reading."

As my body turned to ice, I read John's quotes over Livy's shoulder. "'Christianity will go. It will vanish and shrink. I needn't argue about that; I'm right, and I will be proved right. We're more popular than Jesus now; I don't know which will go first . . . rock 'n' roll or Christianity.'"

Livy peered at me with a forlorn glance. "Maybe we shouldn't read any more."

"Finish it," I said.

"You sure?"

"Yes. All of it." This news had the potential to steal my happiness, kill my fondest dreams, and, most of all, destroy my heart. I nipped at my fingernail, pressed my knee against Livy's. "Go on. Read it."

She tucked her hair behind her ears, then picked up where I left off. "'The Birmingham disc jockeys are calling for a mass burning of all Beatles records and all Beatles items. Then they will be delivering the ashes to the Beatles in *Memphis* when they step off the plane.'"

While glancing around Livy's room at all the Beatles souvenirs and the cutouts of magazine pictures pasted on the walls, I thought about my own Beatles collection—Beatles dolls, Beatles trading cards, Beatles buttons, magazines, *Paul's pictures.*

Livy peered at her mom. "We aren't burning my Beatles stuff. No way."

Mrs. Foster hesitated before answering, though I knew Livy had no reason for concern. "John's words were probably taken out of context. I'm hoping the whole thing blows over in a day or two."

It might blow over for other families, but not mine.

As the newspaper slipped from her fingertips, drifting to the floor, Livy wrapped an arm around me. Her mom moved over to my left, stretching an arm across my shoulders as well. The only sound that could be heard in the room was the prophetic scratching of the record player giving warning that *Meet the Beatles!* had reached the end.

Woodstock

Day One

Friday, August 15, 1969
3:00 p.m.

"Y'all wait!" A comet with a long flowing blond tail blasted past me, holding her hat down with one hand and her cigarette in the other. Our canvas bag lay in a heap where she had dropped it.

The two-lane pathway that looped around the perimeter of the amphitheater had a steady stream of people moving in both directions. Livy stepped over the flattened portion of fence and moved into the flow, maneuvering in and out of the folks in front of her. "Leon! Johnny! Wait up!"

I scooped up our bag in a hurry, scrambled over the same stretch of fence, and trailed close behind.

As soon as Livy caught up with the boys, she grabbed ahold of Leon's arm. When he turned around, Johnny followed. Amid all the noise and clamor, I could still hear the shrill in her voice. "We can page my boyfriend!"

They looked at her with bewildered faces.

"Didn't you hear that announcement about the diabetes medicine?" she asked.

Johnny shook his head. "Wasn't paying attention, man."

"Who has a piece of paper?" Livy asked, jiggling her hands to hurry us all.

I had no paper. Leon didn't either. But Johnny did. He dug inside the front pocket of his jeans before pulling out a small, slim rectangular pack. "All I got," he said with a chuckle.

"Groovy." Livy's hand disappeared into the bottom of her purse until she found a fountain pen. She plucked one of the tiny papers from Johnny's pack, pressed it against her purse for support, and scribbled out a note: *Nick McCarthy. Please meet Livy NOW at the front of the stage.* She waved it in the air. "Think it'll work?"

"I don't have any better ideas," Johnny said, after a glance at Leon. "Unless you want me to shout his name from here." He cupped his hands on either side of his mouth.

"No. No." Livy tugged his hands away. "Don't do that, you silly boy."

Johnny slumped, poking out his bottom lip. "Just trying to help."

She patted his cheek. "You are helping. Follow me." With a scoop of her hand, she beckoned us all, then darted into the two-lane pathway with the moving mass of Woodstockers.

The three of us traced close behind, watching her prance toward the stage.

My insides blazed, knowing Leon was nearby. I longed to strike up another conversation, like the one we'd had over the last four hours, but after our hug I could hardly look at him. *Why is it that Livy finds it so easy to talk to boys? And why can't that be me?* All the wishing in the world couldn't change things, so instead of talking to him, I resorted to what I did best. I took in the sights.

Every few feet something curious caught my eye. For starters, there were just as many clean-cuts at Woodstock as there were hippies. Maybe more. I felt the shock on my face growing when a trio of young nuns in habits walked past. I stopped to pet an adorable collie with a tie-dyed bandanna around his neck, but when I looked up and noticed Livy twenty feet ahead, I left without a word, scurrying to catch up.

All four of us stopped moving at a sharp screech, followed by tapping on the mic. "Emily Kay, please meet Harvey at the information booth," the announcer said. "He has your car keys."

Livy turned around with hands pressed into her hips. "See! I told y'all this would work. People are looking for each other." As she spun back around, her long silky hair flew into Leon's face. He swept it away like he was swatting at gnats.

I pressed a fist to my mouth, trying not to laugh. Because even Livy's hair made me jealous. She could be a Breck Girl, just like Cybill Shepherd, another Memphis beauty queen.

As we got closer to the stage, I noticed something even more shocking than the nuns: a slew of young people seated down front. Some looked as young as thirteen. I couldn't help wondering how in the world they had managed to nab their choice spots. Had they arrived a week early? If so, what kind of whopper had they told their parents?

Livy barreled to the front row, stepping around blankets and sleeping bags until she reached a small clearing. She turned to Johnny. "Lift me up on your shoulders, will ya?"

As if he'd been offered a chance to score the last hamburger on earth, Johnny squatted down in a flash. Livy hiked a leg over his neck, then held on to his head for balance while he effortlessly hoisted her.

She waved her note in the air, trying to catch someone's attention. "Hello!" she hollered. "Can someone please help me?"

You'd have thought Marilyn Monroe had asked the question by the slew of roadies who hustled to assist her.

A shirtless dude beat them all to it. He squatted down at the lip of the stage with a smile that looked like the keys on a grand piano. "I gotcha, doll baby," he shouted. "Is that for Chip Monck?"

"Is he the announcer?" Livy megaphoned back, hands on either side of her mouth.

"One of them."

"This note is very, very important. Would you mind giving it to him right now?"

"Sure will." He looked down into a pit full of film cameras, where several people milled about. "Hey, Joe! Hand me that note."

A random hand appeared over the fence, and Livy passed it off to Joe. "I owe you one," she yelled back at shirtless dude.

"Glad to help." He read the note, then pointed to his right. "We're telling folks to meet up at the information booth. Not the stage."

Livy nodded in appreciation, then kicked Johnny's ribs, like he was her horse. Instead of putting her down, he traipsed back through the crowd holding tightly to her calves. It wasn't until we reached the corner of the stage that he finally let her loose.

She glanced around. "How the heck are we supposed to find the information booth with this mob?"

On the other side of the wooden fence, workers, dressed in blue T-shirts, scurried between trucks and trailers. Roadies pushed cases up a wooden gangway extending from a parking area all the way to the stage. Johnny tried waving one of them down, but no one was paying attention to us.

Out of nowhere a Frisbee appeared, heading straight for Leon. Like a seasoned wide receiver, he jumped three feet in the air, catching it with ease. Drawing his arm back, he scanned the crowd, then, with a skillful flick of his wrist, spun the disc back into the massive audience.

I finally had my in. "Are you a football player? That was quite a catch."

A twinkle of mischief shone in his eyes. "Learned everything I know from the one and only Coach Chaump at John Harris High School."

"What position did you play?" I asked.

But Livy cut in. "Bet you were the quarterback."

"Nope, fullback," Leon said. "Were you a cheerleader?"

"God no. Not my scene."

"Bet you were homecoming queen," said Johnny, exchanging a bemused grin with Leon.

Livy jerked her head back. "How'd you know that?"

Johnny tapped a finger to his forehead. "My superior intellect."

No one asked me if I was homecoming queen. Or a cheerleader. Not that I cared all that much.

While I looked back at the army of festivalgoers from this vantage point, a forever tableau imprinted my memory. It was as if I was standing on the shore of an ocean, staring into the horizon, unable to see the water's end. Blanket to blanket, kids packed in together like a mammoth jigsaw puzzle, each person fitting snugly into the next.

It was hard to imagine how or where we would carve out our own puzzle piece. I could only hope Nick was somewhere in the gargantuan crowd, preserving a decent viewing spot—with four extra seats.

The air reeked of an unfamiliar odor. At first, I wondered about it; then it hit me. *Marijuana.* I wasn't sure what I'd thought it would smell like, but certainly not a skunk. I figured it would have more of a grassy scent, like a fresh-mowed lawn. Boy, was I wrong. I wasn't too fond of the aroma, but it sure smelled a heck of a lot better than the other scent in the air. Cow poop.

Without thinking it through, I leaned over to Livy. "Can you get high from smelling pot?"

She covered her mouth to muffle a full-on guffaw.

But it was plenty loud enough for the boys to hear, and it piqued Johnny's curiosity. "What's so funny?"

"She's wondering if smelling weed gets you high," said Livy.

If only the earth could have swallowed me whole. I wanted to kill her.

As my distress over what my ex–best friend had just revealed about me grew, I longed to reach over, grab her, and slam every single word back into her big fat mouth. But it was too late. The damage was done. What was worse, I had to act like I was fine about it. With the guys eyeballing me, I had no choice but to fake laugh, then disguise my fury—not to mention my humiliation—behind a phony smile.

"I wish!" Johnny said, throwing his head back with a chuckle.

Leon didn't chuckle. "I don't think so, Suzannah," he said.

A pretty hippie girl wearing a brown suede hat like Livy's walked by on her way through the backstage gate. A round white pin, bearing a dove resting atop the neck of a guitar, was attached to her belt loop. Another pin read **JOYCE**.

Livy called out to her. "Excuse me, Joyce."

Joyce turned around.

"We're looking for the information booth."

"That way," she said, pointing to the right. "Next to the Message Tree. You can't miss it."

Livy adjusted her hat; her bracelets jangled. "I just gave an important message to a dude onstage. Do you know when it will be announced? My boyfriend is missing, and I'm desperate to find him."

"Your boyfriend and many others. Try to chill out," Joyce said. "You'll find him."

"I better." Livy kicked at the dirt, as if not finding her boyfriend was Joyce's fault.

Joyce disappeared through the gate in a hurry, leaving us all to sit in the residual muck of Livy's pot comment.

Now what? The guys might not have been aware of my fury, but Livy sure was. With a slight tightening of my eyes, I glowered at her, shooting her a deadly hairy eyeball just like the ones I was famous for in my family.

Right away she hooked an arm inside mine, pulling me away from the earshot of the boys. "I'm so freaked out about not finding my boyfriend" was the first thing out of her mouth.

"You embarrassed the *crap* out of me" was the first thing out of mine. I spoke to her through gritted teeth; she could hear the anger in my voice.

"I'm sorry," she said, laying a hand over her heart. "I shouldn't have said that. It was an accident."

An accident? How does someone say something like that by accident? It reminded me of the day she accused me of spreading her deepest, darkest secret—the first time she betrayed me.

Back at Central High School, Livy and I had been known as the Duet. Everybody had called us that, and it had driven Marianne Gentry insane. Livy was the most beautiful girl in school—worshipped by all the boys—and Marianne couldn't stand it that I was her best friend.

I wasn't dumb. I knew I gained my acclaim from Livy, but Marianne never missed an opportunity to remind me. "Livy's the reason you get invited to the cool parties," she often said when Livy wasn't around.

Marianne got invited to the cool parties because of her outside. On the inside, she was a black widow spider.

Why Livy would confide in that venomous vixen was the question. She'd already confessed to me that she accidentally, regretfully, went all the way with John Dearing our junior year. She had sworn me to secrecy. Even made me place my hand on their family Bible. It wasn't necessary. Never in a million years would I have told anyone. It would be locked inside my vault forever.

But the word got out, and it spread like wildfire.

"You've got to believe me," I'd pleaded, the day Livy confronted me. "It wasn't me."

She was stretched out on her bed, frantically flipping through the latest copy of *Tiger Beat*. She would hardly look at me.

"Livy, please. Look at me," I said. "I'd never betray you. You know that."

She slapped the magazine down on her lap and peered at me. "Marianne swore to God, up and down, on the Bible that she didn't start the rumor. You two are the only ones I told."

"She's a big liar!"

"She's never done anything like this before."

Hot lava spewed from my lips. "Neither have I! Can't you see she's jealous? All she wants is to have you to herself. She's a black widow, Livy."

"I guess it was an accident," she said with her eyes on the magazine. Not me.

Now, all these years later, Livy was calling her words an accident. I almost asked if it was an *accident* that she'd believed Marianne over me. But it wasn't the right time. Certainly not here, in front of Leon and Johnny.

At some point, though, we were going to have to talk about it. Not discussing it in the first place had put a strain on our friendship.

The rumpus from another helicopter made me reasonably sure the boys couldn't overhear; nevertheless, I kept my voice as low as possible. "Don't ever. Embarrass me. Again." It came out like a command. Like I was Dad.

"I won't. Forgive me?" Livy's remorse seemed genuine. It helped but didn't mend it completely.

I gave her a slight nod, followed by a weak smile. I was still angry.

"Leon is beautiful, by the way," she said, her way of diffusing the damage.

"He's even nicer than he is beautiful," I whispered. "I like him, Livy. A lot."

Johnny strolled up behind us and stuck his head in between our faces. "We better get to the information booth, ladies."

Livy whipped around. "You're coming with us?"

"If you want."

"Yes, we want," she said.

Leon, who had also joined the conversation, folded his arms across his chest. "I have a better idea. Let's scope out our spot first. If we don't claim it now, we'll be watching from the top of the hill."

There were no open spots, none that I could see. It seemed we'd have to sit pretty far back.

Seconds later, some random clean-cut strolled up to us with his eyes fixated on Livy. He wore a blue button-down shirt rolled at the sleeves. "Hey, guys, wanna sit with us?" He pointed to his friend, twenty feet back, who gave us a friendly wave.

"Are you serious?" Livy asked.

"I wouldn't lie," he answered.

It was quite an offer. We'd be able to see moles on the performers' faces if we said yes. We wouldn't be smack-dab in the middle—we'd be off to the side—but so what? We'd have some of the best seats in the pasture.

Livy's eyes danced at the chance. "Thank you, man. What's your name?"

"Dave."

By the smile she gave him, you'd never know she'd been crying a few minutes earlier. Or that her *boyfriend* had seats for us elsewhere.

"So, Dave, we need to go to the information booth. Would you mind if we put our stuff down with yours before we leave?" Livy pressed her hands together like she was praying.

"Sure. Whatever you need."

Leon and Johnny beamed at each other. It seemed they were quite pleased with the way things were working out.

Livy led the way as the four of us meandered behind Dave, once again tiptoeing through humans, blankets, and coolers.

Once there, we met Slim, a tall slender clean-cut with greasy hair, who cleared spots out of nowhere. Instead of being irritated that four more people had crowded in, the people seated around them greeted us with friendly *hello*s. All seemed happy we were there. One guy even passed Johnny a bottle of wine.

Turns out, Slim and Dave were brothers from Connecticut—at Woodstock to "*experience* Hendrix." Along with fifty thousand others, they had arrived four days early to make sure they got to see him up close. Now, because of their generosity, we had snagged the perfect viewing spot. A stroke of luck I'd never seen coming. All thanks to Livy's beauty.

Leon turned to Johnny. "I'll hang out here and guard the spot."

I did not want to wait for Nick at the information booth; I wanted to stay with Leon. Besides, I needed a little space from Livy. Mustering all my courage, I asked, "Okay if I hang out here with you?"

"Sure," Boy Beautiful said.

Thrilled, I placed a hand on Livy's shoulder. "Nick's gonna be there waiting. I just know it."

Her face fell. I could tell she would rather have me come along, but she didn't object. "He better be," she said before dropping our bag, and her purse, on the ground. She stuffed her cigarettes in the back pocket of her cutoffs, dug inside the front pocket for her Pink a Pale, and applied a fresh coat.

Within moments we heard the page. "Nick McCarthy. Livy is looking for you. Please go *now* to the information booth to meet her." The announcer chuckled, adding, "The key word is *now*."

Livy jumped in place. "Hurry, Johnny. Let's go."

"Right behind you, love."

Yet again, Livy Foster had another cute boy chasing after her.

Woodstock

Day One

Friday, August 15, 1969
4:00 p.m.

Once they left for the information booth, Leon and I settled in with Dave and Slim, spreading out our blankets as best we could. The couple in front introduced themselves as Cary and Keith, then passed us an open beer and a bag of popcorn. Leon took a swig, then dug a hand into the popcorn before offering the same to me. The girl next to us introduced herself as Anne Marie. She'd traveled to Woodstock all by herself.

Some folks were napping; others were basking in the warmth of the sun while listening to the background music on the PA. Directly in front of us, a guy danced in place with a transistor radio held up to his ear.

I would have loved nothing more than to stand up and dance. Yet my butt was sewed to the blanket like a patch on a quilt, inhibited by shadows of the past. It had been ages since I'd danced. My confidence had vanished. Furthermore, with the absence of Livy and Johnny, I'd reverted to not knowing what to say to Leon. I wished I'd had more of that beer. I didn't like the taste of it, but I'd have guzzled the whole can if given the chance.

"The music is going to start very soon, folks," the announcer informed us around four thirty. "Don't worry."

Leon tilted his head toward mine. "Right on."

"I can't wait." Pulling my knees into my chest, I flashed him a shy smile. He had no idea how flustered he made me.

Right then, the unmistakable first guitar chords of "Suite: Judy Blue Eyes" blasted from the PA. Without meaning to, I gasped.

"What's the matter?" Leon asked.

"Oh, nothing. It's just this song. I love it so much." Hearing their tune gave me chills. I hadn't heard it since I was in my closet.

He leaned toward me, eyebrows raised. "You know this album?"

"Pretty much every word." I reminisced about picking out the chords on the guitar, reading the liner notes, and singing my heart out to "Suite: Judy Blue Eyes" four times in a row.

"How'd you hear about it? It hasn't been out long."

"Livy gave it to me." Guilt bubbled up at the mention of her name. Despite her spending a fortune on records for me, I was still miffed at her. But she deserved it. "I'm just kidding about knowing every word. But it's been a long time since I've fallen so in love with a record. I'm looking more forward to Crosby, Stills & Nash than any other band." I closed my eyes and sang along softly, somehow forgetting Leon sat next to me. "'I am yours. You are mine. You are what you are. You make it haaarrrd. And you make it haaarrd.'"

A few stanzas later, I opened my eyes to find him staring again, the way he'd done when the butterfly was on my shoulder. I stopped singing, abruptly.

He gripped my knee. "Hey, don't stop."

I shook my head.

"Why? I wanna hear you. Please keep singing."

"Not unless you sing with me" was all I could think to say. His touch had caused a butterfly swarm in my stomach.

With a slow shake of his head, he leaned toward me. "You do not want to hear me sing. I have a terrible voice."

"So? I bet you still sing."

After an exasperated sigh, he picked right up with the music. But he stopped a few words in, covering his face with his hands. "Can you at least sing with me? To drown me out."

I gave him a playful push; then we finished the song together, our voices escalating at the end. "Do-do-do-do-do, do-do, do-do!" Clapping along with the crowd, we laughed at our impromptu duet.

The record may have been brand new, but the audience sure knew it.

Once the applause died down, Leon folded his arms across his chest. "Lay it on me. How did you learn to sing like that?"

"I don't know. Church, maybe. I was in the youth choir when I was young."

"No one at my church sings like you."

"Is that a good thing or a bad thing?" I knew what he meant.

"Come on." He lightly shoved me this time. "You sing great."

His compliment sent another flutter to my belly. "You're nice to say that. Thanks."

"It's true. Anyone else in your family sing? I've heard it runs in the family." Even Leon's smile moved me. Bottom crooked canines and all.

"My brother."

He tilted his head to the side. "Ron?"

I nodded, glowing at the idea of him remembering my brother's name.

"What about your parents?"

"My mother sings, but only in church. She's been in the choir her whole life."

During the second track on the album, "Marrakesh Express," a guy next to Leon passed him a joint. Instead of smoking, he leaned over me and passed it to Anne Marie, who put it to her lips straightaway. Her long, tie-dyed skirt was knotted above her knees. She was barefoot and very pretty. Instead of ogling her darling macramé halter top, I studied the way she smoked. How she held the joint. How she inhaled. And the way she twisted her wrist when she passed it on.

"I take it you don't get high," Leon said, once I turned back to him.

I opened my mouth to lie, then thought about Livy's pot comment. So I shook my head.

"I take it Livy does?"

"Oh yeah," I said with a vigorous nod.

"How did you two end up here together? You seem . . . pretty different."

Tilting my head back, I struggled for the right words. "Livy and I have been friends a very long time. And yes, we're *very* different."

That man-giggle of his preceded his next question. "Are you glad you came?"

"So glad. At first, I said no, mainly because of the long drive, but the lineup changed my mind." The Crosby, Stills & Nash record had helped me to relax. The comfort I'd felt earlier with Leon had returned.

He leaned back on his hands. "What other bands are you looking forward to? Besides Crosby, Stills, Nash & Young."

"Young?"

"Didn't you know? Neil Young joined the band."

I shook my head. I didn't even know who Neil Young was.

"Those cats are playing together for the first time tomorrow night in Chicago. Woodstock's their second live show."

"That's so hard to believe."

"All true." Leon smiled. "What other bands are you excited about, Suzie?"

Did he just nickname me? I'd never wanted to be called Suzie—too common—but it sounded like the soft notes of a Mozart sonata coming from him. "I'm excited about Joan Baez and Jimi Hendrix." I tried remembering what other bands I'd heard—Livy had played so many in the car—but between my butterflies and my long hiatus from music, I was stumped. "And Bob Dylan."

"Dylan's not officially on the bill, but there's a rumor running around he may decide to show up. He lives nearby."

Embarrassment bled through me. The last thing I wanted was to look like an amateur. "I hope so. He's incredible."

"Better than incredible. What about the Who? You dig those guys?"

"For sure."

Releasing an appreciative sigh, Leon tucked a lock of loose hair behind his ear. "They're the reason I'm here. Them and the Airplane. Dig them?"

"Oh, definitely. I have *Surrealistic Pillow*." A slight lie. It was one of the records Livy had given me that I never got to hear. And now it was in pieces in a garbage dump. "I'd give anything if the Beatles could be here."

"You and me both," Leon said. "I heard Lennon couldn't get in the country."

I gasped. "Why not?"

"That arrest he had in London for marijuana possession. Nixon won't let him in."

Another fact I was unaware of. Music magazines were no longer allowed in my home. Or my dorm. "That kills me," I said. "I might be their biggest fan."

One of the Connecticut brothers passed Leon another joint. This time he smoked it. But he bypassed me when he was done, handing it over to tie-dyed-skirt girl, Anne Marie. Looking around at all the people smoking dope out in the open blew my mind. The stuff was illegal. And for some weird reason, no one was getting arrested. I glanced around for cops but saw none.

When I turned back to Leon, he was sipping on another passed libation, a jug of red wine. He offered it to me. I took a big slug, then sent it down the row. Gertie's words about not sharing drinks came to my mind. Funny, despite the threat of the Hong Kong flu, no one at Woodstock cared. People shared everything they had.

I had planned to buy food and drinks when I arrived, so I had nothing to offer in return but the Snickers bar I'd bought at the 7-Eleven. I took it from my purse and passed it to Leon, who took a bite, then passed it to the next person. As soon as Livy got back with Nick, I'd head over to the concessions area.

While the Crosby, Stills & Nash record continued over the PA, I couldn't help noticing the couple in front of us. They lay next to one another on a faded quilt. The girl looked deep into the boy's eyes while he tenderly ran his fingers through her long dark hair. He caressed her face. Soon enough he rolled on top of her, moving his hand down to her breast. If I was her, I wouldn't want the whole world watching a boy touch my breast.

Seconds later, *I* was watching. Without meaning to, I tilted my head to the side, eyeballing the boy's hand as he rubbed his thumb across her nipple, so firm anyone could tell she wasn't wearing a bra.

Out of the corner of my eye, I noticed Leon watching me. Embarrassed, I twisted around backward, pretending to search for Livy. "Wonder what's taking them so long?" I asked when our eyes met again.

A tantalizing grin spread across his face. "They'll be back. Don't worry."

"I'm not worried, just curious."

Leon plucked a blade of grass between the blankets. "I'm curious about something."

"What's that?"

"Why you didn't get pissed off at Livy when she laughed at you for asking if smelling grass gets ya high. The girls I know would have clawed her eyes out." He followed with a boisterous chuckle, then took hold of the large bag of Lay's potato chips that had been passed down the aisle. A jug of water followed.

"I did get mad!" I said, indignancy lacing my tone.

"Could have fooled me." With a glance inside the chip bag, he pulled out a handful, then passed it my way.

"I just didn't do it in front of you and Johnny. I didn't want to make y'all uncomfortable."

"We wouldn't have cared." He threw a chip in the air, caught it with his mouth. After swallowing hastily, he added, "Is that what Memphis belles do? Look out for everyone else but themselves?"

"I wouldn't say that. But we sure don't like making people feel funny. Don't Northern girls care about that?" I raised my eyebrows, tossing him a saucy smile.

"Not really. They flat out tell you what they think." Leon laughed that laugh. That adorable laugh. "Chicks from the North do not hold back."

"Neither do I." I crammed a handful of chips in my mouth, felt my taste buds exploding from the salt.

His silly grin made me chuckle. And that made me choke.

"You okay?" he asked, leaning in close.

With a hand over my mouth, I gave him a thumbs-up but struggled for air, coughing my brains out. Everyone around us turned to stare at me as Leon passed me the water jug.

My eyes had filled with tears by the time I recovered. "You know what they say. You can't eat just one."

Roaring cheers sounded from the audience.

"Ladies and gentlemen," the announcer said, "one of the most beautiful men in the whole world. Let's welcome Mr. Richie Havens."

Woodstock had officially begun.

And so had I.

Woodstock

Day One

Friday, August 15, 1969
5:05 p.m.

A few minutes after five, a man dressed in white pants and a long orange tunic strolled out from behind the stage. Richie Havens, an extremely tall fellow, settled down on a wooden stool, propping his acoustic guitar atop his thigh. "Hello!" he bellowed into the mic. "Can you hear?"

As a loud chorus of *yes*es rose from the field, Leon turned toward me with an animated grin.

"Groovy. Okay. Wow," said Richie. "It's really beautiful to see so many people together." He had a gentle presence about him, and I found his voice soothing. Without another word, he started in with a haunting number about a man in prison.

Prison. Had I actually broken out of mine? Or had I stepped into a fantastical dream? It seemed impossible to imagine my courage, but when I eyed Richie on the massive stage in front of me and pinched a hunk of skin on my arm, I *knew* this was no dream.

After several more unfamiliar songs, Richie took things up a notch when he played a tune I knew. Livy and I had heard the Beatles' version of "With a Little Help from My Friends" while listening to *Sgt. Pepper's* in the car. Richie told the crowd he hadn't learned it yet and asked us to fill in the words. I found that strange. Why would he even play it if he didn't know the lyrics? Especially at Woodstock.

I looked curiously at Leon.

He laid a hand on my thigh. "He's stalling."

"How do you know that?" I asked, far more interested in his hand than Richie's song choice.

"Look at the road." He removed his hand, unfortunately, to point behind the stage. No cars or trucks were moving. Total gridlock.

A tap on my shoulder interrupted our conversation. I whipped around to find Livy, shoulders slumped, wearing a sullen expression. Despite the low-hanging brim of her hat, I could tell she'd been crying. Johnny stood with her, but no one else was there.

I leaped up, wrapped my arms around her. "No Nick?"

With a shake of her head, she confirmed her worst fear. She could hardly speak. "We waited over an hour. Other people found their lost loved ones, but he never showed up."

"I'm sorry, Liv," I said, tightening my grip.

Johnny slid his arm comfortably around her waist, as if it wasn't the first time. "We'll page him again, love. Let's just chill here awhile. It'll do you good to sit down and listen to music."

"He's stuck in traffic." I pointed to the road behind the stage. "Just like we were."

"I hope so," she said in a weak voice.

I stroked her hair. "He'll be here soon. Give him more time, okay?"

She squeezed her eyes shut, managing a slight nod.

Despite the anger I'd felt earlier, my heart ached for Livy. Just being at Woodstock was groovy enough for me, but for her, it seemed our epic escapade was more about Nick.

Slim, the greasy-haired brother, patted the ground next to him, all the while flashing a snaggletoothed smile at Livy. Johnny sat there instead, and Livy sat down beside him, with me on her other side.

The music paused, and Richie spoke to the crowd. "You know, we've finally made it! We did it this time. They'll never be able to hide us again!"

With his words, an infectious energy took over. Over the cheers and whistles, Leon told me that Johnny had recently seen Richie play in a Greenwich Village coffee shop. It made me fantasize about singing in a coffee shop. With Leon in the front row.

As soon as Richie strummed the opening chords of his next song, Leon and Johnny eyed one another with knowing smiles and fist pumps. Livy smiled too. It was good to see. She moved her head to the beat like she knew the song, while the guys sang every word.

I listened closely to the lyrics. The song was about a guy named Handsome Johnny, fighting each of the wars in which America had been involved. Depending on the war, Johnny was holding a different gun. Ron creeping through rice paddies, holding an M16, was the last thing I wanted to think about while at Woodstock.

After Richie played the final note, I leaned toward Leon, having to shout over the applause. "This might be a dumb question, but did Johnny get his name from that song?"

Leon pressed his lips together. "You guessed it."

"But the Johnny in the song goes to war, and your Johnny said he'll never go to war."

Jutting a thumb toward his cousin, he said, "My Handsome Johnny got drafted when he dropped out of college. Been living underground ever since he burned his draft card." He leaned across Livy and me to touch Johnny's knee. "Hey, man, Suzannah wants to know why we call you Handsome Johnny if you aren't going to war?"

Johnny shot us a rueful grin. "I'm a conscientious objector, man."

Livy gave Johnny an enthusiastic thumbs-up. I wanted to ask him to please define *conscientious objector*. But I didn't.

A half hour later, completely drenched in sweat, Richie Havens shocked the audience by starting yet another song. With nimble fingers tuning his guitar, he scanned the massive crowd. "Freedom is what we're all talking about getting. It's what we've been looking for. I think this is it." It seemed Richie, strumming with a palpable urgency, was singing for everyone there. "Freedom. Freedom. Freedom. Sometimes I feel like a motherless child."

Johnny leaned forward to get Leon's attention. "He's out of songs, man."

"Right on," said Leon. "Sounds like he's making this one up."

I agreed.

"Clap your hands!" Richie yelled. "Clap your hands."

Most folks did as he asked, in turn standing to show their support.

Electricity was in the air. Everyone could feel it. A girl a couple of rows in front ripped off her shirt. *She ripped off her shirt!* Dancing, swaying, bending like a wild woman, she turned around to face the crowd and thrust her arms in the air, flashing her *bare-naked* breasts for the whole world to see.

I elbowed Livy. "Can you believe that girl?"

She shrugged. "What can I say? She feels free."

"Maybe so, but you couldn't pay me a million dollars to do that! Would you do it?"

With a faraway stare, she answered, "I'm so upset, there's no telling what I'd do."

Although the concert had just started, one thing about Woodstock was abundantly clear. People from every walk of life—no matter the color of their skin, or their gender—were free to do whatever they wanted. Free to smoke pot. Free to have long hair. Free to wear whatever wild clothing they wished. The girls were even free to take off their shirts! Everyone seemed to be claiming the right to live life on their own terms, amid one diverse, like-minded community. Everyone seemed to be filled with the same spirit of love. And of peace. And of hope.

If only for the weekend.

As the percussionist tapped out the beat to "Freedom," I sensed a release of my own. I stood straight up, holding my arms high in the air. *Yes, Richie Havens, this is it. I, too, am free. At last.*

Once Richie had left the stage for good, the announcer returned. "We apologize for the noise of the choppity-choppity. But, uh, it seems there are a few cars blocking the road. So we're flying everybody in. I almost made the worst pun in the world about high musicians, but we'll skip that."

5:50 p.m.

Ten minutes later, a very old Middle Eastern man, with long curly salt-and-pepper hair and a bushy white beard, walked onto the stage wearing a bright-orange robe. He was flanked by two American men in white robes who helped him up to a small platform, where he sat cross-legged on top of a decorative Indian blanket. Several others in long robes knelt on either side of him, like he was a god or someone worthy of worship.

The old man put his hands together in prayer, bowing toward the audience. "My beloved brothers and sisters, I am overwhelmed with joy to see the entire youth of America gathered here in the name of the fine art of music."

He was a gentle, soft-spoken man who squeaked his words. "Through that sacred art of music, let us find peace that will pervade all over the world. The entire world is going to watch this. The entire world is going to know what American youth can do for humanity. So every one of you should be responsible for the success of this festival."

The audience stood and cheered.

"Before I conclude my talk, I would like you all to join me and our group here in repeating a very simple chant . . . We are going to use three seed words, or the mystic words, to formulate the chants. And if you all join wholeheartedly, after the chant we are going to have at least one whole minute of absolute silence. Not even the cameras will click at that time. And in that silent period, that one minute of silence, you are going to feel the great, great power of that sound and the wonderful peace that it can bring in you and into the whole world. Let us have a sample of that now. *Hari* is one word. *Om* is another word. The first chant will have these two words, *Hari Om* . . . The second line will be 'Hari Om, Hari Om, Hari Hari Om.'"

It seemed like the whole Woodstock Nation chanted the "Hari Om" together. And a surprising minute of silence followed.

I leaned into Livy. "That was different."

"Maybe for you, but so calming for me. Especially with my boyfriend missing." She sat up straight, crossing her legs like the worshippers who had just left the stage. She stretched her arms out to the side, flat palms facing skyward. Her thumbs and pointers formed a circle. Eyes closed. Chin lifted. She looked ridiculous. "He was utterly wonderful. Don't you think?"

I thought he was utterly weird. He'd given the strangest speech I'd ever heard. But I still said, "Utterly wonderful."

Maybe it was my tone of voice, but Livy dropped her hands into her lap and glared at me. "*Suzannah.* He's the guru. He's blessing us."

"I know that, *Olivia.*"

Instead of returning to her guru pose, she reached for her purse. "I'm getting high," she said, sliding out a joint. Johnny had pulled a lighter out of his pocket before the thing ever reached her lips. She took two long puffs, then handed it to him. After two puffs of his own, he offered it to Leon, who took one long puff, then passed it to Slim, who passed it to Dave.

Pretty soon the joint disappeared down the row, never to return. I sort of wished Livy had passed it to me. After hearing Richie Havens sing about freedom, my inhibitions were thawing.

6:10 p.m.

Chip Monck appeared at the lip of the stage with an important announcement. "Ladies and gentlemen, if you please. There are a number of reasons that we've run down, I think, why we've requested you not be on the scaffolding. Can we please have your cooperation and ask you to get down? The fact that people behind you also wish to see is, I think, perhaps a point of major consideration."

All heads turned.

It was his next announcement that gave me a thunderous jolt. "To get back to the warning that I've received—you may take it with however many grains of salt you wish—that the brown acid that is circulating around us is not specifically too good. It is suggested that you do stay away from that. It's your own trip, so be my guest. But please be advised that there is a warning on that one. Okay?"

"O-*kay*," I muttered, feeling my muscles leap underneath my skin. Within seconds I conjured up a ghastly image of Ron using LSD. Could Livy be right? It seemed like he would have told me he was using it in one of his letters. Before he slept with that girl, he told me everything.

Woodstock

Day One

Friday, August 15, 1969
6:15 p.m.

Thoughts of Ron using drugs and how long it had been since I'd heard from him gave me a sense of melancholy. My mind had strayed easily, probably because of the band onstage. I didn't care for their music.

Leon must not have liked them either. After the first two songs, he dug into his backpack and pulled out a pale-yellow T-shirt. "Anyone wanna walk around?" he asked. "See what's back there?" He slipped the shirt over his head and stood up, shaking out his legs.

At first, I was shy to speak up, but when no one else offered, I jumped at the chance. "I'll go."

"Cool." Leon offered me his hand and pulled me straight up. "I could use a cold brew. What about you?"

"Sounds great to me," I said and meant it. For the brief time his hand was in mine, tingles shot through me like thousands of tiny comets.

"I need a pit stop first." He looked down at the rest of our group. "You guys need anything?"

"Surprise us" was Johnny's answer.

Livy looked at me but never commented.

When Dave and Slim declined his offer, Leon and I joined the slow-moving line of people walking up the hill to the back of the bowl.

"How about that LSD warning?" he said. "Guess we better not drink anything else that's been opened."

I thought about the bottle of wine and the jug of water I'd already sipped on and felt my stomach drop. "How long does it take for LSD to work?"

"Not long," he said, rubbing his knuckles on top of my head. "You're okay."

Due to the massive crowd, growing larger by the second, it took a full twenty minutes to reach the top. Once there, we found a village of Porta Potties. I took a quick count. Must have been eighty in that location, but the lines were ridiculous. At least a hundred people in each.

Leon glanced at the lines, then back at me. He twirled me around in front of him, pointing toward the woods. "What do you say?"

"Race ya," I said and took off.

I may have had a head start, but he caught up with me in seconds, laughing and waving as he passed me by. With all the people, running proved impossible, but hurrying behind Leon was the most fun thing I'd ever done. Darting in and around folks dressed in every getup imaginable, we passed people in funky costumes, a guy in a psychedelic robe, and even another topless girl.

After reaching the woods, we barreled down the first path we came to, soon hitting a crossroads with three hand-painted signs nailed to a tree: Gentle Path, Groovy Way, and High Way, each pointing in different directions.

"You decide," Leon said, a bit out of breath.

"Gentle Path!" I cried and took off.

We scurried past tents and campfires, ferns, and wildflowers. Once we were deep into the woods, he stopped in front of a large maple tree. "Meet me right here?"

I nodded. "Right here."

Before running off, we both noticed something moving. Not too far away, a couple lay entangled with one another behind a fallen tree. We could hear their heavy breathing, see her bare legs flailing in the air.

I practically spit out my words. "Are . . . they . . . ?"

"Our landmark," Leon whispered with a silly face, then gave me a gentle push.

Once I'd chosen a large enough tree, as secluded as possible, I pulled one leg all the way out of my jeans and squatted, my bare bottom flashing to God knows who. Modesty would have no boundaries at Woodstock. Not when girls were stripping off their tops and couples were having sex in the bushes. It was the most mind-blowing thing I could imagine. *If Dad could see me now.* Just picturing that made me chuckle out loud.

Leon was at the tree when I returned. And our landmark girl was sitting on top of her lover, gyrating her hips, rubbing her hands through her hair. Their breathing had turned into libidinous moans. My eyes swelled into a fixed stare. I couldn't help it.

Muted laughter swept across Leon's face. "Would you like to get closer?"

I turned my head toward him. "I would *not*. Would you?"

"You're the one staring."

"I'm not staring! I'm . . . having a look-see. There's a difference."

He peered at me, eyebrows pinched. "What is that difference, Miss Peeping Tom?"

"That's for me to know and you to find out."

He rubbed his knuckles on the crown of my head again, the way Ron used to do. The way a big brother teases a little sister. My heart stung. I didn't want him thinking of me as one more little sister.

He leaned toward me with an exaggerated stare. "Damn, your eyes are blue."

A thrill coursed through me. My eyes were the only feature I had prettier than Livy's.

"Are those eyelashes real?" He lightly brushed his thumb underneath my eyebrow.

"Of course they're real. Do they look fake or something?"

"Kind of. They're really long."

"They're really mine."

He smiled. "Let's go find that brew."

Gentle Way turned into High Way, with twinkling fairy lights that seemed to go on for acres. Dusk had begun its descent. Swirls of pink clouds, resembling cotton candy, peeked through the trees with an inviting summons. The sun looked like a giant tangerine sinking slowly into the treetops.

We soon stumbled upon an arts and crafts fair, with every hippie item imaginable. Leather goods, handmade beaded jewelry, blown glass, and all kinds of neato tie-dyed clothing were for sale.

"This fair is as cool as the music," said Leon as we strolled along.

I walked right up to one of the booths, gazing at the tie-dyed halter tops. In a different world I'd have bought one, but I knew I'd better hold on to my money. Besides, where would I ever wear it outside of Woodstock? Certainly not at Union University. Definitely not at home. *Home.* Where was home? Would I ever go back?

One booth had a long banner strung from two trees with **Smoke** written in pink letters. A sandwich board out front displayed the menu: pot, rolling papers, pipes, bongs, roach clips, cigarettes, magic mushrooms. Even LSD! All rules were off in the city of Woodstock.

"What's that?" I asked, pointing to an oddly shaped glass vase with a long neck at the top and a shorter one near the bottom. As soon as I asked the question, I regretted it.

Leon winked at the guy manning the booth while handing him two quarters for a pack of cigarettes. "*That* is a bong. You put the grass down here." He pointed to the short neck first. "And smoke it up here."

"Looks cool," I said, kicking myself for acting so naive.

A few minutes later we stumbled upon a stand with a long line of people, all waiting to buy snow cones. Some of the folks had toddlers on their shoulders.

"Don't people care that their kids are around all these drugs?" I whispered to Leon.

"Guess not. I sure am glad I don't have kids here."

"I'm glad I don't have kids, period."

"That makes two of us," he said as something caught his eye. He leaned forward, pointing behind one of the booths. "Wanna check it out?"

A giant tire swing hung from the branch of a maple tree. Close by, an army green tent had been pitched, with the door flaps tied open. I wasn't sure which *it* he was pointing to.

As we moved forward, leaves crunching underfoot, butterflies whizzed around my stomach. Just at the thought of camping with Leon.

"Think we could ride together?" he asked once we reached the swing.

I looked up at where the rope was tied. "Looks sturdy to me."

He patted the top of the tire. "You sit up here. I'll hop through the middle."

Once we were settled, my sandals rested atop his bare thighs. His head, brushed up against my waist, caused goose bumps to rise.

At first, it was hard to get air, but soon enough we were flying. His hair against my stomach tickled and made me deliriously happy.

So delirious I almost missed the monarchs floating into the trunk of a fir tree. Thousands more had roosted within the branches. The tree was shrouded in orange. "Stop!" I shrieked.

He dug his heels into the ground.

"Do you see what I see?"

With his head pressed even deeper into the small of my waist, he peeked around my body. "I see trees."

"Look there." I pointed at the tree in a frenzy. "Don't you see all the butterflies?"

At the sound of his gasp, I knew he had spotted them too. "Holy Mother of God."

We hurried off the swing, then tiptoed toward the tree. I don't know why we tiptoed; I guess we didn't want to startle them, as more were pouring in.

With open jaws, we followed the highway of butterflies out to a small meadow, just beyond the tree line, where thousands of monarchs flickered through the air. Streaks of the fading sunlight pierced their wings, casting an orange glow on the grass. Like a waltz of fairies, they fluttered together, soaring high, soaring low, creating a gargantuan kaleidoscope.

We gaped at one another at the wonder of it all, then crept into the open meadow, moving with caution into the swarm. Neither of us spoke; we were too mesmerized for words. And we sure didn't want to take a chance on scaring the butterflies away. The setting sun above drenched us in warmth as the miracle unfolded. A butterfly tea party was in progress, and we were their honored guests.

With arms stretched open wide, we turned in circles as the butterflies waltzed around us. Many landed on our shirts, causing us to beam with even greater wonder. Leon's yellow T-shirt held so many it looked as if they might lift him up off the ground and fly away.

In the distance, another small meadow abounded with goldenrod. Thousands more monarchs swarmed from flower to flower. With chins tilted skyward, we crept toward the meadow, seduced by our enchanting hosts. As we moved closer, I fantasized about Leon asking me to waltz along with them.

Our presence never seemed to deter the butterflies, so once we got to the second meadow, we lay down on our backs in the tall grass. Neither speaking. Neither moving. Just two stargazers marveling at the extravaganza above.

Minutes passed before Leon broke the silence. "Did your parents give you butterfly kisses when you were little?"

I moved my head from side to side, feeling the soft grass tickle my cheeks. "What's a butterfly kiss?"

He rolled toward me, dipping down toward my face, fluttering his eyelashes. His lips hovered mere inches from mine. I could see my reflection in his eyes as my heart blasted inside my chest. I swallowed, curling my fingers in my palms, waiting for his kiss.

But his kiss never came. Instead of diving into my mouth, he dove into my cheek. His eyelids moved rapidly as his lashes tickled my skin.

When he pulled back, beaming at me, I wanted to grab the back of his head and pull his face down into mine, touching his lips with my lips.

"Feels like butterfly wings flapping," he said. "Don't you think?"

"I think it tickles."

"My mom gave them to me and my sibs when we were little."

A cacophony of voices sounded behind us. Loud. Harsh. Obnoxious voices. We propped up on our elbows, turning at the same time to see intruders spilling into *our* meadow.

One of the girls bellowed, "What the hell? Wow, you guys. This is the grooviest thing I've ever seen!"

"Oh my God!" her friend shrieked. "Stu, look at this!"

Their voices, far too boisterous, caused many of the butterflies to fly away. Leon and I pouted at one another. Our tea party had been crashed by unwelcome visitors.

He sat up. "Ready to head back?"

Heck no, I wanted to say. *I want to stay right here and kiss you. And not with my eyelashes.* But in typical Suzannah fashion I said, "If you want to."

"We should share. We can't be greedy. That wouldn't be the Aquarian way, now, would it?"

"Not the Aquarian way," I answered with a forced smile, pondering the reality that he must have a girlfriend back home. How could this beautiful boy not have a girlfriend back home?

"Let's go find that beer," he said.

"Enjoy the party," I told the crashers on our way out of the meadow, trying to put an Aquarian-way tone to my voice.

On the way back to our seats, we babbled nonstop about what had just happened. "I read about the monarch migration in *National Geographic*," Leon told me. "Blows my mind those little bugs fly all the way from Canada to Mexico."

"It was the coolest thing I've ever seen."

"Right on. I never thought I'd see one."

Happening on one in the first place seemed like a good omen to me. Watching the butterflies flying free, without a care, gave me a sense of hope. For my own freedom.

7:10 p.m.

The lines at the Food for Love concessions area were ridiculous. No telling how long it would take to get food. Even though I wanted to buy snacks for Slim and Dave, to repay them for their kindness, neither of us were willing to spend two hours in line. We agreed to come back later, after the rush had died down.

But Leon still wanted a beer. And they didn't sell beer at Food for Love. There was no alcohol for sale of any kind.

So we traipsed back down Groovy Way and High Way, looking for anyone who might sell beer. Leon stopped to inquire at one of the arts and crafts booths. A girl handed him one of hers—unopened—out of her own cooler. She even gave one to me. The girl told us there were no beer stands because the producers didn't want drunk, rowdy people at Woodstock. "Besides," she added, "you can't drink while you drop."

"Not a good choice," Leon said with his man-giggle.

"What did she mean by that?" I asked as soon as we walked away.

"You can't drink alcohol while you drop acid."

"Oh yeah, right. I knew that," I said. *Lie.*

Leon swallowed a smile. "Let's head back. I can't wait to tell Johnny and Livy about the butterflies."

I was excited to tell Johnny and Livy about the butterflies too. But hearing him say Livy's name made me wonder which of the two he was more excited to tell. He wouldn't have been the first boy to befriend me just to get to Livy.

Woodstock

Day One

Friday, August 15, 1969
7:45 p.m.

Finding our seats took longer than we had expected. Livy's hair became our signpost, even with a hat on her head. I spotted it from several yards back. It draped across her shoulders like a cape.

A tall baby-faced singer with a golden-brown Afro stood at the lip of the stage, singing an unfamiliar tune.

"Who's that?" I asked Livy, settling down next to her.

"Bert Sommer. Isn't he *beautiful*?" Her childlike smile and glazed eyes let me know she was in an altered state. But at least she seemed happier.

With a slight nod, I let her think I agreed, although I did not. He was somewhat cute, I supposed, but nothing at all compared to Leon.

"It was Bert's *beautiful* Afro on the *beautiful* poster for *Hair*," she said, drawing out her words. I understood what Livy meant about grass making people mellow. Other than her flowery adjectives, her voice had toned down several octaves. And she had finally stopped crying.

"You should work for a music magazine," I told her. "You know more about the musicians than they know about themselves."

"That would be *beautiful*," she said, gazing at the sky.

Leon, who had settled down between her and Johnny, spent the next ten minutes talking about our butterfly extravaganza. Even though he had to speak over the music, he went into great detail, recounting the way we had spun around in circles amid the swarm. His voice lifted when he described the golden tones of the monarchs and how they had attached themselves to our shirts. I smiled to myself when he said they may have totaled two million. He didn't tell them about his butterfly kiss—not that I would have expected him to—but it was all I could think about. That, and how I could squeeze in between him and Livy.

By now, it was eight o'clock, and the temperature had dipped. I dug into our canvas bag and pulled out my jacket, silently thanking Mr. Foster for suggesting we bring them along. I slipped an arm into a sleeve. "Any word from Nick?"

The expression on Livy's face changed from rosy to blue. Her shoulders fell. She buried her face in her hands. "No," she muttered. "I can't remember when I've been this upset."

If only I could have taken the question back. "I know, Livy. I'm sorry. But try not to let it ruin the festival for you."

"I can't help it. My heart is broken."

I wrapped my arms across her shoulders. "I'm sure it is. But look around you. We're here together at this ultracool place after being apart three years. Try to put it out of your mind for now so we can have fun. Please? You'll regret it if you don't."

"I really wanted you to meet Nick," she said, with tears flooding her eyes.

"I will meet him. He'll be here soon. I'm sure he's stuck in traffic."

Livy's demeanor bewildered me. I was surprised it was hitting her so hard. She was the most resilient person I'd ever known. And she rarely cried—about anything. I was the crier. What's more, she could have any boy on earth she wanted. What in the world was so great about Nick? As far as I was concerned, he was clearly untrustworthy.

"Just give me a little time. I'll get better," she said with a weak smile, then leaned over to retie her sandals. "You and Leon sure were gone a long time."

I lowered my voice. "He's cool. Don't you think?"

"He's beautiful. That's what I think." She peered over at him, then leaned back on her hands, crossing her legs. "I thought you didn't want a boyfriend."

With a finger to my lips, I gave her a warning gaze.

"He can't hear me over the music," she said, fiddling with her bracelets.

"I admit it," I whispered in her ear. "I have a crush. It's growing bigger by the minute. You'll never believe what happened. We—"

"You were right, SuSu. You can't trust guys. I don't know why I ever thought I could."

"That's not true for all guys," I was quick to say. "I think Leon might be different. Wait till you hear what happened when we were in the butterfly meadow."

She put a hand over her heart and peered at me with an adoring smile. For a second, I thought she wanted to know more, that she might be happy for me. Instead, she switched subjects again. "This is one of my favorite songs in the world. Do you know it?"

The song was lovely. But it was hard to pay attention while thinking about how easily Livy switched from one mood to another. "It's great," I said. "I've never heard it."

"It's 'America,' by Simon & Garfunkel. On their *Bookends* album, the one with 'Mrs. Robinson.'"

As Bert sang the last line, I leaned forward, yelling, "Play it again!" But, of course, he didn't. When he bowed, the audience gave him a standing ovation. *What must that feel like? To have two hundred thousand people standing up for you?* Watching Bert, with the blue-hour sky settling in behind him, I imagined it was me onstage. I pictured myself holding Ron's guitar against my middle, bowing over the strings, smiling at the audience. I heard the roar of the crowd going wild. For me.

8:15 p.m.

A different announcer took the stage after Bert left. "How is it out there?" he asked. "All right, same boring speech about the scaffolds. Hey, look. We've done it all, we've done the threat, we've done the push, we've done the Bill Graham rap number three. The only thing more I can say is . . . fellows, those are scaffolds. They are not cement buildings. Please come down off the scaffolds."

Two hundred thousand heads turned at the same time to look, once again, at the scaffolds.

This turning of heads had become a ritual. When we looked this time, the light towers had become jungle gyms. A billowy haze of thick smoke hovered over the bowl, but you could still see dangling feet twisted in between metal poles.

"Richard Casey or David Bradley from Framingham, Mass, please call the Bradley home or the Casey home," the announcer continued. "With these messages, we'll try to do them in between the bands. Please make sure they're worth it. Make sure that they mean something."

Livy leaned forward like she was talking directly to the dude. "I'll tell you what's worth it. Finding my boyfriend. Why don't you announce *his* name again?"

By then we had figured out the stage announcements were the festival's only means of communication and the sole way she would ever find Nick.

As improbable as it was to ponder, Livy and I had switched places. Here I was, sitting with a boy whom I had a massive crush on, while Livy sat alone. Part of me felt guilty. Like I should be the one in her shoes. Like I shouldn't have a crush at Woodstock because her boyfriend was missing, and she was the one who had invited me. The other part of me knew that was absurd, but I couldn't help thinking it. Livy had a way of putting herself in the center of everything.

After hearing the announcer read note after note from people trying to find their lost friends or lost medication or lost car keys, she turned to me. "Let's go page my boyfriend again. Will you please come with me this time?"

I'd have rather taken off my own shirt and flashed the crowd—that's how bad I wanted to stay put. Leon was talking with tie-dyed-skirt girl, Anne Marie, which made an awful thought cross my mind. Suppose those two started crushing on each other while I was gone?

But I didn't see how I could refuse Livy. Not only did I feel bad for her, but she'd asked me nicely. I had to go.

Before I could reach for my purse, she grabbed my arm. "There's Joan Baez!" She pointed toward a short-haired girl with bare feet, tucked inside one of the stage wings. She looked pregnant.

"I think she's pregnant!" I said.

Livy, of course, knew the scoop. "She is pregnant. And her husband's in jail for resisting the draft."

"That stinks. For how long?"

"I don't know. But good for him. If more of our boys did that, Nixon would be forced to think twice about what he's doing. More of our boys would be alive!" Her hand flew to her mouth. "Forget I said that. Ronny's fine. I swear to God!"

My muscles stiffened as I swallowed renewed anger. Livy was not herself. Even still, I could hardly keep my patience. "I feel bad for Joan Baez," I said. "She has to raise her baby alone."

"You should feel worse for her husband. He's the one in jail." She uncrossed her legs and glanced at her watch. "It's been four hours since last time. Let's page my boyfriend again. Please."

By now we had learned the other announcer's name was John Morris. His exasperated voice rang out into the night sky. "I am informed that somebody somewhere is giving out some flat blue acid. It is poison," he said. "It's deadly serious, man. I've just been informed that we have four or five people who are a little sick from it . . . no, fifteen. Be cool. And whoever you are, man, I'd love to find ya."

"Are you kidding me? That is *horrible*," I said.

"Are you coming?" Livy asked, unfazed by the warning.

"*Yeeees.* I'm coming. Let's get this over with," I muttered under my breath.

As we turned to leave, Leon and Anne Marie glanced at me. I waved, and they waved back. But neither asked where I was going. It made me want to leave even less.

Like before, we squeezed down to the main stage. It took longer to get there because thousands more people had packed into the bowl. Livy handed another note that she'd already scribbled out on one of Johnny's rolling papers to the same girl, Joyce. "Would you mind having my boyfriend paged again?" she asked. "Please."

Joyce read the inscription. "No luck, huh?"

Livy shook her head.

"You'll find him. Don't lose heart."

"I've already lost heart."

Joyce must have taken pity on Livy. *And* me. We'd been at the information booth only ten minutes when we heard the page. "Nick McCarthy, Livy is still looking for you. Please meet her at the information booth *now*."

Livy sucked on a cig, lamenting Nick's absence, while I pretended to listen. But all I could think about was Leon. While she rehashed every reason why she was disappointed, and now furious, at her *boyfriend*, I ruminated on every second at the butterfly tea party, Leon's butterfly kiss, and the moment I thought he might kiss me for real, if not for those horrid party crashers. That led to obsessing over him and tie-dyed-skirt girl until I felt sick. I didn't hear another word Livy said.

An entire hour passed before she was willing to give up and head back to our spot.

While we squeezed between hundreds of people on the way back, a guy named Tim Hardin sang "If I Were a Carpenter." Livy and I stopped where we were to listen. The song was achingly beautiful.

She placed a hand on my shoulder and spoke into my ear. "Can you believe you're here?"

"No, I really can't. I just hope Dad doesn't find out. If he has me paged, I'll die. I'll be the first person in the world to croak of embarrassment."

"That's not gonna happen," she said, like I was crazy to think it.

"Never underestimate my father, Livy Foster."

My Beatles disaster roared back. I couldn't quell the memory to save my soul. It may have been three years ago—and I may not have croaked from embarrassment then—but the horror of it all never faded from my mind. Millions of teenagers had fallen for the mop-headed boy with long dark eyelashes and the face of an angel, but I was the only one with a father mean enough to make me denounce him in front of the whole world.

Three Years Earlier

Mid-South Coliseum (My Beatles Disaster)

Memphis, Tennessee

Friday, August 19, 1966

Dad eased his Cadillac into the entrance of the Mid-South Coliseum, driving slowly through the crowd, where thousands of girls had lined both sides of the street. I ducked my head, praying to go unnoticed. The only reason I could breathe was the bag in my lap. I had left the top open on purpose. To look at him.

Like chocolate diamonds, Paul's eyes sparkled at me from his best photo. Just underneath, more of his other magazine pictures created a thick pile. Each and every one colored my world cherry red, introducing me to fire and passion and a stirring between my legs that I could neither explain nor expel. All I knew was that I had fallen in love. How on earth would I live without him?

After circling the parking lot twice, Dad chose a spot not far from the front door. Before turning off the ignition, he glanced at my lap. "One day you'll thank me for this, Suzannah. When you're raising children of your own, you'll look back and know that your father was right." He held up a finger to emphasize his words. "Your Heavenly Father will bless your obedience. I know what I'm talking about."

Not wanting to look at him—any square inch of him—I kept my head down. Surely my Heavenly Father wouldn't punish me like this. Exactly what had I done wrong?

"Can't you feel his Spirit urging you? Right here?" He tapped his chest, over his heart. All I could feel was rage. Shifting my eyeballs toward my father, I caught a glimpse of the short black hairs poking from his nostrils. *Revolting.*

"Pastor Ralph will be quite pleased with you."

I didn't utter a word.

Dad slipped the keys from the ignition, stepped out of his Cadillac, and then opened the back door. I heard him removing the protest signs he had made earlier that morning. One for him. One for me.

I fantasized about staging a protest of my own, staying in the seat, making him drag me out. Hardly an option. My earthly father was a strict, hardcore military man who rarely considered anyone's opinion but his own. He commanded authority over me, Mama, and especially Ron, who was en route at that very moment from basic training to a blistering jungle.

Resigned, I took a deep breath and reached for the door handle, then stepped outside into my own jungle. The rush of hot stagnant air felt like I had opened the door to an attic.

Dad was waiting for me with a sign in each hand. One read **THOU SHALT HAVE NO OTHER GODS BEFORE ME.** The other: **GO BACK TO ENGLAND! YOU AREN'T WELCOME HERE!** Angst rose in my throat when he handed me that one.

"May I hold the other sign? Please, Dad." No doubt, he could hear the panic in my voice.

With one eye squinted in the sun, he calmly remarked, "It will be more effective if you carry it."

"Why have you gotten so—"

"So what?"

"Mean." I yanked the sign out of his hand. Shame covered my body like a coat of heavy plaster. I wanted to throw up. I wanted to run. I wanted to never see my earthly father again.

What should have been the start of the best weekend of my life had drastically changed course because of something stupid someone had said. Words so powerful they had upended a nation, affecting not only me but millions of other teenagers.

This was all John's fault.

As I walked five feet behind Dad toward the small crowd gathered at the front doors, the back of my throat burned with bile. With each step closer, the whole thing became real, and I became desperate.

"Dad!" I called from behind. "*Please.* Don't make me do this. I'm begging you." I gripped my stomach. "I'm about to throw up."

He turned around slowly, glaring at me with his sign in the air. "*Suzannah!* We've discussed this. The first commandment clearly states that you shall have no other gods before him. Look at that bag you're holding. Idols. All idols. The Bible tells us to flee from idolatry." He stepped toward me, waving his hand over my Beatles collection. "*Beatlemania*, sheesh. I should have never allowed this trash in my home to begin with. I knew better."

"Look at all the girls in the street, Dad. They love the Beatles too." A lump had formed in my throat, which made speaking difficult.

Dad murdered me with his eyes. "I don't care about them," he said through gritted teeth. "I only care about you. Enough of this talk."

His frown morphed into a counterfeit smile as a man from our church broke away from the small crowd. "Colonel Withers!" the man exclaimed, with sweat trickling down the sides of his cheeks. Disgusting rings stained his armpits. Two children lagged behind him—his own, I supposed—who couldn't have been older than ten. Two boys swinging their own protest signs without a clue of what they were doing or why. They thought this was fun.

"You know my daughter, Suzannah," Dad said, stretching an arm across my shoulders. It made me flinch.

The man dipped his chin with a smile. "Of course I do."

Forcing myself to grin back, I noticed a pile of records scattered on the ground. No other mementos, just LPs and forty-fives. A pimple-faced dork around my age stood close by, kicking at the pile. He probably hated the Beatles—felt Pastor Ralph was right—and was happy to be there. I made up my mind to not acknowledge him.

"You can go ahead and empty your paraphernalia," the church man said, ogling my bag. "We'll be burning it all once the concertgoers arrive."

Dad nudged me. But shots fired in the pit of my stomach, causing me to revolt. In a last-second act of defiance, I stood still, muttering, "I can't."

Dad pressed his hand into my back. "Of course you can, Suzannah. Empty your bag."

"I *can't*, Dad!" I said, surprised at my sharp tone.

With stifled anger, my father smiled at the churchman. I'd pay for my outburst later. No telling how many times he'd make me write *Suzannah was a bad, disrespectful girl* in perfect penmanship. Or how many weekends I'd have to stay home, grounded to my bedroom with no TV or music or novels to keep me company, just the Bible to convict me of my sins.

The churchman reached out his hand. "Here, I'll do it for you."

The bag was my ventilator, keeping me alive. How was I supposed to let it go? I considered throwing the protest sign down onto the pile, making a run for it, and hiding in the bushes until the concert was over. I'd call Livy from a pay phone to pick me up. She had offered to share her room with me if I ever got up the courage to run away.

But there was no point. I could never outrun my father. He'd been a marathon runner. Even at fifty-eight, he would still catch me.

With no other choice, I narrowed my eyes at Dad, defiantly pushed past the churchman—there was no way I would let *him* do it—and stepped up to the mound. I turned my bag over and emptied my *paraphernalia*. With every record, every button, every doll, every Beatles card, and every one of Paul's pictures that fell to the pavement, I felt that lump in my throat growing.

I forced back tears when my favorite record, *Rubber Soul*, slipped out of its cover and hit the ground. I never stacked my records together without a sleeve the way Livy did. I kept mine pristine and was extra careful not to scratch them. As *Rubber Soul* landed with the A-side up, I narrowed my eyes on track one, "I've Just Seen a Face." I'd spent a hundred hours playing it over and over while picking it out on guitar. And there it was, scratched to kingdom come, never to be listened to again.

The little boys pushed past me. They jumped up and down on top of *Rubber Soul*, laughing and giggling as if they were stomping on bugs. While each of my records shattered into a hundred pieces, so did my heart, my dreams, and my faith. With tears stinging my eyes, I turned away. I couldn't stand to look at it a second longer.

"'Go home to England! You aren't welcome here!'" the churchman read aloud. "Bet you got that idea from the mayor."

Dad gave him a slow nod.

When the hysteria had broken, Mayor Ingram issued a proclamation saying the Beatles weren't welcome in Memphis. He urged them to cancel their concert. But they didn't.

After John apologized, the mayor lifted the ban. The paper said the real reason he lifted it was because of all the money the city would have lost had he kept the Beatles away.

But that's not what had sealed my fate. Lots of pastors around the country—including Pastor Ralph—had stood at their pulpits the Sunday before the concert informing their congregations that anyone who attended would have their church membership revoked. Pastor Ralph encouraged the ones who had already bought tickets to attend a rally at Ellis Auditorium's North Hall instead of going to the concert. He said it would give the youth of the Mid-South an opportunity to show that Jesus was more popular than the Beatles. Unfortunately for me, Dad felt protesting at the venue was a much better way to show "our family's disapproval."

"Boys," the churchman called in a harsh tone. "Come here."

Out of nowhere, four men in robes and pointy hats walked toward us. Though I didn't want to be close to him, I hid behind Dad and peeked around his shoulder like a child.

Earlier in the week, Channel 5 had broadcast an interview with a Klansman in front of the Coliseum. He claimed they were a terrorist organization promising to use terror in any way they wanted to stop the show.

You'd have thought that would have swayed my father from coming here in the first place. But no. As he'd pointed out, *War colonels aren't afraid of anyone.*

When the Klansmen got to our group, they never uttered a word. They simply laid a hundred or more records on the pile. I noticed the two little boys staring at them as if they were Halloween creatures. One of the Klansmen reached down, picked up my John Lennon doll, and lit it on fire. With a hateful laugh, he threw it back on the heap, causing the pile to ignite.

As quickly as they had arrived, they left. I watched them walk toward the waiting girls at the street. As if on cue, a loud chorus of screams at the entrance startled everyone.

Everyone but me. I knew what was happening. The girls weren't screaming in fear of the Klansmen; they were screaming at the long gray bus turning into the entrance. It moved slowly while fans jostled and jockeyed, moving toward the bus as if it were a giant magnet.

I could see the lads in the distance. Four brunette heads hanging out the windows, waving at the screaming girls as they ran alongside, flapping paper in the air.

The bus halted, and a Beatle hand appeared through the window. A screaming girl reached up with her paper. Another did the same. Like water in my palms, my one and only chance to meet Paul was slipping from my fingers.

I was grateful the Beatles had not come closer. Paul didn't need to see me like this.

Once the bus disappeared behind the Coliseum, the concertgoers headed straight toward me. The majority were girls my age, seventeen. They wore cute hairdos and adorable dresses, each one cuter than the next, a stark contrast to my Bermuda shorts and Peter Pan collar shirt, an outfit Dad had insisted I wear.

As each girl hurried past, tickets in hand, I heard their squealing and laughing . . . right before . . . silence . . . followed by . . . stares. There I stood in front of a burning fire, twenty yards from the front door—on display to the whole world—while eight thousand people approached from all directions. The Coliseum had only one way in. Right past me. And the burn pile.

Each person gawked at me like I was a freak and the burning was my freak show. There was no prayer of anonymity.

A startled cry escaped my throat when I eyed Laurie and Leslie from my class. I spun around, hoping they hadn't seen me. Every cell in my body screamed, *Run!* I even heard Ron's voice urging me to do it: *Run, SuSu, run!*

Run where, Ron, run where?

A man with a press badge clipped to the pocket of his short-sleeved shirt walked over to snap our picture. As he lifted his box camera to his eye, I whipped my head around to avoid the shot and happened to see Livy hustling through the crowd. Making up my mind to leave Dad behind and suffer the consequences later, I stepped toward her. After one more step I froze.

Where was Kim? After John's proclamation, Dad had given my Beatles ticket to Livy's family so her little sister could go, too, but Kim was nowhere to be found. Neither was Mrs. Foster. Yet a blond-haired girl wearing a miniskirt with mod designs of hot pink, lime green, and lemon yellow scurried behind Livy. *Marianne!* It was that lying black widow spider, Marianne Gentry. She had *my* Beatles ticket. And had gotten her wish.

She'd finally managed to come between two lifelong best friends. She must have convinced Livy that I was the one who had betrayed her, when in fact it was her all along.

Our gazes met. But I didn't look away. With the most hateful glower humanly possible, I stared that backstabber down as if poison arrows were shooting from my eyeballs straight to her heart.

Livy didn't react when Marianne smirked at me or come to my rescue when she saw the protest sign. She simply hurried past, pretending she hadn't seen me. Of course she'd seen me. Everyone had seen me.

With that, a dam of shame broke loose, flooding every vein in my body. It was 97 degrees outside; I was used to the heat. Yet my skin perspired in a way it hadn't before, clammy to the touch. I couldn't catch my breath. Each time I tried to breathe, nausea set in. My hands and feet tingled. I trembled uncontrollably. A surge of overwhelming panic paralyzed my body.

What was happening? Was I going crazy? My heart started to pound. A dull pain spread through my chest. I was certain I was dying.

The one man I should have been able to trust more than any other had done this to me.

"Dad, I think I'm having a heart—" As the strength left my legs, I peered in desperation at my father, then crumpled down onto the pavement below.

Woodstock

Day One

Friday, August 15, 1969
10:30 p.m.

"I would never underestimate your father," Livy said as we zigzagged down our row, trying not to step on anyone. "There's no way he's gonna find out you're here. He's not a wizard."

"Oh, yes he is!" I called from behind. "He can figure out anything." I was seconds away from confronting her about what she had done at the Beatles concert when I spotted Leon sitting all by himself. Tie-dyed-skirt girl was no longer talking with him. She had moved down to sit with the couple in front. Relief coursed through me, and I forgot all about challenging Livy.

As soon as I walked up, Leon patted the ground next to him. "My curiosity about you continues, Suzie," he said after I'd settled down on the blanket, like he'd been pondering things to ask me while I was away. Hearing him call me *Suzie* again made my heart soar. It had been caught in his butterfly net.

"About what?" I asked, a little afraid to hear the question.

"Nothing bad—I just want to know more about you."

No boy had ever asked to know more about me. When he grinned, I could hardly look at him. He was, without a doubt, the most adorable boy alive. "What do you want to know?" I asked.

"For starters, I don't know your last name."

"Withers."

"Suzie Withers," he said with a cute smile.

"I've never really loved my last name, but I suppose it could be worse."

"Yeah, man. You could be Suzie Butts, or Suzie Cobbledick."

I pushed his thigh. Laughed out loud. "That's not a real last name."

He chuckled through his words. "Yes, it is. I have a buddy named Cobbledick."

Hiding my face in my palms, I said, "Withers is just fine. What's your last name?"

"Wright."

"That's a good one."

"I like it."

"What else do you want to know about me, Leon Wright?" I flipped my hair behind my shoulder, a bit flustered but happy he was next to me.

"Let's see." He squinted one eye. "I know you're from Memphis. And you sing like a songbird. What'd you do all summer?"

While the stage lights bounced off his face, I studied his darling chin dimple. I wanted to curl up inside that dimple. "I worked. Read lots of books—"

"Where'd you work?" As I opened my mouth to explain, he said, "Wait, let me guess. At a restaurant?"

I shook my head.

"You helped at your dad's office."

I chuckled. "He's kind of retired."

"Already?"

"He was old when I was born."

He gave me a crooked smile. "Were you a camp counselor?"

"No, but that would have been fun."

"A lifeguard?"

"No, but that would have been even more fun."

"I give up, Suzie Withers. What's your job?"

I considered making up something glamorous—telling him I'd been on the Cypress Gardens waterski team all summer or had had an internship at Sun Records—but I'd decided to give up lying earlier in the day, so I told him the truth. Something about Leon gave me the courage to be honest. "I worked as a bra clerk at a fine department store," I said, with a definitive nod. "And no. It wasn't in the least bit fun."

If the way he gawked at me wasn't so hilarious, I might have cussed myself for not lying.

"Whoa!" he said, throwing his head back. "I was not expecting that."

I leaned toward him. "It wasn't my choice. All the cool departments were full."

His face glowed like a harvest moon. He tapped his chest. "It would have been *my* choice."

I sat up straight with a glow of my own. "Why's that, Leon Wright?"

Thrusting a finger at my breasts, he sang a line from "My Favorite Things," then hung his head. "I told you I can't sing."

"Stop saying that. Yes, you can."

He looked up, touched the tip of my nose. "Better be careful, Pinocchio. Your nose is gonna grow." At that exact moment, we heard a loud thunderclap. "See there. God's warning you."

"He is not," I said, giving him another push.

He grabbed ahold of my wrists. I wriggled. I pulled. I yanked. As hard as I tried, I couldn't move my hands from his grip. He twisted my arms behind my back, pulling me into his chest with his chin resting on my shoulder. "Say *uncle*," he said.

"No."

He pulled tighter. "Say it."

"No."

"You better say it."

"Uncle!"

He let go, and we beamed at each other just as it started to rain.

11:00 p.m.

It had never once crossed my mind it might rain at Woodstock. It started out light, but thirty minutes later it poured. Instead of raincoats, all Livy and I had were the light jackets her dad had insisted we bring. And mine was getting soaked. Come to think of it, Livy had said Nick would be in charge of our rain gear. And our tents. And our food and drink. Nick the no-show. What in the heck would we do now? He was even more untrustworthy than I'd thought.

"Don't look at me," Livy said as the rain made splotches on her brand-new suede hat. She closed her eyes, leaned her head back, and yelled into the night sky, "Dammit, Nick. This is all your fault!" When she opened her eyes, she caught me peering at her with frustration brimming from every pore on my face. "I don't know why you keep looking at me like that," she said.

"I'm not looking at you like it's your fault; I'm looking at you because . . . Okay, I'm frustrated. I wish we'd brought our own rain gear and not relied on your untrustworthy boyfriend." *Untrustworthy* just slipped out. I felt a little bad for saying it, but it's not like I hadn't warned her.

"I'm much more frustrated than you are," said Livy. "Trust me."

Meanwhile, this strange music flowed from the stage. No harmony, no pretty chords, no singing, just steady unmelodic tones. I couldn't stand it. It grated on my nerves and added to my frustration. "Who is this guy?" I asked, dying for a pair of earplugs.

"Ravi Shankar." Livy—well, the old Livy—wouldn't have liked his music, either, but she swayed her head from side to side with her eyes closed, pretending like she did. "Ravi's music is transcendent," she said, like all was well. "Don't you think?"

I glared at her. It was raining. I was starving. I was thirsty, and I sure didn't want to talk about—much less listen to—transcendent music.

A large pumpkin-shaped guitar with an abundance of strings and tuning pegs lay across this Ravi guy's lap. So big he had to play it sitting down. "What's that instrument he's playing?" I asked, in an irritated tone.

She answered me in her signature know-it-all voice. "A sitar. Ravi taught George Harrison how to play so he could use it on 'Norwegian Wood.'"

Ravi. Livy acted like she knew him personally. Before I could respond, another thunderclap crashed. Seconds later it started to pour. People stood up and yelled, cursing at the rain to go away. But the rain didn't listen. It only got worse. And Ravi played anyway.

In my mind, we had two choices. One, we could stay put, like most of the Woodstockers. Two, we could run for cover. We could head into the woods and use the trees as a leaky umbrella. But that option meant we'd lose our seats. And, worse, we could lose each other.

There was no second option. We had to ride it out.

Johnny removed his jacket and placed it over Livy's head. He wrapped his arm around her shoulders like he was keeping her warm. And left it there. They looked like boyfriend and girlfriend huddled together. I expected him to kiss her at any moment.

Leon had a better idea. "Let's do this, you guys," he said, unzipping his rainproof sleeping bag. "Huddle in." He tried placing it over all four of us, but it was too small. So Johnny unzipped his and laid it half across Leon's, creating a much bigger umbrella.

Now, this was a wonderful choice—all of us squeezed in together. It got even better when Leon poked his head out and invited Slim and Dave to join. Because that meant I had to scoot closer to Leon. So close our arms and legs looked glued together. Just touching him sent a jolt of electricity from my head down to my toes.

I peeked out into the crowd. Everyone else had had the same idea. It looked like one giant patchwork quilt hovering over the pasture.

Livy's mood changed again. This time for the better. With a shimmy in her shoulders, she rubbed her palms together. "This is cozy," she said before looking right at me. "Ready to get high?" I hesitated just long enough for her to add, "We have to make it through this rain somehow. It'd be a hell of a lot easier if you were high."

With only a second's thought, I answered, "Sure." From the corner of my eye, I saw Leon turn his head toward mine.

"I scored this lid from one of the booths at the bazaar," Johnny said, pulling a baggie out of his back pocket. "Cat called it great stuff." With fervent curiosity, I watched as he spread the grass onto a rolling paper. Leon held his lighter close while Johnny picked out the seeds and sprinkled them on the ground. "Next year they'll be turning this pasture into one helluva pot farm." He chuckled, twisted an end on the robust joint, and then handed it to me. "You get the first toke, love."

My readiness to be daring trumped my nerves. Besides, I knew just what to do. I'd been watching everyone around me smoke since I got there. Without another thought, I took the joint from Johnny, pinching it between my thumb and index finger. Dad's voice rang in my ears, warning me that I'd go straight to hell.

But I did it anyway.

While Johnny lit the end, I put the joint to my lips and sucked. *Hard.* I drew the smoke into my lungs like a pro. But the second I did, my lungs hurt so bad I hacked it out like a capital-A Amateur. Embarrassment lit my skin on fire. I wanted to die.

Leon pounded my back. He thought he was helping, but he only helped to embarrass me more. I didn't need a mirror to know my cheeks had turned bright crimson. *God's already punishing me,* I thought but went right back for a second puff.

This time I didn't cough. But I didn't feel anything, either, so I smoked the joint a third time, then passed it to Johnny.

After it came back to me for a fourth round, with Johnny's "roach clip" attached to the butt, Leon whispered in my ear. "Not trying to be your keeper, but since this is your first time, I'd stop." He gave my thigh a gentle squeeze.

Livy noticed. And cut her eyes toward us. My shoulder was tucked inside his armpit, my thigh on top of his. I might as well have been sitting in his lap. I met her eyes with a look that said *Don't you dare say a word.* Because that's normally what she would have done. She would have brought attention to how close we were sitting, and I would have been mortified.

Within seconds, fireworks exploded in my head. It buzzed like bees were trapped inside. Livy had been right. The grass made me feel so damn alive! My nostrils took on a life of their own. Holding my hand outside the sleeping bag, I let the water pool inside my palm. Then I took a big sniff. Each raindrop had its own odor. And its own face!

My cheek was so close to Leon's, I almost kissed him—in front of everybody. If he'd been facing me, I probably would have. Because every time he moved, brushing his thigh against mine, heat spread from my toes up to my nose.

If this was what Nick called *euphoria*, I had it.

Fifty Years Later

Woodstock 50th Anniversary Celebration

Bethel, New York

Saturday Morning, August 17, 2019

"Wait a minute. *You* smoked weed?" Adelaide's eyes look like giant blue marbles. I've blown her mind.

"Don't look so shocked. It was Woodstock."

"But you don't even drink."

"I used to. Plenty. I got ahold of myself before it became a problem. At Woodstock I was young and dumb."

"Young and in love."

"Young, dumb, in love, and desperate to fit in. That's not a reason to smoke marijuana." I dip my chin and give her a loving glance.

Adelaide shrugs, with her hairbrush in one hand and a cup of coffee in the other. She sits down next to me on the bed.

"Have you tried it?" I ask, trying to remain cool. It's important she knows I won't be angry even if she has.

She bristles, won't look me in the eye.

I lift her chin so she has no choice. "How many times? I won't be mad."

"Two. Maybe three," she says shyly.

"Did someone pressure you?"

"No. It just seemed like a cool thing to do."

"It seems cool now. But you never know what it'll lead to. Some people have genetic predispositions to drugs and alcohol. It's best to stay away from it." I give her a light tap on the nose.

"They use it for medicinal reasons now. It couldn't be all that bad. Besides, it's legal in Washington and Colorado."

I laugh out loud. She's so much like me. "This is not about the law. It's about common sense. Young people think nothing bad can ever happen to them. Will you at least think about what I'm saying?" Here I go, preaching to her again. I don't mean to. I just want her to make good choices.

Her arms are around me before I can utter another word. "I always think about what you tell me, Grammy."

I breathe a sigh of relief. Hopefully she knows by now I love her more than life itself.

Woodstock

Day Two

Saturday, August 16, 1969
12:40 a.m.

Once the pouring rain had slowed to a drizzle and Ravi had finished his set, Chip Monck returned to the stage. "To the gentleman that's climbing down the scaffolding tower, that is not a piece of rope that you are hanging on."

All heads turned.

"But a four-conductor cable. And it would sort of weld you to the side of the tower if you missed."

"That would suck," said Dave. "Even more than the rain."

Slim, whom we'd come to know as a fellow of few words, piped up with a suggestion. "If we drop acid, man, we wouldn't even know it's raining, man."

Despite the dire warnings from the stage, Livy Foster actually said, "I'm game."

"I second," said Johnny, holding his hand up. Dave shook his head no. Leon never responded, and I sure didn't.

Had Livy lost her mind? Despite her high intelligence, at times she seemed to be void of common sense. We'd all been warned about poisonous acid, yet she still wanted to experiment. I almost pulled her off to the side to knock some sense into that hippie brain of hers, but the last thing I wanted, or needed, was another clash with Livy. Especially while she was high. There was no telling what she might *accidentally* reveal to the group about me or my family.

The scales were beginning to fall from my eyes. No doubt Livy was physically perfect, but how much did that matter if someone lacked good judgment?

1:00 a.m.

With a light mist hanging in the air, a singer named Melanie strolled onto the stage. Not a soul with her, just this beautiful sable-headed young woman alone with her guitar, wearing the coolest pair of boots I'd ever seen. Melanie couldn't have been much older than me. I wondered if she was afraid. Looking at her all alone up there, facing hundreds of thousands of people, I put myself in her boots. I'd have been terrified.

After her set ended, John Morris made a shocking announcement. "It's a free concert from now on. That doesn't mean that anything goes. What that means is we're gonna put the music up here for free. What it means is the people who are backing this thing—have put up the money for it—are going to take a bit of a bath, a *big* bath. That's no hype; that's truth. They're gonna get hurt. But what it means is that these people who put on this thing here have it in their heads—and it's worth being grateful for—that your welfare, and their welfare, and the music, is a hell of a lot more important than a dollar."

Roars and applause sounded for the longest time; most people stood up. Over the cheering, Leon shouted, "Did you already pay for a ticket?"

"No," I said. "Did you?"

He shook his head.

"Now, let's face the situation," John Morris continued. "We've had thousands and thousands of people come here today. Many, many more than we knew or even dreamt would be possible. We are going to need everyone to help each other to work this out because we are taxing the systems that we've set up. We are going to be bringing the food in. But the one major thing you have to remember tonight, when you go back up into the woods to go to sleep or if you stay here, is that the man next to you is your brother. And you damn well better treat each other that way, because if you don't, then we blow the whole thing."

Loud whistles and whoops radiated from the audience. "There is a bit of acid sickness going around. Let's not pass anything to anybody else tonight. Let's just hang together. Anything that could be dangerous, let's just forget about it. Let's just make the festival, not the other stuff. There ain't nothing that can make you high as this."

Once the applause died down, John introduced us to the next singer. "Ladies and gentlemen, Mr. Arlo Guthrie."

"Yes! Far out, man," Arlo said, looking out into the audience. "I don't know how many of you can dig how many people there are, man. There's supposed to be a million and a half people here tonight—can you dig that? The New York State Thruway is closed, man. Lot of freaks."

I whipped around to Livy. "See! I told you. Nick's stuck on the thruway. That's what happened."

She gave me an exhausted sigh. "Dear God, I hope so."

Regret set in. "I shouldn't have called him *untrustworthy*, Livy. I'm sorry." I pulled her into a side hug. "He'll be here soon. He won't give up."

"Before today, I'd have told you he'd never give up." She leaned back on her hands, turning her attention to Arlo, who rambled on about a lot of nothing, like he was having a one-sided conversation with the audience.

Out of nowhere a wave of fatigue washed over my body. I had to *make* myself listen. Maybe it was the pot, but I had to force my eyes to stay open. I turned to Leon, hoping a conversation with him would spring me back to life. "What do you wanna do when you graduate?" I asked, clenching my jaw to suppress a yawn. I didn't want him to know I could fall asleep at any moment.

"I don't know yet," he said, as peppy as he had been all day. "But I'm not in a hurry to find out. The sooner I graduate, the sooner I may have to head to Canada."

That woke me up. "You'd really go?"

"I love my country, but I will not fight this war. People are dying on both sides. For what? So the South Vietnamese won't fall to communism? Why is that our problem?" He pressed his lips together as he shook his head in disgust. "It's all about money and power in Washington. Always has been, always will be."

Ron had said the same thing the day he left. "This is Johnson's war," he'd said. "He craves power." His overstuffed green duffel bag hung from his shoulder, weighing him down physically, mentally, spiritually. He could hardly hug me.

"Please don't hate me," I whispered in his ear. "I can't take it if you do."

"I don't. I'm just scared." He laid his head on my shoulder.

"I'm scared too." *How can he ever be a soldier?* I thought. *He's just a boy.*

"Pray for me," he'd said. "Promise?"

"Every day."

Leon chanted, "Hell no, I won't go."

I gave him a weak smile. "My poor brother. He's so scared over there."

Leon put his cross to his lips. "If something happens to my kid brother, my mom will lose her mind."

"Same with mine. I think about that a lot."

"Mom said she'd drive me to Canada herself. So did Dad."

I was tempted to tell him how cool it was that his parents were against the war, tell him about my dad's opinions and how he had insisted that his own eighteen-year-old son enlist for three tours. But that was a part of my life I preferred to keep private. The last thing I wanted was Leon knowing I came from a nutso family. "Sounds like you have really cool parents," I said.

"Yup. They're pretty cool." He skimmed his fingertips slowly across his jawline. "They've hounded me to keep my grades up ever since Andy got drafted."

"What about graduate school?" I asked, sure I'd come up with a way to keep him out of Vietnam *and* Canada. "That's a way to drag out your deferment."

He shook his head. "Ended last year. *Unless* . . . I go to divinity school." He chuckled. "I could never be a priest. A reverend in a different church where sex is allowed, *maybe*. Hey, I'd do just about anything to avoid 'Nam."

"You'd make a good minister."

"I don't know about that," he said with a grin. "But I'd be a better minister than a soldier. Would you sing in my choir?"

I smiled back. "Definitely." That was a delicious fantasy.

Johnny leaned over Livy and me to tap Leon's knee. "Guthrie's tripping, man. Can't you tell?"

Leon nodded without comment. It was hard to talk over the music unless you were sitting next to the person. When Johnny turned back around, Leon leaned closer to me. "He's moving to Canada as soon as we get home."

"He's really gonna do it?"

"Hell yeah. He got called up for his physical. Never showed."

"Uh-oh."

"Yeah, uh-oh. He's been listed *delinquent* by the selective service. They'll throw his ass in Leavenworth if he doesn't get out of here."

"That's awful," I said, imagining Ron locked up in prison.

"Better than Vietnam. Canada's his only option. Thousands of American boys have already crossed over," he said, scratching the back of his head. "Bad thing is you could lose your citizenship."

Leon's words dripped through me like hot wax from a burning candle. And gave a jolt to my sleepy head. What a terrible choice. Keeping your American citizenship while locked up in prison, or losing your birthright to move to Canada for freedom. Or, worse, risking death while fighting a senseless war.

What young American boy ever considered he'd have to make that decision?

Woodstock

Day Two

Saturday, August 16, 1969
3:00 a.m.

"There's nothing you can say, except the fabulous lady," the announcer said. "Let's welcome Joan Baez."

When the person I wanted to hear most on Friday finally made it to the Woodstock stage—amid yet another round of drizzle—I had nothing left. Drowsiness, the kind that was impossible to battle, overtook my body. I couldn't fight it. I'd been up since four in the morning. I'd walked ten miles, even more since arriving. My bones ached. My eyelids drooped. And my head hurt. I was soaking wet, cold, and ravenous. All I could do was blink, in a comatose state, at the great Joan Baez.

Everybody in the audience stood up and cheered when she walked out. Desperately trying to rouse myself, I clapped like she was Paul McCartney. I cheered. I hollered for her. "Yay, Joan!" I yelled. Yet fatigue wrapped around me like a heavy blanket.

A few stanzas into her first song, "Oh Happy Day"—my favorite gospel tune—Joan abruptly stopped singing. "Sit down," she commanded, in a nice tone.

As soon as I felt the quilt cradle my butt, it called me to recline. But I refused to give in.

During Joan's next two songs, I literally held my eyes open with the tips of my fingers pressed into my cheeks and eyebrows. Short of jogging around the farm in the chilly night air, or finding an elusive carafe of hot coffee, my luck was running out.

I rallied a little when she told the audience about her husband, who had indeed been imprisoned for draft resistance. "David is fine," she said. "And we're fine too." She patted her pregnant belly, then explained how he had been shipped from county jail to federal prison, which, she said, "is a big summer camp after you've been in county jail long enough."

The thought of Ron and which choice I'd have rather he made ran across my weary, near delirious mind. Would he have been better off standing up for what he believed in federal prison or fighting a senseless, heinous war because the government—and our dad—required him to do so? The odds of Joan's husband dying in a federal prison camp were almost nil. Obviously, that was his point.

Joan's next song had a much slower tempo. It was precisely the lullaby I needed to send me off to slumberland.

3:45 a.m.

A half hour later I awoke with my head on a hairy thigh. With a quick jolt I bolted straight up, humiliated. The hairy thigh was Leon's.

"Morning," he whispered.

I raked a hand through my tangled hair, mustered a weak "Hi."

Yasgur's dairy farm had grown deathly quiet, except for an occasional whistle. And Joan's astonishing a cappella voice.

"Is this her last song?" I asked.

He scrubbed a hand across his chin. "Might be."

"'I looked over yonder, and what did I see? Coming to carry me home? Saw a band of angels coming for me, coming for to carry me home. Swing low, sweet chariot.'" Joan hit notes I could only dream of.

As she serenaded the crowd with my second-favorite gospel tune, I leaned into Livy. "Wonder if Joan Baez ever sang in a choir?"

"Maybe," she said. "Her grandfather was a Methodist minister."

That night—I would be willing to guess—Joan sang "Swing Low, Sweet Chariot" with a five-octave range. I imagined bottles breaking all over the pasture when she reached her highest note.

She played one more protest song, "We Shall Overcome," an anthem to the civil rights movement. She dedicated it to her husband and invited everyone to sing along.

When it was over, Joan waved and told the audience good night. She exited the stage, never to return. As the Woodstock Nation jumped to their feet, cheering for our Friday-night headliner, my heart stung. I had missed most of it.

John Morris appeared back at the microphone sometime after four in the morning. "That brings us fairly close to dawn. The word I get is that maybe the best thing for everybody to do, unless you have a tent or someplace specific to go, is carve yourself out a piece of territory. Say good night to your neighbor, and say thank you to yourself for making this the most peaceful, most pleasant day anybody's ever had in this kind of music. We'll give you a little bit of recorded music in a little bit."

Since Livy and I had no tent or anywhere specific to go, and no dry blankets to keep us warm, we had no other choice but to carve out our own piece of territory right there in the bowl, in the drizzle. And pray the massive amount of body heat might keep us from freezing to death.

As for the good news, Leon and Johnny had no place to go either.

"Guess we'll crash here. Night, neighbors," Leon said, settling down on his back, knees up.

I settled down, too, on top of my wet blanket, happy that I was already next to him. Livy scooted in close to me, and Johnny lay down on her other side.

The four of us talked a little while, mostly about the music and which bands we were most excited about hearing over the weekend.

Shortly thereafter, Livy fell asleep. How she could do it in the cold rain blew my mind. It couldn't have been higher than sixty-five degrees. And since I was soaked to the bone, it felt like forty. It seemed like I'd never get warm again as I stared up at the night sky. I tried to keep it to myself, but shallow breaths gave me away.

Leon rolled over on his side. "You okay?"

I nodded, even though I wasn't. I'd missed most of Joan Baez. My blanket was soaked. I was soaked, cold, and hungry. As jubilant as I was to be at Woodstock—lying a foot away from Leon Wright—my body still screamed in agony.

"Softest bed I've ever slept on," he said. A faint chuckle followed.

I forced a grin while my teeth chattered.

"You sure you're okay?" he asked again.

"I'm fi-fine."

Without another word, I felt him slip his arm underneath my waist, pulling us together. He pressed his full body into the back of mine, then wrapped his arm around my middle, resting his hand just underneath my breastbone. One move of his finger and he would have known the curve of my breast. "This better?" he asked.

I'm wrapped up in your arms, I wanted to say. *What could be better than this?* "Much better" was all I said.

He dipped down to my ear. The stubble from his chin grazed my cheek. "It's not that cold, you know."

"Maybe not for you. You're a Ya-Yankee."

His loud Leon laugh woke Livy. She peered at us. But thankfully never said anything.

As exhausted as I'd been earlier, sleep should have come easy, but Leon's nearness made it impossible. All I could think about was turning around. Kissing him. Loving him. But I knew boys were supposed to make the first move. Then I remembered his knuckle massage, the way a brother teased a sister. As much as I wanted to kiss him, there was a big chance he thought of me as only a friend.

Silence fell between us. After a few minutes passed, I said, "I'm much better now."

He didn't answer. Soon enough, I heard his breathing slow. In and out, air whistled through his nose. I shifted, hoping he'd respond. Hoping he'd kiss me.

He didn't.

So I lay there in reflection. *Am I really here? Or is this a dream I'll wake up from at any minute? Did I really break free of Dad's heavy hand and drive 1,100 miles to a dairy farm in the middle of nowhere to hear some of the best bands in the world? Is the cutest boy I've ever met tucked behind me, with his arm wrapped around my middle?*

All these wonderful things had happened because I'd made the decision to take control of my own life. It was the best decision I had ever made.

It's hard to know when I finally gave in to sleep. The last thing I remembered was saying a prayer of thanks to God for sending Leon to me. Even if he was meant to only be my friend.

Woodstock

Day Two

Saturday, August 16, 1969
7:30 a.m.

A boisterous broadcast from a new announcer roused me from a deep slumber. I had no idea of the time, but when I cracked my eyes open, I saw daylight. And more misty rain.

"Why don't we just clean up our areas," the dude bellowed. "We're going to pass along garbage bags for you to put your trash in, and then we'll pick them up."

Shut up! Can't you tell people are asleep? I lay there on my side, desperately trying to fall back asleep, but it was no use. When I tried swallowing, it felt like someone had pushed a vacuum hose down my throat and sucked out the saliva. My head banged like a kick drum, and I needed to tinkle. The only reason I had the energy to open my eyelids was Leon. Sometime in the wee morning hours, he had rolled away, but his leg still touched mine. The mere feel of it made my heart dance.

With one hand pressed into my aching forehead, I pushed myself up with the other. The bowl resembled a war zone. Mud. Collapsed tents. Smoldering campfires. More mud. People scattered everywhere.

Some looked dead. The stage looked like it was floating on top of a giant mud soup and might sail away.

The soggy air clung to my skin, the grossest weather possible for an epic music festival. On the bright side, the temperature was on the rise. I had finally stopped shivering.

Nothing was as gross as the garbage. I couldn't get over all the waste the Woodstock Nation had managed to accumulate in one day. Empty garbage bags had been placed in a long line on both sides of the bowl, and people were already filling them.

Since Leon had slept through the announcement, I lay back down on my wet blanket to watch him sleep. Even that was magical. I counted the freckles on his arm and studied the new growth of stubble poking through his chin dimple. The rise and fall of his chest sprang new life into mine. Just looking at him aroused that ecstasy I'd felt when he was glued behind me.

He must have sensed my eyes upon him, because his popped open wide. I quickly shut mine, pretending to be asleep. Through gaps in my eyelashes, I watched him turn toward me, then prop up on his elbow, cradling his head in his hand. "Wake up, little Susie," he sang. The cutest thing about that—besides his bad voice, which by then I found simply enchanting—was that he felt comfortable enough around me to sing without apologizing. That, I loved.

I peeked out one eye, then spoke between slits in my fingers. The thought of having morning breath was horrifying. "I'm awake," I said, feeling a strong urge to visit the woods. As soon as I got there, I'd sneak off to brush my teeth.

A Bob Dylan song I'd never heard blasted from the PA. Seconds later, I smelled marijuana.

Leon inhaled the aroma with an exaggerated sniff, then gave me a wink. "Hey, Livy," he called. "Can you get high from smelling pot?"

No answer.

His lips curled into a grin as he sat up, raking his fingers through his hair.

Loving this unspoken alliance between us, I shot him a knowing smile and sat up along with him.

He glanced around at the wreckage before picking up his wet sleeping bag. "I'm gonna hang this over the fence. Want me to take yours?"

"It's still misty."

"I'm counting on it going away," he said with a wink. "It's rained enough."

While he meandered down to the stage, my eyes never left him. He hung both of our blankets over the wooden fence, where others had done the same. One of the massive cranes had been moved close to the stage, not far from where he was standing. I kept my eyes glued on its long neck while the driver pushed the bulging canopy to the rear of the stage, dumping hundreds of gallons of water onto the ground below. The deafening noise made him jump.

By the time he returned to our piece of territory, his white Converse tennis shoes looked like giant chestnuts. He kicked Johnny's butt, leaving behind a long brown streak. It made me laugh. "Let's go find grub, man," he said. "I'm starving."

Handsome Johnny sat up, rubbing his face with both hands. He looked down at Livy, who, by some miracle, was still snoozing. "Should we wake her?" he asked me.

Before I could respond, Livy grumbled, "Who has an aspirin?" No one answered, so she rolled onto her back. "Somebody please shoot me."

What amazed me most about Livy's beauty was that she looked just as pretty when she opened her eyes in the morning as she had the night before, no matter what she'd done or how late she'd stayed up.

Johnny leaned into her ear. "I'll find you one, love. Hey, Slim, do you or Dave have an aspirin?" he shouted. "Livy's got a helluva headache."

Poor ole Slim popped right up. "No, man, but I'll find her one." The back of his greasy bedhead was all we could see as he sprinted toward the medical tent, not all that far away.

"I'll take one too, please," I hollered.

Slim waved without turning around.

"Who wants to come with me to page my boyfriend?" Livy asked, in her ultrascratchy morning voice. If I had to hear her say *my boyfriend* one more time, I'd scream bloody murder.

I sure didn't volunteer. No one did. Not even Johnny. So she asked again. "Will somebody please come with me?" This time she sat up and looked straight at me.

"Before I can do anything, I have to visit the woods," I told her. "My head hurts, and I'm really, really hungry. I need to find food first."

"Okaaay," Livy said, drawing out the word, then followed it with an exasperated sigh. Frustration oozed from her eyeballs.

It astonished me that Livy wasn't ready to give up on Nick. I sure would have. She should have listened to me yesterday when I questioned his trustworthiness. Still, she wrote out another note on one of Johnny's rolling papers and tucked it inside her purse. For later.

After Slim returned with a handful of aspirin and everyone took turns in the woods, our little group gathered to formulate a plan for finding food. It was decided we'd have to split up. To be fair, we'd all take turns so no one would lose their seats. Slim and Dave set out first.

All morning long, the announcers had been keeping the audience abreast of life outside Yasgur's dairy farm. They informed us that the media had declared Woodstock a disaster area. A disaster area? Even with the rain, the cold, and the mud, I'd still call it a *wonder area.* Chip Monck announced that the New York State Thruway had been reopened, and state troopers were finally allowing cars back into the site. He said a hundred thousand more people were expected to roll in throughout the day.

Instantly I turned to Livy. "Nick's on the way. He'll be here soon."

"I still wanna page him," she said. "Please, please come with me."

I closed my eyes with a heavy sigh. "It's not that I don't want to go with you. I just don't want to lose Leon. I really like him, Livy."

"I can see why. He's beautiful."

"Not just that. He's really nice and really funny. All I can think about is making out with him."

She chuckled, patted my knee. "I'll ask Johnny to go with me."

9:00 a.m.

An hour after Livy and Johnny left in search of food, they returned empty handed. She claimed the Food for Love concessions area was an even bigger madhouse than it had been the night before, and she refused to stand in line. Hamburger or no hamburger, hot dog or no hot dog, she didn't care—the lines were far too long. She was positive somebody somewhere would take pity on her and share their food like people had done yesterday.

I overheard Johnny telling Leon most of their time away had been spent at the info booth, and the long wait for Livy's *boyfriend* had been brutal. Thank God it wasn't me.

Now it was our turn. Despite Livy's warning about the long lines, I was not deterred. My stomach growled, and my mouth watered at the thought of a juicy hamburger.

By the time Leon and I made it to the top of the bowl, we were up to our knees in mud.

The scene looked just as Livy had described. Thousands of people in slow-moving lines. To make matters worse, you had to stand in one line to buy your food tickets and another to receive your food.

A full two hours later, we walked away with a canned drink for each of us and a cold hot dog for Leon. The hamburger I'd set my heart on was sold out by the time we made it to the front of the line, so I'd ordered a hot dog. When I'd spied a dude serving them right out of a cellophane package, my hunger vanished. Not to mention, they had upped the price from twenty-five cents to a dollar overnight. No way I'd waste my money on something that unappetizing.

Another disappointment: My Coke wasn't a Coke. Or even a Pepsi. It was something called a Best Cola.

Once we'd been served, we stopped at a stand with a variety of condiments so Leon could dress his hot dog. Watching him zigzag the ketchup onto his bun made me queasy. Cold dog, cold bun, cold ketchup. Gross.

As we turned to leave, I neglected to look behind me, consequently slamming head-on into a solid mass. My face literally planted inside a dense jungle of chest hair.

Gagging from the scent of severe BO, I jerked back so violently my Best Cola splashed all over this hairy guy who looked like a woolly mammoth.

"Excuse me!" I said. "I am so sorry. I didn't see you."

Instead of speaking, he simply shrugged, then looked down at the cola seeping through his chest fur.

Utterly fascinated by the sight of him, I just stood there, taking him in. First off, he wore this towering pink top hat at an angle on his head. A little odd, but it was Woodstock—what did I expect?

It's what I didn't expect that caused my eyes to bulge out of their sockets. Woolly Dude wasn't wearing any pants! And without realizing it, I was staring at the burly upside-down toadstool between his legs, just dangling there—in front of God and everybody. I almost passed out.

Feeling a flush sweep across my face, I squeezed my cheeks. "Oh! Wow!" I accidentally blurted out before making matters worse. *Way* worse. Instead of looking away like a normal person, I *kept staring*! I gave that thing a full-on gawk, with my mouth hanging wide open.

Then for some reason—God only knows why—I extended my hand to make sure it was okay. It was an instinct I had. I did this sort of thing without thinking about it. The day before, I had done it to Leon's knee after banging it with the car door.

My fingers were mere inches from it when I realized what I was doing. I snatched my hand back as if it was an anaconda, gasped like I was terrified, and pressed a palm to my mouth. Naked Woolly Dude and I just stood there staring at one another for the longest five seconds of my life.

You'd have thought he'd have been embarrassed too. Not a chance. He held up those two Woodstock fingers and said "Peace, baby" in a jovial voice.

Right after that—I swear on a stack of Bibles this happened—while giving me the peace sign with one hand, he reached between his legs with the other. He picked up that toadstool and waved it at me, as if *it* was telling me goodbye.

In a daze, I stumbled away from the concessions area with a hand pressed against my stomach, praying Leon hadn't noticed. But when I whirled around to make sure, there he stood, only a few yards away, with a Cheshire cat grin on his face.

As soon as our eyes met, he burst into wild laughter. He crumpled over, holding on to his Best Cola with one hand and his cold dog with the other. I just stood there—glaring at him—as he shook his head from side to side. With no regard for my feelings whatsoever, he gazed up at the sky, all the while cackling like a farm hen. His face flushed as he gasped for air. Tears rolled down his cheeks. The only thing redder than his face was mine.

"Are you kidding me?" I bellowed. "I can't believe you're laughing. I'm traumatized."

Leon howled so hard he snorted, placing his hand that held the hot dog on my shoulder for support. He could hardly spit out his words. "As long . . . as I live . . . I'll never . . . witness *anything* that good."

By then we had attracted a crowd. People had stopped to watch, looking at the two of us as if we were a sideshow. A few even chuckled along with Leon, having no idea why.

"Hey, man, what's so funny?" one dude asked.

I glared at Leon, as if to say *Don't you even think about it*, so he raised a hand, flapping away the dude's question. "Nothing. Just a private . . . *joke*," he managed to spit out before dissolving once again into hysterics, like a deranged hyena.

"Looks like a good one," the dude answered before strolling off. Fortunately, the rest of the onlookers left when he did.

I stared Leon down with one of my signature scowls, crossing my arms in front of my chest. "Are you satisfied?"

He shook his head.

"I'm delighted I could be your entertainment today. Maybe I should charge you admission."

He leaned his head back, moving it from side to side. "If you could have seen that cat's face when he saw you staring at his johnson. Holy shit, Miss Peeping Tom!"

I leaned in toward him with hands dug into my hips. "I did not mean to stare! I was taken by surprise. Nobody told me Sasquatch was at Woodstock. *Naked.*"

After making another embarrassing pig snort, Leon grew oddly still. "Oh God, that's good. Say it again."

"Say what? Sasquatch?"

"No. *Nekkid.* I love your Southern drawl."

"No way." He'd have to beg me for it.

"Please," he said, with a crooked smile. "For me."

"No. You don't deserve it."

"Pretty please." He cocked his head, pouted his bottom lip.

I fought back a grin, but the sight of his silly face softened my resolve. After an eye roll, I finally muttered, "Nekkid," but not very loud.

With that he removed the hot dog from its bun and stuffed it inside his mouth. He bobbed his head up and down, waving the dog at me like Woolly Dude had waved his wiener.

I lunged at him. But he leaped out of the way, holding his Best Cola out to the side. With both hands I tried grabbing the dog, but he turned his head. Every time I tried to yank it away, he backed off, waving it at me again. I sprang toward him, but this time he ran, juking in and around the people in front of him, proving once more he knew his way around a football field.

Seconds later, when he let me catch him, I yanked that wiener from his mouth and whipped him with it, right across the face. Mustard and ketchup streaked his cheeks and nose. "You better watch out, buster,"

I shouted, shaking it in front of his face. "Or I'll lash you with this again." He tried grabbing it, but I beat him to the punch. I threw that dog down on the muddy ground and stomped on it.

Watching him laugh got me going, and I shrieked with glee. We just stood there, doubled over with bellyaching laughter. No help from marijuana, just good old-fashioned funny. *How many moons have passed since I've howled like this?* I wondered.

Our bodies were coated in mud, but I didn't even care.

Leon slipped an arm around my waist, pulling me into his chest. A match the size of Texas struck deep down inside, igniting a roaring fire. Fire I didn't know I had. As I looked up, square into his green eyes with mischief tucked inside the outer crinkles, I wanted to take my finger and outline his pretty lips. Because I craved those lips. I'd been longing to taste them for the last twenty-four hours. I'd spent the wee morning hours pressed into his abdomen, yet our lips had not touched. *Kiss me, you fool! Put your mouth on top of mine and kiss me. Right here, right now.*

But he didn't.

"Ready to head back?" he asked instead.

I slumped, ever so slightly, but straightened in a hurry, determined to steel myself against the sadness eager to clog my veins. The last thing I wanted was him sensing my disappointment.

"Sure," I said, trying to match his upbeat tone.

He has a girlfriend. That's what's going on here. Why else hadn't he kissed me? He wanted to. I saw it in his eyes. Surely he wasn't worried about people watching us. It's not like folks at the festival were making out behind bushes. People were having sex out in the open, for goodness' sake. A guy in a pink top hat was walking around buck naked.

So why hadn't he kissed me? As soon as the opportunity arose, I'd screw up all my courage and ask him. *Just wondering, Leon, do you have a girlfriend?* I'd say.

He glanced back at the multitudes waiting in line for their manna. "Do you want another soda?"

I shook my head. "I'm not getting in that line again. But I'll take yours—thank you very much." I snatched his Best Cola away. "You owe it to me after making fun of me."

"I wasn't making fun of you, little darlin'. I was teasing you." He tapped a finger to my nose. "There's a big difference. Let's head over to the Hog Farm. Dave told me we might find food there."

Food was now the furthest thing from my mind. His touch was the sustenance I craved. "What's the Hog Farm?" I asked as we maneuvered in and around the crowd.

"A hippie commune from . . . New Mexico, I think."

"So you don't mean an actual hog farm?"

"Not hardly," he said. "They're our festival security. I saw it on the news. Instead of the *police* force, they call themselves the *please* force." He chuckled. "They're using cream pies and seltzer water in lieu of guns. Should anyone get out of line."

"You need a cream pie to the face. I should turn you in for what you did to me."

"So this is war, huh?"

"You better believe it, buster."

Leon smiled, wrapped his arm around my shoulders, and gave me a gentle squeeze. Euphoria settled in until I felt another darn knuckle massage.

Instant buzzkill.

Woodstock

Day Two

Saturday, August 16, 1969
11:15 a.m.

Just beyond the woods, down a winding path with a hand-painted sign reading **Ho Chi Minh Trail**, we stumbled upon the Hog Farm. Strung up between the trees like a piñata, a pink winged papier-mâché pig dressed like Uncle Sam welcomed us in. How befitting. Having frolicked in the mud, we looked like sloppy pigs ourselves.

Once inside, I noticed a camping area with a bountiful number of tents and tepees and hay bale huts. An open-air kitchen had been set up on the opposite side, where a line of hippie girls sliced vegetables and cantaloupe. More girls dumped veggies into giant pots. The aroma smelled amazing. And made my stomach lurch. I'd have just about killed somebody for a McDonald's cheeseburger, fries, and a real Coke.

In the center of the camping area, graffiti-laden psychedelic school buses, painted in all colors of the rainbow, encircled a wooden stage. A hundred hippies or so stretched out on the damp ground, relaxing and listening to live music. Little children ran about—some clothed, others naked—and several dogs darted to and fro. Girls my age, dressed in halter tops and flowy skirts, danced around freely, like butterflies floating from flower to flower, enjoying the tranquility of commune life. I'd never heard of a commune before coming to Woodstock. And now I was in the middle of one.

On the stage, a four-piece band with a lead singer whose voice reminded me of John Lennon sang an unfamiliar tune. Leon and I sat down among the other listeners, settling in on the back row. There was no mud, just grass—a welcome chance to sit in a clean place and rest for a while. A couple named Linda and Wes passed us a joint. We each took a couple of tokes and sent it back. *Look at me,* I thought, *freely smoking marijuana out in the open, when I was scared of it a day ago.*

As the band exited the platform, the man we'd seen directing traffic yesterday—the one wearing the white jumpsuit—ambled over to the center microphone.

Leon leaned close to my face, whispering, "That's the commune leader, the one I saw on the news."

I turned toward him, felt our cheeks grazing. "He was the one blowing the kazoo when we came in yesterday," I said. With Leon's face brushing mine, more butterflies waltzed inside my stomach.

"I think he's an actor or a clown. Something like that."

"Let's give a big thank-you to Dylan McDonald and the Avians," the commune leader bellowed, with both hands holding on to the microphone stand.

People clapped and cheered. But when his chin hit the mic by mistake, making an awful screeching noise, everyone covered their ears.

He apologized for his error by giving us a silly, clown-like face, then glanced at his watch. "We have time for one more." He peered into the audience, shading his eyes.

From where we were sitting, I saw a few people turn to one another, as if they were considering his request. But no one actually volunteered.

"Aww, come on. It would be *groovy* if somebody sang us another song. You don't even have to be good! Just lead us in 'Kumbaya' or something. Don't be shy. We're all family here."

Leon took the Best Cola from my hand, sipped it, and then placed it down on the grass in front of him. "What about you?" he said, raising his brows.

Purely for effect, I turned my head slowly, looked him square in the face. "Have you lost your mind? I've never sung in front—" Before I could finish my sentence, his hand shot up in the air. From outside my body, I watched him pointing down over my head. By the time I gained the wherewithal to yank his hand away, it had already caught the attention of the commune leader.

"Groovy! Come on up here, milady." He beckoned me with both hands and a wide grin. The man truly did remind me of a clown, jovial and lighthearted. His missing front teeth didn't stop him from smiling at all.

But I wasn't budging.

As I sat there like a stunned mouse, paralyzed, unable to speak, he called on me again. "Don't be timid. What's your name?" His voice sounded hoarse, and the weekend wasn't half over.

"Suzannah," I mumbled. It was hardly loud enough for the people in the next row to hear, much less him, many yards away. "I'm gonna kill you," I said to Leon, ventriloquist-style.

"I can't *hear* you," the leader singsonged, sounding just like Gertie.

Leon cupped his hands on either side of his mouth, belting, "Suzie."

In an instant, almost everyone turned around to look at me. Hundreds of smiling eyes pierced through me. One guy in front turned and said, "Go ahead, Suzie. Nothing to be afraid of." The girl to my left wrapped an arm around my shoulders. "Give it a try. We're all family here." The tenderness on her face, and in her voice, comforted me somewhat, but I was still glued to the ground. A *tiny* part of me wanted to try, but deep down I was terrified. Not only did I have zero experience singing in front of a real audience, but I looked like Pig-Pen. Hardly the look for a singing debut.

The temperature couldn't have been more than seventy degrees, yet at the thought of getting up in front of that many people—on a real stage—beads of sweat had already formed in between my breasts. And under my arms. Feeling pressured, I called out from my seat, "I don't have a guitar."

"What's that?" the leader asked, with a hand cupped to his ear. "Speak a little louder, milady. You're on the back row."

"She didn't bring a guitar," someone yelled, a few rows ahead.

He waved away my excuse like he was swatting a fly. "Eh, that's easy." He glanced at a band member from the last act who stood at the side of the stage. "Ian, can Suzie borrow your guitar, man?"

I watched Ian remove the strap from his neck and hold his guitar high in the air. But I still wouldn't budge.

When the commune leader led everyone to chant my name, the reality of the situation finally sank in. As much as I wanted to resist, there was no way out. And of all people, Leon was to blame.

"Su-zie. Su-zie. Su-zie," I heard the Hog Farmers chanting. They wouldn't stop.

With no other choice, except chickening out like a pantywaist, I peered at Leon. "I'm gonna kill you. I am honestly going to kill you."

Covering his head with the crook of his arm, he winced. "My mom will be sad."

I had to consciously resist the urge to run as fast as my legs could carry me.

As if he sensed my thoughts, Leon stood up and extended his hand. My legs were jelly bowls, and my heart a sledgehammer, but I still took his hand and rose to face him. He gripped my shoulders. "I know you're scared shitless. But you can do this, Suzie. I believe in you."

His words melted onto my heart like a salve. No one but Ron had ever said anything like that to me.

"Singing is your destiny," he said.

Call it the marijuana. Call it the brotherly love of Woodstock, or flat call it Leon and his words of encouragement, but something inside me split open. Courage bubbled up. My feet took on a life of their own as I scooted past Leon, floating in a daze out to the edge of my row. Sensing every person's eyes moving along with me, I strode confidently toward the stage. With my head held high, I stepped onto the platform.

The commune leader smiled. "Welcome, milady, Hugh Romney. Glad to meet ya. Would you rather sit or stand?"

I didn't know, but something told me I'd be more comfortable sitting, as if I was on my bed at home. "I think I'd rather sit," I said.

While watching Hugh fetch a wooden stool at the back of the stage, my heart raced as fast as a cheetah. He placed the stool down in front of me with a thud, then patted the seat. "She's all yours."

"Just so you know, I've never done this before."

"That's why we have this stage." He lowered the mic stand to my level. "To give everybody their first time. Nothing to be afraid of. We're your family, hon." Hugh slipped an arm around my waist and gave me an encouraging squeeze.

Ian plugged his guitar into a small black box at my feet, then handed it to me. It was a beautiful Martin, with mother-of-pearl encircling the sound hole and rimming the edges. *A Martin.* Like Ron's. It had to be an omen. What's more, it looked like the one Joan Baez had played the night before. With pulse pounding, I took it from him, slipping my arm through the strap. I settled down onto the stool and placed the guitar waist against my thigh.

I peered out into the audience. Hundreds of nameless faces stared back. Suddenly I lost all confidence. What were they expecting? Another Melanie? "I'm not sure what to play," I told Hugh.

He gave me a toothless smile, then leaned in close, lowering his voice. "Do something easy. Like I said, sing 'Kumbaya.' Do you know it?"

Of course I knew it. By heart. From Young Life camp. Though I wasn't sure I wanted to play it at Woodstock. It would be cooler to sing one of Peter, Paul and Mary's other songs like "Michael Row the Boat Ashore" or "Puff, the Magic Dragon." I knew those by heart too.

At least I used to.

This was my shot, my chance to reignite my dream. I should be daring. That was what this epic escapade was all about. I'd done all kinds of gritty things in the last week. I'd stood up to Dad. I'd run away. I'd smoked marijuana. *Twice!*

Deep in my soul, I knew exactly what I wanted to play. But not only did I need a pound more nerve to do it—I needed a capo. If Ian didn't have one, I'd know it wasn't meant to be. "Do you have a capo by chance?" I asked him.

I'll be darned. Ian reached inside his pocket and held up a capo, then gladly handed it over.

"Thanks," I said, then placed it on the second fret, turning my G chord into an A. Although it had been shattered into a million pieces, I could still see *Rubber Soul* spinning on my turntable. The American version, first side, first track—the first all-acoustic song Paul had ever written: "I've Just Seen a Face." I was destined to play it.

With a shaky left hand, I found E minor, playing two notes together, a sixth apart. *Here goes. No turning back now.* As my fingers struck the chords with a second-nature sureness from all the hours of monotonous practice, I launched into the quick tempo. With my lips inches from the mic, I closed my eyes and let the lyrics flow.

By the time I got to the chorus, I had regained my confidence and sang with an intense fervor.

People in the audience were clapping to the beat, so I opened my eyes. Most were singing with me. Every cell in my body erupted with joy. I couldn't remember a time in my life that had been any more fun.

The last verse came before I knew it. Then two short minutes later, when I strummed the final chord, the impossible happened. The audience jumped to their feet. Their applause seemed to go on forever. You'd have thought I really was Melanie or Joan Baez or some other famous person. Certainly not me.

Bouncing off of the stool, I smiled at the crowd, then handed the guitar back to Ian. I stepped off the stage, with my head held high.

"Su-zie, Su-zie, Su-zie," the Hog Farmers chanted again. As ecstatic as that made me, I couldn't appreciate it fully because I was scanning the crowd for Leon. He was no longer in our spot in the back row. Dear God, had he left?

Behind me, Hugh Romney belted out, "Where do you think you're going, Suzie Q? Get back here!"

I swung around to see him waving me back to the stage. It hadn't been as hard as I'd thought. And I had loved every second of it. But where the heck was Leon?

Once again, Ian handed me his guitar. I settled back down on the stool. This time I knew exactly what to play: "I'll Follow the Sun." It was the first Beatles song I had ever learned. The way the minor two chord leads into the minor four chord makes the song achingly beautiful. I'd sung it over and over when I was seventeen, dreaming of Paul and me. *Beatles '65*, first side, fifth track. A perfect tune with simple, beautiful chords. *Under* two minutes. It was in the key of C, so I didn't need a capo.

Without overthinking it, I placed my fingers on the frets and strummed the short intro. With a sudden burst of confidence, I opened my throat and sang my heart out.

As quickly as it started, the song ended. "Thank you," I said to the audience once I'd strummed the final chord. "I really appreciate the chance."

Once more, all one hundred of my new friends, including the little children, stood up and cheered, as if they truly were my family. I'd never felt the kind of love and acceptance they offered. It made me long for more.

After handing the guitar back to Ian for good this time, I stepped off the platform like I was Joan Baez. Like a crocus blooming in the springtime, I had awoken from a long dark winter. Never had I felt more alive.

It got even better when I spotted Leon. He had moved to the side of the stage, with his arms open wide. I headed toward him and folded inside.

"You did it, Suzie. You were so, so great," he said, stroking the back of my head.

Hugh Romney made another announcement. "Wow! Isn't it great when life surprises ya? Let's give Suzie Q another big round of applause."

The Hog Farmers continued to cheer and clap—at least I think they did—but I had left my body and levitated to the top of the commune, the same way I had when I'd first heard Crosby, Stills & Nash. Two of my favorite Beatles songs had flown out of my mouth without a hitch, in front of a hundred people. All the drugs at the festival couldn't have given me that kind of high.

"Who wants to follow Suzie?" Hugh asked. "Just kidding. Quill's starting down in the bowl anyway. We'll pick back up later."

"Great job," a hippie dude with a ponytail said while walking past. His hair was as long as mine.

"Hope you'll come back," a girl told me. "I'd rather hear you than Quill any day."

"Your lady sure has a nice set of pipes," another hippie said to Leon while walking past. "Come back tonight, Suzie. Sing us all a lullaby."

I smiled in appreciation but found it hard to look at Leon. Someone had called me his *lady*.

The time had come. I had to find out if he had a lady back home. But how? Phrasing the question just right was critical. I couldn't say, *Hey, Leon. Do you have a girlfriend back home?* That seemed abrupt at this point—weird, even. What about *Am I your lady?* Lord no, that sounded even worse. I was just about to muster the courage to say *Do you have a lady back home?* but we were interrupted.

A topless girl with giant boobs painted as if her nipples were daisies stopped in front of Leon. "Come back later, why don't you?" she said. "We could take a trip together." She brushed a long, seductive finger all the way down his arm. Then followed it with a slow wink.

A slight smile crossed his lips, but he didn't say a word.

When Daisy Tits left, Leon looked at his feet, scrubbing a finger across his brow. "Not sure what to say to that."

I didn't know what to say either. Because I wanted to *slap* her. She had ruined my chance to ask him about a girlfriend. "Did you have any idea people would be walking around here without their clothes on?" was all I said, with a slight hint of irritation in my voice.

"It's all part of free love, baby. Ready for some chow?"

He seemed eager to change the subject. So I just dropped it. For now. Until I could muster the courage to ask him if a lady was indeed waiting for him back home.

Woodstock

Day Two

Saturday, August 16, 1969
Noon

After standing in line at the Hog Farm kitchen, which was a piece of cake compared to the madhouse at Food for Love, we inhaled our brown rice, vegetables, and cantaloupe in minutes. It wasn't all that great, but when you're starving, quality doesn't matter much. It was far better than cold hot dogs, that's for sure. What's more, the food was free, piping hot, and made with love.

We lingered in the soft grass before throwing away our plates.

"Who taught you to play guitar?" Leon asked. "You're really good at that too."

"Thank you. Ron taught me. He's the one who's good."

"That's right. You told me he's a musician. Is he a Beatles fan?"

"Big Beatles fan. He taught me to play those songs before he left for Vietnam."

~

I'd been doodling *Paul, Paul, I love Paul* in my school planner when the sound of Ron's guitar wafted down the hall. I jumped from my bed, paced over to his bedroom door. "Will you teach me to play something?"

He lifted his eyes but kept strumming. "What do you wanna learn?"

"'I've Just Seen a Face.'" I wanted to learn all Paul's songs.

Ron patted the space next to him. "You'll need a capo for that one." He reached over to his nightstand and pulled out a capo, then clamped it onto the neck of his guitar.

"What does that do?"

"Changes the pitch," he said. He went on to explain that even though a chord is fingered the same way, a capo shortens the strings and takes the music up a step. He handed me the guitar. "Find your E chord."

I did as he asked.

"Now find E minor, and play two notes, together, a sixth apart. Got it?"

I glared at him. "No."

He chuckled. "Watch me." Ron took back the guitar, starting the song in a slower tempo. But when I joined in to sing along with him, he notched it back up, and we finished the song together.

"You're a much better singer than me," he said.

"No way."

"Oh yeah you are. Emotion bleeds through your voice in every note. I have dreams for us, SuSu. We're gonna be the next big family duo. Like the Everly Brothers."

I crooked my pinkie and reached for his. "Pinkie swear?"

"Pinkie swear. What should we call ourselves?"

With a finger to my chin I said, "*Suzannah and Ron* sounds pretty good to me."

He laughed and rubbed his knuckles atop my head. "Yeah, but *R* comes before *S*. *Ron and Suzannah.* Much better."

I couldn't have cared less what we called ourselves. All I knew was I wanted to sing in a band. With my brother.

~

We threw away our plates in an overflowing garbage can, then headed back toward the bowl. As we strolled down Ho Chi Minh Trail, I obsessed over asking Leon about a girlfriend. I knew I had to ask him, whether I wanted to or not. My crush had blossomed into something I never thought possible, certainly not at Woodstock.

In a matter of hours, we'd be saying goodbye. I couldn't afford to fall for someone whose heart was elsewhere. Not even for this weekend of free love. Maybe others could do it, maybe Livy could do it, but I sure couldn't.

I had to find out.

As we passed through an opening in the woods, he led me over to a flower patch—a weed patch, actually—with tiny daisylike blooms. He picked several, then tied the long stems together before placing the wreath on my head. "Can you pretend these are lavender blossoms from France?"

I reached up to touch the wreath. After taking an exaggerated sniff, I said, "I smell the lavender. It smells sweet. Like you."

Leon sneered. "I bet my sisters would argue with you about that."

"Why? Aren't you sweet to your sisters?"

"Sometimes."

I drew my shoulders back, peering at him in jest.

With a toothy, kindhearted smile, he said, "Just kidding. I love my sisters. I'm not ashamed to say it."

"Are you sweet to your girlfriend?" I asked casually, even though my pulse blasted inside my eardrums. It seemed like a benign way to find out. I expected him to say, *What are you talking about? I don't have a girlfriend.* Instead, he blinked, jerking his head back like he'd been caught red-handed. A dazed look transformed his face as he shifted his eyeballs skyward.

My heart plummeted. A heaviness settled inside my stomach, like a tapeworm shredding my intestines apart. A tear or two, much to my dismay, sprang into my lids, stinging my eyes. *No! You will not cry,* I told myself, biting down on the insides of my cheeks.

"Not anymore."

A beat passed before his words sank in. "You aren't sweet to your girlfriend anymore?" I blurted out, rather sarcastically.

"I don't have a girlfriend anymore."

The relief was undeniable. My body even felt lighter. But the word *anymore* gave me pause. "Since when?" I asked.

Leon swayed his head from side to side. "A month. Or so."

"That's like yesterday. What happened?" I tried to say it in a sweet tone, but it was pure fake.

He breathed in, then exhaled slowly. "It ran its course."

"Are you sad?"

"Not really."

What was *not really* supposed to mean? "Aw, that's too bad." I acted aloof, pretended I didn't care, even though I cared far too much.

It got weird when he didn't respond. He looked down at his muddy high-top tennis shoes, wouldn't even make eye contact with me. "Shelly is . . . complicated," he finally said.

Still feigning indifference, I fidgeted with the tail of Livy's pink top—now brown—all the while conjuring an image of what *Shelly* might look like. Livy's face flashed in my head, along with her big boobs. "Lots of girls are complicated," I said, thinking about Livy, not me.

Leon peered at me earnestly. "Are you complicated?"

Was this an interview question? If so, I had to give the correct answer. I tugged at my earlobe. "Not particularly. In some ways, maybe, but I think I'm pretty normal."

"Normal's good," Leon said, as if there was no other way to be. *Note to self.*

"I agree."

"So what about you?" he asked. "Do you have a boyfriend back home?"

Without missing a beat, I lied straightaway. "We broke up." I blinked. "At the end of the school year."

"Are *you* sad?"

I twisted my mouth, playing like I was giving his question serious thought. "Sometimes."

When neither of us spoke, creating a long awkward pause, I was sure I'd blown it. I cursed myself for lying. Now I'd have to tell even more lies to make sure I wasn't caught in the first one. What's worse, I always got paid back when I lied. Like what had happened in my closet the night I'd left home. What would God's punishment be this time?

We both looked away, wondering what to say. More seconds passed before he broke the silence. "Looks like we've got something else in common, Suzie Q."

Determined to hide my deceit and even more determined that it would be my final fib, I forced myself to look at him. His somber expression had changed to a grin. It no longer felt awkward between us.

He tilted his head, letting his face drift toward mine. As heat rushed up my body, I lifted my chin and closed my eyes.

At that second a stoner stumbled past, high out of his mind, tripping down at our feet. I nearly fell on top of the dude, trying to get out of the way.

Leon bent down to help him. "You okay, man?"

Without a response, the dude pushed up on his forearms and stood. After he regained his balance, he wobbled back down Ho Chi Minh Trail toward the Hog Farm, never even saying he was sorry.

A wave of more people streamed past. Maybe they had heard about the free kitchen too. At that moment, I didn't care if anyone got fed. They were interrupting a crucial moment. Leon may have kissed me for real. It sure seemed like it.

Once we were alone again, instead of kissing me, he gave my head another damn knuckle massage. "What do you say we find Johnny and Livy to let 'em know they're friends with a star?"

This knuckle massage was the biggest disappointment of all. It made me think I was imagining the whole thing and that friendship was all he wanted. Maybe Livy was all he wanted, and he was using me to get to her.

Whatever the case, Leon slung his arm around my shoulders, tucking me in close. He sang a bit of "Suzie Q," letting me know he liked the way I talked and the way I walked. Then he cracked up at himself. "If John Fogerty could hear me, he'd send me to jail for murdering his song."

I'd heard Creedence sing "Suzie Q" on Thursday, in the car with Livy. If someone had told me in less than forty-eight hours a boy as beautiful and wonderful as Leon Wright would be singing the song to me, much less tugging me in next to his beautiful body, I may have had a stroke and died on the spot.

Fifty Years Later

Woodstock 50th Anniversary Celebration

Bethel, New York

Saturday Evening, August 17, 2019

"Why didn't you just kiss *him*? That's what I would have done," Adelaide says. "I love kissing."

Hold back, Big Mama, I tell myself. *Let her talk. She trusts you.* Mustering all my will to simply listen, I just nod with an excited grin.

We are in my Mustang with the top down, headed to hear Santana at the luscious new amphitheater at Bethel Woods.

"You should have kissed him first," she says.

"I guess girls don't wait for boys to make the first move anymore, huh?"

"Not always." She pats the dashboard. "My first kiss was in a convertible. A really cool Corvette." She crosses her arms in front of her, shifts in her seat to look my way.

"Sounds romantic," I say, then nudge for a little more. "How old were *you* when you had your first kiss?"

Now she's fumbling with the car radio—stalling, I suppose. She stops on Adele, "Make You Feel My Love," a perfect song—Adele's voice, Bob Dylan's lyrics. There's a long stretch before she answers. "Fourteen."

"How old was the lucky boy?"

"Eighteen."

My heart stops. What else happened in that Corvette?

A pause settles in. "Daddy thinks girls should wait till marriage to, you know, *have sex*." Adelaide giggles. In a nervous sort of way. "I don't talk to him about guys. He doesn't need to know everything."

The pounding against my chest accelerates. Instead of pushing her for more, I simply ask, "Are you still dating this fellow?" I didn't think she'd dated anyone, much less a grown man.

"We never actually went out. He found a prettier girl. My age." Her voice trails off, and I detect a hint of sadness.

"Well, he goofed."

"She's got long blond hair and a perfect face. She thinks she's the shit."

"What does that mean?"

"It means she thinks she's all that. All the guys are in love with her."

"Ahh. The beauty queens. The boys are always chasing after them. There was a time when I was crazy jealous of Livy because she could have any boy she wanted. I finally learned that *real* beauty comes from right here." I lean over and tap her heart.

She shrugs.

"Hey. You are plenty beautiful. And your heart"—I touch it again—"is even more so. Beauty is not about having a perfect face. It's about the way you love others and how you make them feel."

"I know, Grammy." She sings along with Adele, and I have to admit she's got what it takes to make it as a singer. Or an actress. She's darn good at both.

"Just do me one favor," I say, patting her leg.

"What's that?"

"Be careful when you're kissing. Before you know it, you're going all the way."

She cracks up laughing, shakes her head to and fro.

"What's so funny?"

"Nobody says 'go all the way' anymore." A beat passes before she adds, "I know what I'm doing." There's conviction in her voice.

By now we have arrived at the Bethel Woods amphitheater, and I get in line to park.

"There's a spot!" Adelaide exclaims, pointing left. "Over there."

I take a quick turn, and sure enough, she's right.

Once I put the car in park, she jumps out and helps me roll up the convertible top. There's no prediction of rain, but I'm not taking any chances. It wouldn't be the first time an unexpected rain shower showed up in Bethel, New York.

As we walk toward the front gate, I slip my arm around her shoulders. "I know you know what you're doing, lovey. Your Grammy is just old school sometimes."

"My parents have talked to me about that."

"Have they?"

She gives me an exaggerated nod.

Instead of asking for details, I give her a wry grin. "Your father may think he knows everything about me, but he does not. You'll know more about me after this weekend than he's ever known."

"Cool!"

Squeezing her shoulder, I say, "And that's just between us. Like you said earlier, he doesn't need to know it all."

She laughs. "Mom and I say that all the time. Daddy's old school too."

"And what about your mom?" I know the answer. I just wonder what she'll say.

"She took me to get the Gardasil vaccine when I was thirteen."

It's time to shut my mouth. I have no business asking questions about things I don't want to know.

Grandmothers don't need to know everything.

Woodstock

Day Two

Saturday, August 16, 1969
1:00 p.m.

Quill had finished their set by the time we found our seats. And our friends were right where we'd left them. As for Nick, he was still AWOL.

A guitar player wearing sunglasses and a bandanna tied around his forehead was onstage, singing solo. He wore an army green military jumpsuit with stripes on the sleeves, looking like a soldier fresh out of Vietnam. Not many people paid attention to him.

Meanwhile, a constant stream of army helicopters flew in and out of the backstage area. It was unsettling, like Woodstock was a military zone. It made me think about Dad. Unfortunately.

"What's shakin', y'all?" I asked, noticing there was very little room to sit. The Woodstock Nation had doubled in size since yesterday. New people had edged into our piece of territory while we were gone. Squeezing in anyway, we settled down on the waterlogged ground. I'd rather have sat in Leon's lap.

Livy had braided her hair into pigtails. While she and Johnny swayed to the music, I noticed wooden blocks in their laps. "What are those?" I asked, pointing at them.

"Quill threw tons from the stage." She tried knocking her blocks together like cymbals but missed. "It was killer, man." She pointed at my head. "Where did you get that?"

I reached up to finger my flower wreath. "Leon made it for me."

"Lucky." She smiled, but there was sadness behind it. "If my boyfriend had bothered to show up, I would have gotten a crown too."

After his no-show, I'd decided to never bring up Nick's name again. "Johnny will make you one," I said. "Just ask him." I certainly wasn't going to volunteer Leon.

"Give me an *F*!" the singer shouted from the stage. The audience, who had been unresponsive until then, echoed back with a loud "F."

"Give me a *U*!" the singer shouted.

Everyone yelled, "U."

"Give me a *C*!"

The echo happened again.

"Give me a *K*!"

"K."

"What's that spell?"

"Fuck."

He asked the question three more times, and by then every person seated at Woodstock shouted *"Fuck!"* like a meadow full of mynah birds. Without missing a beat, the singer slid into a song about Vietnam. Glancing around, I was surprised to see everyone singing the chorus along with him. The guys, the girls, all of Woodstock knew the words. All except me.

"And it's five, six, seven, open up the pearly gates. Whoopee! We're all gonna die."

Livy knew every word. So did Johnny and Leon.

"I don't know how you expect to stop the war if you can't sing any better than that," the singer shouted. "There's about three hundred thousand of you fuckers out there. I want you to start singing."

"Be the first one on your block to have your boy come home in a box." The Woodstockers sang the whole song along with him.

Everyone thought it was upbeat and fun—the highlight of the festival. Everyone except me. As the lyrics washed over me, all I could think about was Ron's body coming home in a box. And that was not fun. If I hadn't been such an idiot, he would be here, sitting next to me. Enjoying the festival. Not risking his life in a 110-degree jungle.

"What is this song?" I asked the group as soon as it was over, having to yell over the thunderous applause.

"'Fixin'-to-Die Rag.' Best protest song ever written," said Johnny. "I saw Country Joe perform it last summer in Manhattan. Helluva show."

"Do you like it?" I asked Leon. His brother was in Vietnam. I couldn't imagine he'd think much of it.

With two comforting fingers under my chin, he lifted my head to meet his eyes. "It's all in fun, Suzie. Try not to take it seriously."

Just when I thought it was over, Chip Monck called Country Joe McDonald back to the stage for an encore, and he sang the whole song all over again.

The only way I could suffer through it was to muse over the last few hours. While Country Joe and everyone around me sang, I re-created the day, moment by moment: bumping into Naked Woolly Dude, chasing Leon for the hot dog, my singing debut, finding out he didn't have a girlfriend, our kiss that almost happened. By the time I had rehashed every minute detail, the "Fixin'-to-Die Rag" encore had come to an end.

Country Joe disappeared for good, giving the audience a short break. I tapped Livy's knee. "Guess where Leon and I were all morning?"

Her gaze wandered over to Leon. "Going all the way?" she asked, shimmying her shoulders. She leaned in close to my face. "Tell me he used a condom."

"No! He didn't. I mean, *no*, we didn't go all the way. Jeez, Livy. We just met."

"So? You're at the biggest music festival ever. It's the perfect place to lose your virginity."

"Do you want to know where we were or not?"

"Of course I do," she said, after a long sigh. "Sorry. I'm even madder at Nick today than I was yesterday. Where were you?"

"Singing! To a real audience."

She sat up straight, wearing an authentic smile. "Seriously? Where?"

"At the Hog Farm stage. They have an open mic."

"That's so cool, SuSu. What'd you sing?"

"Two Beatles songs."

She gasped, threw her arms around me. "Which ones?"

"'I've Just Seen a Face' and 'I'll Follow the Sun.'"

"Oh my gosh. Did you play guitar? Or did someone accompany you?"

"I played. Some guy named Ian loaned me his."

"Right on! Did you . . . do okay?" she asked hesitantly. Livy knew me well enough to know I'd be terrified.

"I know this sounds cliché, but it really was like riding a bike. Every word and every note came flooding back."

"Maybe you'll take my advice from now on. You've got to sing at open mic nights when you get to college. I'm serious."

"I told you. There are no open mic nights at Union." I hesitated a moment, then added, "If Leon hadn't been there, I wouldn't have done it."

"Yes, you would have."

"No," I said, shaking my head. "I wouldn't have. At first, I said *no way*. But he was so sweet and encouraging; all the Hog Farmers were. They treated me like family."

"That's the beauty of commune life."

I couldn't stop smiling. "Can you believe it, Liv? *I* sang Beatles songs in public. Me! They even stood—"

"What I can't believe is Nick McCarthy." Livy's smile, which only moments prior had shown genuine happiness for me, faded as fast as footprints on the shoreline. She glanced down at her muddy sandals and held her head in her hands. "I am so mad!"

I longed to tell my best friend more about my performance and how the Hog Farmers had given me a standing ovation. I was dying to tell her that Leon didn't have a girlfriend and that I was almost positive he would have kissed me if not for some drunk idiot. But Livy had moved on. *You can't force someone into wanting to know the good things in your life. They either do or they don't.*

"I still say he got caught in traffic," I said. "Who knows; maybe he got pulled over and was arrested? Did he have drugs with him?"

She hesitated, swiping away dirt on her knees. "I don't know. Probably. Wait, shh." She put her hand on my knee to let me know we needed to listen closely to what Chip was saying.

"Once again if we may." Chip had laughter in his voice. "All lost persons—those wishing to be *lost*, those wishing to be *found*—again, the information booth is somewhat swamped, please go to the field behind it."

Livy peered at me with angry eyes. "Either he was arrested, or he met someone else when he got here and doesn't wish to be found."

"Oh no, Livy."

"Oh yes, Suzannah. Any girl would kill to be with him. He's beautiful."

"I'm sure he is, but—"

"He's probably somewhere in this crowd." She twisted around, sweeping her hand through the air. "With the prettiest girl here."

I gaped at her with a sneer. "I highly doubt that. Not many girls are prettier than you."

"I bet he's been camping with her since Wednesday. Ignoring my pages."

I grabbed her by the arm, determined to knock some sense into her. "Livy. Listen to me. You're letting your mind run away with you. Just because Nick isn't here yet doesn't mean he's camping with another girl. Or that you can't have fun without him. The last thing you want to do is let his absence ruin your good time."

She didn't comment, but I knew she was listening, so I seized the opportunity to give her more. "I get that you're crazy about him. But you're not acting like yourself. I've never known anyone as fun and resilient as you. Not to mention headstrong. You can still have a good time without Nick. You said it yourself: The best bands in the world are here. Pick yourself up and cut loose, Livy Foster. You'll regret it the rest of your life if you don't."

Livy looked skyward, like she was seriously considering my advice. It took a minute, but a smile appeared. "You know what?" she said. "You're right. Two can play his game. We've met good-looking guys too." She looked over at Leon. Then Johnny.

I swallowed a flash of jealousy. If she had to pick between our two new friends, I had a sixth sense she'd rather choose Leon.

Over my dead body.

2:00 p.m.

The rain decided to stay away in the afternoon. Bits of blue peeked through the clouds like tiny forget-me-nots, giving everyone hope fairer times lay ahead. The air felt sticky and humid, though. And the smell of urine and cow poop hung heavy in the air. At times I wanted to gag.

"Marilyn Cohen, Greg wants you to meet him at the information booth," a shirtless Chip Monck announced. "'Cause he wants to marry you." People whooped and hollered. "There goes Marilyn. Sydney McGhee, come immediately to backstage right. Your wife is having a baby." Folks were still whistling and cheering when he gave his next announcement. "Helen Savage, please call your father at the Motel Glory."

Poor Helen Savage. *If Dad finds out my whereabouts and has me paged, I'll die a thousand deaths.* I imagined him in the copilot seat of one of the military choppers we'd been eyeing, flying in to chastise me. Just as I thought about it, another chopper flew overhead.

"Those of you who have partaken of the green acid," Chip continued after the helicopter buzzed away, "if you would, as soon as convenient, please go to the hospital tent."

With each of Chip's chilling words about LSD, I kept asking myself why anyone would "drop acid" in the first place. It made no sense.

After a few more announcements, my new friend Hugh Romney walked out onto the main stage and tapped Chip on the shoulder. Seeing him up there gave me a sense of pride.

"My name is Hugh Romney. I'm with the Hog Farm, and I'm working on a scene," he told the audience. "Some people call it bum trips. I don't think there's such a thing as a bum trip. We've handled over three hundred, and everybody's worked out all right. A half hour after we release someone from our section, we turn them into doctors. And they care for the people that were tripping just like they were when they came in. Now people been saying that some of the acid is poisoned. It's not poisoned. It's just baaad acid. It's manufactured poorly. So anybody that thinks they've taken some poison, forget it. And if you feel like experimenting . . . only take half a tab, okay? Thank you."

Chip followed. "Uh, there's a little tremor of paranoia running through the audience about going to the first aid tent if you're on a bummer, if things are not going well for you, or whatever. Please be assured—again, I repeat, *please be assured*—there is no bust; there is no hassle. And they'll make every effort to make no unfortunate occurrence for you if you can't handle what's been going down."

There was no point in talking to Livy about it, so I turned to Leon. "With all that's been said, why would someone even want to take LSD? I don't get it."

"It's a psychedelic experience." He chuckled as he said it, but I found nothing funny about LSD.

"Can you define *psychedelic experience*? Because I'm not hearing anything that makes me wanna try it."

He gripped his chin as he glanced skyward. "How can I define *psychedelic experience*?" He swirled his fingers next to his ears. "When you drop acid, things get distorted. You might see colors or swirling patterns. A buddy of mine thought the walls in his pad were breathing."

"*Breathing?* That's wild."

"You've seen *Alice in Wonderland*?"

I nodded.

"Remember all the swirling colors? Alice drinks from the bottle. Then she's small enough to fit through the keyhole."

"Shut up. *Alice in Wonderland* is not about LSD."

"Remember the caterpillar sitting on a mushroom, smoking a hookah pipe? He tells her if she eats from one side of the magic mushroom, it'll make her large. The other side makes her small."

My hand flew to my chest.

"Grace Slick wrote 'White Rabbit' about it. Listen to the words. I'm sure they'll play it tonight."

"So that's why they call it a *trip*," I said, nodding.

"Yeah, man. LSD takes you on a journey to wonderland. You experience things you've never seen before."

I hesitated, then asked, "Have *you* done it?"

He nodded. "Yeah. I don't think I'll do it again, though."

"Why not?"

"I don't dig the feeling of not knowing what's real. It's groovy in some ways. But you're right. You could take a good trip or a bad one."

"You mean you don't know if you'll be poisoned."

"I've never heard of poison acid before this weekend. What I mean is some trips make you paranoid. You could hallucinate, for example, that your friend is trying to kill you."

I gasped.

"It's the risk you take. On the other hand, it could take you to *wonderland*." Leon's man-giggle followed as he crossed his legs.

"Livy thinks my brother's doing it in 'Nam."

"My little bro is shooting up heroin. We've talked about it in our letters. Something he'd never have done had he not been drafted. He's gotta get the images out of his head somehow." *Exactly what Livy said.* When he dropped his chin, I could see the wolves of worry on his face.

Although he hadn't meant to, he scared me to death. I pictured Ron on a bad acid trip. I pictured him pressing a needle into his arm.

But I'd become a master at blocking out the bad, so I pushed away the unsightly images just as Chip Monck leaned into the microphone. "Ladies and gentlemen, Santana."

A thin, curly-headed Hispanic dude stepped onto the stage, wielding his guitar like he was taming a tornado. He wriggled and writhed as if he was locked inside a jar with that tornado, fighting to get out. No one in our group had ever heard of him, but if his first song was an indication, he was on his way to stealing the festival.

Woodstock turned into a gigantic dance party. The stomping was so intense I could feel the ground rumbling underneath my feet like an earthquake.

For the first time all weekend, I cut loose. I spun around in circles, laughing with every turn. With every shift of my shoulders and every twist of my hips, I felt life returning to my soul.

The way Livy danced was so Livy. She pouted her freshly painted Pink a Pale lips while shimmying to the ground. Seconds later she twisted over to Leon and stuck out her thumb, bouncing it to the beat of the music. My heart sank. The Hitchhike had always been her favorite dance move, but what bothered me was the way she laid it on thick for Leon.

She thrust her thumb in front of his face, seductively moving it from side to side, like she wanted his ride and his ride only. Johnny stood next to him, but she never asked him for a ride. If she'd bothered to look at me, that thumb of hers would have become a bull's-eye, split in two by the poison arrows jutting from my eyeballs.

But a still small voice told me to let it go. *That's just Livy,* the voice said, before something else occurred to me. Old Livy had made a comeback. She was taking my advice.

Sometime during the next tune, the couple in front started a limbo. They invited everyone around them to join in. We all took turns dancing underneath.

Livy, on her second turn, slipped and—*splat*—fell down into the mud. Scrambling back up with a smile, she pretended she was fine. I knew better. She was mortified. She wouldn't look at any of us.

Once Santana's set ended, the mud looked a hundred times worse. Three hundred thousand fuckers, as Country Joe McDonald had called us, jumping up and down had obliterated what was left of the grass.

Dave and Slim, who had missed Santana's performance, scooted into our row wearing wet, yet clean, clothes. Livy, coated head to toe in mud, tackled them with questions. "Where did y'all find a shower? Was there shampoo? How about towels?"

"No shower, man," Slim said. "We found the lake." He pointed toward the lake behind the stage, then whispered into Johnny's ear.

Livy waggled her finger. "Hey, man, secrets are rude."

"I just said it's a beautiful scene, man." With his palms lifted, Slim gave us all a silly face.

"Very beautiful," Dave said, exchanging a knowing smile with his brother.

One by one Livy met all our gazes. "If I don't wash this dirt off soon, I'll self-destruct."

I glanced down at my own mud-coated body. A dip in the lake sounded good to me too. "I'm game," I said.

"Let's all go," said Slim.

"Who's gonna save our seats?" Livy asked. When no one volunteered, she picked up our overnight bag and slung it over her shoulder. "We can always find more seats."

Dave sat down in the mud. "You guys go on. I worked too hard for these seats." He turned around to look at the crowd. "Can't promise there'll be five more when you get back."

John Sebastian, one of my favorite singers, strolled up to the microphone in a tie-dyed pantsuit. Despite the chance to hear him sing, and the threat of losing our choice piece of territory, the five of us, including Slim, disregarded Dave's warning and headed to the lake.

Woodstock

Day Two

Saturday, August 16, 1969
3:30 p.m.

The lake wasn't all that far, but it still took twenty minutes to get there. With each step, I looked more and more forward to cleanliness. A body coated in cow pie mud was not the way I pictured our first kiss, which I had not given up on. I peeked at my watch. We still had time to make it happen. Didn't we?

In the distance, we saw hundreds of Woodstockers had had the same idea. It was hard to tell who was male and who was female. They looked like androgynous stick figures wading in the water.

Fifty yards out, their bodies came into focus. I caught myself before gasping out loud. We were entering a nudist colony.

Sweat sprang from my pores. My chest caved in to my ribs. I heard myself clearing my throat. Because I was on the brink of heart failure. Would I be expected to strip off *my* clothes? Would Livy? Would *Leon*? I considered turning around and hauling back to sit with Dave. But that meant I'd look like the biggest goody-goody on planet earth. The only choice I had was to keep putting one foot in front of the other toward the colony.

Even though I had the feeling of jumping out of an airplane, I held my head high, marching on like nothing was wrong. Like it was just another day in the deliciously free, cool, hippie life of Suzannah Withers. *You cannot stare,* I told myself. *You must act unfazed. Especially in front of Leon.* I didn't want him thinking me any more naive than he already did.

Forty yards away, I spotted people bent over, rinsing their clothes.

At thirty yards out, I saw three girls, naked as jaybirds, tiptoeing into the water, holding hands.

Twenty yards away, I spied Slim rearranging the crotch of his blue jeans.

Ten yards from the lake, Miss Olivia Foster—*undaunted*—broke away from our group and hustled toward the water. By the way she hurried, I expected her to take a racing dive into the lake. Instead, she halted at the water's edge, removed her sandals, and dipped them up and down in the water. She then carried them over to a boulder where others had left their clothing.

Livy was somewhat hidden by reeds, but we could still see her unbuttoning her suede top. She let it slip from her shoulders, exposing her big beautiful bare breasts. I watched in shock as she shed her shorts. Surely she would leave on her pretty new panties. Nope, they came off too.

After a quick full-frontal wave to our group, Livy turned and paraded toward the lake with her muddy clothes in her hands, gifting us all with a view of her magnificent posterior. Tan lines streaked her back, one just above her bottom, and the other flaunted the line from her bikini top.

Like a parliament of great horned owls, we all just stood there stock still, watching naked Livy step into the lake. Someone handed her a bar of soap, which she proceeded to swab over every inch of her body. When done, she bent over—mooning everyone on the shoreline—then soaped down her clothes and rinsed them in the pond. Once her clothes were clean enough for her liking, she turned around to our group with a big smile, flapping her hand like a flag caught in a mighty wind. She then cast her clothing onto the rocky ledge, piece by piece.

Handsome Johnny stumbled in his haste to remove his own clothes. After ripping off his T-shirt lickety-split, he stepped out of his first pant leg at breakneck speed, leaving it inside out. The boy wore no underwear. While stepping out of the second pant leg, he tripped, landing on the ground like a big klutz. Twenty-four hours earlier, when I'd first met Johnny, never in a million years would I have dreamed that I would soon be eyeing his tally whacker, *in broad daylight*, or any tally whacker, for that matter. Yet there was Johnny's, as virile and happy as the Apollo 11 rocket blasting to the moon.

"Let it all hang out, baby," he shouted, bolting in after Livy. Slim followed. He had ripped off his clothes so fast I didn't even see him do it. Miraculously, Leon didn't follow, which left the two of us to sit in the second-most awkward moment of my life.

Now what?

Despite the boulder-size knot in my stomach, I smiled confidently at Leon like I was just fine. I peered over at our naked friends with the same confidence. I even waved. Until Woodstock, I had thought *embarrassment* meant the time I'd tripped and face-planted onstage in front of the whole school while accepting my dorky perfect-attendance award. But this weekend had redefined *embarrassment*. The thought of people seeing me nude, in broad daylight, was as unimaginable as eating escargot. Truth was, I couldn't imagine anyone seeing me nude. No one had since I was a little girl. Not even Mama. Or Livy. Or Penny. Modesty was the policy in the Withers family.

Leon and I just stood there, mute, looking from the pond, back to one another, and then back to the pond, and when our eyes met again, we burst into wild laughter. We carried on like we had earlier; only this time, it was not at my expense.

"Okay, Suzie Withers. I don't see you stripping off your threads," said Leon, with that intoxicating man-giggle of his. "But hey, feel free if you want to. I promise not to *stare*." He jutted bug eyes toward me, then tickled the skin between my jeans and top.

"Stop." I brushed his hand away. "I'm not going to stare at anybody."

"Bet ya can't do it."

"Bet ya I can. How much?"

"Five bucks."

"Deal," I said, reaching out to shake his hand. I stepped toward the lake, then quickly turned back around. "Are you going in naked?" I gave him an exaggerated stare, square in the face.

"There it is. Can you say it once more? Please?"

Cocking my head to the side, I said it. "Nekkid."

Cocking his head to the other side, he said, "Good luck!"

"You'll see," I told him with a confident smile.

Leon laid a hand on my shoulder. "I don't have a problem with nude bathing, but I'm more than happy to dip in my shorts. If it makes you feel better."

The idea of Leon bathing in the nude came with a treasure trove of emotions: angst, excitement, titillation, *euphoria*. "Whatever works for you," I said, feeling my cheeks flush and praying he didn't notice.

He gave me a tantalizing grin, then pointed to a boulder, where the two of us sat down and removed our shoes.

"You could swim in your undies. No different than a bikini." Leon pointed to a group of girls who were doing just that. "But not if it would make you uncomfortable."

"I wouldn't be uncomfortable." Lie. Big lie.

Leon stripped down to his underwear, then pretended not to watch while I peeled off my jeans and slipped Livy's top over my head. My heart blasted out of my chest while I just stood there smiling at him, in my bra and panties. I didn't even own a bikini. One-pieces were the only bathing suits allowed in my family.

But my new underwear looked like a bikini. Gertie was the one who had convinced me to buy the set. Between my discount and the sale price, I'd paid only four dollars and fifty cents for a yellow floral Maidenform with matching panties.

I had to keep myself from staring at the four young boys sitting on a rocky ledge. They couldn't have been older than fourteen or fifteen, all nude. One boy, a clean-cut who had yet to grow facial hair, had his mouth hanging open and, like Johnny, was quite happy to be there. So was the boy next to him. All four sets of eyes were fixated on the bare breasts in the pond. The big ones, the little ones, the pointy ones. There were floppy boobs and firm boobs, large brown nipples and tiny pink ones. I smiled to myself, thinking about the variety of breasts in the world.

We stepped across the pebbles toward the pond. As soon as my feet touched the icy water, I flinched but resisted the urge to complain. A group of naked guys and girls in a canoe waved at us as they passed. The same person who had handed Livy a bar of soap handed one to me. I dipped my muddy clothes in the water, then rubbed the soap across my jeans and top. Leon did the same.

As soon as we were done, he waded out of the lake and placed each piece of our clothing on a boulder to dry. While his back was turned, I stared him down, weakening at the sight of wet underwear clinging to his butt cheeks.

Once he had waded back in the pond, we took turns scrubbing down our bodies with soap. Lots of people were washing their hair. Leon swam over to a girl and asked to borrow a squirt of her shampoo. He held up his hand and sidestroked it over to me.

First, he put a little on his own head; then he dumped the rest on mine. Only he didn't remove his hands. He lathered it for me. With his smiling eyes resting on mine, I lathered his, too, all the while experiencing . . . *euphoria*.

Was this Boy Beautiful, the one I'd met by chance on the road to Woodstock, really washing my hair? And I his? As if his fingertips against my scalp didn't feel good enough, add to that the fact that they were his, and I could have sworn I was on fire.

"Did you buy that at your fancy department store?" he said, *staring* down at my cleavage. It was small, compared to some I had seen that day, but he didn't seem to mind. He traced his fingertip along the lacy edge of my bra, making every pore on my body squeal with pleasure.

"As a matter of fact, I did." With my toes squished into the pond's muddy bottom, I gloated in the irony. I'd have never bought a pretty lingerie set if I hadn't worked at Goldsmith's. Here I'd spent the summer hating my job, having no idea of the ecstasy that lay just around the corner.

We dunked under the water at the same time to rinse off the shampoo. When I came up for air, my bra strap dangled from my shoulder. Leon traced my tan line with his finger, then pushed the strap back up. "I thought all you did was work and read this summer," he said.

"That's all I did."

He gave me a wry grin. "Liar."

I leaned toward him. "I'm not lying! I live in the South. Everybody gets a suntan."

He looked down at his chest. His torso shone bright pink from walking without a shirt the day before, but he had no suntan. "Maybe I need to come for a visit. Do you guys have a swimming pool?"

"I wish!" I said. "I swim at our club. I was on the swim team in high school."

"Is that so?" Leon tilted his head to the side, squinting one eye. "What's your best stroke?"

"I'd say . . . butterfly."

"What is it with you and butterflies?"

"Nothing! I've never thought about butterflies this much in my life."

"I thought you'd say breaststroke." He took his time tickling the top of my breast.

I let him. It felt so, *so* good.

He turned around and propped me on his back. I wrapped my arms and legs around him. Holding tightly to my calves, he strolled us through the pond.

"Does this hurt your sunburn?" I asked, feeling his muttonchop sideburns against my cheek. He smelled nice and clean.

"Nah, the water's helping. But thanks for asking."

Six more nudists, holding on to one another's shoulders in a straight line, passed us by, singing, "'Row, row, row your boat, gently down the stream. Merrily, merrily, merrily, merrily, life is but a dream.'"

Willing myself not to gawk, I just gave them a quick glance.

Until that second, I'd forgotten all about Livy. I hadn't known—or cared—about her whereabouts. But the nude singers brought her to mind. Fun. Carefree. *Naked.*

I turned to look for her, and there she was, ten yards away, with her big boobs on display for all, including Leon, to behold. Queen Livy holding court, with her knights—Johnny, Slim, and two new guys—all feasting their eyes upon her. When she saw me, she waved. Then made a look-at-you face.

I knew that face. I'd seen it a hundred times over the years. As hard as I tried to ignore her and swallow the jealousy, it boomeranged back, streaking through me like a speeding locomotive. Livy's big bare breasts were in Leon's direct line of vision. He had said it himself: Breasts were a few of his favorite things. What was going through his mind?

As I tightened my grip around his chest, another horrific thought wormed its way into my consciousness. There were only thirty-three hours of Woodstock left. Were Leon and I supposed to part ways as friends, without ever kissing, and never see each other again? The word was Jimi Hendrix would close the festival Sunday at midnight. After his show, we were all leaving, going our separate ways. Would it be the end of us? Could we, would we, ever be an *us*? Or was this all a figment of my imagination?

A few minutes later, Leon turned around in the water and guided us back toward the shore. When he let me go, I felt a wave of disappointment. We stepped out of the lake and shook off the excess water. I wrung out my hair. Without a towel to wrap up in, goose bumps popped up all over my arms and legs. He pointed toward the boulder holding our clothes and offered me his hand.

When we sat down on the ledge, he noticed my goose bumps. "I wish I was Merlin," he said, flicking his wrist like he held a magic wand. He lifted his chin to the clouds. "I command ye to shine."

"A wish shared by everybody," I said. Hoping to absorb his body heat, I scooted in closer. He wrapped his arm around me. My body warmed instantly. And burned on the inside.

"How tall are you?" he asked.

"That was random," I said with a chuckle. "Five three, maybe two."

With a warm grin, he tapped my nose. "Shrimp." His face was inches from mine.

"How tall are you?"

"A lot taller," he said.

His next grin was different, unlike the ones I'd seen before. There was something new there, on his face. Something mysterious. Whatever it was made me lightheaded. Blood rushed to my cheeks as I watched his head float toward mine. He looked into my eyes, like he longed to know the depth of them. Then it happened. He rested his lips on top of mine. Soft and warm, they felt so right. As he gently opened my mouth with his, I felt my body catch fire.

It may have been my first time, but I was no stranger to French-kissing. I'd been practicing on my palm for years. I'd examined the kisses in movies and reread the love scenes in my novels over and over. I was determined to prove to Leon that I was a better kisser than Shelly.

We had just settled into a lyrical, divine kissing rhythm when Livy's flea-bitten voice called from the water's edge. "Suzannah. Where are you?"

Reeds grew around us, sure, but no doubt she could see us. Why would she interrupt our kiss? That was the burning question. She knew how much I'd longed to make out with Leon.

I wanted to wrap my hands around her throat and *squeeze*.

Although I shouldn't have, I answered. "Over here." Both Leon and I looked straight at her and waved.

When Aphrodite and her apostles stepped out of the lake, ten feet from the boulder where we had just started kissing, a jealous rage more potent than the green acid at the festival sped throughout my body like a Formula One race car. Not only was Livy the prettiest girl at Woodstock; now she was the prettiest *naked* girl at Woodstock, and she was walking straight toward Leon.

His gaze traveled from her head to her toes. It was quick, but I saw it. How could he not look? Livy's hair, thick as a horse's tail, covered most of her breasts, but her nipples peeked between blond strands. Surely Leon noticed the pond water dripping off the dark triangle between her legs.

But what the heck could I do about it? Nothing. Absolutely nothing. Livy had an excuse to be naked. It was Woodstock.

Woodstock

Day Two

Saturday, August 16, 1969
4:45 p.m.

Once Johnny, Slim, and Aphrodite had shaken out their nude bodies and she had twisted her ponytail to squeeze out the water, they sat down on the rocky ledge beside us. Sunbeams streaked through gaps in the clouds. Without a word, the three of them closed their eyes and stretched out in the warmth to sunbathe.

My heart grew fists. They banged on the inside of my chest.

I tried to let it all go, but the longer I lay there in the sun, the madder I became. Livy knew I had a mountain of a crush on Leon. Why would she do this to me? Free love or not?

I yearned to take Leon's hand and run. But to where? There was no other choice but to grin and bear it, lest they all think I was a prudish, possessive baby.

Even though my clothes were sopping wet, I stood up and put them back on, hoping Livy would take the hint and do the same. Maybe body heat would help them dry faster. I had no idea, nor did I care. The only thing I cared about was Livy lying casually in the nude in front of Leon, as if all was well.

All was not well. She had crushed me to the bone. And betrayed me, yet again.

After a while, my betrayer sat up, gazing at our group with chocolate brown eyes. "I've never felt so free. What about y'all?" With both hands she finger-brushed her long wet hair from the scalp to the ends. It cascaded onto her shoulders like a waterfall. Livy knew she was beautiful. What's more, she was well aware of the power it gave her. It made me give serious thought to who she would be if her outer beauty was stripped away.

"Hey, Leon. Are you a Leo?" Livy purred, then shot him one of her sexy, kitty-cat smiles.

"Nope," he answered. "Aquarius."

"*Really?* I could have sworn you're a Leo. You have all the traits."

He smiled at her, but his eyes conveyed a different message. I didn't know what that message meant, but I hoped he was as annoyed by Livy as I was.

"I figured your parents named you Leon because you were born a Leo," she said.

He shook his head. "I doubt my parents even know the zodiac exists."

Livy actually batted her eyelashes. "Maybe you should enlighten them."

Now my blood had reached the boiling point. She had told me in the car that Leo was her favorite sign. Watching her sit there like a nude model posing for a French painter, flirting with the boy I liked—make that *loved*—made me choke with fury. When I had told her to cut loose, I had never expected this. Woodstock or not, how was I supposed to be okay with her casual nudity? And what about her *boyfriend*? Three hours ago, she'd claimed to be in love with him. If so, why flirt with Leon?

As soon as our eyes met, I shot her a nasty look a hundred times more powerful than an M16 assault rifle. I fingered my top, then my jeans. Even without words, Livy knew what I was saying. Ever since we were little girls, we'd been able to read each other's hand signals.

It worked. She stood up, strolled over to her clothes, and picked them up off the boulder. She peered at me with a look that said, *You are acting ridiculous*. But her actual words were "Still not dry."

"Neither are mine," I was quick to say, adding a look of my own that said, *Thanks a lot, Benedict Arnold.*

Likely sensing the chill in the air, Leon glanced between us. First at Livy, with her unclothed, erect-nipple breasts. Then at me, my breasts hidden underneath wet clothes. Yet he never uttered a word. Neither did Johnny. Or Slim.

But I did. "Put your clothes on, Livy." I just said it. If someone could have counted my rapid heartbeats, there's a good chance I would have been hospitalized. I was that close to a heart attack. When the guys weren't looking, I shot her yet another fierce hairy eyeball.

Everyone in the group watched as Livy re-dressed, then sat down next to Johnny, snuggling up to him for warmth. He wrapped both arms around her waist.

The disappointment in Slim's eyes broke my heart. Not sure why, but I felt sorry for him. His hair may have been greasy, but he sure was sweet. And generous. He had shared his food and drink with Livy and me. He was the reason we had snagged an epic piece of territory. If it weren't for him, Joan Baez would have been a tiny shell on the seashore, and I would never have seen Melanie's cool boots.

"I'm gonna head back," he said. "I'll see you guys later."

"Aw. Sure you don't want to stay, man?" Livy asked.

"Dave's probably having a hard time saving the seats. I better head."

"We understand. See you soon, man," she said.

I thanked him for his generosity. I even gave his naked body a hug. There was no way we'd get those seats back. Nor would we ever see him again.

Once Slim had dressed and told us all goodbye, Johnny—the only one still in the buff—moved over to his dry, mud-caked jeans. He pulled a bag of pot from his pocket, rolling papers, and a lighter. But he never put his clothes back on. After sitting down cross-legged, he slid a single paper out of the pack, then emptied a healthy serving of marijuana on top. As soon as he finished rolling what he called "a fat doobie," he licked one side of the paper, then twisted an end closed. "Who wants the first toke?" he asked.

The words had barely left his lips when I raised my hand. "Me!" It would be the only way I'd survive Livy.

Johnny passed me the joint. He held his lighter to the tip. I took a hit, then another, hoping it would give me an immediate sense of serenity. Putting Livy's vanity behind me was critical.

Three rounds later, my brain buzzed. The boulder of anger I'd been carrying went up in smoke. Where it went was anyone's guess, but I sure felt better. I silently thanked God for putting marijuana on the earth.

The sun, now peeking through the clouds, had obeyed Merlin's command, so we all lay down on our backs to catch the warm rays.

No telling how much time passed before I caught a glimpse of Johnny. The sight of him, in his birthday suit while the rest of us were clothed, struck me as *the* funniest thing I'd ever seen in my life. My shoulders started shaking. I clutched my stomach and gasped for air. Tears rolled down my cheeks. I tried to make them stop, but every time I did, the sight of Johnny became even funnier. Pretty soon I was suffocating in soundless laughter, and no one else knew why.

Seconds later, Leon started. As soon as our eyes met, it worsened. His breaths turned into wheezes. Now neither of us could stop. I had no idea whether he knew why I was laughing, but it didn't matter. Just seeing his face beet red made the whole thing a hundred times funnier. I turned on my side and howled.

When Johnny and Livy joined in, I thought I might need a stomach operation. Pressing both hands to my middle, I screamed out in pain. My face hurt so bad I had to squeeze my cheeks shut. The thought of Handsome Johnny hooting at himself without knowing it was funnier than all the Carol Burnett skits put together.

"What the hell is so funny?" Johnny asked, scrambling to a seated position. He had tears rolling down his cheeks too.

I could hardly spit out the word, but I managed a faint *"You."*

"*Me?* What's so funny about me?"

With a fist pressed into my mouth, I clamped my lips together, pulling back just enough to say, "Not you. Your *willy*!" With that I rolled over on my back, kicked my legs in the air, and squealed.

Johnny spread his knees apart and looked down. "What's so funny about my willy?" He eyeballed Leon, who shook his head, unable to speak. But when Johnny stretched out his legs on the rock, tucking his willy inside, the rest of us nearly fell over the cliff, roaring with laughter.

It was the cure I needed.

5:30 p.m.

After the chilly night we'd had, lying in the sun felt heavenly. None of us said anything for the longest time, at least thirty minutes. I was nearly asleep when I heard Leon say, "Too bad you guys missed Suzie Q this morning. She stole the show."

Johnny propped up on his elbow. "What show?"

"She sang her heart out on the Hog Farm stage. Got a standing O!" He stood up to clap, all the while beaming down at me. In light of Livy's physical perfection—dressed or nude—it boosted my confidence.

Johnny sat up straight, peering at me. "Hang on a minute. You're a singer?"

I shook my head. "I enjoy singing, but I'm not a real singer."

"She had to give it up a few years ago," Livy explained, her voice raspier than ever. "I was the one who told her to sing at open mics."

With a deep furrow between his brows, Leon sat back down next to me. "Why would you ever give up singing?"

I released a slow sigh before answering. "It's a long story."

Livy pushed herself up, gathered all her hair to one side, and then raked her fingers through, like she was brushing. "Her dad's psycho. That's why." With a crazed, wild-eyed face, she wriggled her fingers on either side of her head.

Leon stole a quick glance in my direction, as if he was waiting for me to say something.

I was still gathering my thoughts on how to respond when he took it upon himself. "That's not nice, Livy."

"I'm not saying anything she wouldn't say herself. Right, Suzannah?"

It wasn't the disrespectful gesture that bothered me; I was well on my way to forgetting Dad existed—at least for the weekend. What riled me up was Livy's perpetual know-it-all attitude and, yes, her audacity to prance around nude in front of Leon. As hard as I had tried to put that out of my mind with the pot and the laughter, the anger came roaring back. I was so mad I couldn't look at her. "Yep. He's a psycho," I said to Leon, not Livy.

But Aphrodite couldn't let it rest. "When John Lennon said the Beatles were more popular than Jesus, Psycho Dad burned her concert tickets." She paused. "They were her seventeenth-birthday present. Paul was her whole world."

The Paul comment was mortifying. My chest tightened. I could see red. With pulse pounding, I sat straight up, glaring at Livy. "He wasn't just my whole world." I tapped my chest. "Millions of other girls felt the same way. Still do." I took an angry breath. "George was your whole world. Davy Jones was too." Shifting my gaze away from her, I stared at the lake.

The time had come. Even though Leon and Johnny were with us, I had no choice but to finally confront her about what had happened three years ago. As I opened my mouth, intending to say, *Are you ready to admit your lie? And tell me the truth that you gave Marianne Gentry my Beatles ticket?* something she had said hit me like a baseball bat to the face. Did she just say Dad *burned* my Beatles tickets? I slowly turned my head toward her, as if I had a crick in my neck. "Dad banned me from the concert. But he did not burn my tickets. He gave them to you." I pointed straight at Livy's face, a real Southern no-no.

With a slight shake of her head, she squeezed her eyes shut, then opened them wide, as if she was not hearing me correctly. "*What?* No, he didn't."

"Oh yes he did. So you could take your *mother* and *little sister*."

A loud gasp spewed from Livy's throat. "That's not what happened! You must have forgotten."

The tension, thicker than a copy of *War and Peace*, caused a hush to fall over all four of us.

It was high time I stood up to her. Unable to hold back another second, I leaned toward her. "I have not forgotten one single detail about that day. I still think about it way more often than I should." My nostrils flared as I crossed my arms in front of my chest. "I know what you did, Livy. Did you think I wouldn't find out?"

"Find out *what*?" There was a sharp edge to her voice.

"You know very well what I'm talking about." With fresh daggers hurling, I dared her to look me straight in the eye and lie to my face. Yet again.

Her shoulders fell. She picked at her toes. "I didn't think you knew."

With a loud sneer, my voice escalated. "Are you kidding? Of course I knew! You saw me standing there with those protesters, but you hustled past, pretending you didn't." I disregarded Leon and Johnny, not caring that they were watching the showdown or learning about my crazy family. I was nearly shouting when I added, "I saw you with Marianne! I know you gave her my ticket."

Air blew from Livy's lips as she pressed a palm to her heart. "Can you please let me expl—"

"Of all people!" I interrupted before another lie could leave her lips. "You knew I couldn't stand her. She was the one who spread that rumor about you and John Dearing. Not me. I would have never betrayed you like that, and you know it. Why would I want Marianne to be the one to get *my* birthday present?" Livy tried to interject, but I wouldn't let her. "You told me Kim was using my ticket. You lied to me."

She stared down at her feet as if she was contemplating a response. Her voice was neither defensive nor angry when she said, "Marianne did not use your birthday ticket. Neither of us did."

"Then how did you go to the concert, Livy? The tickets were sold out." At this point, I was so upset I could hardly get the words out. "Dad gave all three of my birthday tickets to your family."

"Suzannah," Livy said, in that authoritative tone of hers. "That's not what happened. Your dad *burned* your tickets. Or so he told my dad. He said he didn't want anyone going because the Beatles were making devil music."

Hanging my head in shame, I felt heat rush to my face. Livy had exposed my darkest stain.

"He left me at the last minute with no way to go. Thank God for Marianne. If she hadn't invited me, I'd have missed out on the concert of a lifetime. Your dad's the one who lied to you. Not me."

I was the one who had missed out on the concert of a lifetime. And spent three long years thinking Livy had betrayed me. When, in actuality, it was Dad. "If what you're telling me is true, then why didn't you call me for three years? It wasn't my fault Dad burned the tickets. Was that a reason to walk out on our friendship? You were my *best friend*!" My voice broke. Tears blurred my vision.

Leon placed a hand on my back, rubbing his fingers across my spine. It gave me much-needed comfort.

"Your dad told my dad I couldn't see you anymore," said Livy. Her voice softened as she scooted toward me. "That's why."

"He *what*?" My mouth fell open. "My dad said that? Why?"

She lifted her shoulders. "He's psycho."

I covered my ears. I couldn't hear anymore.

Johnny, still naked, piped up. "Ladies, ladies. There's no reason to fight. This weekend is about peace and love. You said it yourself, Suzannah. You guys were best friends. Can't you kiss and make up now?"

Livy laid a hand on my knee. "My parents weren't making me burn my Beatles stuff. Or boycott the concert. Your dad was. He told my dad he thought it would be best if we didn't *keep company* anymore. Who knows what goes on in his head? That's why I didn't call you."

With a palm to my forehead, I muttered, "My God."

Leon clutched my shoulder, saying in a soft voice, "I'm sorry that happened to you."

I peered at him, my world shattering all over again. "I'm sorry you had to hear this. You too, Johnny."

"Suzannah." Livy's voice was gentle, laced with compassion. "I'm sorry it happened to you too. You and Ronny have been through a lot."

Johnny clapped his hands together. "Hey, man, can you guys kiss and make up now?"

Livy pulled me into a hug. But all I could give her was a limp embrace.

A choppy sea of emotions surged through my head. On one hand I was relieved to learn she had not betrayed me. Part of me wanted to break down—right then and there—and weep over all the wasted time away from my best friend. Sob over the endless energy I had expended on anger. But the other 50 percent of me couldn't get past the gall of her to prance her nude body around the boy she knew *I* wanted. Sure, it was Woodstock. Lots of people were into free love. But still. Who does that to a best friend?

With a look of exasperation, Livy pulled away.

I couldn't muster up the energy to feign goodwill; I was exhausted from hardly any sleep. Awkwardness returned, but I owed Leon some sort of an explanation about my father. "My dad's super strict," I told him. "He's an army colonel. Very tough on my brother and me."

"Is he in 'Nam?"

"No. He's retired. He probably wishes he was so he could whip my brother into sha—"

"The brother he *forced* to enlist in this horrific war." Livy straightened, pressing her fists into her waist.

I glared at her. "If you would hush your mouth, maybe, just maybe, I could finish my sentence."

"Yeah. Let her finish." Leon's deepened tone surprised me. It must have surprised Livy, too, because she shuffled next to Johnny, buttoning her lip. For once. She stretched out her legs, tapping her feet together.

"My dad probably wishes he was in Vietnam," I said. "So he could slap my brother and all his rebellious soldier friends into shape."

Livy couldn't let it rest. "Poor Ronny. He didn't have a chance."

I looked at her with renewed resentment. "You say that like he's dead."

"I didn't mean it like that," she said. "I meant he didn't have a chance to go to college first. With his friends."

"Son of a bitch," said Johnny. "I'd kick my dad in the nuts before I'd let him make me go to 'Nam."

"You don't know my dad," I said. "It's impossible to say no to him."

"The army colonel thing is rough," Leon said. "I had a teacher my freshman year at Penn State. Old guy. Retired high-ranking officer in the army. Biggest dick who ever lived."

"That's just the tip of the iceberg," said Livy. "He's over-the-top religious."

"What's your religion?" Johnny asked me.

I'm seconds away from slapping her across the face, I thought but answered Johnny anyway. "Southern Baptist."

"Did your brother try for conscientious objector status?"

"I have no idea, Johnny. I don't even know what a conscientious objector is."

He started to explain that it would have gotten Ron out of combat, but Leon interrupted, "My mom grew up Southern Baptist."

Surely this was a joke. "Really?"

"Yup," said Leon.

"Is she from the South?" I asked.

"Well, yeah. Georgia. She's a peach. She talks just like you."

I couldn't believe my ears. We had something else in common.

"When she married my dad, she converted to Catholicism. So they could appease my grandparents and get married in the Catholic Church. Why do you think I have so many sibs?" Leon said, letting one of his man-giggles fly.

"Catholics are against the pill," Livy explained, like we were all—including Catholic Leon—morons. "Blows my mind every time I think about it."

"That would be my parents' philosophy. Not mine." Leon stood. "Let's get back to the bowl. I'm ready to boogie."

"Me too!" said Livy, quickly rising to her feet. She was done with the conversation.

And so was I.

She turned to Johnny. "Let's go find grub first. I'm starving."

"You and me both," Johnny said, finally putting back on his filthy clothes.

Leon snickered. "Good luck. This joint is all out of grub." He offered me his hand and pulled me up. My ankle turned on the uneven rock, but he caught me before I fell.

I couldn't have cared less about finding food. All I wanted was to go back to our kiss.

Woodstock

Day Two

Saturday, August 16, 1969
6:30 p.m.

On the way back to the bowl, we made a pit stop in the woods. It made me wonder how many thousands of others had avoided the nasty Porta Potties and done the same. The ones not wanting to lose their seats had simply wet their pants. I'd seen their pee spots. I'd smelled their urine.

On top of that, the pervasive smell of cow dung, which had gotten worse after the rain, refused to go away. Woodstock wasn't the best-smelling place I'd ever been, but I wouldn't have traded my spot for all the tea in China. Even with the Livy showdown, I couldn't have been happier. Leon had kissed me. For real.

The distinctive sound of Chip Monck's voice wafted throughout the farm. After a few announcements about more missing people, he made yet another plea to the idiots who refused to come down from the scaffolds. "Those of you still on those towers," he said, dog tired from the asking, "I don't really know how to approach you. Please come down. I think it's a reasonable request. If it's out of reason, I trust someone will tell me."

At first, I was surprised Livy hadn't mentioned paging her boyfriend again. But the more I considered it, I wasn't surprised at all. She had reverted back to her wild, carefree self. And the most astonishing part about that—I was the one who had suggested she do it. Look where that had gotten me. Mad as hell. I wasn't sure how much longer I could stand the sight of her. I snickered to myself as I wondered why I'd ever thought she was attractive in the first place. Like Mama often said, "Pretty is as pretty does."

Since we were all starving, and sure we'd lost our seats with Dave and Slim, we made our way up the hill to the Food for Love concession area. We wanted to make sure—and prove to Queen Livy—that they were still out of food. They were. Quite a few mad patrons milled about. I was in the middle of a fantasy about spending the remainder of Woodstock alone with Leon, when Johnny noticed a helicopter. "Look, you guys." He pointed to a pink-and-white whirlybird that had landed in a nearby field.

From where we stood, we could see people unloading what looked like massive amounts of food. Livy threw her arms up, looking heavenward. "Thank you, God," she exclaimed, then took off running, with Johnny two steps behind.

Although I was hoping to somehow distance myself from Livy, Leon seemed eager to help. So we headed over too. Sure enough, thousands of sandwiches and hard-boiled eggs had arrived at Woodstock, as well as canned goods, water, and fresh fruit. The four of us jumped behind several others who were passing the food in an assembly line toward a waiting truck. "Where did this come from?" Johnny asked the dude in charge.

"The townspeople heard about the food shortage," he shouted over the whir of the helicopter. "Donated all this from their own pantries."

It took thirty minutes to finish the unloading. For our assistance, the guy in charge offered volunteers first dibs on food. We graciously accepted the handouts and found a place to sit down at the back of the bowl. You'd have thought none of us had eaten in a year by the way we devoured our boiled eggs and slurped peaches from a can.

We hung out there for a while and listened to the acoustic sound of the Incredible String Band.

Just being around all the nice people at Woodstock and thinking about how kind the townspeople had been made me consider what it would be like to live in a Northern town like Bethel. I wondered if a college happened to be close by. Maybe I could get a student loan and transfer. It couldn't be all that far from Penn State, could it?

After disposing of our trash, Livy insisted we try and get our seats back, even though the odds of that were slim to none. As we passed the bank of pay phones, I thought about calling Mama. But the lines stretched on forever, most likely an hour wait. I didn't want to leave Leon that long. By now, I craved everything about him. He had protected me from smoking too much marijuana. He was the reason I had gained the courage to sing at the Hog Farm. He understood why I hadn't wanted to strip off my clothes at the lake. Even better, he had stood up for me in front of Livy. Whether I wanted to admit it or not, I had fallen in love with the boy in less than twenty-four hours, after one short kiss.

And that boy would be leaving tomorrow night.

The sun, which had finally decided to show her glory, dipped closer to her cradle, taking away my warmth. The thought of being that cold again made me dread nightfall. My Southern skin was far too thin to live outside in the North for three days. Thank God it had stopped raining.

Once we made it down front, we attempted a search for Slim and Dave. I thought it was ridiculous, but Livy insisted. With all four of us trekking up and down the Woodstock highway, it proved impossible to tell where we were once seated. Thousands upon thousands of newcomers had arrived. The brothers had become tiny minnows, swallowed up by the sea.

Canned Heat had taken the stage. A lapis blue-hour sky provided a lovely backdrop for the band. The spotlights from the towers illuminated the lead singer, who blew his harmonica from another universe. I so wished we had our seats back.

"Any ideas?" I shouted over the music. "I think we should just sit anywhere."

"Yeah, you guys, let's figure this out," Leon yelled.

The words had just left his lips when Livy spotted someone she knew. An hour ago, Chip Monck had announced 450,000 people were at Woodstock. Yet Livy, a girl from way down South, spied a familiar face. Her mouth dropped open. She grabbed the sides of her head, prancing in place. After she screamed, "Oh my God, I cannot believe it," I glanced at Johnny to gauge his reaction. He was blank-faced dumfounded. We all were.

"Nick?" I asked casually.

"Hell no!" Livy's smile widened as a gorgeous guy with a full black beard and silky dark hair hanging past his shoulders stepped around blankets and coolers to head her way. The moment he reached her, Livy leaped into his arms, wrapping her legs around his waist. He swung her around. Twice. She beamed at him while he flashed her an equally happy grin.

The dude set her down but kept his arm around her waist. Now that he was close, I noticed he wasn't very tall; he and Livy were the same height. "Everybody, meet Henry," she yelled over the music. "He's my political science professor."

It was loud where we were standing—no point in carrying on a conversation—so Leon, Johnny, and I just waved.

Pushing her hair aside, the professor spoke into her ear. She nodded vigorously, then announced, "Henry's making room for us, y'all!"

So just like yesterday, we traipsed behind Livy as she and Henry led us to our new piece of territory.

These seats were even better than the ones with Slim and Dave. Oddly enough, a thin rope had been stretched ten feet back from the stage. Even more bizarre, no one crossed it. Henry and his bevy of intellectual hippies had managed to snag a spot twenty feet behind the rope. But there was no extra room. None that I could see.

Henry's presence commanded enough authority for everyone around him to move over a couple of inches, creating four microscopic viewing spots. So puny we had to press our arms into our sides. I looked like a pickle in a pickle jar. I could hardly breathe, especially with the heavy cloud of skunk smoke impregnating the air. It made me cough.

As Canned Heat jammed onstage, I longed to dance. Yet there was no room. So I lightly shifted my heels and tapped my hands against my hips, determined to ban Livy and her men from my consciousness.

It didn't last long. Once Canned Heat finished their set, I overheard her say to Henry, "When did you grow that beard? I almost didn't recognize you."

Combing it with his fingers, he replied, "Over the summer. Like it?"

"Love it."

Watching Livy flirt with her professor made me want to vomit. Had she no shame? I was beginning to think Nick was a figment of her imagination. How could she be so flirty with Henry if she had a boyfriend? How could she prance around naked in front of other boys if she was truly in love? No wonder I couldn't be a hippie freak.

Chip appeared at the lip of the stage. "Come on. Get yourself together. It's really a drag. Every time we begin a set, we have to ask you to come down. If you go up there for attention, I'm sure you could throw yourself somewhere else and get the same effect. So if you *please*, leave the towers *now*, and *stay off* the towers!"

"Look behind you," Leon said, tugging on my sleeve.

I turned around to see, yet again, a barrel of monkeys tangled between metal poles like it was a jungle gym. "What's their problem?" I asked him. "I feel bad for Chip Monck. This has to be getting old."

Leon shrugged. "Some people are just selfish."

Yeah, and the blonde I came with tops the list.

Woodstock

Day Two

Saturday, August 16, 1969
10:30 p.m.

After the crew had spent time shuffling gear on and off a giant turntable in the middle of the stage, the Grateful Dead appeared. Over the weekend I'd overheard conversations about Jerry Garcia. People talked about him as if he was a demigod. I couldn't wait to find out what all the hype was about.

Since darkness had fallen, I didn't notice the clouds sneaking in. When the wind picked up, so did my angst. I looked around at folks standing near me. Hair was blowing around their faces. Their shirttails looked like they might catch sail. A gust caught my pink top and blew it straight up as high as my chin.

The canvas top over the stage undulated with the wind as it whipped through Woodstock as fiercely as a lion's roar. Not five minutes later, the skies opened. With no warning whatsoever, a gully washer returned, falling much harder than it had the night before.

Yet again, I was soaked to the bone.

The rain blew onto the stage. Jerry Garcia looked at the water pooling underneath his feet and gave the cute guitar player to his left a horrified look. Their giant light show screen, hanging above them, flapped like a sailboat caught in a mighty wind. Someone climbed up and slashed it right as some crazy dude ran onto the stage and flung LSD pills into the audience. If we hadn't been seated so close, I would have missed the whole thing. I thought back to all the warnings about the poisonous acid and wondered why in the world this guy was allowed on the stage in the first place.

Fifteen minutes into their annoyingly slow first song, Livy turned around to the people behind her with hands pressed into her hips and a rageful stare.

"Stop talking!" she yelled, even though she couldn't have possibly heard anyone over the music. "People are trying to hear the band." With that she turned back around, crossing her arms over her chest like she was mad as hell.

I'd never seen her act that way. Her sudden mood change came out of nowhere. Swallowing my growing resentment, I stood up, put my arm around her. "You okay, Liv?"

She shook her head from side to side for what seemed like a full minute, then pointed frantically at the stage. "Do you smell that?"

"Smell what?" I asked. She didn't answer, so I got in front of her face and asked again. "Smell *what*?"

"The flowers!" Her smile warned me that her mood had flipped again. I had to get next to her face to hear what she was saying, because the music muffled her voice. "Aren't they beautiful?" She pushed me aside and thrust a hand toward the stage, seemingly picking flowers—one by one—until she had formed a bouquet. "Gardenias. My favorite." She dipped her nose inside the bouquet, then handed the thing to me.

"There are no flowers," I shouted over the music, with rain dripping off my nose.

She ignored me. "Look at the red wine bubbling from the stage!" With a wide-open mouth, she leaned her head back. Her jaw moved, like she was guzzling it down her throat. Or so she imagined. She started singing something familiar, but the music drowned out her voice. Then tears sprang into her eyes. Seconds later she wailed like a grieving widow.

Einstein may not have been my last name, but I knew what was happening. I turned around and peered desperately at Leon. He'd been watching the whole affair. "After all the announcements?" I said. "Tell me she's not that stupid."

He shrugged.

"For a Harvard student, she has no common sense."

"Wait a second. Livy goes to *Harvard*?"

"Well, Radcliffe."

"Damn." He pushed his wet hair back from his forehead. "She's one complicated chick."

As happy as his remark made me, my panic over what she had done escalated. "Suppose she took the brown acid? Or the green acid? I need to take her to the medical tent right now." I may have been furious at her earlier, but now I was scared. I didn't want Livy poisoned.

"Suzie." Leon cupped my wet shoulders. "You don't need to worry about Livy." He pointed at Johnny. "Look at him. He's tripping too."

Johnny had a faraway look in his eyes, but he sure wasn't crying. Or shouting. He was dancing.

"He'd never be dumb enough to take the bad shit going around here. They probably got it from Henry. Just ignore her. She'll come down eventually."

"Ronny! You are beautiful," Livy shouted at the stage. "I'm so happy you're here!"

What the hell? I turned around to Leon again. He simply raised his palms.

My patience was growing razor thin. With a scowl on my face, I stepped right in front of her. "Ron is not here. He is in Vietnam!"

She stepped aside—I had blocked her view—then waved and hollered at the good-looking guitar player onstage. "I'm right here, Ronny."

With eyes pinned on the dude, I studied him head to toe. There was an uncanny resemblance between him and Ron. "What's that guitar player's name?" I asked Leon. "The one next to Jerry Garcia."

"Bob Weir."

I twisted back around. "Livy!"

She wouldn't look at me.

"Livy." With hands on both shoulders, I shook her. "That's. Not. Ron. It's. Bob. Weir!"

She flat ignored me, like she was unaware of my presence. "Play 'For Your Love,' Ronny!" she shouted. "Play it for me."

Ron loved the Yardbirds. He even wore their signature sunglasses.

"Get a *grip*, Livy!" I shouted, inches from her face. "Ron is not on that stage."

Leon wrapped his arm around my waist and spoke into my ear. "No point in trying to talk her down. The LSD has to wear off."

Laughing like a lunatic, Livy reached out and placed her hand on my forehead. "Your head. Your head. It's huuuuge!"

"No, it's not," I said, growing more incensed. "You're the one with a big head."

Leon shook his. "No point in arguing with her."

"Why did you drop my ring, Ronny?" she shouted at Bob Weir.

Drop your ring? Okay, that's it. Drenched to the bone, I turned away, scheming how to get as far away from her as I could. Meanwhile, the Grateful Dead continued with an instrumental number that had been going on for at least twenty minutes. I wanted to slit my wrists.

"It was my favorite ring," Livy cried, with real tears in her eyes. Then she started to wail for the second time in minutes.

As much as I wanted to ignore her, I couldn't. Unable to hold back, I shook her again. *Hard.* "What? Ring?"

Finally recognizing my presence, she held up her pinkie finger. "My signet ring. It's gone."

I remembered that ring. Signet rings were all the rage. Of course, Livy got one. It was a birthday gift from her parents, gold with cursive initials—OAF, for Olivia Adele Foster, named after her grandmother. We had always joked about her initials spelling *oaf.*

It was all coming back. I remembered her telling me that she had lost her ring over Easter break.

She placed her hands on either side of her mouth to yell at Bob Weir, "I said you could try it on. Not drop it behind Rosie's bed."

Rosie's bed? Rosie was our housekeeper. She slept in the little bedroom off our kitchen whenever my parents were out of town—

Oh. My. God.

My brain flatlined as a steady, high-pitched hum took over. The ground tilted underneath my feet. I felt dizzy. Nauseous. And, worse, *betrayed*. The girl in Rosie's bed. Ron refusing to tell me her identity. How could I have been so stupid?

I had been bushwhacked with the lie of the century.

~

Easter had come right on time, mid-April of '66. Memphis city schools had a holiday on Good Friday, but it didn't mean I'd get a holiday from my piano lesson. Thank goodness it had been moved up to one o'clock. Ron and I had big plans for the afternoon.

"See you next Friday, Mrs. Bohannon," I said, once my lesson was over.

"Good work today, Suzannah. You have a terrific grasp of this Beethoven piece." Mrs. Bohannon had often told me I was her best, most advanced student, a compliment that made my parents prouder than it did me. Dad believed the piano was meant for church hymns and classical compositions. I believed it was meant for Beatles songs. Paul played the piano.

"Aw, thanks," I said, peering out the front window. Ron was late. Again.

Mrs. Bohannon and her next pupil had already entered the lesson room, and the door was nearly shut when I asked, "May I please borrow your phone?"

"Be my guest. You know where it is."

I certainly did. On the wall, in the kitchen. Punctuality was not my brother's strong suit.

I dialed home. Twenty-five rings later, I hung up, waited thirty more minutes, and called again. Ron had forgotten about me and was in the basement playing music too loud to hear the phone. He often turned up the volume when our parents were away.

The next time I called—fifteen minutes later—I let it ring *fifty* times. When I got no answer, I could feel anger rising inside my throat. Ron had promised we would spend the afternoon learning a new Beatles tune on his guitar.

At three o'clock, after sixty rings, my anger turned to fear. The ghastly thoughts of what might have happened were impossible to dismiss. I plopped down in a chair on the front porch with nothing to do but twiddle my thumbs. And worry.

"I thought you'd be long gone," Mrs. Bohannon said, once her last pupil had left.

"I can't get in touch with Ron."

"Have you tried your parents?"

"No ma'am, they're at church. Setting up for Good Friday supper. I'm worried about him."

"I'll take you home, honey. Just let me grab my pocketbook."

A minute later we loaded up in Mrs. Bohannon's Buick Skylark, and she drove the ten minutes to my house. Cuda was parked out front.

"He must have lost track of time," I said with a sigh, stepping out of the car. "Thank you so much for the ride." I flew inside the house, so damn mad. Ron often lost track of time. And often got in trouble for it.

"Ron," I called as soon as I opened the front door. After no answer, I sprinted up to his bedroom. He wasn't there, so I barreled back down the stairs and flew to the basement. Not there either.

Convinced something was terribly wrong—like he'd been hurt or kidnapped, even—I hurried back up the basement steps and happened to hear a funny noise coming from the little room off the kitchen. Rosie's room. The one we rarely entered.

Pressing my ear to the door, I heard someone's heavy breathing. It scared me, to be honest. Even so I pushed the door open, afraid of what I'd find.

What I found was a shirtless Ron propped up in bed with his head against the wall and his eyes closed.

"I've been waiting at piano for two . . . hours." It was then that I noticed a hump underneath the sheet, strategically positioned.

Ron jerked the covers up to his chin. He just stared at me, mute, while the nameless hump stayed stock still.

I stared back, unable to speak myself, as the reality of what I'd walked into crystallized.

With a mixture of dread and embarrassment tingling through my body, I slowly backed out of the room, shocked that Ron had taken such a big risk. *You are such an idiot,* I wanted to scream. *If Dad had been the one to catch you, there's no telling what he would have done.*

After softly shutting the door behind me, I flew up to my bedroom and yanked my diary out of the nightstand.

~

Breathing solely on life support, I stared at the stage, unable to move. While the drizzle continued to coat 450,000 people listening to the Grateful Dead rock Yasgur's dairy farm, the lie rocked me, encasing my body in a thick coat of plaster.

Though I grappled to put the last pieces together, the puzzle had been solved. Looking back now, I could see all the signs were there.

My sophomore year in high school, when Livy and I were having a sleepover, I'd found her in Ron's room propped up on his bed, flipping through his albums in her nightgown. She didn't want to come back to my room even though I had asked her to.

That should have been the harbinger.

There was the time I had looked everywhere for Livy and found her in the basement dancing with him. I'd never thought anything of it. We always danced with Ron when our parents were away.

The times Livy had sneaked off with him at the University Club to smoke cigarettes should have been another clue, as well as the many occasions she had hitched rides home with Ron from school. It had all seemed normal. She'd told me she considered Ron the brother she never had. Sure, she flirted with him, but she did that with every boy.

The unanswered questions tumbled through my mind like balls in a bingo cage. *Where is Livy's signet ring now? Is it still underneath Rosie's bed? Was she in love with my brother three years ago, or did she just want to go all the way with him, like she had with John Dearing?* At that moment, I didn't know all the answers. All that mattered was that I had been lied to by my very own brother and my very best friend, two people I should have been able to trust.

Something else occurred to me. It had the worst sting of all. It was Livy's fault my brother was in Vietnam. *Not mine.* I had been stupid and left my diary on the bed for my nosy parents to discover, but Livy was the one to seal his fate. Even more despicable, she knew I blamed myself.

Livy Foster was the most screwed-up individual I had ever met.

There was only one way to extricate myself from this quagmire. I had to get the hell away from her. That instant.

Woodstock

Day Two

Saturday, August 16, 1969
11:45 p.m.

I squeezed my lips together to keep from screaming. The last thing I wanted was to pull Leon into the quicksand with me, but if I didn't get away from Livy, I'd have to go to the medical tent myself.

Sopping wet, with my arms wrapped around my chest—as if that could keep me warm—I peered at Leon in desperation. My words tumbled out in a jumbled mess. "I'm trying to be a good sport, but I just found out something horrible. Everything makes sense now. I should have known. I'm such an idiot. I wish I had—"

"Slow down, little darlin'. Everything's gonna be okay."

My teeth chattered. "No, it's not."

"Sure it is." He draped an arm around me, tucking me inside his chest with a firm grip. "What the hell happened?"

"I want to tell you, but . . ."

"But what?" His voice radiated tenderness and calm, especially when he lifted my chin and looked into my eyes. "Tell me."

"I don't want you to think I'm complicated."

His smile calmed me even more. So much so I stood on my tiptoes and kissed *him*.

"You aren't complicated," he said, once my lips left his. "You're here with Livy. That's what's complicated."

"I need to take a permanent leave of absence from her. Right now."

His response was a hearty laugh.

"It's not funny."

"Sorry. It's the way you say things sometimes."

"Can we please sit somewhere else?"

Without hesitating, he bent down and picked up his backpack.

As quickly as the relief arrived, something dawned on me before I reached down to gather my things. The best of Woodstock was yet to come. All Leon's favorite bands were due to perform thirty feet from where we were standing. I didn't have to be a Harvard student to know this night would be historic. Creedence Clearwater Revival and Janis Joplin, Sly and the Family Stone, the Who, and Jefferson Airplane would be performing. It wouldn't be fair to ask him to leave our prime piece of territory. On top of that, how could I ask him to leave Johnny, when he was moving to Canada on Monday?

"Never mind," I said, waving a hand in front of my face. "I'll go alone."

Leon peered at me, confused. "Huh?" When I didn't respond fast enough, he said, "You're leaving me?"

"I can't ask you to leave Johnny. Or this spot. All your favorite bands are coming up."

"I don't care about this spot."

"You don't?"

"No. We'll find another one." He slipped the backpack through his arms. "I'm surprised you've made it this long. Grab your stuff."

"What about Johnny?"

"Johnny will be fine. He can have me paged before the festival's over."

I hugged him with more vigor than I'd ever hugged anyone. In ten seconds flat I had dug into our overnight bag and pulled out a fresh pair of panties, my toothbrush, and our only tube of toothpaste, jamming all of it inside my purse. Livy could find her own damn toothpaste.

11:59 p.m.

Leon was right; we found more good seats. Just the two of us wading inside the sea of humans proved to be easier than I'd thought. Because everyone at Woodstock was too high to care. We settled not all that far from where we'd been the night before. With plenty of distance from Livy.

Getting away from her was my good luck charm. The rain stopped as soon as we sat down. My clothes were wet, and I was chilly, but Leon's nearness made me forget the cold. I could hear my stomach growling, but having him all to myself could satiate my appetite for a month.

Paranoia bloomed shortly thereafter when John Morris made his next stage announcement. "I've just had a conversation with a gentleman from the medical center and a gentleman who's been looking to try to trace down some of these little blue-and-green pills. They are *quite* dangerous. We went through this last night. We gotta try not to take anything from anybody else. Just hang on to it. Especially the little pills."

I grabbed Leon's knee. Fear rang through my voice. "Suppose Livy did take one of those little pills? And now I've left her. Who's going to take her to the medical tent?"

"I thought you never wanted to see her again."

"I don't. But I don't want her to die."

"Look. The way Livy reacted back there, jumping from one emotion to another, is a telltale bad acid trip. Will you please trust me on that?"

I nodded. He had given me no reason to distrust him.

He grinned, then tilted his head. "Are you ready to tell me what happened back there?" He shook a cigarette from its pack, then pulled it out with his lips. Shielding it from the breeze, he lit the end, then tilted his head back, blowing the smoke into the night sky. There was a break in the music, a perfect opportunity to fill him in.

"Are you sure you want to hear it? It's complicated." For him to thoroughly understand, I'd have to start with Dad.

And I wasn't sure I could do it.

"Lay it on me," he said.

The notion of telling Leon about my father felt like cutting a slit down my chest and opening it up for all to see. "I'm so embarrassed," I said, drawing my knees up and gripping my elbows. I hung my head as the shame Dad had inflicted on me for the last three years crawled up my spine.

Leon gently lifted my chin. "Please don't be. There's all kinds of shit in my family." Compassion sang through his voice. And gave me the courage I needed.

So I did it. I dived down deep into the treacherous waters I'd been avoiding since we first met. With tears threatening to fall, I told him everything about Dad, A to Z. While detailing how tough it had been growing up in a church with all the sins I considered unfair—like no dancing and, worst of all, no listening to the Beatles or any rock and roll after John's Jesus comment—he pressed a palm to his forehead. Every line on his face seemed to be filled with my pain when I told him how Dad had embarrassed me at the Beatles concert.

"He shouldn't have done that," Leon said tenderly, like he truly cared.

For some odd reason, I defended Dad. "He hasn't always been a monster. Don't get me wrong; he's the biggest square ever born. He wears Hush Puppies and he has bad dandruff, but there was a time when he was . . . sorta nice. The old Dad left when Ron left."

Leon didn't say anything at first. I was afraid I'd spilled too much. "Sounds like he's a tortured soul," he said at last.

I thought about the emotional torture he'd put me through the night I'd left home. "He did something so mean the night I ran away. It made me hate him more than ever." The tears I'd been struggling to hold back fell anyway.

Leon entwined his fingers with mine. "Sounds like you need to get it out."

I did need to get it out. I'd been holding in the horror of it all since Tuesday.

Four Days Earlier

Home

Memphis, Tennessee

Tuesday, August 12, 1969

Livy was right. The world was changing. Even though I was headed back to my conservative college in a few weeks, the last thing I wanted was to be ignorant about the goings-on in the country. If Ron's life depended on it, even more reason to listen to the rest of the records.

Disobeying my father was a necessity.

I was going to hell anyway. At last count, I was breaking six of the ten commandments on a regular basis. One, I wasn't honoring God; I was often mad at him. Two, I still idolized the Beatles, and now Crosby, Stills & Nash. Three, I lied—a lot. Four, I did not honor my earthly father. Mama yes, Dad no. Five, I sometimes cussed and on occasion took the Lord's name in vain. And six, I coveted Livy Foster's face, hair, and body more than anything in the entire universe.

I might as well listen to rock music.

Like last time, I pulled the record player from the top shelf, stretched the power cord underneath my closet door, and turned off the light. There was just enough light from the space underneath the door to see what I was doing.

As my eyes strained to adjust to the darkness, I pulled the Jimi Hendrix record from the stack. Like last time, I cracked the cover open and pressed my nose inside the fold, inhaling its new-album aroma. Music was as much a part of me as the blood running through my veins. It was my sustenance, vital to my organs. I needed it like I needed water and was beginning to realize I'd die if I couldn't have it.

As soon as I heard the first chords of the first song, "Purple Haze," I knew I was in for a ride. Jimi's sound was different than anything I'd ever heard.

The bass guitar thumped through my body, even at low volume. "Purple haze," Jimi sang. From the first note, I fell in love with his voice. I'd never known the definition of *sexy* until that moment.

When the tempo changed, picking up speed, I jumped up from the floor, whirling like a dervish. Swinging and twisting like a kite's tail in the wind, I was at Livy's house again—seventeen years old—dancing my feet off.

Beads of perspiration had gathered on my temples. Holding up my ponytail, I twisted it into a tight bun. It was scorching hot inside my closet. Ask me if I cared.

At the end of the first side, a song called "Foxy Lady" began. By then I knew the nuances in Jimi's voice. He was delicate in places and robust in others, and the variations in his guitar chords sounded downright mesmerizing.

Halfway through the song his words dragged, sounding thick and low. At first, I thought it was a technique he used, but then the music stopped completely. *The power's gone out,* I thought. Yet the light peeking underneath the door assured me I was wrong.

Swoosh, swoosh. I heard house shoes shuffling on the hardwood. I froze, scared out of my mind. My heart thumped out of control. Before I had time to hide behind my dresses, the closet door flew open.

The light from the bedroom illuminated the imposing six-feet, four-inch figure with hands shoved inside his bathrobe pockets. "Is something wrong with your bed, Suzannah?" the imposing figure asked.

"No sir." My pulse roared inside my eardrums, nearly drowning the sound of my own voice. How had he heard the music? I had the volume turned down low, and he was downstairs sleeping. The floor must have creaked while I was dancing. *Dammit. I am such an idiot.*

"Then why are you in your closet?"

"Sir?" I asked, desperate to delay the inevitable, my arms wrapped tightly around my knees.

Dad raised his voice, slowly enunciating each word. "I said, Why are you in your closet?"

That familiar pang of fear I'd tried so desperately to forget over the last three years bubbled up like a geyser, strangling my throat and tying my tongue. I felt dizzy.

"I asked you a question, Suzannah." Dad crossed his arms in front of him.

With every limb quaking, I answered with a terrified stammer. "I didn't want to disturb you and Mama."

"What would be disturbing?" Without warning, he flicked on the light.

My eyes ached from the sudden brightness. I shielded them with my hand.

"Sounds like you've decided to bring rock and roll into our home again. *Without* my permission."

"It's not the Beatles" was all I knew to say.

"Why don't you bring your phonograph out here so we can listen together?"

Rising up on shaky knees, I grabbed hold of my coat for support, but it tumbled off the hanger. Mustering all the strength in my body, I rose to face my dad.

"I'll go get your mother. I'd like her to hear it too." Whenever I got in trouble, Dad's voice remained calm and steady, such a contrast to my quivering lips.

While listening to his footsteps on the stairs, I knew I had to act fast. Like a convict with moments to devise a breakout plan from prison, I grabbed three dresses, four blouses, and two pairs of shoes, shoving everything inside my suitcase. I yanked open my drawers, frantically adding shorts, my new floral bra with matching panties, more underwear, jeans, and a pair of pantyhose for work the next day. I grabbed the wad of cash I kept hidden in my drawer and jammed it inside my purse. I started to make a run for it but heard whimpering in the hall.

"Ronald. Please. She's twenty years old."

My heart plummeted. Poor Mama. She wanted to protect me. But she was no longer herself. Ever since Ron had left for Vietnam, she'd become increasingly mournful, and her husband had become increasingly mean.

The two of them walked inside my bedroom. "Going somewhere?" Dad asked.

Instead of answering, I ran to Mama, who folded me inside her arms. I'd always found comfort in the security of Mama's embrace. Now, it tempered my fear and gave me courage for what was sure to be a long night.

Wrapped up together like newborn puppies, Mama and I watched as Dad took the record player out of my closet and plugged it back in. Jimi's seductive voice picked up right where it left off, in the middle of "Foxy Lady." I hung my head while Jimi's lascivious lyrics floated from my turntable.

When the song ended, Dad snatched off the record and picked up the album cover from the floor. He sat down on the edge of my bed, studying it with a stoic expression. "Have you forgotten the rules in this house?" he asked, with a surprising calm. He crossed his legs and turned the record over to view the other side.

I offered him only a blank stare; not a single word left my lips.

"I'm going to say this one more time. I hope you'll heed my warning. As much as you love that powder-yellow Mustang in the driveway, I'd hate to see her go to someone else. I will *never* allow this trash in our home again." He held up the Jimi record. "Do you understand me?"

This time I stared into space, nodding in slow motion. Here I was, twenty years old, yet he still talked to me like a child—the way he always had—like I had no say in the matter.

Moments later, I experienced what I considered a sin far more egregious than any of the sins for which Dad insisted I'd go to hell.

With murder in his eyes, he glowered at me. "What makes you think you can bring this garbage into our home? You are as trashy as this record." With that he lifted his knee and split my Jimi Hendrix record in two.

The jagged edges in each of his hands mirrored my heart, and his tongue had assassinated my spirit.

A long guttural moan dislodged from Mama's throat.

While his words, as sharp as a bayonet, sank down into my soul, I felt dissociated from my consciousness, like the world around me wasn't real. My eyes glazed over. It seemed like I had left my body.

The creaking of the mattress snapped me out of it. Dad padded over to my closet to retrieve the rest of the records and placed them on the dresser. One by one he lifted his knee and split each in half. He lingered when he held the Beatles, the White Album, studying the cover like he admired it, then cracked it open. Running a finger down the track listing, he said, "You are aware of what happened last weekend in California, are you not?"

His frosty voice sent a fresh chill down my spine. I had no idea what he meant.

"That vulgar hippie freak Charles Manson, along with his savage thugs, stabbed Sharon Tate and her unborn child sixteen times. All high on LSD!"

Mama released another guttural moan.

"Her father is a lieutenant colonel with the army and happens to be a friend of mine."

Of course, I knew about the tragedy—everyone was talking about it—but what did it have to do with the Beatles? "That's horrible, Dad. I'm sorry it happened."

"The words 'Helter Skelter'—a song from *this* very album—were written in her blood." He thrust the record toward me. "Shame on you for wanting anything to do with this band of *hippie heathens*."

A poster included with the White Album poked out of the cover. He removed the poster and also the enclosed headshots of all four Beatles. One by one, he held up each photo for me to see, then tore it down the middle. The ripping of each picture sounded like the sharpening of a blade.

"You are a *disgrace* to our family, Suzannah. A heathen yourself. How do you expect to attract a man with godly character? Or any man, for that matter? Aren't you afraid of God's wrath?"

With a hand pressed into her stomach, Mama crumpled over and wept.

"Dad! You told me yourself my musical talent is a gift from God. Just like Mama's gift and Ron's gift."

"Your mother has devoted her musical gift to the Lord. As should you."

The pain from his name-calling had settled into my bones. Although terrified, I knew I had to talk back to him, no matter the cost. "Am I really that horrible of a person just because I love rock music?" I asked, my voice dripping with anger.

Dad dipped his chin, answering me with the same ire. "Yes."

Whether I could continue to swallow the rage bubbling inside my throat was anyone's guess. But I took a deep breath and tried. I knew the consequences of challenging my father. The Beatles concert was proof of that.

I also knew something equally dire. I had to leave. That night. I couldn't endure his cruelty another second.

On second thought, I could never leave. My mother's bleating cries were killing me. She was already dead from the constant worry of whether her only son would make it home alive. If I left, what would happen to her? She couldn't afford to lose another child.

Stand up to him! I heard my brother's voice echoing at high volume. *Do it for me, SuSu. Do it!*

In that moment I didn't care what Dad had called me. I only cared about what he had done to Ron. "I hate you!" I blurted out, softly at first; then the fury I'd been suppressing for three years exploded like three million sticks of dynamite.

"*I . . . hate . . . you!*" I yelled, turning into someone I didn't recognize. Heat rushed to my head. My body shook with rage. "How can you treat your own daughter like this? I'm sorry I'm such a big disappointment." My voice cracked as tears flooded my eyes. "You've destroyed beautiful music by talented people who God himself created! Why—"

Dad cut me off mid-sentence. "I'm trying to save you from burning in hell with all the beautiful beatniks you think so highly of." His eyes were cold. Sharp. Murderous. But he did not yell. "You'll thank me on Judgment Day."

"I'm *already* in hell!" I screamed. "And so is Ron! Why did you make him go to Vietnam? He had his student deferment! He should be going to college with his friends, not killing innocent people!" Tears streamed down my face. "He's not a soldier, and you know it. He's a kind, caring person who just wants to make music and bring love to the world. You saw in living color what happened at the Tet Offensive. How can you still believe in this war?"

My father remained silent. In his mind, he owed me no explanation. But I could tell, by his crimson cheeks, he was furious. Beads of sweat sprang on his forehead. His face tightened as he rubbed the back of his neck.

"He's my only sibling. I *miss* him!" I yelled. "He never writes us anymore. Do you know why that is? He doesn't write"—I thrust my finger toward him, bouncing it with each word—"because he. Hates. You. Too!"

Dad stood there with his lips mashed together. His shallow breaths provided the only sound in the room. I had awoken the hornet's nest.

He stepped closer, raising his voice. "You're absolutely right! Not only is your brother not a soldier—he's not a student, an athlete, or even a man. He is a *coward*!" he yelled, nose flared, fists clenched. "Going to Vietnam was the only way to change him." His yell ricocheted like bullets off my bedroom walls, terrifying me. "Not writing to his family is his choice!"

My first instinct was to cower. Instead, I stood tall. "Maybe so. But here's my choice. I'm moving to Arkansas. Or Kentucky."

Dad lowered his chin, peering at me down his nose. Clearly, he didn't think I was serious.

"And you can't stop me."

With arms crossed over his chest, he leaned against the doorframe. No longer yelling, he asked, "How will you survive? No money, no car."

I hadn't thought that part through. He'd never allow me to take my car. "I'll figure it out," I said. "I'm smart." Between my fury and what I'd just threatened, I couldn't bring myself to look at Mama. I felt guilty already.

I knew Dad so well. On one hand he figured I'd never leave. On the other, he'd never seen me like this. Until I could formulate a definite plan, I knew I had better calm myself down. He may try and stop me.

Seizing the lull, Mama glared first at Dad, then at me. "For *God's* sake!" she said through gritted teeth. "College starts soon. Can't we just make it through the next three weeks?" Her gaze darted between the two of us. "My son has had to fight to *stay alive* in Vietnam. Is it too much to ask the rest of my family to stop fighting in our own home?"

A sidelong glance between Dad and me confirmed we'd better do as she asked. I'd never seen my mother this way. She rarely made a fuss. And she never, *ever* took the Lord's name in vain. Come to think of it, how could she make a fuss? Her every move was controlled by her husband. Whether it be meal planning, folding the laundry, or making the bed just so, my mother had strict guidelines to follow. The poor thing had dominion over nothing in her own home. Right then and there I made a silent vow never to get married.

Pinching the bridge of his nose, Dad closed his eyes. If I didn't know better, I'd think he regretted his behavior.

He let a few moments pass before darting his gaze between Mama and me. "It's late," he said. "We'll discuss this in the morning." By then his voice was laced with a surprising calm. And a tinge of kindness.

Psycho. "Good night, Suzannah." Turning toward the door, he stretched out his arm. "Come back to bed, Jean. All will be well."

From the despair on Mama's face, I could tell she didn't want to go. But, like always, she relented. "I'll be there in a moment, Ronald."

After he stepped away, she pulled me toward her, pressing a watery cheek against mine. Together our tears formed a weeping wall of torment.

Nestling my face into my mother's neck, I breathed the scent that had comforted me all my life. "Let's get out of here," I whispered. "Let's run away."

Mama squeezed harder, whispering back, "I love you with all my heart, my sweet girl." As her breath sailed across my face, I detected an unfamiliar odor. It was faint, barely noticeable, but it was there. It smelled like liquor.

Seconds away from challenging her, my better sense grabbed ahold. Who could blame her?

"I love you too, Mama. Let's go. Let's leave. Right now," I pleaded. "I can't take living here anymore."

"I can't, honey," she whispered. Dad was waiting for her in the hall.

"Why not?"

"I just can't. But do what you must. I'll understand." She paused, squeezing me tighter, and looked me dead in the eye. "Suzannah, you are *not* who he says you are. You are loving and good, joyful and kind. You are a child of God."

I'd heard those words from her many times before, but Dad's hateful words always drowned them out. "Please, Mama. Please come with me. When Ron gets out of the army, we can all live together in peace. Free of *him*."

Her blank stare revealed it all. Even if she wanted to, my mother would never leave her husband. He had manipulated her into believing she could never make it on her own.

But he would not do that to me. Maybe I was all those things he claimed, but I'd never let him say it to my face again.

Home

MEMPHIS, TENNESSEE

Wednesday, August 13, 1969

I watched the minute hand on my bedside clock stand straight up and the little hand point toward three. My bag was packed—everything but the toiletries—so I tiptoed down the hall into the bathroom. I climbed onto the sink and pulled my toiletry bag from the top shelf of the linen closet. A large stack of letters, held together with a fat rubber band, tumbled to the floor.

Scrambling down, my heart pummeled against my chest. I recognized the handwriting right away. All the letters were addressed to Mama. At a PO box. *What the heck?*

I sat down cross-legged on the cold tile floor, picked out a letter at random, and read it through to the end.

April 1, 1968
Long Binh, South Vietnam

Dear Mama,
I had a big surprise when I got back from our 14-day mission. Four new tapes! Man was it a happy welcome

back. Thank you! Music is the only thing that keeps me sane out here. By the way, next time you send paper and envelopes, please put them in a plastic bag because they get wet otherwise. It's monsoon season, been raining three times a day. I've never seen so much rain. Not sure which is worse, the rain, the heat or the mud. Most of the guys in my platoon have rashes. Thank God for calamine lotion! (And our medics.) How is the weather there? I bet the azaleas are looking nice about now. Makes me miss Memphis in the spring.

Before I forget, our CO has a request. More cigs! Also, we'd love cans of stew or soup, Oreos, Cheese Whiz and crackers, and packages of Kool-Aid. Mama, your care packages are the best. You are everyone's favorite mom!

I don't want to scare you, but you asked me in your last letter to be honest. Monday, we hid in the swamp and waited. That part wasn't so bad, even though we stayed wet for three days.

Getting there was the worst part. The crunching sound under your own feet while creeping through rice paddies is enough to scare the living daylights out of you. We don't know where the enemy is hiding. They could be anywhere. They know this thick terrain inside and out. The US is dropping this herbicide from airplanes to clean out the brush so the soldiers can see the enemy. Surely that will help.

Dad wouldn't understand. This war is different from his wars. He doesn't get how bad it is here. The enemy doesn't wear a uniform! How are we supposed to know if they are the Viet Cong or villagers? All of their pajamas look the same. By day they are barbers, by night they are the VC. Dad never had to wonder about the enemy in WWII or Korea. Innocent Vietnamese civilians are getting killed every single day. Washington is lying to everyone over there. Don't believe them.

Dad and my grandfathers didn't face what we're facing over here. You said I'm to be totally honest with you. Here goes . . . I don't want to die for my country. Is that an unforgivable sin as Dad suggests? If so, I can only pray God will forgive me. I'm not the only soldier who feels this way. Many, many do. None of us believe any of our boys should be dying because our politicians are trying to save the Vietnamese from communism. The Vietnamese don't even care. Johnson craves control. I'm only here before college because someone else made that decision for me. AMERICA SHOULD NOT BE HERE. It's not our problem.

I have not had a shower in six weeks. And I've been wearing the same clothes. It makes me really appreciate all you did for me when I lived at home. You are a stickler for clean clothes. I didn't know how good I had it. I'm sorry I didn't thank you more.

I picture you driving to the post office, getting out your key, and sticking your hand in the slot only to find it empty. I'll try my best to write more. I know you love getting my letters. I also know I ask for a lot of stuff.

I'll make it through this somehow. God keeps sparing me. He must have something big for me to accomplish. I've been talking to Him a lot. I don't think He believes in this war either. I'll write more soon. They are coming for the mail now. I don't mean to upset you. I just need to vent.

Thank you for loving me. I miss and love you.

Your loving son,

Ron

P.S. Don't worry about what you say in your letters. The army no longer censors them. That ended after WWII. You can say whatever you want.

Learning nothing new, I read another. And another. They made me even angrier at Dad. I thought about taking all of them to read later but quickly decided they were my mother's prized possessions, like my own letters were to me. She probably read them for comfort the way I did. Ron needed a way to write to our mother apart from our father's judgmental eyes, the same way he wrote to me at Penny's house and at college.

Even if they were hard to read, they were proof he was still alive. At least he was when Mama saw him over New Year's.

I put them back where I found them, gloating with pride. Mama held a secret from Dad.

~

With my suitcase in one hand and my purse hanging across my middle, I floated down the stairs, moving as softly as a butterfly. I lingered on each step as if it was a flower. Our old house groaned whenever we walked her halls.

With equal caution I tiptoed into the kitchen, then slinked toward the back door. Ever so carefully I put my suitcase down, removed the chain, and turned the knob. You could have heard cotton growing in the silence with how quietly I shut the door behind me.

I calculated my route. If it took eight minutes by car, I figured thirty to forty-five on foot. If I traveled down the back streets of Midtown Memphis, the only busy one I'd have to cross was Peabody.

The moon was my friend, carving a lighted path. I was not afraid. Inside my wallet was forty-eight dollars and twenty-three cents. It was all the money I had in the world, save my final paycheck from Goldsmith's.

Instead of focusing on the long walk, I dreamed of the future. Discovering the true Suzannah was so near I could taste it. The how, the what, and the where of it all looked daunting—practically impossible—but I would not let that stop me. Where I'd live and what I'd do to support myself was anyone's guess, but it would work out somehow. For now, I would focus on my freedom.

Maybe I'd go back to Union, and maybe I wouldn't. One thing was certain. I'd bring music back into my life. I'd sing and dance every chance I got. It would fill up the gorge inside my heart and make me whole.

Eyeing the Foster mansion in the distance, I jogged the rest of the way. By the time I reached the front door, I was out of breath. My suitcase felt like a safe after the long haul. With a steady finger, I pressed the bell.

Several minutes passed before Livy's parents peeked through the sidelight and opened the door. I didn't apologize for waking them. I was too numb for apologies. All I said was "Hi, Mr. and Mrs. Foster."

Livy's mom wrapped an arm around me with an understanding smile, guiding me inside their home. The lingering scent of stale cigarettes filled the air. It had been three years since I'd been there, but it felt like three weeks. That warm-apple-pie sensation I used to have rushed back, and I knew I was safe. I knew I could trust them.

I caught them staring at my swollen eyes, but they didn't ask why I'd been crying. Mr. Foster simply picked up my suitcase, and the three of us hiked up the grand center staircase. Mrs. Foster held a finger to her lips when we passed Kim's room.

Not wanting to frighten his daughter, Mr. Foster tapped on Livy's bedroom door. "Livy. Livy, honey," he said softly. "Look who's here."

My best friend sat up in bed, squinting her eyes. The full moon shone brightly through the sheers on her bedroom window, illuminating my face. "Are you okay?" she asked in a groggy voice.

"I'm great." My voice sounded clear and steady. "I've changed my mind. I'm going with you to Woodstock."

Fifty Years Later

Woodstock 50th Anniversary Celebration

Bethel, New York

Sunday Afternoon, August 18, 2019

"I feel so bad for you, Grammy." Adelaide turns over on her side, props up on her elbow.

"Thank you, lovey. I know you do."

"At least you did something about it."

"I stood up for myself. And for what *I* believed. I had to discover my own truth."

We are at the motel, resting on our beds after a big day at the festival site. Rain delayed our tour of the grounds the day we arrived—which would have made the tour more nostalgic, in my opinion—but we had fun today. Adelaide didn't want to leave until she'd walked the Bindy Bazaar trails and turned circles in the butterfly meadow. Neither did I.

While we were at the museum, we'd met the Ercolines, the couple who'd been huddled together under a blanket on the Woodstock album cover and now serve as docents. They met a few weeks before the festival and married two years later. Woodstock must have sealed their love.

It made me think of Leon. And young love. And how much I thought I knew about it at the ripe old age of twenty.

Adelaide had peppered the Ercolines with questions and arranged for us all to pose for pictures. She couldn't wait to post them on my social media accounts. And hers.

I'm exhausted. But John Fogerty's playing tonight. Wild horses couldn't keep me from his concert.

"Being here this weekend has been so cool," she says, "but it seems like it's dredging up hard feelings for you."

"I suppose it is," I say with a sigh. The quilt at the end of the bed is calling my name. I reach down, wrap it around me. "Life has a way of doing that. We have to take the good with the bad. Can't let the trials define us."

She pulls at the tail of her new Woodstock T-shirt, releases a heavy sigh. "Livy was right. Your dad was scary."

"I've been hesitant to give you the gory details about him. But there's something deeper and more important I want you to know."

"What?" The gleam in her pretty blue eyes makes me glow. She inherited them from me.

"I don't want you to ever let a man mistreat you."

She sits up, with a defensive tone in her voice. "Daddy's not anything like your dad."

"I'm not talking about my sweet son. I'm talking about boys your age, the ones you know from high school and now the ones you'll meet at college."

She gives me a blank stare, then scoots back against her headboard.

"And the men you'll meet later in life. You are a beautiful girl, and you sing like an angel. Men will be more attracted to you because of it." I swing my legs off the bed to look her in the eye. "I don't want you to ever compromise yourself. Promise me."

"I won't." There's even more defense in her tone.

"Don't be pressured into doing something you know in your heart isn't right. If a man *or* a woman talks to you disrespectfully, let them know you won't stand for it."

"I do that already," she says.

I have my doubts.

"If a boy talks you into smoking dope, then tries to sweet-talk you into bed, *run*!"

She laughs, diverts her gaze to her painted-black toenails.

I know she must learn from her own mistakes, but I can't help wanting to protect her. She's my heart. "You don't have to put up with it. I don't care who he is. He could be the biggest rock star on the planet. No woman deserves to be spoken down to or taken advantage of by a man—or a woman—under any circumstances!" My voice rises a little more than I had intended, but so what? Never having had a daughter of my own, it thrills me to think I can pass along the trial-by-fire wisdom I've gained to my granddaughter. Unlike her father, she's actually listening to me.

"I'm never gonna let that happen. I'm a badass. Like you!" Adelaide looks up at me with a smile that I could crawl inside of and live contently in for the rest of my life.

"You are definitely a badass. But you never know what kind of situation you might find yourself in. Just remember that your grammy gave you permission to tell that asshole to go to hell!"

Adelaide laughs out loud, pulls her legs to her chest. "You're so cool. None of my friends have grandmas half as fun as you."

"Well, I doubt that, but I'm glad you think so," I say after a hearty laugh of my own.

"You're the only grandma I know who still has long hair. Most of my friend's grandmas have short gray hair." She leans toward me and gazes at my head. "You're lucky yours isn't gray."

I chuckle. "Oh, it's gray. I pay my stylist, Jennifer, good money to make sure it's covered up." My mousy-brown hair became a nice, frosted blond many years back.

In one fell swoop, Adelaide leaps over to my bed and rises up on her knees. She digs her fingers through my scalp. "Where? I don't see any gray."

"You better not. I just had it colored." I close my eyes, relishing in the sensation of her fingers against my scalp. My head hasn't been caressed like this in years. One of the many crimes old age allows. "That feels amazing, by the way."

Adelaide moves behind me, gently guiding my head into her lap. "Close your eyes. I'm gonna give you one of my famous head massages."

"I had no idea you were famous for head massages."

I feel her gently closing my eyelids. She lowers her voice. "Keep your eyes closed. And don't talk."

Without another word she goes straight to work. Separating her fingers from her thumbs, she moves in slow circles around my scalp, then takes her time traveling down to my neck. She presses her thumbs into the base of my skull with just the right amount of pressure. And when I think it can't get any better, she lightly scratches the circumference of my entire head, sending me into euphoria.

I consider asking how she came by this acclaim. Part of me wants to, but I've asked enough personal questions this weekend.

"No wonder you're a famous head masseuse," I say. "I might have to fly to New York every week. Can you fit me in your schedule?" My words are beginning to sound slow and low. They are laced with fatigue. "You must be booked solid."

Her darling little laugh is even more reason to make me wish our weekend would never end. "I told you not to talk," she commands.

As Adelaide continues her famous head massage, I daydream back to my time at Woodstock. It's impossible not to recall the head massage Leon gave me while we watched Creedence Clearwater Revival together. I've never forgotten it. Nor have I forgotten my first kiss. *Our* first kiss. The way his lips felt against mine. The spell he put over me.

Adelaide is right. This weekend has dredged up all kinds of feelings. Not only hard feelings about my father and my brother, but intense emotions about Leon too. Emotions I thought would have gone away by now.

Woodstock

Day Three

Sunday, August 17, 1969
12:15 a.m.

After confessing the gory details about my family, I leaned into Leon. "My life's pretty complicated, huh?"

"It's not *Leave It to Beaver*," he said with his Leon laugh.

"More like *Dark Shadows*."

He grinned, then took a drag of his cigarette before blowing the smoke skyward. "You should be very proud of yourself."

"I am proud of myself. It's about time I break free from my . . . *unworldliness*." I squeezed my eyes shut and gave him a bashful smile.

"It's high time you break free of your dad," Leon said before holding my face in his hands. He met my gaze. "I rather like your unworldliness."

"Thank you, but I don't."

He let his hands slip from my cheeks. "You still haven't told me what happened with Livy."

"Ahh, Livy." I looked skyward at the mention of her name. "Well . . ."

I took him back to that fateful Good Friday when I'd discovered Ron in Rosie's bed with the girl. I confessed I'd written about it in my diary and accidentally left it out for one of my nosy parents to read.

He told me his sisters had diaries. And there was no telling what they'd written about him.

But when I told him that Livy's LSD trip had revealed *she'd* been the one in bed with Ron, and that I had no idea they'd once had crushes on each other—until that moment—I could read the shock on his face. He hung his head when I explained they'd hidden it from me, allowing me to blame myself for Ron's enlistment, when the fault lay with Livy.

"You've blamed yourself for three years?" he asked.

"See why I never want to see her again?"

He didn't comment about that. He just asked, "Do you think your parents know it was her?"

"I doubt it. Ron refused to tell any of us who she was. That's why Dad got so mad. But if they know now . . ." I looked down, wondering if they'd found her signet ring. "Katy, bar the door."

Leon roared with laughter, then shook his head like he'd made a mistake. "Sorry. It's not funny. It's just you and your Southern sayings."

"It's okay," I said with a reassuring smile.

"After what you've told me about your dad, I'm guessing Ron having sex in the first place was a pretty hairy deal."

"Very hairy. Sex before marriage is a *big* sin in our family." As soon as I said it, I had a flash of regret. Leon thinking of me as even more of a Goody Two-shoes was unbearable. "I mean, it's a sin as far as my parents and my church are concerned."

"No sexual revolution going on at your house, huh?"

"Not hardly."

"And they sure didn't want the girl getting pregnant."

"Heck no."

"And now your brother's in Vietnam because of your dad's beliefs." He shook his head. "Man. A puritanical army colonel. Tough combination."

I leaned my head back with a sigh.

"It's cool your brother wouldn't snitch on Livy, though. He's a good guy."

"He's so good. I wish you could have met him. He'd have been here if not for me."

Leon scratched his head. "Don't say that. It's not your fault."

"You're right. It's Livy's."

"All that drama because of a roll in the hay. No wonder a half a million people showed up here in support of the sexual revolution. 'We're Not Gonna Take It,'" he sang into his fist. "Know that song?"

At first, I wanted to lie. Then I realized there was no need to pretend. I was back from a long, bad trip and could finally be me. "I don't."

"Last track on *Tommy*. I'm hoping the Who plays it tonight."

I wished I knew more of the music he loved.

"Now I'm curious about something," I said, remembering how he'd said those exact words the day before.

"What's that?"

"Does your family believe sex before marriage is a sin?"

A slow smile embellished his face. "Sex outside of marriage is a *mortal* sin for Catholics."

"What's a mortal sin?"

"A grave sin committed with full knowledge and deliberate consent," he said theatrically. "Catholics learn that early in catechism class. It is forgivable." He raised a finger. "As long as you confess to the priest and receive Holy Communion."

"There's gonna be a long confession line after the festival," I said. "Might wrap all the way around New York City." We both laughed. It felt good to laugh.

"Can you imagine sliding into a small dark box, telling some old fat dude you have lustful thoughts?"

"No!" I said with a chuckle, happy my church didn't require that.

Leon grew quiet. That same mysterious grin appeared, the one he had given me at the pond. A moment later his face floated toward me, and he gently opened my mouth with his. His tongue searched for mine. I felt lightheaded. I wanted to melt on top of him, feel every cell on his body, never regaining my own form.

I slipped one hand through his hair and caressed the back of his neck with the other. I wanted him to want me, the same way I wanted him. To never forget this moment. Never forget me.

As his lips left mine, he looked into my eyes, gently tucking my damp hair behind each ear. "You are something special. You know that?"

I didn't say *yes*. I didn't say *no*. I just peered at him, wishing he would run away with me.

"You didn't deserve that kind of treatment from your father. Or your best friend." With my cheek cradled in his palm, he kissed me again, then, inches from my lips, whispered, "I wish I could have protected you."

As his hand slipped from my cheek, I longed for him to put it back. Instead, he took my hand in his. "Despite your dad's shit, you're gonna thrive. You're strong. You're smart, *funny*, a gas to be around. I've learned all that about you in less than two days." He held up two fingers.

"You're sweet to say that."

"Know what else?" he whispered, grazing his lips against mine.

I shook my head.

"I *love* how naive you are."

I dipped my chin, covered my face with my hand.

"Hey. Look at me." Our eyes met. "I think it's endearing." He kissed me again. "And refreshing."

"I'm glad somebody does."

"You're gonna be famous," he said.

I pulled away to catch his gaze. "Yeah, right."

"You'll be singing in arenas and festivals soon."

"Street corners, maybe. But I appreciate your vote of confidence."

He nudged his knee against mine. "I'm serious, Suzie. You're really, really good. I've never heard anyone sing like you." He pointed at the stage. "You'll be on the bill for the second Aquarian festival."

I rolled my eyes, pushed him playfully. "You're blitzed!"

"I wouldn't be surprised if I turn on *The Ed Sullivan Show* and there you are. Ladies and gentlemen, Suzie Withers!" he mimicked, like he was Ed himself.

"Now you've entered *The Twilight Zone*."

"Will you still know me when you're famous?"

I shoved him again. Harder.

Crouching low, he protected his face with the back of his hand. "Will you wave if you see me in the crowd at one of your shows?"

I leaned toward him, with hands on my hips. "You should know the answer to that, buster. You just said you've learned a lot about me." As dear as his compliment was, it reminded me that the sand in our hourglass was falling fast. "I don't want to think of you as another face in the crowd."

Leon's shoulders drooped, as if the thought made him sad too. Instead of talking about it, though, he changed the subject. "This time tomorrow night we'll be watching Crosby, Stills & Nash."

"And Young," I added.

In the background, we heard the tapping of a kick drum and the tuning of an electric guitar.

"Wait till you see the way Neil smokes," Leon said, moving his fingers up and down an imaginary guitar.

The pasture darkened. Blue lights lit the stage. A smattering of whistles and cheers sounded from the audience. Creedence Clearwater Revival had arrived.

Spotlights illuminated John Fogerty's mop top as Creedence strolled over to their instruments at about twelve thirty in the morning. Seconds later "Born on the Bayou" rang out into the night sky. Only a small number of audience members roused. Most were asleep.

Even so, song after song, Creedence showed us why they belonged on top of the charts. "Green River." "Bad Moon Rising." "Proud Mary."

They played their hearts out for the Woodstockers. But all they got in return was meager applause. The band members looked frustrated.

"Don't worry about it, John," some guy in the audience yelled. "We're with you!"

The only reason I wasn't asleep was because Leon had scooted in behind me with his legs on either side of mine. He played with my hair, gently pulling it back into a ponytail, stroking his fingers in circles against my scalp. I'd never had a head massage. *Luxury comes in many forms.*

With his chin resting atop my head and his arms encircling my shoulders, his body felt like a security blanket. While John Fogerty sang "I Put a Spell on You," Leon put a spell on me. It was the same chilly temperature as the night before, yet I didn't care.

"You're so small," he whispered, caressing my waist.

I leaned back into him, feeling his chest curl around me. A current of electricity jolted inside my veins as he reached around to kiss my cheek. He lingered on the tip of my ear, kissing it softly. I closed my eyes as he combed my hair to the side and brushed his lips across my neck. For the first time since falling for Paul McCartney, I ached to make love.

Unfortunately, Creedence left the stage without playing "Suzie Q." I was disappointed, but Leon whispered, "They'll be back. I told them to save the best for last."

He must have. It took only a minute for them to return to their instruments. The unmistakable first chords of "Suzie Q" roused the sleepy crowd. Many people, including Leon and me, stood to dance.

Leon sang all the words to me. Even the *I love you* part. My heart exploded into a cascade of red fireworks.

Once the song was over, Creedence left the stage. And Chip came back to the microphone. "After a very short intermission, we will continue."

The audience booed.

"Hey, it'll happen. All in good time," he said. "It's gonna be a very long evening."

Just not long enough for me.

Woodstock

Day Three

Sunday, August 17, 1969
2:00 a.m.

While the stagehands switched out the band gear, the Woodstockers who were awake chanted "We want Janis; we want Janis" over and over until she finally showed up at two in the morning.

Wearing a velvet tie-dyed pantsuit with a flowy jacket and a foot's length of bangle bracelets on her arms—and an equal number around her neck—Janis Joplin strolled onto the stage. The clamor must have woken the rest of the sleepy crowd, because the audience went ballistic. The volume sounded like a rocket launch.

"Sorry about those who got the green," she said, once the screams had died down. "We got a whole lot of orange. And it was fine. And it's still fine. Everybody's vibrating."

Leon leaned toward my ear. "She isn't yelling or crying. See the difference?"

Janis floated around the stage, dancing like she was one of the Woodstockers—not a superstar. She even talked to the audience like we were her family. "Look to your left. That's your brother. Look to your right. That's your sister. What I have is yours; what you have is mine. I relate differently to the human family around me." A few minutes later she asked if everyone had enough water and a place to sleep.

Watching Janis Joplin was like witnessing a cosmic explosion. Her energy roused every person there. She took us on a wild ride, her raspy voice reaching places only available to a few freaks of nature.

Amid a thunderous roar, the supernova ended with "Ball and Chain," and I thought the producers might just call it a night. In my mind, the festival had reached its zenith. But in Leon's mind, the best was yet to come.

Now it was three in the morning. Despite the energy flowing through our bodies only minutes prior, exhaustion settled in. We dozed while the roadies switched out the band gear. But we woke up thirty minutes later to an energetic mania. Sly and the Family Stone had arrived.

They were decked out in cool white fringed costumes, bringing along a new energy the minute they stepped onstage. The band started with a song called "M'Lady," but when they got to "Everyday People," followed by "Dance to the Music," the crowd went berserk. My idiotic three-year gap in music had caused me to miss this band. Judging by the screams, I was willing to bet I was the only person there who didn't know the words. But they were easy to learn; I picked them up right away.

The ground rumbled underneath while every person on Max Yasgur's property—all 450,000 of us—bounced up and down like tennis balls. I had never danced so hard in all my life.

"Now what is happening here is we are gonna try to do a sing-along," Sly Stone said. "Now a lot of people don't like to do it because they feel that it might be old fashioned. But you must dig that it is not a fashion in the first place; it is a feeling. If it was good in the past, it's still good! We'd like to sing a song called 'Higher,' and if we can get everyone to join in, we'd appreciate it. What I'd like you to do is say *higher* and throw the peace sign up. It will show you no harm."

Every time Sly threw up his arms in a peace sign, with a xylophone of fringe hanging from his sleeves, the audience responded by holding up their own peace signs.

Sly and the Family Stone was the first racially integrated band I'd ever heard. While I stood there, absorbing and loving every note of their music, something dawned on me. Like atoms and molecules, music binds people together, no matter what kind of family they grow up in. Or what they look like. Black, white, brown, yellow, or red. Music is the golden thread of commonality that joins us all. It's our universal language, our perfect form of communication.

And we sure had it that night in Bethel, New York.

5:00 a.m.

The Who showed up at five o'clock Sunday morning. As soon as Roger Daltrey—whom I found extraordinarily beautiful—walked onto the stage, Leon's face lit up like a torch. He wore a jacket with white fringe like Sly's, but unlike Sly, he was rock solid, bare chested underneath. Like Leon, he wore a chunky silver cross around his neck.

"He's copying you," I said, fingering Leon's cross.

"I think it's the other way around." Leon's shiny white smile mirrored his euphoria, which made me beam, too, just looking at him.

No doubt about it, the band's voices were far out, but the music didn't keep me grooving the way Sly's had. As much as I tried, I struggled to keep my eyes open. I wanted to lie down but was afraid someone might step on me. So I bit down on the insides of my cheeks, trying desperately to stay awake.

Just after "Pinball Wizard," this crazy dude rushed out from the side of the stage, taking over Pete Townshend's microphone when his back was turned.

"Is he part of the band?" I asked Leon, who'd been mesmerized ever since the Who took the stage.

"I don't know who that guy is."

"Hey, all you people out there having fun while John Sinclair is being held a political prisoner," the guy said with a heavy Boston accent, then proceeded to berate the audience, like we should all feel guilty about it.

"Who's John Sinclair?" I asked.

Leon raised his eyebrows. "All I know is he was sentenced to ten years in jail for marijuana possession."

Pete Townshend whacked the guy in the head with his guitar. The dude fell into the camera pit, then scrambled over the wooden fence before disappearing into the crowd.

Once he was gone, Pete, also in head-to-toe white, yelled into his microphone, "The next fucking person who walks across this stage is going to get fucking killed!"

Lots of people laughed; maybe they thought he was joking. But this close, I could tell he was furious.

The Who ushered in a splendid sunrise. As the band concluded with the one song I knew, "My Generation," Pete Townshend leaped into the air, banged his guitar multiple times on the stage floor, and then tossed it to someone in the front row.

I wished that someone could have been Leon.

After a two-hour break, Jefferson Airplane finally strolled onto the stage at 8:00 a.m. Grace Slick was another star dressed in white, the picture of *sexy* with her sleeveless fringed leather vest, cut so low you could see her tan lines. "All right, friends," she said. "You've seen the heavy groups. Now you will see morning maniac music. Believe me, *yeah* . . . it's a new dawn!"

That's the last thing I could remember before falling fast asleep.

Woodstock

Day Three

Sunday, August 17, 1969
9:40 a.m.

I awoke to Hugh Romney's gravelly voice booming throughout the pasture. I recognized it right away, even though his voice was nearly gone.

"Good morning," he said. "What we have in mind is breakfast in bed for four hundred thousand. Now, it's not gonna be steak and eggs or anything, but it's gonna be good food, and we are gonna get it to you. It's not just the Hog Farm either. It's the Ojai Mountain family and the Pranksters and everybody else that has volunteered and put in their time. In fact, it's everybody. We're all feeding each other! We must be in heaven, man! There is always a little bit of heaven in a disaster area . . . Okay, here it comes, mess call."

If a person was still asleep, an out-of-tune reveille on the bugle made sure they were wide awake. I had to cover my ears, it was so annoying.

Just as Hugh promised, an open-bed truck with garbage cans filled with granola made its way down the two-lane pathway around the circumference of the bowl. Two Hog Farmers dipped the granola into paper cups while others handed it out to the crowd. It tasted heavenly.

The music wouldn't start again for several hours, so Leon and I headed back to the arts and crafts fair to take another look around.

Just down Groovy Way, a dude recognized me. "Hi, Suzie," he said, without stopping. "Really enjoyed your performance yesterday."

"Thanks," I said, over my shoulder.

Leon wrapped his arm around my waist with a gentle squeeze. "See. You are a star."

Once we arrived at the fair, I picked up one of the tie-dyed halter tops, admiring it all over again. I didn't notice Leon digging inside his pocket until he handed the girl a five-dollar bill.

I tried to stop him. "You don't have to do that."

"You won the bet. Never stared at a single person at the lake."

Not true. I stared at every inch of you. "But you still don't have to do it," I said.

"I almost bought it for you last time we were here. Just didn't want you to think I was a weirdo."

"I wouldn't have thought you were a weirdo. I would have known how sweet you are a lot earlier." I held it up to my chest, twisting my body toward him like I was a model. "What do you think?"

"I think I love it."

"Me too." Standing on my tiptoes, I kissed him. He clasped the back of my head, and we just stood there, five whole minutes, making out in front of the booth.

Never in a million years would I have thought I'd be going braless, much less kissing a beautiful boy in front of so many people. I chuckled to myself, imagining Gertie's face if I showed up at Goldsmith's wearing my new tie-dyed halter top with bell-bottom blue jeans hugging my hips, far below my belly button.

Truth is, Gertie would have loved it. Mama, on the other hand, would have been horrified.

Leon took my hand. "Let's go see if the butterflies are still there."

"Race ya," I said and took off down the familiar path.

Once we reached the open meadow, past the tire swing, past the random green tent—the flaps were down and the zipper up—we slumped our shoulders in frustration. Our butterflies had vanished. But we stretched out our arms and turned circles anyway, pretending the monarchs were swarming around us. There was only one couple at the far end of the meadow, and they looked like they were asleep.

We fell onto the soft grass. This time we left no space between us, lying on our sides next to one another, our faces inches apart. Leon stroked my cheek with the back of his hand. "I can't believe out of all the hundreds of thousands of people at this festival, I got to meet you."

I didn't know what to say. It was the loveliest thing anyone had ever told me.

He stared into my eyes as if he was peeking inside my soul. "Your eyes are so blue. They look like forget-me-nots."

My breath hitched. "I love forget-me-nots," I whispered, having never realized words could be so titillating.

"Will you forget me not?" he whispered back.

I gently shook my head. "I could never forget you."

Entwining his fingers with mine, he raised my hand to his lips. One after the other he kissed each of my knuckles, slow and easy, as if he had a year to do it.

Sensations I didn't know existed shot through me. They started as ripples, then exploded into waves. That ache between my legs spread through my body like wildfire. I liked it but was afraid of it at the same time. The stubble on his chin tickled as it brushed across my flesh. He kissed my forehead. Then my nose. And both of my cheeks. I felt his breath on my face. Breath from his beautiful face.

He kissed my ear, moving his tongue along the outside of the lobe. He learned the inside too. It was as if he wanted to know all of me. It made me yearn to know all of him. Softly, he placed his lips on top of mine. That wave in my stomach crashed against my ribs. I had to stifle an urge to gasp because his touch felt that good.

Leon rolled over on his back, pulling me along with him. My hair spilled across his face. With my hips on top of his, I could feel how much he wanted me. We rolled over, again and again, until we landed side by side. His hand slipped from my neck, then inched closer to my breast. At first, I was nervous. But remembering our tender conversations melted away my fears. He'd been understanding and kind.

I trusted him.

His lips swept across mine before he worked his way down my neck, pausing to taste every inch of my skin. Slowly he kissed my chest, following the gold chain to where my cross hung between my breasts. I felt him slip the first two buttons on my top through the holes. He pulled my new bra down, exposing my bareness to the warm breeze. My muscles tightened. I felt timid for him to see me; it was daylight. But the gentleness in his eyes helped me to let go.

While I watched his lips move slowly across each of my breasts, learning their curves, the blush of my nipples, my heart pounded against my chest. With jittery fingers I slid the next button of my blouse through its hole. His gaze traveled with my hands as I opened another. As my need for him to love me exploded, I thought about what it would be like. I'd dreamed about it for so long. Would it hurt? If so, could I do it? Would I even know how?

More than anything I wanted my first time to be with Leon. Here in the butterfly meadow. I had fallen deeply in love. I was sure of it.

The last button was through the hole when he pulled me up straight, guiding the pink top off my shoulders. He reached his hands behind my back, unhooking my bra. As it fell into my lap, my bashfulness returned. I crossed my arms over my chest, but he gently pulled them away. My body tingled as he peered at me, like I was pretty. Like I was Livy. "You are beautiful," he said in a soft voice. "Has anyone ever told you that?"

I slowly shook my head.

He pulled his T-shirt over his head, then moved his lips toward mine. We reached for each other at the same time, falling back onto the grass. His bare skin against mine felt better than anything I'd ever known. I nearly suffocated in anticipation of what would come next.

I heard him unzip his pants. Then felt him unzipping mine. Visions of our lovemaking danced through my mind, until Livy's words stalled the fantasy. *You may not want a boyfriend, but you're on the pill, right?* Our pants were at our knees when I whispered, "Are you gonna use a condom?"

With a sudden urgency he rolled away from me, covering his face with his hands. My heart sank, down into the depths of the earth. I felt the pounding. Heard the pounding. I placed my hand over my chest to somehow stop it, but it wouldn't go away.

It seemed like ten minutes passed before he asked, "You're not on the pill?"

I shook my head against the soft grass.

"Shit," he blurted out, in a tone I didn't recognize. He ran his fingers through his hair, sweeping it back from his forehead. "Sorry. I got carried away."

"Don't be sorry," I whispered, dying to climb on top of him again.

Instead of answering, he pulled up his shorts and stayed two feet away, while my heart continued to hammer. *Bam. Bam. Bam.*

Pain punctured every pore on my body as I pulled up my jeans. I may as well have been lying on a bed of nails.

Our silence stretched into lethal awkwardness.

"Are you mad or something?" I said at last.

"Mad at myself. I knew you were a virgin."

It shamed me that he knew and now, because of it, we were lying two feet apart instead of on top of each other. "What makes you think that?"

He turned his head toward mine. A slight smile shaped his lips.

"I know I said it's a sin in our family, but I'm not psycho about it. I don't really think it's a sin. I—"

"Shh." He rolled toward me, pressing a finger to my lips.

The image of a gorgeous Shelly appeared out of nowhere. "I guess you're not a virgin," I said.

A long pause stretched into nowhere before he answered. "No."

I wished for the courage to say *Did you lose your virginity with Shelly? Or was it with someone else?* But I couldn't make myself say it. The words I did say were something I instantly regretted. "Couldn't you just, you know, maybe pull out before—"

"No way. I'm not willing to take that chance. Are you?"

"No. Of course not," I said.

Yet I was. It was crazy to think about how willing I was to take that chance—how quickly I would have compromised myself—just to be close to him. Just to feel his love. Just to have my first time be with him. Even there in that rank cow pasture with strangers close by, doing the same thing.

I had dreamed my first time would happen differently—with a *husband*—yet I was perfectly willing to tempt fate. Without thinking about it, much less praying about it, I had taken off my clothes at an outdoor music festival and given myself over to . . . what . . . *love*? Or could it have been lust?

As I lay there, with my arms covering my bare chest, a sharp pang of remorse strangled my throat. I was disappointed, not only in what had happened but in myself. From there the remorse snowballed into fear. Fear that Leon still had feelings for Shelly. Fear that I'd never see him again. Fear that I would never find anyone as cool and wonderful as Leon Wright. As much as I tried holding them back, tears welled up in my eyes.

I could see him looking at me from the corner of my eye.

"Why are you crying?" he asked.

"I don't know," I lied, then rolled over on my stomach to hide myself. "I guess I'm just disappointed."

In one motion, he reached over and pulled me back on top of him. Once again, my hair spilled across his face. After sweeping it away, I folded my arms on top of his chest and buried my head. I couldn't look at him.

"It's gonna be okay," he said tenderly. "Please don't cry."

How could you tell a boy you just met that your head was warring against your heart? That you sincerely wanted your first time to be with him, even in a cow pasture, even though his first time was with someone else? How could you let him know that telling him goodbye in less than twenty-four hours would rip your heart down the middle?

Perhaps he read my mind. He tapped my nose, then rolled me onto my back. "We could still have fun without birth control. I promise you won't be disappointed."

"Show me," I whispered, then reached up to kiss his lips.

Woodstock

Day Three

Sunday, August 17, 1969
Noon

An hour later I awoke sore.

For the first time in my life, I had an achy chin and imagined it a bright ruby red. I'd seen red chins on my friends coming home from making out all night but had never been able to boast one of my own. The ache made me deliriously happy.

Leon's heavy breathing was more reassurance I was not dreaming. With his arms around my body, my cheek burrowed inside his neck, I was very much awake. And very much alive. Every time the air left his nostrils, a draft warmed my ear. I never wanted the memory of us lying together under a warm, partly sunny Woodstock sky to fade. For that matter, I never wanted to move again.

I ogled the hair on his forearm, exactly the color of the hair on his head. Noticing the dirt underneath his fingernails—and mine—conjured up an unwanted image of Dad. He would have never stood for dirt underneath my fingernails. It made me even prouder of myself for taking charge of my own life. And for having dirty fingernails.

Seconds later, panic eclipsed my happiness. How many hours did we have left? Would we part after Jimi Hendrix closed the show tonight? Or would we spend another night together and say goodbye in the morning? Imagining our farewell punched a hole in my lung. I could hardly breathe. How could I do it? Leon was the coolest, most beautiful person I'd ever known.

And we lived a thousand miles apart.

A screeching noise from the main-stage microphone made Leon stir. It was a wonder we could hear it this far away. His arm slipped from my waist. His whiskers crackled as he rubbed his chin. As quickly as he had moved his arm away, he wrapped it back on top of mine, adding a gentle squeeze. "Wake up, little Susie," he sang, so beautifully out of tune. It made my insides beam. And burn, all over again.

Wiggling in deeper, I let him know I was awake. "No one's ever called me Suzie before you."

"Are you cool with it?"

"When you say it, I am."

"Would you rather I call you Suzannah?" He kissed the tip of my ear.

"I'd rather you call me Suzie."

"Wonder what time it is, *Suzie*."

I could have looked at my watch, but it would mean he'd have to move his arm. "No idea."

"What do you say we find one of those outdoor showers? I feel gnarly." He sat up, pulling me along with him.

"I'd say I love that idea."

Leon's gaze roved across my chest. Only then did I remember I was shirtless. At first, I resisted the urge to cover myself, but modesty roared back. So I pulled up my knees to hide behind them and reached for my bra, lying in a heap on the ground. As soon as it was in my hand, I remembered my new halter top, balled up inside my purse. I slipped it over my neck.

"Will you tie this for me?" I asked, turning my back toward him.

Instead of tying it, he reached under my arms to touch my breasts. One of his delicious man-giggles followed as he kissed my neck. His hands felt lovely and warm, so I leaned back against him, relishing in his touch. *How am I supposed to leave this?*

Once he'd tied the bow, he turned me around by my shoulders. "Looks rad on you. How do you feel?"

"I feel . . . like a brand-new me." Truth was, I felt like the butterfly that had landed on my shoulder when we first arrived. Totally carefree. And beautiful.

1:00 p.m.

We never found one of those outdoor showers. It must have been a rumor. But we did find water—or *wooder*, as Leon pronounced it—in a nearby pasture. Faucets had been installed from underground pipes. Thousands of folks stood in line.

The two of us waited forty-five minutes to rinse our faces and hands, brush our teeth, and quench our thirst. Fortunately, we had saved our paper cups from the granola. We passed them on to the person behind once we'd downed a few cupfuls.

We stood at the top of the bowl, peering down in awe on the city of Woodstock. There must have been one hundred acres' worth of bodies. New piles of muddy sleeping bags dotted the perimeter. The stench of dirty humans, vomit, and garbage, mixed with the scent of marijuana and campfires, hung heavy in the air. The smell of urine met my nostrils, but it no longer grossed me out. Just as Grace Slick had predicted, a new day had dawned.

Although still humid, the weather was nice and warm, and the sun on my skin felt sublime. A few clouds hung low in the sky, but they didn't seem to carry a threat of rain. I decided not to think about us parting ways until I had to. I'd simply enjoy the time we had left.

An unknown musician from England named Joe Cocker was slated to kick off the Sunday music. We meandered down the two-lane pathway in search of yet another choice place to sit, then settled halfway down, at the edge of a row.

Livy crossed my mind. Although she was headed on to Cambridge after the festival, she was supposed to help me figure out how I would get home. Where was home? I didn't want to think about that yet. Leon was all I wanted to think about.

Like normal, John Morris's voice floating throughout the pasture city caused everyone to listen up. "We have a gentleman with us," he began. "The gentleman upon whose farm we are. Mr. Max Yasgur."

Applause and whistles followed as Chip escorted our festival host to the microphone. Almost everyone, including Leon and me, gave him a standing ovation.

Max wore hefty black glasses and a crisp white dress shirt. "Is this on?" He tapped the mic twice, looking to Chip for affirmation. "I'm a farmer. I don't know—" The roar from half a million people caused him to pause. "I don't know how to speak to twenty people at one time, let alone a crowd like this, but I think you people have proven something to the world. Not only to the town of Bethel or Sullivan County or New York state. You've proven something to the world! This is the largest group of people ever assembled in one place. We had no idea that there would be this size group, and because of that you've had quite a few inconveniences, as far as water and food and so forth. Your producers have done a mammoth job to see that you're taken care of. They deserve a vote of thanks."

Another explosion of applause. The largest so far.

"But above that, the important thing that you've proven to the world is that a half a million kids—and I call you *kids* because I have children older than you are—a half a million young people can get together and have three days of fun and music and have nothing but fun and music, and I—God bless you for it!"

It was a super cool moment. Someone my parents' age affirming the ideology behind Woodstock. No one had forced Max Yasgur to lease his land. He didn't have to hold the festival on his property, no matter how much the producers paid him. He must have favored the youthful, rebellious spirit spreading rapidly through the country.

After Max left, Chip made a few more announcements. "Okay, let's run through these before we invite Mr. Joe Cocker to the stage. Michael and Will Brown, your mother would very much appreciate you calling home. Elise Crockett, please meet your boyfriend, Robert, at the foot of the stage. He's a little slow but has finally arrived. Leon Wright, you have an important message at the information booth."

"Ugh," I moaned. "My leave of absence from Livy is over."

Leon laughed. "Don't you wanna tell her goodbye?"

"Not really."

"Then let's ignore it. Johnny will page me later."

I wasn't ready to share what little time Leon and I had left with Livy and Johnny, not to mention Professor Henry, but I was afraid to ignore the page. "We should make sure he's okay," I said. "After the acid and all."

He pressed his lips together, trying not to grin. He knew Livy was the one I was worried about.

Hand in hand, we strolled toward the information booth. I couldn't remember a day in my life when I'd been as happy. Nor could I have fathomed the kind of freedom Woodstock had offered. As we approached the Message Tree, I felt weightless. None of my family problems encumbered my mind. Not Dad, not Mama, not even Ron's enlistment in Vietnam. Music had come back to my life, and I had danced the night away without anyone telling me not to. At last, the world seemed like a beautiful, peaceful place.

Hundreds of notes and paper plates were pinned to the Message Tree. Many more than the last time I'd been there with Livy. We scanned the writing on each, reading about people in search of people, rides home, hunts for good LSD, lost car keys, even a notice about a poor lost dog. But we found nothing for Leon.

We spied a girl with curly brown hair manning the inside of the booth and stood in line. We waited five minutes while she finished her conversation with a girl who rambled on and on about nothing. Once she left, Leon stepped up to the window. "Hey, man, I'm Leon Wright. I heard Chip Monck say I have a message here."

The girl searched around the inside of the booth before shuffling papers and Best Cola cans. She picked up a bag of pot, looked underneath, and put it back down. She even peeked inside a pair of muddy cowboy boots on the counter. "No messages for Leon Wright that I can see," she said, in a Boston accent. "Have you guys checked the Message Tree?"

"Yeah, man. We'll check again, though. Thanks." He tapped the counter with both hands.

Before walking away, the girl handed me a *Life of Yogi* pamphlet, then took a sip of her Best Cola. "Good luck."

"What gives?" I said, fanning myself with the pamphlet. For the first time all weekend I was hot.

"My cousin's a master prankster. He's somewhere looking at us right now laughing his ass off."

We turned circles, scanning the area for Johnny—and I for Livy—but saw neither. Leon even shouted his cousin's name. "Come out of hiding, Handsome J. You got me." He waved both hands in the air, crossing one over the other. But Johnny never showed up.

"What do we do now?" I asked.

"Go listen to Joe Cocker."

Joe's backup band, the Grease Band, had already been introduced and was jamming in the background.

"Sounds good to me," I said. "Let's go."

Leon didn't answer.

"You ready?" I asked, but his gaze had fixated over my head on something else.

I pulled on his sleeve. "Leon? Are you ready to head over?"

He shifted his eyes toward me, but only briefly, then diverted his stare back into the crowd. I looked, too, curious as to what had captivated his attention. A gorgeous blonde was waving at him. She must have just arrived, because she wore a spotlessly clean white dress.

A ring of white daisies crowned her long, waist-length blond hair. She could have passed for Livy's twin.

Leon waved back, with a curve in his lips.

Another gorgeous girl, wearing a matching white dress and daisy wreath, waved too. After a second look, I realized they were not only dressed like twins; they were twins. Identical twins.

The two Livys moved swiftly in Leon's direction.

He shot me another brief glance. This time with a pall of panic on his face. With a mere six-foot distance separating him from the twins, he ran a hand through his hair. He held it back from his forehead, then slowly let go. "Shelly" was all he said. Then gave her a wide grin.

My heart dropped like an elevator. Shelly, the girl he was "*not really*" sad about breaking up with, answered him, but the roar of my pulse inside my ears drowned out her voice.

Both girls melted into his arms.

"Good to see you, Leon," I heard Shelly's twin sister say before they all broke from the embrace. She looked at me curiously. "Hi."

All I could do was offer a shy wave. And a tight-lipped grin. An empty pain gripped my stomach.

"I didn't know you guys were coming," said Leon.

"It was my idea," Shelly's twin told him. Her tart New York accent puckered my nerves.

Shelly looked straight at me but asked Leon the question: "Who's your friend?"

He gestured to each of us as he made the awkward introduction. "This is Suzie. Suzie, meet Shelly and Sarah. That's a lot of *S*'s."

I heard the discomfort in his voice.

While the three of us managed an exchange of weak *hello*s, all I could think about was how much the twins looked like Livy. And how gorgeous they were. And how I'd been trailing behind Livy's gorgeous shadow my whole life. I couldn't do it anymore.

I reminisced on the last few hours of our time together in the butterfly meadow. For me, they were the most magical hours of my life.

For Leon, they were nothing special. The girl, the gorgeous girl, with whom he had most likely lost his virginity was standing in front of him. They would always share that special bond.

I took a step backward. *I can't do this.*

"We tried to get here yesterday, but the cops told us they weren't letting anyone else in," Sarah said. "We had to spend the night in Poughkeepsie."

Shelly's eyes sparkled like two stars in a midnight sky. "We heard the Who was outta sight!" The Who. Shelly knew it was Leon's favorite band.

As I listened to them ramble on with idle conversation, the situation became crystal clear. I wasn't the kind of girl he found attractive. He may have told me I was beautiful, but that was a lie. He only wanted a weekend fling, a way to get in a girl's pants. I thought maybe I'd found someone different, a boy who liked me for me. He had me convinced he liked me just the way I was. He had told me he couldn't believe that out of all the hundreds of thousands of people at Woodstock, he got to meet me. That was pure unadulterated bullshit.

I will not fight for someone who's interested in drop-dead-gorgeous, complicated girls like Livy. I won't.

While Leon and the twins prattled, I took another step backward, silently thanking God for protecting me. I told him I was sorry for the bad things I'd done and I'd try my best to do better. I especially thanked him for helping me to remember Livy's wise words about birth control. Not going all the way with Leon was the best decision of my life. How many other girls had he coaxed into removing their clothes?

I had thought I could trust him, but I was wrong.

I took a third step backward. When a tall dude strolled past, I positioned myself next to him, matching his stride. We walked together for several yards, as if we were a Woodstock couple. Step by step I followed along with him until I was sure I had melded into the massive crowd.

I never looked back to see if Leon had noticed I was gone. Or if he was searching around frantically. It would have hurt too much to learn he wasn't.

Woodstock

Day Three

Sunday, August 17, 1969
2:00 p.m.

"Our Father, who art in heaven. Hallowed be thy name . . ."

God, please, please forgive me for going too far with Leon. And for lying. And for smoking pot. If you'll see me through this, I'll never do anything bad again. I swear.

Picking up my pace, I sped through the crowd. With expert footwork I managed to dodge all the happy people strolling around aimlessly, like they hadn't a care in the world. Like their hearts hadn't been shattered into a trillion pieces. Couples—the only people who caught my eye—were holding hands, snuggling necks, lying on top of one another, making out in the sunshine. Every couple I passed gazed into one another's eyes as if they were madly in love. Like me.

My head spun like a top out of control, whirling into a vortex of confusion. *Where do I go? What do I do?* With no inkling, I stumbled past smoldering campfires, abandoned coolers, and piles of muddy clothes and blankets. When I tripped on a flashlight hiding in the mud, something dawned on me. The Woodstock aura I'd grown to love—grown to crave—had vanished. The beauty I'd seen with Leon only minutes prior had mutated into a wasteland of stink, sludge, and filth. For the first time since my arrival, Woodstock looked ugly. All I wanted to do was go home.

But I didn't have a home.

You will not cry; you will not cry. If time could be reversed, I'd beg Leon to ignore Chip's page. Come to think of it, he'd wanted to ignore it. It was me who had encouraged him, leading him straight into Shelly's arms.

What a stupid imbecile.

As the audience welcomed an unknown Joe Cocker with a deafening roar, I searched for Slim and Dave; tie-dyed-skirt girl, Anne Marie; any familiar face. I even looked for Livy. I missed her in that moment. If I could have spotted her movie-star mug, I would have forgiven her for everything. *Almost* everything.

Having no luck, I wormed my way back into the nameless crowd, determined to find another spot near the front. No one stopped me. I pretended as if I knew right where I was going.

As soon as I inched between two total strangers, who welcomed me with warm smiles, I turned to face the stage. Instead of Joe Cocker, I saw Leon and me up there, with a massive theater curtain slowly closing between us. The moment the sides met, oscillating from the blow, my eyes stung. As hard as I had tried to keep the tears at bay, they fell anyway.

While Joe Cocker serenaded the crowd with an otherworldly, enormous voice, I just stood there, a tiny krill inside the vast Woodstock ocean. Each salty tear that slipped into the corner of my mouth turned into a bitter taste of loneliness. And more reflections of Leon.

I looked down at my filthy toenails, ran a hand through my tangled hair. Why, why, why did I have to meet Leon's old girlfriend looking like this? Shelly looked as if she'd just stepped off the runway. Why the heck hadn't she and Leon come to Woodstock together in the first place? It would have saved me an ocean of heartache. I'd been right. You couldn't trust boys. Not one of them.

Determined to concentrate on Joe Cocker instead of Leon, I forced myself to give him my full attention. With his gritty, soulful gravel, he sounded like Ray Charles. He certainly screamed like Ray Charles. I stared at him up there on the stage, noticing everything about him. His bell-bottoms and tie-dyed Henley T-shirt, his cool blue cowboy boots speckled with white stars, his handsome face, his muttonchop sideburns, which, of course, reminded me of Leon.

Everything reminded me of Leon.

As Joe's set continued, it crossed my mind there might be something wrong with him. At first, I thought he might be having an epileptic seizure by the way his eyes rolled back and how he crippled his fingers. He'd flail his arms in spasmodic movements, endlessly strumming an invisible guitar. I considered he might have taken LSD like Janis Joplin or Arlo Guthrie, and we were all witnessing his acid trip.

"We're gonna leave you with, uh, the usual thing," a sweaty Joe Cocker told us a few minutes past three. "But all I can say, as I've said to many people, this title just about, uh, puts it all into focus. It's called 'With a Little Help from Me Friends.' Remember it."

No way anyone at Woodstock could forget it. From the moment the song's first B3 organ chords sounded, you could sense the spirit of Woodstock catching fire. The weekend of peace, the communal love, paralleled with the best music in the world, all blended into one alleluia.

I thought about Richie Havens's version. It might not have been as dynamic, but it sure had been a great way to open the festival.

After the last note, Joe waved, then leaned in to the mic a final time. "The Grease Band. And meself. Thank you all for watching. See you again. Beautiful." He left the stage amid engine-like roars from a half a million people. A star was born.

But that star never returned for an encore. Black thunderclouds had gathered out of nowhere.

John Morris did return, pointing behind the audience. "While we switch over, it looks like we're gonna get a little bit of rain, so you better cover up. If it does, if we should have a slight power problem, just glue it up. We'll sit here with you. You'll be okay."

I turned around to see a sky so dark and eerie it looked like a tornado was headed straight for the festival.

Minutes later, a fierce wind howled through the city of Woodstock like a pack of angry wolves. Stagehands scurried about, trying to cover the gear with plastic sheeting, but the wind made it impossible. Cracks of thunder shook the ground, while lightning strikes squiggled across the blackened sky. People scattered like beetles. Yet plenty of others, like me, had nowhere to scatter.

Meanwhile, John Morris stayed true to his post. "All these people in the towers, all of you up in the towers, please come down! You are making it very, very dangerous. Please come down off those towers. If it does rain, it will be slippery and dangerous. *Please.* Come. Down!"

What is wrong with you people? A lightning strike could take your last breath. As Chip had said the night before, their bodies could be welded to the poles. I shuddered at the ghastly image.

Five minutes after John Morris said the word *rain*, his prediction came true. It started out slow, but within seconds the raindrops felt like BB gun pellets hitting my bare shoulders. They bounced angrily against the bare earth, pooling into giant puddles. When I looked down, my feet were gone, sunk inside the mud soup.

"All right, everybody, just sit down; wrap yourself up. We're going to have to ride it out. Hold on to your neighbor, guys," John told the audience with a growing panic in his voice.

I had nothing to wrap up in but my own bare arms. I'd abandoned my muddy blanket a long time ago. A few people around me had umbrellas, but there was no extra room underneath. Some took cover under water-soaked blankets, and others under sheets of plastic, but lots of people had no covering at all. No neighbor to hold on to. I had accidentally left the jacket Livy gave me in the butterfly meadow when I'd changed into my new halter top—the one Leon had given me. Come to think of it, I'd left Livy's pink top in the meadow. And my new bra. *Dammmmmmit.*

Some new guy took over the microphone, yelling, "Hey, if you think really hard, maybe we can stop this rain!"

We were all drenched and the storm fierce, yet the audience responded with enthusiasm, cheering like mortals had the power to stop the rain. Looking around at the people near me, I noticed most of them weren't even bothered by the storm. They were cheering.

Not me. Dad would say God was punishing me for all the terrible things I'd done. Dancing, lying, smoking pot, drinking alcohol, going too far with Leon.

I was doomed.

I checked my watch for the time, but it was no longer ticking. It was ruined. My new purse was ruined. My new tie-dyed halter top was definitely ruined. The ink had bled onto my chest and stomach. My soaking-wet jeans were cemented to my body. I'd lost my blanket. And my jacket. I was freezing cold. I hated my new life.

I hated Woodstock.

"Thanks a lot, Livy," I yelled. "I tried to tell you there was no way I could go with you. But, like always, you refused to listen. And now I'm in an even bigger pickle. This, like everything else, is *your fault*!"

Looking up at the black sky, John Morris pleaded, yet again, "Everybody just get away from the towers, and clear them. Like Barry says, let's think hard to get rid of the rain, please. Everybody needs to think hard. Let's go! Let's think! We've done all of this. We can keep doing it." He sounded like a motivational speaker.

It worked. The crowd started a new roar, shouting and clapping as if they were enjoying themselves. "No rain! No rain! No rain," people chanted over and over and over, as if they truly believed they could make it go away. Along with the wooden blocks Quill had thrown from the stage, they banged cans together. They banged flashlights together. They banged anything they could find to make lots and lots of noise, all the while imploring the rain gods to cease their fury.

John had one final announcement. "We're gonna have to turn off the microphones for a minute. Hang in there with us. God bless you. Watch those towers. Kill the power!"

Some girl in front of me screamed, "Hey, Joe Cocker, isn't the rain beautiful?" But Joe was long gone.

As the beautiful rain pelted my body, my loneliness turned into frustration. At myself. Here I was with only forty-two dollars to my name—in the middle of freaking nowhere—with no clear vision for my afternoon, much less my future. Or my ride home. Should I even go home? If so, I'd have to go back to Dad treating me like I was some unholy, unlovable devil instead of his beautiful loving daughter. After this weekend, after meeting Leon, I didn't see how that would be possible.

Why should I waste any more of my life not listening to rock music or singing the songs I loved most? Who was Dad—or the whole Southern Baptist Church, for that matter—to tell me I couldn't dance or listen to rock music? Even King David danced and played music before the Lord. Why shouldn't I?

The worst part of the storm lasted only twenty minutes, but the rain refused to let up. I glanced around the bowl, thinking they should name the place Mudstock. It was one giant, muddy pigsty. Although some people around me were crying, plenty of others turned the pigsty into a party.

Caked in red clay, they danced. They played tag. They limboed. Someone started a giant Slip 'N Slide at the top of the bowl. People not wearing a stitch of clothing took a run for it, sliding down the hill all the way to the stage. Nudity didn't faze me anymore. By then the sight of a penis was as common as a nose.

Jealousy ensued when I spotted two girls turning walkovers in the mud, laughing like they were euphoric. I wished I could join them, forget my troubles, just have fun.

But I couldn't do it.

My heart was in shambles.

Woodstock

Day Three

Sunday, August 17, 1969
4:30 p.m.

A long forty-five minutes later, they restored power to the stage. And Chip told the audience there would be another long rain delay before the music started again.

That started the mass exodus. It looked like a city of people the size of Jackson, Tennessee, was moving toward the exit.

Okay, Suzannah, this is a sign. You should leave too. I got in line with the evacuating Woodstockers and moved slowly to the back of the bowl. Water pooled everywhere. People stepped right through the puddles; some even hopscotched.

Walking in my sandals became impossible. Every time I picked up a foot, a sandal would get sucked in by the mud. I did it one too many times. The strap between my toes broke. So I took it off and left it. Along with the other one. Right there, sunken in the mud. Now I had no shoes. Folks in front of me slipped and fell. It made me even angrier. Getting the hell out of Woodstock was all I cared about.

At the top of the hill, I noticed a bank of telephones in the distance, each covered in a black trash bag. Even with the rain falling, the lines were fifteen people deep. I hurried to the shortest line. More than anything, I needed a familiar voice. Not just any voice. Mama's.

Someone had put boards down for folks to stand on. Although by now, they, too, were sunken in the mud. I searched through my coin purse. It yielded seven quarters, three dimes, four nickels, and fifteen pennies. Surely that was enough for a long-distance telephone call.

Once it was my turn, I pushed back the trash bag, picked up the phone, and dialed zero. I'd just hang up if *he* answered.

"Operator," a lady said, in Shelly's tart accent.

"I'd like to make a long-distance call to Memphis, Tennessee, please."

"Phone number?" the tart operator asked, like she couldn't be bothered. Maybe she thought I was a hippie freak and couldn't stand hippies? But still, why be rude?

"Fairfax3-6180."

"That's three dollars and fifty cents for the first three minutes. Seventy-five cents for each additional. Deposit now," the rude operator said. *Tersely.*

I panicked. "I don't have that much change, ma'am. I—"

Click. She never bothered to say *goodbye*, or *thank you*, or *kiss my butt*. She just dial-toned it in my face. Calling back collect crossed my mind, but I dismissed that bright idea. I'd have rather strutted around the place naked myself than tell my parents where I was. I could see Dad now, using his state department connections to fly in on one of the military choppers, land on the heliport, step onto the state, and page me himself.

Frustrated, I slammed the phone back on the hook. Then spent the next ten minutes asking random people if they had change for a dollar. Instead of taking my dollar, each person gladly gave me all the change they had.

Thirty minutes later, after another wait in line, I asked a second surly operator to please give me Memphis, Tennessee. As soon as she gave me the cue, I dropped fourteen quarters into the slots. With each ring I could feel my angst growing. *Please, Mama, please be the one to answer.* Six rings later, a starving sense of loneliness engulfed my body as soon as I heard my mother's soft "Hello."

"*Mama.*" My voice cracked when I said her name. I missed her desperately.

The pops and whizzes from the connection made it hard to hear, but there was desperation in her voice too. "Suzannah! Honey. Are you okay?" She asked the question as if she was afraid to learn the answer.

Instead of responding, I wasted the first minute of our phone call weeping. Mama asked what was wrong, but that only made things worse.

"I'm *sad,*" I finally muttered. Although my words were practically inaudible, Mama understood me. She always understood me.

"We are too, honey. Your father is truly sorry. For *everything.*"

"Stop, Mama! I'm not sad about *him.*"

A long moan sounded on her end. She so wanted our family to be normal. "Is it Ron?"

"*No!* I mean yes, I'm always sad about Ron, but right now I'm sad because . . ." I couldn't finish my sentence. I just sat on my end of the phone, wailing.

It made Mama cry too. "Sad because why?"

"Because . . . I'm in *love.*"

There was a long, long pause, then finally, "If you're in love, why on earth are you crying?"

"Because I'll never be able to measure up to his old girlfriend." My nose jammed with mucous. I heaved for air. "She's so beautiful."

"So are you."

"Not compared to her."

"Come home, honey. We can talk about it here."

Going home sounded pretty good. At least I'd be warm. And dry. And have a soft bed to sleep in, with food on the table. I had enough money for the bus ticket. Plus a candy bar or two and a Coke along the way. I knew the pain I'd be up against at home. That pain seemed better than this pain.

"Maybe," I said, my chin trembling.

"Your father and I miss you terribly. He has so much to tell you. We both do."

I panicked. "Please don't put him on the phone. I don't want to talk to—"

"He's not here, honey. He's at church."

My veins burst with relief. But it was only four o'clock at home. Sunday-evening services started at five thirty. "Already?" I asked.

"There was a deacon meeting. I'm to meet him there."

"A deacon meeting." The stench of bitterness traveled through my nostrils and lodged inside my throat. "Dad is such a hypocrite, such a pharisee. Why can't you see that, Mama? The rules he makes us follow are *messed up*. Do you honestly believe God minds if I listen to rock music? Or if I dance? If loving either of those things means I'm going to hell, then I guess I'll be on fire for eternity."

"*Suzannah!* Don't you ever speak that way again!" she exclaimed, adding a loud groan. "Your father feels terrible about what happened. He—"

"He called me *trash*, Mama."

I could hear her pain in the long silence that followed. "You are *not* trash. And he knows it. He . . . has realized all kinds of things. He wants to apologize."

I sneered. "With what? A present? Forget it."

The operator broke through with a demand for seventy-five more cents. I dropped all the change I had into the slots.

"Your brother's deployment has changed everything," Mama continued, after our conversation had been restored.

"I'll say it has. Our family is screwed up. You can't even see it."

Mama paused. "I do see it. I just don't know what to do about it." Her voice trailed off, as if all her energy had been depleted.

"I do. You can leave him. We can move somewhere else. It's nice up here." As soon as I said *up here*, I knew I had goofed.

Instead of challenging me, she just wasted our phone time with a long stretch of silence. Thank God she didn't ask me to define *up here*.

"Please, Mama. You don't have to stay with him. When Ron gets home, we can all live free from Dad. In peace! Ron and I can start a band, and we'll make money to support you. I've realized how important music is to me. I'll never go without it again. Never."

She took another pause before asking, "Are you still at that jamboree?"

Pressing a hand to my forehead, I took a step backward. "How did you know? Never mind." I rolled my eyes, devastated to learn the truth. "Livy's parents called you."

"They didn't want me to worry."

"Please don't tell Dad!"

"I wouldn't dare. Ron will—"

The operator cut Mama off mid-sentence. "Deposit seventy-five more cents."

Frantically, I dug around in the bottom of my sopping-wet purse. "I don't have seventy-five cents, ma'am. Please give me more—"

The line went dead.

"Time." Depressing the hook with my forehead, I banged the handset against the pay phone, reeling from the unfortunate fact that Livy's mom had ratted me out. Another person I had thought I could trust.

Instead of placing the handset back on the hook, I handed it to the girl behind me. The only thing clean on her body were the whites of her eyes. She looked like a fudgesicle.

Staring at my tearstained face, the girl pouted her bottom lip. "I guess you heard about the kid who died yesterday morning."

My heart lurched. "No. Was it from the brown acid?"

The girl shook her head. "He was wrapped up in a sleeping bag, fast asleep. A sewage truck ran over him. The driver must have thought he was garbage."

The driver thought he was garbage. What a horrific way to die. The boy wasn't even fighting in Vietnam. He was at a peaceful, love-filled music festival, trying to get some sleep.

And now he's dead.

I stepped away from the phone bank with an ache in the pit of my stomach and no clearer answer about my future than I'd had before calling home. Where would I go? Memphis? Union? Or should I move to Kentucky or Arkansas so I could live on my own as a legal adult?

There was so much to think about. So many choices to be made. When I had arrived on Friday, I hadn't considered two days later I'd be making life-changing decisions. I'd rushed pell-mell out of Memphis, turning a blind eye to my future until I had to. And now I had to. More than anything, I longed to discover who in the heck I really was. The *real* Suzannah.

What would Ron tell me to do? Thinking about what he would say reminded me of his letters. I pulled one out the stack and saw that the ink had run on the envelopes, bleeding onto the lining of my purse. *No!*

After noticing a line of trees in the distance, I sloshed over and sat down underneath the canopy of a large maple, then opened the first envelope I touched. My heart throbbed as soon as the letter was in my hands. The ink had run all over the paper. Ron's words were barely legible. I opened another. Same thing: unreadable.

Not my letters! I lifted my chin skyward, screaming at God. "They are all I have left of him!"

Frantic, I tried another. The ink had run, but I could still make out his words. It was the most disturbing letter he'd ever sent. But I still wanted to read it. Just to be close to him. Just to hear him talking to me.

November 6, 1968
Long Binh, South Vietnam

Dear SuSu,
On purpose I have not written to you about the worst horrors of war. I wanted to protect you and keep you from worry. But now I need your prayers. I'm having a really hard time.

Yesterday, we saw Vietnamese soldiers standing near the road in a straight line. We had a feeling they were

SVA (South Vietnamese Army—our allies) but when they opened fire on us, we got our answer. They were the Viet Cong. We lost two of my platoon brothers, Philip and Mason. Their bodies will be sent home tomorrow. Billy G lost an eye, and Damon had both legs blown off. After they recover, they'll be sent home to live with their families, minus an eye and two legs. We are all in grief. My gun jammed in the middle of our firefight. I have never been so scared in my life. Freddy C is the one who fixed it. I don't know what would have happened if he hadn't. Guns jam all the time, my CO says.

I have intense fatigue. I can't make a decision, even about dumb things like which boot to put on first. The worst part is I can't get the flashbacks out of my head. And the nightmares are so real, SuSu. CSR, they call it in the military, Combat Stress Reaction. Shell shocked is a better term if you ask me but they don't call it that anymore. I asked my CO yesterday if I get a discharge because of my CSR. No way, he said. Everyone has it.

The longer I'm here I realize war kills all soldiers, whether they live or die. Some just handle it better. Like Dad. Part of me wishes I'd lost my leg. At least I'd be free to get the hell out of here. I sometimes wonder why I've been spared. I also wonder if I'll have to die to get home. I know that scares you. But I've got to get it out.

I don't believe in this war. And I'm not alone. Most of us feel the same way. AMERICA SHOULD NOT BE HERE. It's not our problem!

I know I sound angry. I am angry! There is not one safe place over here. Johnson knows very well we can't win this war. He refuses to stop the bombing, even though his advisors tell him he should.

I will see you again, I swear.

I love you,
Ron

I slipped the letter back in the envelope, then stuffed it inside my purse. I was starting to wonder if Livy could be right. Maybe Ron was wounded with his friends, and he didn't tell me.

Maybe Ron is missing in action.

Maybe Ron is dead.

Refusing to give that thought any more oxygen, I stood up and looked around for the last time. Still unsure what to do with my life, I got behind thousands of others walking toward the exit. No point in staying at the festival. Woodstock was about community. I had lost mine.

Hoping the answer about my future would come, I kept moving forward, knowing this much: I was sick and tired of the rain, the mud, the cold, the growls in my stomach, and, most of all, the loneliness. A cold dark mist hung over my heart, coating it in grief. Pain spread through its chambers like a hornet's sting. My nerve endings felt as though they had been pricked by needles.

I was a hundred yards down Hurd Road when someone shouted, "Look at the sky, you guys!"

With dropped jaws, an army of folks turned to watch thousands of flowers floating down from the clouds. An army helicopter flew overhead, spilling fresh white daisies over the filthy city of Woodstock. Our beauty among the ashes.

I stood in the middle of Hurd Road as the answer came into focus. *The Hog Farm.* Hugh Romney had said they were my family. Kind, loving people who treated each other the way a family should were just on the other side of the forest. I could pitch in, help prepare the food. Maybe I could babysit. Best of all, I could sing when I got back to the Hog Farm!

I turned an about-face. I would not miss Crosby, Stills, Nash & Young or Jimi Hendrix. I'd already missed the Beatles. There was no way I'd miss another concert of a lifetime. No one would deprive me of that.

Woodstock

Day Three

Sunday, August 17, 1969
6:00 p.m.

The psychedelic school buses were still there when I arrived. So were the tents and tepees. The stage was right where it had been yesterday. It seemed none of the Hog Farmers had left. Feeling abundantly relieved, I stepped up to the free kitchen and stood in line.

Only a minute passed before I heard a guy's voice calling, "Suzie!"

I whipped around, hoping it was Leon—sure it was Leon—only to find a dude I'd never laid eyes on flashing me the peace sign. I smiled and signed him back. Within seconds his arm lay across my shoulders. It felt nice and warm. And he was sort of cute.

"I heard you sing yesterday," he said. "Outta sight, milady."

I smiled, felt goose bumps rising from the compliment. "Thanks. What's your name?"

"Brady." He tilted his head, studying my face. "What's the matter?"

"Nothing," I answered in a low voice.

"*Nothing* doesn't give a person red eyes." He touched my nose. "Or a red beak."

I glanced at the ground, embarrassed. *I must look awful from all the crying.*

He lifted my chin and tilted it toward his. Tenderly. The way Leon had done. "Wanna talk about it?"

I shook my head.

"Wanna go somewhere dry?"

I gave him an enthusiastic nod.

Once we'd both been served a plate of warm veggies atop more brown rice, my new friend, Brady, pointed toward tepee city. "Follow me to my wigwam, milady."

On the way over, we passed the Hog Farm stage, doused in puddles. A hippie dude swept the water away with a wide broom while dogs frolicked in the spray underneath.

"When will the music start?" I asked Brady as we passed little children playing tag in the buff. I could hardly wait for the chance to sing again.

"Not sure we'll have more music on our stage. But don't hold me to that."

I was disappointed but shrugged it off. And kept following Brady.

His "wigwam," one of the largest in the Hog Farm campground, had a round hole for a door, which had been tied open with rope. "After you," he said, gesturing toward the opening. Holding tightly to my plate, I stepped through the hole, then settled down on top of a Native American blanket that had been stretched out as a rug.

The smell of patchouli was the first thing I noticed, with the scent of marijuana lurking underneath. The amber glow from two Mexican prayer candles gave me the impression I had stepped inside a hippie lair.

Brady followed me through the hole, then sat down next to me, cross-legged. While he chowed down, I looked around at the colorful decor.

"How did this wigwam not blow down in the storm?" I asked, noticing everything around me, particularly the absence of mud.

He rushed to swallow. "I've done this a time or two. This is my home."

"It's so cool," I said and meant it. It looked straight out of the magazine photos I'd seen of Haight-Ashbury. Flags with peace signs sewed into the fabric had been hung on the canvas walls; long strips of tie-dyed cloth dangled from the tiptop, like icicles. More Indian blankets were rolled up and stored off to the side, while brightly colored tapestry pillows encircled the circumference. A small wooden table held a brass shoe with a glowing triangle of incense tucked inside. Next to the shoe, a large bong had taken up residence, along with a transistor radio, Janis Joplin's "Work Me, Lord" playing softly from the speaker.

While the thumps from the bass guitar rumbled through my chest, I swayed to the beat, my mood lifting with each note of Janis's raspy voice. I touched Brady's knee. "Can I ask you a question?"

"Yeah, hon. Shoot."

"Why are y'all called *the Hog Farm*?"

After a loud chuckle, he leaned into my face, far too close for my liking. I could smell his veggie breath. "We used to live on a hog farm. We cared for . . ." He tilted his head, squinting one eye. "Fifty hogs. Or so."

"Wow. Where was that?"

"Tujunga." After I furrowed my brow, he added, "In the Hollywood Hills."

"Hollywood sounds dreamy. Where do y'all live now?"

"Pretty much in the buses. We move around from show to show. When we aren't traveling, we live in Llano, New Mexico." Brady stretched out his legs, nudging my foot with his sandal. "Everybody in the commune pitched in together. We bought thirteen acres."

"Cool. How many people live in your commune?"

"Three hundred, give or take. Thinking of joining us?"

I drew in a short breath. This took me by surprise. "I don't know. Maybe."

"Why *maybe*?"

I gave his question serious thought. When I had come back to the Hog Farm, I hadn't considered joining their commune. I had come back for a place to fit in. *Temporarily.* Until Woodstock was over. I had come back to be around nice people. To sing, eat, do my part, earn my keep. While at Woodstock.

"I've never thought about joining a commune," I said at last.

He leaned into me again. "You'd never look back."

After a long sigh, I tucked my hair behind my ears. "I have a lot of big decisions to make right now. My life needs a readjustment."

Again, Brady stretched his arm around my shoulders. I didn't really want his arm around my shoulders. I wanted Leon's. "That's another reason to come with us," he said. "We don't make big decisions. The biggest one I've made lately was where to set up my wigwam here on the farm."

"That sounds pretty good, actually," I said with a hearty laugh.

"It's the only way to live, milady." I was just about to ask how they supported themselves when Brady said, "How long have you been a singer?"

"I'm not really a singer. I just wish I was."

"Maybe not professionally. But who's to say you can't be?"

With downturned eyes, I answered. "I hope I can. One day."

"I bet Hugh could get you a gig at the Whisky. Elmer Valentine's a friend of his."

What's the Whisky, and who is Elmer Valentine? Livy would know. I smiled like I knew but wasn't sure Brady believed me. He reached over to his table and handed me a shiny red box of matches with raised gold lettering: **WHISKY A GO GO, 8901 SUNSET BLVD. OL2-4202.**

I turned the box over, then handed it back. "Looks like a cool place."

"The Whisky's launched some pretty famous careers."

I straightened. "Really? Like who?"

"The Byrds, the Springfield, the Doors. Frank Zappa and the Mothers got a record deal after playing there *one* night." He smiled, scooted in a little closer. "Why couldn't you? We'll all say she got her start on the Hog Farm stage."

Goose bumps rose on my flesh. I grinned at him but didn't know how to respond. I didn't want him sitting so close.

"Where do you live now?" he asked.

"Memphis. But I'm going back to college soon." I inched away.

He took both of our plates—I'd barely touched mine—and set them off to the side. "Memphis, Tennessee. Beautiful views of the Mississippi."

"You've been there?"

"Once. Drove through on my way from coast to coast." He reached for his bong. "I just filled this with fresh water before the storm."

The water may have been fresh, but the bong was well loved. Brown residue stained the glass. It looked gross.

I watched him stuff chunks of marijuana inside a funnel on the bong's neck and sprinkle them with smaller grinds. He covered the top with his mouth and lit the funnel. Smoke filled the water chamber. His lips disappeared into the mouthpiece as the water bubbled. He removed the bowl of pot before sucking in the smoke, then blew it toward the door hole. After two hits, he handed both the bong and the lighter to me.

Confident I knew what to do, I took it from him. I did it exactly the way he had done, but when I inhaled, I hacked and coughed like I had tuberculosis. I made an even bigger fool of myself than I had that first night in the bowl. *With Leon.*

"Uh-oh," said Brady. "Let me help you." He took the bong back to demonstrate. "Don't inhale right away. Just draw in a little smoke, and let it fill the chamber. Watch me." I heard the water bubbling as soon as he placed his lips inside the glass.

Once he'd blown the smoke out the wigwam hole, he handed me the bong. He put his hand over the top so the smoke wouldn't escape. This time, I took a hit without choking. I tried handing it back, but he stopped me. "Take a couple more."

I took a couple more.

Within sixty seconds, a meteor shower exploded inside my head. *Wow. Wow. Wow!* I glanced around the wigwam. The pillows were dancing. So I stood up and danced along with them, with Mick Jagger singing "Under My Thumb" in the background.

When the song was over, I plopped down on his Indian blanket. "I've decided," I announced loudly, settling down on my back. "I'm definitely joining your commune." I pulled up my knees and crossed one leg over the other. With my head cradled in my hands, I stared up at the top of the tepee, fantasizing about singing at the Whisky.

Brady stepped over to the wigwam door and untied the rope so the flap would cover the hole. He stepped back and lay down next to me, turning his head my way. "Good choice, milady. You'll never look back."

I wished he'd stop calling me *milady*. "How much money will I need to join?" I asked, thinking about the forty-two dollars in my wallet.

"None. We pool our money. Everyone earns their keep."

"Far out, man," I said, in a daze. "Works for me."

What else would I need to join the commune? First and foremost, I'd need clothes, many more than I had at the festival. It was dusk now. As soon as it got light, I'd go back to the butterfly meadow. I'd find my jacket, Livy's pink top, and my new bra. Although I'd never wear a bra once I became a Hog Farmer, I still wanted to keep it. It matched my panties.

Would I change my clothing style completely? Wear flowy skirts and halter tops every day? A photo slideshow of all the adorable things I'd bought from Goldsmith's played in my head. I'd never see a single one of them again if I joined the Hog Farm. *Who cares?* I thought. *I'll never miss a stinking one of them.*

"It's exactly what I'm supposed to do," I said out loud, feeling relaxed and euphoric. I didn't care about Leon. I sure didn't care about Dad, or Livy or Shelly or that I had no home. I didn't care about much of anything. Except singing at the Whisky a Go Go on Sunset Boulevard.

"One. Two. Three. Four . . ." With my finger held high, I counted Brady's tie-dyed ribbon icicles. I stood up and batted them through the air like they were dancing. Then I lay back down and stared up at the point of the wigwam, imagining Santa Claus squeezing through on Christmas morning. Belly laughter erupted. My shoulders shook. Nothing I could do would make them stop shaking. But it felt heavenly to laugh.

Brady turned over on his side, propping up on his elbow. "Wanna do windowpane?"

Do I wanna do windowpane? My brain whirled with visions of windowpanes dancing in the air. I glanced slowly around the wigwam, studying every inch of the walls. Not a windowpane in sight. Not even a peephole. "Where do you find a windowpane around here?"

He moved over to a bag propped up against one of the perimeter pillows, then slipped his hand inside. After crawling back, he sat down next to me, holding out his palm. A tiny paper square, no bigger than a dime, lay in the center. "Got it on the West Coast. It's rad. And safe," he said with a chuckle.

What could be rad or unsafe about a tiny little piece of paper? The windowpane correlation was obvious, but that was about it. I plucked it from his palm to give it a closer look. "What's so rad about this?"

"Takes you on a trip to wonderland, man." Brady raised his eyebrows sky-high.

I sat up, curled my legs underneath me. If I hadn't been on a serious bong high, I would have dropped it like a hot potato. Instead, I gave it a hard look. Leon was gone. It could be a way to forget him. I was on my own now, headed for commune life. I'd do it eventually, wouldn't I? I'd done everything else since I'd arrived. Might as well drop acid. I'd be a bona fide Hog Farmer if I did. Why not take a trip to wonderland?

I sure didn't want to admit to Brady that I'd never done acid before, so I smiled at him, like it was a good idea.

Brady took it back and tore it in half. "Stick out your tongue and say *ahh*."

As soon as I stuck out my tongue, a still small voice whispered, *This is not the real you, Suzannah. You don't have to prove yourself to anybody. You are wonderful the way you are.*

That voice sounded authentic. Somehow, I knew it spoke the truth. Brady's fingers were hovering above my tongue when I jerked it back inside my mouth. I didn't want to take a trip to an artificial wonderland. I didn't want to be a Hog Farmer either. Truth was, I didn't want to be anyone but me. Not Livy, not Shelly, nor any other drop-dead-gorgeous, complicated girl. Just me. The *real* me.

I shook my head. "No thanks."

"Come on."

"Really. I'm good."

He cocked his head to the side and gave me a shrug. "Suit yourself."

In one motion, I grabbed my purse and rose up on wobbly knees. A heaviness gripped my eyeballs.

"Wait. Don't go." Brady rose with me. "I didn't mean to make you uncomfortable. Please stay. Stay as long as you want, milady."

Fatigue clamped on to my body like a vise. "What I want is to take a very short nap." I dropped my purse and lay down on the blanket, curling up in a ball. As much as I wanted to leave, a catnap sounded better.

That's the last thing I remembered before falling into a deep slumber.

Woodstock

Day Four

Monday, August 18, 1969
12:30 a.m.

An abysmal darkness filled the wigwam. I sat up, confused. "Where in the heck am I?"

The steady breathing of a sleeping hippie produced the memory. Grady the Hog Farmer, his wigwam, our bong high, the windowpane. *What else happened?* I wanted out of there. That instant.

I scooted slowly away from Grady. *Wait. Is his name Grady or Brady?* With no choice but to crawl on my hands and knees, I searched for my purse, fingering everything in my path. My elbow hit the small table holding the bong. It crashed onto the blanket where I'd been lying, spilling bong juice everywhere. *Gross.*

Brady stirred.

I froze, praying he'd go back to sleep. *What time is it? Dear God, please tell me I haven't missed Crosby, Stills & Nash. Or Hendrix.*

Once I was sure Brady was snoozing again, I inched along in what I hoped was the direction of the wigwam hole, thankfully discovering my purse nearby. Pushing the flap open ever so carefully, I peeked outside to the glow of campfires. The night air chilled my face. So I wrapped up in one of Brady's spare blankets before slipping away to freedom.

Several Hog Farmers were gathered in lawn chairs around a campfire. I didn't want them to see me, so I tunneled around each tent like a mole, finding my way in the darkness. Leon's smile lit my path. His emerald eyes colored the coal-black sky. The sting of leaving him had returned, filling me with deep regret.

Why, *why* had I left him? I didn't know for sure he would stay with Shelly. He had told me she was complicated. They had broken up. I'd just stood there like a fool and let someone else have the boy I wanted. I'd made it easy for Shelly. All because of my low self-esteem. And lack of trust.

Trust is a curious thing, especially when considering the blind trust people have in strangers. We trust pilots we've never met to take us safely to our destinations. We trust nameless pharmacists to dispense the right medications and unknown surgeons to operate with a steady hand. Dentists are trusted by millions of patients every day to drill holes in their teeth. We blindly trust drivers not to cross the yellow line.

Trust is in most every decision a person makes. How could I have called all men untrustworthy just because Dad had treated me wrong? The more I thought about not trusting Leon just because Shelly had decided to show up, the more I knew, 100 percent, I had to page him. I had to at least try to get him back. He had given me no reason to distrust him.

All I had needed was to learn how to trust myself.

Seconds later I sped down Ho Chi Minh Trail barefoot, in the direction of the main stage.

1:00 a.m.

By the time I made it to the bowl, the crowd had thinned dramatically. Hard to say, but it looked like the population of Woodstock had been cut by two-thirds. I plodded up to a gathering of people hovered around a warm campfire. "Excuse me. Has Crosby, Stills & Nash played yet?"

"Not yet," said one of the girls in the group. "Blood, Sweat & Tears is next. Those guys are supposed to follow."

My muscles softened. "Do you happen to know what time it is?"

The girl used the glow from the fire to check her watch. "One o'clock."

"Thank you!" With the lull in the music, I had to get to the stage in a hurry. If not, Leon's page could take another two hours. I wanted to watch Crosby, Stills & Nash—and Young—with him.

I bolted down the two-lane pathway. With fewer people, it didn't take as long to make it to the front. Once there I scribbled out a note on a deposit slip from my checkbook and handed it to a stagehand. *Leon Wright, you have an important message at the information booth.* Shelly's exact words.

Heading straight there, I pondered what I'd say when he showed up. I'd thank him for all the fun and laughter, and for buying me the halter top. I'd tell him he's a great kisser. Most of all I'd thank him for helping me to discover my truth. For helping me to see myself for who I truly was . . . a survivor. A singer with a future. A girl who, given a little freedom to trust herself to make her own wise choices, could love her life. And herself.

I would tell Leon he was a kind, beautiful soul any girl on earth would be lucky to have. And maybe, just maybe, I'd tell him that girl should be me.

Chip delivered my message fifteen minutes after I made it to the info booth. "Leon Wright, you have *another* important message at the information booth. Popular guy."

While waiting, my heart fluttered. In the background the unmistakable sound of Blood, Sweat & Tears rang out through the night sky. Fifteen more minutes passed while I circled the booth, darting my eyes in every direction, waiting for Leon to show up. With or without Shelly.

Another fifteen minutes slipped away. Although I knew it was futile, I asked the same girl with the Boston accent—the one who had been manning the booth earlier—if Leon Wright had answered his page.

"I don't think so," she said. "But I've talked to thousands of lost souls this weekend. I couldn't tell ya for sure."

An hour later, Blood, Sweat & Tears told the audience goodbye, and I said goodbye to the information booth.

Woodstock

Day Four

Monday, August 18, 1969
3:00 a.m.

Illuminated by a blue cast from the spotlights atop the towers, three handsome faces appeared onstage. Even from where I stood toward the back of the bowl, I knew exactly who they were. Shouts and applause loud enough to silence a hurricane exploded from the audience while I stood there, alone, watching the band I'd looked forward to hearing the most.

Once the trio had taken their seats atop wooden stools, Stephen Stills leaned down toward his microphone. "Hey, man, I just gotta say that you people have gotta be the strongest bunch of people I ever saw. Three days, man. *Three days!* We just love ya. We just love ya." He looked over to David. "Tell 'em who we are."

"Just sayin' hello. Test. Forty-nine. Sixty-five. Hi," said David Crosby, right before the magical guitar chords from "Suite: Judy Blue Eyes" filled the night sky.

Chip's offstage voice could be heard underneath Stephen's guitar. "Ladies and gentlemen, please welcome with us Crosby, Stills & Nash. And Young."

I didn't know why he announced Neil Young. He wasn't onstage.

Although their harmonies delighted my ears, I couldn't barricade the pain. It felt like a knife had ripped a gaping hole in my heart. I had never once considered Leon wouldn't answer his page, even if he had decided to stay with Shelly. I thought he was a much nicer person than that. I considered the possibility that he may have left when the storm blew in. Either way, I couldn't stop the heartache. Or the regret.

When the final note from "Suite: Judy Blue Eyes" faded, the crowd cheered madly. And Stephen Stills spoke again. "Thank you. We needed that."

"This is our second gig," David Crosby said. "This is the second time we've ever played in front of people. We're scared shitless."

I was the one scared shitless. I didn't even know where I would sleep that night. Or the next.

After they finished a beautiful version of the Beatles' "Blackbird," Graham Nash spoke to the audience in his lovely British accent. "Let's do a Stephen Stills song. I think one of the best ever written. It's called 'Helplessly Hoping.'"

I couldn't have agreed more. While their angelic, unmistakable harmonies wafted through the pasture, I listened closely. "Helplessly Hoping" was a poem about two people who love each other but must say goodbye, for a reason unknown. I hadn't understood the song when I first heard it in my closet, but after meeting Leon, its meaning crystallized. While Stephen sang about the empty place inside, I knew what he meant. The poet was lost, helplessly in love. He was wondering if he would ever have another love to fill the void she had left.

As their three-part harmony faded, and one of the prettiest tunes I'd ever heard came to a close, I grew not only weary but sick and tired of sadness. Sick and tired of tears.

Stop obsessing over someone you can't have. Stop it right now! What are you going to do, cry for the rest of your life? Of course you'll love again. For God's sake, girl, don't let this moment pass you by. You are at Woodstock. This is your once-in-a-lifetime concert! Go down front and enjoy the rest of it.

While David Crosby sang lead vocals on "Guinnevere," I shimmied through the crowd in a hurry, squeezing between hundreds of people, determined to get as close as I could. I finally made it to the front, then nudged my way in between two guys who smiled at me, glad I was there. One passed me a joint, but I declined. I wanted to be as clearheaded as a child while watching my new favorite band.

Wrapped up in Brady's Indian blanket, with my bare feet sunken in the cold mud, I allowed their melodies to once again lift me high in the air. I felt my confidence rising. And my resolve taking root. One day I'd get a record deal too. As soon as Ron got back, we'd be that family duo he always talked about. We'd play at the Whisky a Go Go to a sellout crowd.

I just knew it.

Woodstock

Day Four

Monday, August 18, 1969
6:00 a.m.

After the Crosby, Stills, Nash & Young set was over, I chatted for a long time with some of the Woodstockers in my row—all of us raving about the far-out performance—then headed straight for the butterfly meadow in search of my clothes.

While strolling down Gentle Path, I mused over my time at Woodstock. Although I was riding high with hope about my future as a singer, my heart still groaned from the thought of never seeing Leon again. Perhaps he was only meant to be a signpost, I reasoned, a guiding light on my path to freedom. Whatever the case, I was a stronger person for having met him. He had helped me to discover the real me.

I'd do my best to stop blaming myself for leaving my diary on my bed. I hadn't meant to; it was a mistake. I didn't cause Ron's enlistment. I knew that now. Leon had helped me to understand.

This weekend had helped me to see that someone could be the most beautiful girl in the world, but if her inside didn't match her outside, so what? All the hours I'd spent obsessing over Livy's beauty had been a big waste of time.

As I made my way down Gentle Path, I saw the sun's first rays sparkling from the tips of the trees like diamonds. Once I spotted the tire swing, I knew my way. Following an imaginary train of butterflies, I strolled out to the first meadow. People were sleeping. So I crept through the dewy foliage with my eyes pinned to the ground, softly kicking at the weeds. Finding my jacket was imperative. It was the only one I had. The tall, dew-glistened reeds of goldenrod made my search more difficult, but I knew my clothes would be there. No one at Woodstock would take anything that didn't belong to them.

Once I'd made it to the second meadow, I noticed a dude sitting with his back against a tree. His legs were stretched out on the grass below. It was hard to tell if he was awake or asleep, as his head hung to the side. I tried to be quiet, but the stillness amplified the sound of my feet shifting through the grass.

"Hey," he called, startling me.

I wanted to ignore him, but that was not the Woodstock way, so I glanced over my shoulder, gave him a quick wave, and returned to my search.

"Morning," he said louder.

I knew that voice. Relief melted throughout my body, yet I was caught so off guard words escaped me. I just stood there gaping at Leon, while he did the same to me.

"It's about time you decided to show up," he said.

"How long have you been here?" I asked, walking toward him.

He picked at something in the corner of his eye, then scratched the top of his head. "Four hours. Maybe more—"

"*Four* hours?"

"You didn't answer your page, so I figured it was the only chance I had of seeing you again."

I stopped moving as my relief crashed and burned. "You paged me? When? I never heard it."

He moved back and forth against the tree, like he was scratching his back. "I paged you. I went back to the Hog Farm. I camped out at the information booth. I've basically gone back to every place I thought you'd be within three square miles. Where have you been?" There was a harsh tone to his voice. Cords in his neck bulged as he ogled Brady's Indian blanket.

Lying crossed my mind. Yet I knew if I lied, I'd be taking a giant leap backward. "Sleeping. Inside a wigwam. A dude named Brady invited me to get out of the rain."

"Brady? Who the hell is that?"

"Where's Shelly?" I retorted, with the same amount of sarcasm.

"Hell if I know. If you hadn't disappeared so quickly, you would have known I had no desire to spend what little time *we* had left with Shelly."

We just stared at each other. Without words.

"Didn't you know that?" he asked.

I shook my head. My resolve was waning.

"How could you not know that?" His eyes were tight.

Unable to shake the feeling of deep regret, I broke eye contact with him and wrapped the blanket tightly around my body.

"What's the real reason you walked away, Suzannah? I need to know." He hadn't called me by my real name since we first met.

I just stood there with the sad realization that my lack of trust—and my immense insecurity—had caused every bit of this. What's worse, we had missed our last day together because of it. My insecurity roared back. "When I saw Shelly, I . . . guess I figured you wanted to be with her. She's—" I stopped short of saying *beautiful, like Livy*.

"Complicated. I told you that. She's the looniest chick I've ever known."

"You didn't exactly say it like that." I forced a nervous chuckle, wishing I knew what made her so loony.

He didn't answer me. And I didn't say anything else. The silence between us stretched so long it seemed even the droopy, dew-laden necks of goldenrod sensed our despair.

Not able to stand the distance any longer, I sat down next to him. Only then did I notice my clothes in his lap.

He shifted until we were facing one another with our knees touching. "Shelly was important to me *once*. She's not anymore. She's nuts."

"Maybe so. But she's . . ." As much as I wanted to say *beautiful, like Livy*, I stopped myself. Was her heart beautiful? Was she kind? Loving? Good to others? Leon had just said she was nuts.

"She's what?"

"I figured she was your first love. And that y'all had lost your virginity together. I figured you'd always be bonded because of it."

He didn't confirm or deny my suspicions; he just said, "I'm not bonded to Shelly. Look, Suzie, I know we just met two days ago. And maybe it's ludicrous to think down the road when we live in opposite directions." We caught one another's eyes. Deep inside those pretty green irises of his, I saw an earnestness I hadn't seen before. "I don't want this to be the end of us."

There. He said it. *Us*.

He took my hand in his. "I don't know what the future looks like, or if I'm nuts to think we can have a long-distance thing, but I don't want to be another face in your crowd." He had remembered my exact words.

"I don't want that either."

"Johnny and I have to split right after Hendrix. That's in a couple hours." At Leon's reminder of the time, I felt the hornet's sting again. Our hourglass was almost empty.

"When I was alone during the storm, I realized a lot of things about myself," I said.

"Like what?" he asked, with that tender expression I'd grown to crave.

"Like how hard it is for me to trust boys. Trust anyone, really. So many people I should have been able to count on have let me down."

Leon sighed, shaking his head slowly. "I know, and I'm sorry."

At the mere thought of my complicated, psycho family, I pulled my legs up close to my body and hung my head. "I'll never be able to forgive Dad for what he did to Ron. Or me."

Leon parted his lips to say something but stopped.

"What? Say it."

"I understand why you're mad; I'm on your side. But who knows what war did to your dad? There's no telling what he witnessed."

I let his words sink in before answering. "I've never thought about that."

"War changes people. It's done it to my kid brother, and it'll do it to Ron."

Thinking about how Ron would have changed made my heart burn.

"Besides that, unforgiveness has a way of poisoning *you*." He tapped my chest. "It locks you in prison and throws away the key. I learned that the hard way. Johnny and I didn't speak for a year."

This surprised me. The two cousins seemed closer than brothers. "Why?"

"He totaled my car. It was an accident, but the way he handled it was shit."

"What did he do?"

"It's what he didn't do. I'd saved for that thing since I was thirteen. He knew how much I dug it. One night, he begged me to loan it to him so he could impress this chick. So I loaned it. Gladly. But on his way home, he hit a fire hydrant. He'd had too much to drink. Messed the engine up so bad the car was toast. I was mad for a long, long time."

"Were they okay?"

"Fine. No cops, no blood, no whiplash, no nothing. But they left my ride there and walked home. Johnny called me the next day to tell me he'd pay for the tow charge but didn't have the dough to fix the car."

"Why didn't insurance cover it?"

He shook his head. "Johnny was driving. I didn't realize I'd declined that coverage."

"How did you forgive him?"

Leon rubbed the back of his neck, then met my gaze. "I chose to forgive him."

I narrowed my eyes. "You make it sound easy."

"It's not easy. It's a choice. Not an overnight choice—one you keep working on. Know what I mean?"

A big shrug was my answer to that.

"One night I was lying in my bed, so pissed off I couldn't sleep. That's when I realized I'd spent too many hours angry over something I couldn't do a damn thing about. So I decided to take the high road. And forgive him. It took a long time. But I knew it's what I needed to do."

I just stared at him. Forgiving Dad would be a much bigger challenge than forgiving Johnny. It might have worked for him, but it would not work for me.

"You can't let your dad ruin your life, Suzie."

Visions of Dad breaking my records over his knee made me shudder. So did the ones of me holding the protest sign. "I know that, *Leon*. It just seems unfair that I have to forgive him when he's the one who's caused me all the pain." My voice cracked. "He should be begging *me* for forgiveness. He's said so many hateful things to me."

"Come here." Tenderness blazed in his eyes as he reached out.

Once I'd settled inside his arms, my blood flowed again. Thoughts of Dad had tightened my muscles into giant knots. But not as many as I had had from missing Leon.

He kissed the top of my head. "He might not ever do that. But like I said, forgiveness is for you. So *you* can have peace. Not him."

Pulling away, I looked him in the face. "But *how*? How do I do that?"

"Well, if it were me, I'd say a prayer to God for help, then make a choice not to let him ruin my life. Forgiveness is a gift you give yourself. It's the place where healing starts."

No one had ever talked to me like that. I didn't quite understand how it would work, but his words had softened the calluses on my heart. Maybe not a lot, but it was a start. "I guess I could try," I said.

He smiled. "That's all you can do."

"You just said something else interesting."

"Yeah? What's that?"

"You said there's no telling what my dad witnessed in war."

He nodded.

"I'd never thought about that before you said it. Maybe that's what drives him to do all the mean things he does."

"Who knows what's under all his rocks?" said Leon. "Or what he thinks will happen if he uncovers them? I bet he's terrified not to comply with all the rules in his life."

"He's terrified he'll go to hell if he doesn't."

"Hey, man, Catholics feel the same way." Leon laughed through his words. He wiggled his eyebrows and put a deep tone in his voice. "Unless you confess your sins to the priest."

Releasing a loud sigh, I leaned my head back. "I suppose you're gonna tell me I need to forgive Livy too."

Leon circled his head with his hands, like he was conjuring up magic. "To free the mind. To get out of jail." After a long pause, he added, "We're *all* in need of forgiveness. I know I am."

His words seeped into my heart like blood from a wound, coating me with the realization that I needed forgiveness as much as anyone. I'd hurt people too. I'd sinned like everyone else. *Perfection* was not my middle name.

"Have you really been here four hours?" I asked, tapping his chin dimple. I was tired of such serious talk.

"Yup. Sang along to 'Suite: Judy Blue Eyes' from right here." He patted the ground. "Bad voice and all. Good thing there's a decent sound system in this joint."

I thought about telling him I'd had him paged but decided he didn't really need to know that. I needed to keep a few cards to myself. "How did you know I'd come back for my jacket?"

He peered at me with a crooked smile. "You're cold when normal people are hot."

I shoved him. He grabbed hold of my wrists, pulling me down on top of him. Then he rolled us both over in the damp grass until we were side by side. Using his fingertip, he dotted the freckles on my cheeks. "You're the cutest thing I've ever seen, Suzie Withers."

Guiding his chin toward mine, I whispered, "You're my miracle, Leon Wright."

The words bounced through my head, until they had crystallized into a lyric with music behind them. *Who could have thought, who could imagine, the time it would not take. To find my miracle, in the shape of you. Just in time, just for my sake.*

As more words flowed, I committed them to memory. For later. Right now, my attention was better spent inside the miracle of his kiss. Soaking up every second I had left with him was all that mattered. Because as much as it killed me to think about it, there was a high chance I'd never see him again.

7:10 a.m.

"Livy Foster, please head to the information booth. Nick is here. *At last.*"

Chip's page made me belly laugh. "Well, good for you, Livy!" I said out loud. "You've got Handsome Johnny on one arm, the professor on the other, and poor ole Slim off to the side. Where's Nick gonna fit?"

Leon laughed. "You crack me up, little darlin'." He leaned in to kiss me. Then did it again, and again, and again.

I considered ignoring the page. But the more I thought about it, the more I knew it might be the only chance I had to see Livy again. And, dare I say it, begin the process of forgiveness. "I guess I should go to the info booth to tell her goodbye," I said. "And make that choice you told me about."

Leon propped up on his elbow. "Good for you. I need to find Johnny anyway."

We sat up at the same time, holding one another's gazes. It was 7:15 Monday morning. The Paul Butterfield Blues Band had just left the main stage, and Sha Na Na was up next. Hendrix would follow.

Then Leon would leave. And I didn't even have a picture to remember him by.

Silence fell between us. I suspected we were both thinking the same thing. We kissed once more before standing up. With our arms wrapped tightly around one another's waists, we meandered back down Gentle Way toward the information booth.

From thirty yards out, I spotted Livy by her hair. She was folded into Nick's arms. I giggled at the thought of her wearing the yellow baby doll negligee, splashing through mud puddles to get to him, with all her Woodstock suitors—Johnny, the professor, and Slim—tagging behind.

Until that moment, I hadn't stopped to think about what Nick might look like. I'd never even asked Livy if he was cute; I'd taken that for granted. From this vantage point, I could tell he was tall and thin with long wavy brown hair that hung past his shoulders. He had a full beard, like Professor Henry's. For a second, I considered he might be Henry but noticed Nick was much taller. And Henry was nowhere to be found.

Ten yards apart, I got a better look at him. Nick's jeans hung low, as if he was too thin to hold them up. He wore a loose green T-shirt and Jesus sandals on his feet. He held tightly on to Livy, as if he never wanted her to move from his grasp.

Johnny, bless his heart, stood in front of them with his hands shoved inside his front pockets, rolling a Best Cola can underfoot. Poor thing. Even though Leon claimed Johnny wasn't the relationship type, I knew Livy had a way of seeping under someone's skin. I was pretty sure Johnny was feeling the sting of Nick's arrival.

Johnny happened to look up and noticed Leon and me approaching. He held his hand high, flashing us the peace sign. That caused both Nick and Livy to look over their shoulders.

Nick's deep-set blue eyes caught mine. I shuffled back a step before the air left my lungs. Nick was my brother.

Woodstock

Day Four

Monday, August 18, 1969
7:25 a.m.

Time stood still. Ron and I eyeballed one another as if we were statues. With firecrackers exploding inside my veins, I pushed Livy out of the way. I literally pushed her. Then stumbled into my brother's arms. Dizziness ensued. Tears sprang out of nowhere. I opened my mouth to say something, but the words wouldn't flow.

"SuSu," Ron said, stroking the top of my head.

I looked up at him. Stunned. Dazed. Confused. Fit to be tied.

Ron pulled away slightly, meeting my eyes. "You must feel like you've been hit by lightning."

"Try a nuclear bomb."

"That's fair."

I took a step back. To get a good hard look at him. His hair hung on either side of his face, covering his cheeks. It was the first time I'd ever seen him with long hair. Or a beard. No wonder I hadn't recognized him.

"Wh—*how* are you here?" I asked, with an angry fire nipping at my words. Guilt crawled all over me for my tone, but what the heck?

Ron gave a quick glance to Livy, then looked right back at me. "I'm out of the army."

"No *duh*!" I shouted. "For how long?"

He took a deep breath, dipping his chin. "For good."

This news overwhelmed me with elation, but I had a strong sense something was seriously wrong. It snapped me out of my fury. I grabbed hold of his forearm. "Ron, what's going on? Are you okay?"

When he turned to look at Livy again, I noticed a gap in his beard. Whiskers no longer grew on the side of his cheek. I reached up to tuck a long lock of hair behind his ear. Ron's beautiful face, once the longing of every girl at Central High School, had a crater stretching from his ear to his mouth. Crimson burn scars covered a large portion of his cheek. I moaned, tapping the scars.

"Stepped too close to a land mine," he said. "You should see my leg." He reached down to massage his calf. "I'm one of the lucky ones. I've still got it."

Before I could inspect the damage, Livy threw her arms up. "Yet the army sends him back into combat," she said in a mocking tone.

"Why didn't you tell me?" I asked him. *Not her.* The very idea that Livy Foster knew things about my brother that I didn't made me furious all over again. And to think I had wanted to forgive her.

"I didn't wanna scare you," Ron said, with caring eyes.

"He begged me not to tell you anything," said Livy, placing a hand on my shoulder.

It made me flinch. "Get away from me, you liar."

"Hey, now." Ron guided me back into his chest, where the familiar scent of English Leather hung around his neck.

But I pulled away. "Why haven't you written? And when did you get out?" I looked back at Livy with a pointed finger. "And how does *she* seem to know everything?"

Ron twisted his watch back and forth on his wrist. "She helped me."

I glanced between the two of them. "Helped you how?"

He squeezed his eyes shut. "There's a lot I need to tell you."

"I'll say," I said with a sneer.

"He'll explain everything," said Livy, in that sickening authoritative voice of hers. "I'm exhausted from covering it up."

"Covering what up?" I gave her a cold stare. This fresh betrayal was excruciating.

"Let's go somewhere to talk," said Ron. His voice sounded as if he would choke up at any second.

I held my head between my palms and squeezed as a hideous image crossed my mind. "Wait a minute. Are you her *boyfriend*?" I asked my brother.

Ron and Livy looked at each other; then they both answered at the same time. "Yes."

As an angry sigh blew from my lips, I looked heavenward, muttering, "God help me." We all sat there in silence before I said, "I don't get it. Who is Nick?"

"I am," said Ron. "At least while I'm in America."

"Yeah. We have a *lot* to talk about." I spun around, catching sight of Leon. *Leon!* He and Handsome Johnny stood ten feet away, chatting among themselves. This had to have been awkward. I stepped over to him, slipping an arm through his. "Ron. I have someone I want you to meet. This is Leon Wright. Johnny's cousin."

Ron looked at him curiously.

"Hey, man," Leon said, reaching out to shake Ron's hand. "I've been hanging out with your cool sister all weekend. She's told me a lot about you. Welcome home."

Ron smiled. "Thanks, man, happy to be here. I thought I'd never make it."

"Sounds like you guys have some catching up to do. Let me grab her address, and I'll let you two talk."

"No!" I said in a panic. As happy as I was to see my brother, I was not going to let Leon just *leave*. We had our "What's next" to discuss. Leon had said it himself; he didn't want Woodstock to be the end of us. Sha Na Na was stepping onstage. This was not the right time for Ron and me to "go somewhere to talk." I squeezed Leon's arm. "Can't we all listen to Jimi Hendrix together?"

"Cool with you, man?" Leon asked Ron.

"Way cool with me. I thought I'd missed him."

This new plan gave me solace, but I knew it would be short lived. We had only a couple of hours left.

"Hey, man," Ron said to Leon. "How about I borrow her for a short talk first?" When Ron smiled, I noticed three of his teeth were chipped.

"Sure, man," said Leon. "Take all the time you need."

Time? There was no time. I was aching to know the details about Ron's scars and how he'd gotten an early release from the army, and I needed to know what he meant when he said Nick was his name while in America. But not right now. I didn't want to leave Leon. Not even for a second.

But I didn't have the heart to tell my brother he had to wait.

"Let's find our seats first," I said, sounding a bit desperate. "It's easy to get lost around here."

"Good plan," said Ron.

As the five of us stepped through the war zone of trash, left behind by a half million people, Livy sidled up next to me. Her voice was low, so no one else could hear. "I'm sorry I've acted weird. Does everything make sense now?" She raised her eyebrows with a smile, like she was proud of herself.

But my fury had reached a new high. "No. Absolutely not."

Her shoulders curled as she sighed in frustration. "I've been dying to tell you, but Ron begged me not to. When he didn't show up on Friday, I became frantic. Not for myself. For *you*. I knew how happy you'd be to see him, and I didn't know how to handle it if he never showed up. It was all on me."

There was sincerity in Livy's voice. It genuinely seemed as if her concern was for me instead of herself. It still didn't excuse her lie about being the one in the bed with Ron. Or prancing naked around Leon when she knew I loved him. That betrayal was a splinter I would never be able to remove.

"When Ron never showed up, I was so freaked out, man," Livy said. "The only way I knew how to handle it was to drop acid. I had to escape the pain. I was tormented, SuSu. Ron and I planned this whole trip so you two could reunite. He wanted to be the one to tell you why he's out of the army, and about his horrible wound." Livy's eyes swelled with tears. "You'll learn the whole story when you talk to him. I'm just happy I could help him."

Something told me to give Livy a hug, but I couldn't do it. All I could give her was a blank stare.

Meanwhile Leon's words echoed: *Forgiveness is for you, so you can have peace.*

Woodstock

Day Four

Monday, August 18, 1969
7:40 a.m.

Once we'd picked a good place for all of us to watch Hendrix, and I was positive I could find Leon again, Ron and I stole away to the back of the bowl, far enough from the music to talk without yelling.

We found two abandoned lawn chairs and turned them to face one another. It would have to be a short discussion, for now anyway. I missed Leon already.

As soon as we sat down, Ron twisted the tail of his T-shirt. He crossed and uncrossed his arms, like he was a bundle of nerves. His legs jiggled constantly.

"You're as nervous as a cat," I told him.

"I've got some heavy shit to tell you."

He looked down at his feet, instead of at me, so I reached over and pressed my hands into his knees to ease the jiggling. "It's okay, Ron. Just tell me."

He chewed on his bottom lip, pondering his words, for what seemed like a full minute.

I became impatient. Leon was waiting. "Just say it, Ron."

"Okay." He took a deep breath. "Remember when I took my R & R in Hawaii?"

"Of course I do. I wanted to go with Mama. I told you so in my letter. But you never wrote me back," I said, angrily.

Ron's head was down, but he raised his eyes, begging me for patience. "It wouldn't have worked for you to come to Hawaii."

"Why not?"

"I need you to try and understand what I'm about to tell you." He drew in another deep breath, blew it out slowly.

I could tell he needed me on his side, so I leaned toward him with our knees touching. My voice was suffused with tenderness. "I already know Livy was the one in bed with you. I figured it out when she was on her LSD trip. She's a pretty good actress. I'll give her that."

Ron never flinched when I mentioned Livy had taken LSD. "That's not what I need to tell you." He punched his fists against his thighs. "SuSu, I tried to be a soldier. I gave Vietnam over two years of my life."

"It's been three."

Ron's palm, inches from my face, told me to hush and let him finish. He rubbed his thumb across the long scar on his cheek. "I lived through artillery fire, bombs, land mines . . . you think this mud is bad?" He looked around. "You should see the waist-high sludge I trekked through in Vietnam. Snakes and leeches everywhere."

I flinched. "Ew."

"That's not the worst part. Not by far. I got my cheek blown off." He touched his face, then rolled up his pant leg. A scar snaked an uneven path from his thigh down to his calf. Pockmarks covered leathery flesh with no hair. "But the best friend I've ever had in my life got his fucking head blown off. Right in front of me."

"Freddy C?" I asked, with terror ringing through my voice. I leaned over, gently caressing his leg.

He nodded, squeezing his eyes shut like he was trying to flush it all away. "There's only so much of that a body can stand before they lose not only their mind but all sense of what's right and what's wrong."

I started to say something, but Ron raised his palm again. "Let me finish. Please." He gripped his head with both hands, zoning out for a bit.

"Ron. It's okay. I'm so sorry." I had to press his bouncing knee again to bring him back to the conversation.

"Rage develops for the enemy so intense you can't lay your head down without fantasizing about the worst way you can make the son of a bitch suffer." He finally looked me in the eye. "That's not me. You know that."

"Of course not." I reached over and pulled him into my chest.

"That's what war does," he said into my ear. "It's hard to talk about even now, but I need you to understand my decision."

I pulled away. "What decision?"

"To not go back."

"But you did go back."

He shook his head. "I never boarded the plane from Honolulu to 'Nam. I was given a fake Canadian passport with the name Nick McCarthy. Then I took a jet to Vancouver, where I met up with this dude who works with an organization that helps American soldiers blend into Canada."

My mouth dropped open. My bulging eyes met his. "You *deserted*?"

"It was either that or suicide. I couldn't do that to Mama. Or you."

"God, no," I said as a horrific thought crossed my mind. "Don't they shoot soldiers for that?"

"Not since World War II."

"Don't they send them to jail?"

"Not if the soldier goes to Canada. But honestly, I'd rather be in jail than Vietnam."

Like Joan Baez's husband. I didn't know what to say. Desertion was the last thing I had expected to hear. "So that's where you live now? Canada?"

He nodded. "Along with fifty or sixty thousand other American war resisters. I live in Montreal. About six hours from New York City."

This was difficult to hear. My head spun from one end of Yasgur's farm to the other before another hideous thought crossed my mind. "Does Dad know?"

Ron grimaced, gnawing on his bottom lip. "He knows I never reported back to 'Nam. Someone from the State Department called to tell him. But he doesn't know where I am now. There's nothing he or the US government can do about it. Canada harbors American deserters. Sweden offers amnesty, but that's too far away from you."

I released the breath I'd been holding. "No wonder Dad's been so hateful. He got progressively meaner after you left, but much worse after Mama got back from Hawaii." I pictured him breaking my records over his knee and considered the anger behind each crash, all the hateful things he had said to me.

"I'm so sorry, sis."

"It's not your fault."

"Yeah it is. I shamed him in front of his military comrades. Worst thing I could have done. It's not like I'm proud of it—truth is I feel like the scum of the earth most days. When I wake up every morning, the first voice I hear is his. 'Good morning, coward,'" he said, in Dad's voice, then peered at me with a deep longing. "Please don't hate me, SuSu."

Looking at my brother—with his hair hanging in front of his face, hiding his war wounds—aroused deep anger. Not at him. At Dad, the army, President Johnson, Robert McNamara, and President Nixon. Livy was right. Vietnam was a horrific, senseless war. I leaned over and pulled us together. "I'd never hate you. I understand why you left."

Ron laid his head on my shoulder. "I couldn't bear one more day of war." He lowered his voice. "I couldn't kill one more person."

A chill froze my body as his reality sunk in. I pulled away then touched his marred cheek. "Ron. Listen to me. You are not a coward. Cowards don't have scars like this."

"I feel like one most of the time. Giving up my country is the hardest thing I've ever done. I just didn't see another way out."

"Does that mean you can never come home?"

"Not unless the government changes its stance."

I let go of a frustrated sigh. "That makes me so sad."

"Makes me even sadder." He hung his head for a moment, staring at the ground. Then met my gaze. "I honestly don't know how or why I made it home alive. I feel guilty about that too."

We sat in silence awhile before I asked, "How did you get here? To the festival, I mean."

"Hitched a ride."

A chill raced up my spine. "Were you scared to cross the border?"

"No. Plenty of roads into New York without border patrol. I wanted to see you so bad." This time Ron leaned over to hold me. And he wouldn't let go.

After a minute passed, I pulled away to look him in the eye. "This is all Dad's fault."

Ron glanced away for a second, then met my gaze. "You know what? I honestly don't blame him."

My mouth fell open. "Are you serious?"

"Yeah. Three years away has given me a lot of time to think about him. And what it was like for us to be his kids. When Freddy's head got blown off, it got me wondering how many times Dad saw the same thing. He was a foot soldier once, before he moved up the ranks in World War II, then made it all the way to colonel in Korea. Can you imagine how war has affected him?"

"Leon said the same thing this morning. I'd never thought about it before."

"Neither had I till I got to 'Nam. Think about it: Dad grew up in a military household, then went to West Point when he was eighteen. The army is the only life he's ever known. He had to be a rigid SOB with the thousands of soldiers under his authority. He just didn't know how to pull it back when it came to his family."

I let his words marinate before answering. "Are you saying you're not mad at him anymore? I sure am."

"I'm saying I can't live my life estranged from our one and only father forever. I don't know what that looks like, but there has to be a peace treaty at some point."

"I called Mama yesterday. She told me Dad wants to apologize, and he's realized all kinds of things." I rolled my eyes.

"Good! Let him apologize. He's got a lot of it to do." Ron crossed his arms over his chest. "Our father is so full of pride; I'm surprised he would consider admitting he's wrong about anything."

"We'll see," I said, unconvinced it would ever happen.

A memory of Dad holding my hand at the zoo when I was little crossed my mind. I saw love in his eyes while he handed me pink cotton candy on a long stick. He had tenderness in his voice when he told me the cotton candy was twice the size of my head.

The remembrance of my younger years with Dad filled me with a surprising warmth. "Dad hasn't always been a monster." Tears stung my eyes. "Maybe he does this stuff because he truly believes he's saving us from burning in hell."

Ron leaned toward me. "Our chaplain back in 'Nam says that's bullshit. When I told him I was gonna defect, even if it meant I'd burn in hell, he said God wouldn't do that." He put his hands on my knees to meet my gaze. "He said God loves us unconditionally, no matter what we've done. And forgives us for all of it. All we have to do is believe."

"I wish your chaplain could talk to Dad."

Ron chuckled. "That ain't gonna happen." His broken-tooth smile killed me.

"Dad should have come to the festival," I said. "Maybe smoking a little weed would have set his soul free."

Guttural laughter spewed from Ron's throat. And mine. We held on to our stomachs. It was the first time we'd done it in ages.

After the laughter subsided, I remembered Leon's words about forgiveness. "Maybe someday I can forgive him. It's just gonna take me a while."

Ron caressed my freckled cheek with the back of his hand. "I know you can do it."

We gazed at one another a few seconds before I said, "Can I ask you a question?"

He nodded.

"How does *Livy* fit into this? I mean, I get she's your girlfriend and all, but she told me she was happy she could help you. What'd she mean by that?"

"She's the one who came up with the defection plan."

I gripped the arms of the chair and leaned back. "Figures."

"Hold on a minute. If it weren't for her, I wouldn't be alive. I . . . would've shot myself."

That was hard to hear.

Ron tugged on his beard. "I'm sorry I never told you about her. I, well, we didn't want you mad—"

"Mad?" I said, all riled up again. "You both knew I blamed myself. Livy deserves part of that blame, doesn't she? If it weren't for her, you would have picked me up from my music lesson, I wouldn't have written about it in my diary, and you wouldn't have gotten in trouble. Look what happened to you!" I leaned in again, touched his leg.

"Hey," he said tenderly. "I don't blame either one of you. War doesn't take long to humble a guy. *I* got myself to 'Nam."

"Why didn't you write me? Nine months is a long time to go without hearing from you. I imagined all kinds of terrible things."

"I didn't think writing you from Canada was a good idea. That may have been a bad decision; I don't know. I just did what I thought was best at the time."

I glanced longingly toward the stage. As much as I wanted to be sitting here with him, hearing more of the story, I was tangled up in blue from having to say goodbye to Leon.

"Livy's connected with protest organizations here in the US and in Canada. She had the whole thing set up when she met us in Hawaii."

"*Livy* was in Hawaii with you and Mama?" With a deadly eye roll, I slumped low in my chair. This new revelation about Livy pushed me over the edge.

"There was a reason for that. Honolulu is where couples go for R & R. Whether you're already married or you want to get married."

I bolted straight up. "Are you and Livy married?"

"No."

Sighing loudly, I placed a hand over my heart.

"But she posed as my fiancée. She went through the wife training program at the base on Waikiki Beach. Instead of taking me to the wedding chapel, she took me to the airport to catch a flight to Vancouver. She got me a fake passport. I couldn't have done it without her."

I thought back to Livy showing up at Kress out of the blue, then buying me the records for no reason, and not giving up when I told her I couldn't go to Woodstock. She kept her promise to Ron that she would let him be the one to tell me about his defection. She was a much better friend than I'd given her credit for.

"Everything finally makes sense," I said with a sigh. "Everything except Mama. Are you telling me she helped Livy?"

Ron nodded. "She's been in on it from the beginning. We've been corresponding through a secret PO box. I couldn't risk sending letters to the house."

"I found them the night I left. She hides them in our bathroom."

"We couldn't tell anyone. Not even you. That's why Livy and I came up with this festival plan. So I could tell you face-to-face."

A ghastly notion sent shivers down my spine. "Does Dad know Mama helped you?"

"God, no," Ron said, with a firm shake of his head. "And he never will. Our mother is not weak. She's as strong as steel. She risked everything for me."

My head reeled. All I could do was give him a painful stare.

"I told you I had some heavy shit to tell you."

"Heavy indeed," I said with a groan. I pictured our mother's sweet face. "I'm so proud of Mama. But she must be so worried about you up there."

"Not as worried as she was when I was in 'Nam."

"Are you lonely?"

"Not really. I've got friends. Been writing music with a cat from Memphis named Jesse Winchester. He fled the draft and moved up to Montreal a couple of years before I got there. Great musician."

I wanted to hear more, but the thought of leaving Leon was starting to consume me. With a firm grip on the handrails, I glanced at the bowl. "Leon and Johnny have to leave right after Hendrix."

With a growing smile, Ron said, "You like him, don't you?"

I stared at him like he was the biggest dumbass on planet earth.

"No, you don't. You love him."

I smiled.

"We'll finish this later." Ron stood up and cracked every one of his knuckles, a habit of his that used to drive me insane. "Where are you going after this?" he asked.

With a tilt of my head, I lifted my eyebrows. "*That* is a very good question."

Woodstock

Day Four

Monday, August 18, 1969
8:55 a.m.

"Please, there's been reports that due to wet mud underneath the towers, they are slowly moving downhill. The guy wires are getting a little tighter. Well, I am a little worried about my lamps on top of them—as well as you—and the people underneath. So if you'd be kind enough to come down, you'd save us a great insurance hassle. And perhaps broken bones. Please come down if you will." Chip sounded mighty patient this morning.

"Damn," said Ron, staring up at the jungle of monkeys on the towers. "I can't believe that dude's having to ask people to get down. You'd think it would be obvious."

A collective laugh sounded from our group.

"You don't know the half of it, man," Johnny said. "That's his four hundredth announcement. He's had a helluva time."

Chip made another plea. "Before we begin, and close, could we ask you once again to leave the towers. And then in the same breath, thank you for making all of this possible. It's been a long one, but it's been delightful."

"Four hundred and one," said Leon.

We all laughed.

Five minutes later, at nine o'clock Monday morning, exactly three years minus a day after missing the concert of a lifetime in Memphis, I got a second chance in Bethel. Woodstock's headliner strolled onto the stage with only a fraction of the audience left, but the cheering sounded like a full house.

Chip gave his final introduction. "Ladies and gentlemen, please welcome the Jimi Hendrix Experience."

With his white Fender Stratocaster guitar hanging from a colorful shoulder strap, the one and only Jimi Hendrix strolled onto the Woodstock stage wearing a white leather jacket with beaded fringe on the sleeves. He looked uncommonly cool, and oh so patriotic, in his faded blue-jean bell-bottoms and a red bandanna tied around his forehead.

After what must have been a long weekend for him, too, Jimi walked straight over to the microphone and spoke in this sexy, deep-throated voice. "I see that we meet again. Hmm. Yeah, well, well, well. Dig, dig, dig. I'd like to get something straight. We, uh, got tired of the Experience, and every once in a while, we're just blowing our minds too much, so we decided to change everything around. I call it 'Gypsy Sun and Rainbows' for short. 'Cause we're nothing but a band of gypsies."

A girl in the audience yelled, "Jimi! Are you high?"

"I am high, thank you. I am high, thank you, baby," he said.

Ron pointed to ten girls on the side of the stage. "Holy shit. Look at his groupies."

"They're not all with him," I said.

"You better believe they are," my brother answered, wiggling his eyebrows.

"Ew."

Leon, who'd been watching me, reached over and tugged my body into his, with a tantalizing grin.

"What?" I said. "That's gross."

He cracked a crooked smile, then looked right back at the groupies.

Jimi played six songs before I recognized the opening chords to "Foxy Lady." Visions of my closet sprang to mind. Instead of crying, I hollered out loud, "Look at me now, Dad!"

Ron gave me a high five with an ear-to-ear grin.

In the middle of the song, Leon and Johnny exchanged fist pumps, as if this was the moment they'd been waiting for their entire lives, especially when Jimi played the guitar with his teeth.

Unable to take his eyes off the superstar, all Ron could do was stand perfectly still, staring at the stage in disbelief. Jimi wielded his Stratocaster like he was riding a bucking bronco. It sounded like one hundred wild Chincoteague ponies locked inside a corral, squealing to get loose.

"I'll never be able to pick up a guitar again," Ron said. The blissful look on his face warmed me with a bliss of my own.

But it didn't last. Instead of seeing Jimi on stage, I saw a giant hourglass with only three grains of sand left. On top of the hourglass hung a banner with a message reading **It is coming to an end.** I tried blinking it away, but the image wouldn't leave.

Jimi played another song I didn't know before slipping into one that sounded vaguely familiar, not from the album Dad had destroyed but from somewhere else. It took a minute for the melody to resonate before I knew exactly what he was playing. In fact, I knew it by heart.

It was "The Star-Spangled Banner," but no words left Jimi's lips. Instead, they warbled through his guitar. It started out tame, but as soon as he got to "the rocket's red glare," the melody shifted into rage. Simulating the fury of battle with his fingertips, Jimi Hendrix unleashed the nightmarish sounds of the Vietnam War onto the audience.

My blood ran cold as he mimicked machine-gun fire, wailing emergency sirens, and sonic bombs bursting in air. *Stop it!* I wanted to scream. *Please stop it!* I was afraid it would remind Ron of his friend Freddy and send him into a full-on panic attack.

Glancing around, I saw other folks grabbing their heads, some even pulling their hair, as if they wanted to rip it out because the sounds were too excruciating to bear. Jimi replicated the turmoil that existed in the country right there on the ravaged war-torn pastures of Yasgur's dairy farm. I could hardly stand it. No one could. We could only look at each other with agonizing, painful stares.

Jimi's guitar personified the Vietnam soldier ripped apart and abandoned by his own country. *Ron.*

As our distorted national anthem came to an end, Jimi segued into "Taps," making the experience even eerier. When it was over, I overheard someone behind me saying Jimi had served in the US Army. While that shocked me, it also made me wonder: Was Jimi's version protest or patriotism?

The first chords of "Purple Haze" induced a loud roar from the audience. Each person left sang along with him, knowing every word. Even me. Thanks to Livy, I'd learned it from listening to Jimi's eight-track in the car. I was sure it would be his last song, but Jimi knew I didn't want him to stop. He played three more, plus an encore.

Then, after a simple "Thank you," Jimi Hendrix exited the stage.

11:10 a.m.

Once the ballistic cheering died down to a low-level murmur, Chip Monck appeared for the final time. His hollow, sluggish voice sounded every bit like he'd been up four days without sleep. "Ladies and gentlemen, thank you so very much. We've got one little last trip we'd like to lay on you if it's at all possible. There are a couple packages of garbage bags here. If on your way out you wouldn't mind taking one, filling it up, and leaving it where you fill it, that certainly would be appreciated. Anything you can do to give us a hand to leave this area somewhat the way we found it—I don't think it will ever be quite the same—but somewhat the way we found it, it certainly would be appreciated. It's been a delight seeing you. May we wish you anything that the person next to you wishes for you. Good wishes, good day, and a good life. Thank you."

The remaining Woodstock stragglers clapped for Chip, but their applause was silenced by the helicopter flying in to whisk Jimi away.

That was it.

The end.

Woodstock was over.

And our hourglass was empty.

Woodstock

Day Four

Monday, August 18, 1969
11:30 a.m.

The five of us stepped around mountains of trash, strolling behind thousands of others toward the exit. Good Woodstock Samaritans were attempting to pick up the trash, but our group didn't have time. By the looks of it, the cleanup would take a month.

With the taste of despair lodged inside my throat, I felt tears pricking my eyes. But I refused to cry. I'd cried enough.

My long face must have been hard to hide. Leon tried to inject some humor. "Wait on me, will ya?" he said, tugging on the sash of my halter top. "I'm going back to look for my sleeping bag."

It made me laugh. But only a little. Because I was unraveling. The uncertainty of our future had gnawed a hole in my soul. How could I say goodbye to the best thing that had ever happened to me? Only seventy-two hours prior, I'd had no idea of Leon's existence. Now he was pretty much the reason I had air in my lungs.

With the second hand ticking, we stepped back over the flattened fence onto Hurd Road, exactly the way we had come in on Friday. Arm in arm, Livy and Ron led the way. *Livy and Ron.* It was a lot to swallow.

Thirty minutes down the road, Livy stopped in her tracks. Her shoulders slumped forward. "My feet hurt, y'all," she said, in a whiny voice. "I'm so tired of walking."

I was barefoot, too, but no one heard me complaining.

"You always were a baby," Ron told her.

"That's not true. Woodstock has worn my ass out," she said. "It'll take me weeks to recover."

Ron pinched her worn-out ass, then poked out his bottom lip. "Poor baby. Want a piggyback ride?"

I wanted to vomit.

She leaped onto his back. The two of them proceeded on like that for a quarter of a mile until Ron finally gave up and put her down.

"I have a great idea!" she said as soon as her feet hit the pavement. "Let's hitch a ride back to our cars."

I shot her a discreet hairy eyeball. She still didn't get it. Why would I want to leave Leon a second sooner than I had to?

"Actually," she said, with a smile, "on second thought, I can make it."

The closer we got to town, the more Leon's words echoed over and over. *I don't know what the future looks like, but I don't want to be another face in your crowd.* I didn't know what my own future looked like, much less ours. Instead of discussing what that future might look like, our conversation turned coy, like it had on Friday.

What were we to say? *I'll write you every week. I promise to call you every Sunday.* I couldn't help wondering how long it would take for those vows to tarnish, like a forgotten piece of silver. Long-distance telephone calls cost a lot of money. Money neither of us had. I was twenty years old. Leon was twenty-one. Neither of us owned a car, and our colleges were a thousand miles apart.

Paper was cheap, though. So were stamps. At six cents a letter, we could afford to mail one every week. How long could that last? How soon would it be before Leon tired of the "long-distance thing" he'd talked about?

We'd been walking in silence for five minutes when he gripped my hand, like he never wanted to let it go. I had the sense he was having some of the same thoughts I'd been having and couldn't help wondering if the uncertainty was bothering him half as much as it was me.

Unlike Friday, the forty-five-minute return trip to White Lake seemed to pass in ten. As we strolled into town, many of the locals sat along the road in front of their houses with buckets full of juice and water, urging people to help themselves.

I glanced around at the cars that were still left and thought about how this tiny little town had been invaded by a half a million hippies whom the townsfolk had so desperately tried to keep out. Yet in the end, they had pitched in to help. They'd made thousands of sandwiches and sent canned items, fruit, and hard-boiled eggs out of their own pantries. Despite their inconvenience, they had been incredibly generous. And here they were in front of their homes, still nourishing the hippie freaks. A testament to the beautiful human spirit and the weekend itself.

My time at Woodstock had shifted my thinking about many things. No longer did I feel ashamed by the gaps in my rock-music education. I just knew I could never live without music again. It wasn't God's will for me to give up singing and dancing. He had given me the gifts in the first place. And I sure wasn't going to hell for them. Having been steeped from the cradle in Dad's dogma and his impossible expectations, I had accepted his truth as my own.

It definitely wasn't God's will for me to be put down and humiliated by my own father. I wasn't the worthless, trashy person he'd made me think of myself as. I was a kind, loving person who tried to find the best in people. Albeit, I had my issues, but I sure wasn't the only person who had made mistakes. Everyone had. Life could be harsh, but there was still plenty of joy to be found, especially while spending life with those we love.

The weekend had helped me to grasp that real beauty is not about how we look on the outside. It is found in who we are as human beings, the way we treat one another, the way we love one another, and our willingness to consider someone else's feelings before our own. Love, joy, peace, patience, kindness, goodness, faithfulness, gentleness, and self-control. When I was a little girl, Mama had helped me to memorize all the fruits available to me as a child of God. I couldn't throw him away just because of Dad's wounding.

The five of us grabbed juice and took a moment to quench our thirst. Livy plopped down on the grass and stretched out her legs, moaning loudly.

Ron looked at her with puppy dog eyes. I'd never seen those eyes. And frankly, I wasn't sure how much more of them I could witness.

"What do you say we make a game plan?" Ron said to the group, while tossing his empty juice bottle into a nearby trash can.

"Please call me a taxi," Livy whined.

Johnny whipped around to the lady handing out juice. "Any taxis around here, ma'am?"

"Closest taxi is New York City," she said.

Johnny tapped Livy on the head. "Can't say I didn't try."

"Thanks, man," she said, then looked at me with apologetic eyes.

Ours was a complicated relationship. We were vastly different people, but Livy had risked her life for my brother. She had reunited me with him, and for that I would be forever grateful. No wonder she had wanted me with her at the information booth.

I had fallen in love, thanks to Livy. How could I stay mad at her forever? I leaned over and whispered in her ear. "We've had our rough patches, but we're cool now, right?"

"So cool," she whispered back. "I'm happy you met Leon. Make sure you get on the pill, okay?"

I just shook my head.

Ron looked at Leon and Johnny. "Do you guys have time to grab a bite?"

"I wish we could," said Leon. "My mom needs her car. I was supposed to have it back last night."

"My folks are waiting on me too," said Johnny. "We're having a big family dinner before I leave in the morning."

Noon

With only a mile left in our journey, it felt like a boa constrictor had wrapped itself around my chest. And by the time we got to Highway 55, where Leon and Johnny would turn off toward their car, I thought I might be having one of those anxious episodes. Like the one I'd had in front of the Mid-South Coliseum three years earlier. I felt lightheaded. I could hardly breathe. Leon and I hadn't even exchanged phone numbers.

I dug inside my purse for paper, finding Ron's letters and my checkbook. Once I'd found a fountain pen, I pulled on Leon's arm and handed him one of the envelopes. "I need your address, please."

He took the pen from my grasp. Instead of writing on the envelope, he tattooed his name on the inside of my forearm, in large all-capital letters. Underneath he added his parents' address, phone number, and the name of his dorm at Penn State. "I don't know the number at my new dorm, but Mom will," he said, then let loose one of his man-giggles. I would so miss that man-giggle. Handing me back the pen, he held out his own arm. "Give me yours."

"I don't know where I'm going," I said with a slight tremor in my voice. I could feel tears threatening to fall.

"Just give me something. I'll find you."

Biting down on the inside of my cheek, I printed my name, home address, and phone number on the inside of his arm. I added the name of my dorm—the one I was supposed to live in should I end up going back to Union.

He plucked the pen from my grasp and encircled my name with a heart.

Eyeing that heart made the tears I'd been determined to block fall anyway.

"Hey," he said, clasping my cheek. "This isn't *goodbye*. It's *see ya soon*."

"How do you know?"

"I just know." Leon tapped his heart, not his head. "Can you trust me?"

I gave him a slow, but confident, nod.

He slipped the chain holding his silver-and-turquoise cross over his head, then slid it over my neck, pulling my hair out from underneath.

"You don't have to—"

"You can give it back next time we see each other," he said with a wink. Slipping his arms underneath mine, he lifted me off the ground, guiding my legs around his hips. I buried my nose inside his neck. To memorize his smell. And breathe him one last time.

We held on to each other until Johnny placed his hands on our shoulders. "I don't mean to be a killjoy, man, but we gotta split."

Feeling Leon's arms give way, I slid slowly down his body until I felt grass underneath my bare feet. As I pulled away, he reached out to tickle my stomach. "You look sweet in that halter top."

"I'll keep it forever."

Ron stepped between us. "Great to meet you," he said, shaking Leon's hand first, then Johnny's.

"Likewise," Leon told him. "Good luck in Canada, man."

"Thanks. I'm gonna need it," said Ron.

"See you there, man," said Johnny.

"You've got the address of my crash pad, right?" Ron asked him.

"Right on," Johnny answered. "Thanks for your help."

The hug Livy gave Johnny lasted much longer than the one she gave Leon. "You and Ron will be fast friends in Montreal," she told him. "I'm always here to help." She turned to Leon with a knitted brow. "Are you sure you're not a Leo?"

"Positive. Aquarius," he said.

As if on cue, Johnny sang, "'The Age of Aquarius.'"

"You are a helluva terrible singer," Leon told him.

"And you're any better?" said Johnny.

Livy pinched Leon's cheek. "FYI. Aquarius is an air sign. Intellectual, thoughtful, charismatic."

"That's me," said Leon, shifting his eyes my way. "Let me know where you land, Suzie Q. Promise?" He pushed his hair back from his forehead, then rubbed the back of his neck.

I didn't answer.

"Promise?" he asked again.

"Promise," I forced myself to say. Feeling utterly powerless, I longed to yell, *Don't leave. Don't take another step. Please run away with me.*

But there was no point. His life had to go on. My life had to go on.

He took two steps backward, then stopped.

I held up my hand, fluttering my fingers.

With eyes pinned on mine, he took ten more steps backward until Johnny turned him around forward. As the cousins strolled off down Highway 55 toward their car, my eyes never moved from the back of Leon's dishwater-blond waves, hoping against hope I'd be lucky enough to spot them again.

Someday.

They made it twenty yards down the road before Leon glanced over his shoulder. Once he knew I was still watching, he held his arms high in the air. Instead of peace signs, he used his fingers to form a heart.

By the time the cousins reached the crest of the hill, Leon's arms were still raised, his heart still in the air. But with each step he took down the other side, his heart grew smaller and smaller and smaller, until it slowly disappeared.

Livy looked at my tearstained face. "I thought you were smarter than that."

I whipped around with an annoyed stare. "What's that supposed to mean?"

"Are you really gonna let him walk away?"

"I didn't know there was an option."

"There's always an option, man," she said.

My mind spun as Livy's words seared into my heart.

"I know love when I see it." She glanced at Ron with that Livy smile.

"He has to get back to school," I said. "So he's not drafted. And Johnny has to get to Canada."

"So do I," said Ron. "Might as well get there together. You need more time to figure out what you wanna do next. Let Leon help you."

I peered at my brother with his long hair, his gnarly war wound, and his crystal-blue eyes. I did not want to live far away from him ever again. "How far is Montreal from here?" I asked.

"Five and a half hours. Not a bad bus ride unless the freeways lock up."

"It's even closer to Cambridge," said Livy, in her post-Woodstock ultrascratchy voice.

Ron's eyes shifted to the top of the hill. "We can catch them if we run."

With bullets firing inside my chest, daring me to take a chance, I took two steps forward, then stopped. Three days of music, peace, and love had changed me into a different person. Part of me wondered if the high I felt was more about self-discovery than Leon.

"Don't overthink it," said Livy. "The Northeast is full of possibilities. Penn State. Coffee shops. Broadway. *Carnegie Hall.*" She gave me a gentle push. "What do you have to lose? If it doesn't work out, so what? You'll find someone else just as good."

Would I? Was three days even long enough to know? About Leon? About love?

I had to find out.

Without giving it more thought, I picked up my pace and jogged. Livy caught up and grabbed my hand. Ron took the other. "Leon! Wait!" I yelled.

Shrieking and laughing, the three of us raced up the hill.

Barefoot and braless, footloose and unfettered, I felt my soul breaking free. With the wind in my hair and the sun on my face, I lifted my chin and blew a kiss to the sky.

Fifty Years Later

Woodstock 50th Anniversary Celebration

Bethel, New York

Sunday Evening, August 18, 2019

"You look so cute, Grammy." Adelaide's eyes travel from my head to my toes. "I have the coolest grandmother, like, ever."

We look like twins in our bell-bottoms and tie-dyed tops. Actually, mine is a tie-dyed silk tunic, to cover my rear end, but hers is a tiny little halter top accentuating her tiny little waist. It reveals far too much, in my opinion anyway, but what can I say? I wore the same top right here in this very spot. Fifty years ago, to the day.

"Smile!" Adelaide snaps our selfie. "I'm adding this to my story right now. And yours." Her thumbs fly across the keys of her smartphone.

Adelaide loves posting pictures of us on Instagram. I put her in charge of my account since I haven't the foggiest idea how to make a post on my own. Learning how is on the top of my to-do list.

"Are you nervous?" she asks.

"Maybe a little."

A twinkle of mischief shines in her eyes. "Sounds like you could use some green acid."

"As I recall, the brown was much more potent." I add a little shimmy to my shoulders.

She looks up from her phone. "They say if you remember Woodstock, you weren't really there."

"I can assure you, my darling, I was most definitely there."

Adelaide giggles in a schoolgirl way. Despite her youth, she considers herself the picture of sophistication. My pride swelled to the size of a fat watermelon the day I opened her text with a picture of her holding her NYU acceptance letter. Their premier music program is reserved for the most talented of singers.

"Just teasing," she says. "I think acid is dumb. I'd never be that stupid."

Like grandmother, like granddaughter. "Music to my ears, my love."

I love her confidence. Her parents have raised her to believe in herself, stand up for her truth, and speak her own mind. That mind, however, is the reason she's been allowed to drill a hole in her belly button so she can flaunt two jeweled studs. That mind has paved the way for the tiny gold ring that fills the hole she drilled into the side of her darling little nose. She claims it lessens her period cramps. I know a lie when I hear one.

That butterfly shoulder tattoo she boasts whenever she has the chance was supposedly done in my honor. *At least it's not her zodiac sign,* I've thought time and time again. After these four days, I've decided to get out of the way and trust Adelaide to make her own choices, in the same way I let her father make his. She is smart as heck and has a good head on her shoulders. After all, it's her journey, not mine. She'll have to carve her own musical path in the world. Just as I have carved mine. Despite the obstacles.

It took several years, but with the help of my brother, I forgave my father. Despite his deep psychological war wounds, Ron humbled himself, carving a path to reconciliation between him and Dad, and that led the way to my forgiveness. I credit Ron for helping Dad to release his legalistic theology that had hurt and confused us all. Dad decided to embrace the miracle of God's grace and unconditional love. It saved not only our relationship but also my parents' marriage. Mama would have never left him, not physically, but at least her final years were joyful.

She never confessed to Dad what she had done for Ron while he was in Vietnam, God rest her brave, beautiful soul. And none of us ever shared their secret.

Sadly, our family folk-rock group, Ron and Suzannah, never materialized. Ron wasn't able to move back to America, something that caused him, and my parents, deep regret. Although President Ford instituted a conditional amnesty program for all draft evaders and deserters in 1974, Ron had already fallen in love with a darling Canadian girl, a musician whom he treasured. They have raised a beautiful family together, all of them singers, and have their own folk-rock quartet. Livy was never the ultimate girl for him, but they remain friends to this day.

"The music this weekend has been dope," Adelaide says, scrolling through her phone. "Especially Ringo and Santana. I've already gotten three thousand likes on the pictures I posted from the museum party. So outta sight."

I grin when she says *outta sight*. She loves the sixties lingo.

~

While we were at the museum party, she'd been sure she saw me in every photo. "Is that you?" she must have asked thirty times. "Grammy, look, this girl has your hair. I think it's you." When she spotted a blowup of a gorgeous blonde wearing a floppy hat, with multiple love beads around her neck and wrists, she said, "Look! It's Livy."

"No," I said, pointing to a picture of one of the nudists dipping in the lake. "This is Livy."

"For *real*?"

"Just kidding," I said with a wink. "Livy would never do something like that." I'd left out most of the details about our visit to the lake.

"Grammy." Adelaide peered at me over her eyelids. "She was a Playboy model. Of course she would swim naked in the lake."

"How did you know she was a Playboy model?" Despite her intellect, and even though she had posed one time only, for a college spread, Livy's common sense has often come into question.

"Daddy told me." Adelaide clicked off her screen and slid her phone inside her back pocket.

"How does he know?"

She lifted her shoulders so high she nearly touched her ears.

"Well, some big shot movie director talked her into it. He told her if she posed for one photo, he'd get her a major movie role. You see where that landed her."

"On *The Love Boat*."

I held up a finger. "One episode."

"It's still cool."

I nodded. "Very cool. Thank God she quit all that and went to law school. She's a darn good entertainment attorney."

I wouldn't call Livy my best friend, not in the way my husband and I are best friends, but we certainly love each other. She and both her daughters live not far from us in California. Her husband left her for a younger woman ten years back. I told her a long time ago she shouldn't trust him.

Adelaide rubbed her hands together. "Did you take off your clothes? You can tell me the truth. I'm a grown-ass woman now."

Indeed. Almost the age I became a grown-ass woman, right here in this pasture.

I simply gave her an elusive shrug. *Adelaide, darling,* I mused, *I won't answer that. I took off my clothes in a butterfly meadow with a lovely man I'd only known forty-six hours. That, however, is something I will keep to myself.*

Granddaughters don't need to know everything.

~

Each second of my time at Woodstock is still very much alive. The ecstasy of hearing Crosby, Stills, Nash & Young live. The thrill of happening upon a monarch migration. The constant butterflies I had while falling in love with a boy who seemed to want me as much as I wanted him. Silly. It's been so long. Yet the festival is every bit as vivid as it was fifty years ago.

Someone dressed in a flannel shirt with red, white, and blue fringe dangling from the sleeves walks past my dressing room before backing up. He pokes his head around the doorframe. "Suzannah Withers!" he exclaims, as if he's the luckiest man alive. "I was hoping I'd get to see you."

My smile opens wide. "John! How are you?"

"Super! Now that I'm with you."

Waving away his compliment, I say, "Have you met my granddaughter, Adelaide?"

"I have not." John steps inside the doorway, places an arm behind his back, and gives her a bow. "John Fogerty. Glad to know you, young lady. Your granny is something special."

Adelaide's eyes practically pop out of her skull. She can hardly speak. "So nice to meet you, Mr. Fogerty. Would you mind if we take a selfie?"

"Not one bit." John moves in between us and stretches his arms across our shoulders.

When she snaps the picture, I glow, remembering Saturday night of Woodstock, when I'd first heard John play. That night is still very much alive in my memory.

"Have you guys heard?" John asks. "We've got a full house. Fifteen thousand folks here tonight."

"A drop in the bucket from the last time you played here," I say with a wink. "You put a spell on me that night, John Fogerty."

"You were here?"

"All four days. I got this top at the Bindy Bazaar." I pinch the fabric circling Adelaide's pretty little neck.

John smiles. "Wish I'd known you were here."

"Oh, you," I say, tousling his hair.

"I still kick myself for not waiting around for Hendrix."

"He was something else," I say.

"I was born in the wrong era," Adelaide exclaims, with a cute stomp of her foot. "I would have stayed till the end. I'd have helped with the cleanup and been one of those guys forming the peace symbol out of the trash." She'd been fascinated by that photograph in the museum.

A man pokes his head inside my dressing room. "Miss Withers. You're up."

John steps aside, leans over to kiss my cheek. "Great seeing you, baby. See you after the show?"

"You better! Great seeing you too, John."

When I moved to California, back in the latter part of 1970, John was a frequent visitor around Laurel Canyon. It's still hard to believe I had the privilege of living around and learning from some of the best musicians who ever lived and that I'm lucky enough to call the incomparable Joni Mitchell my friend.

Leon was the one who encouraged me to go. After receiving a student loan and a small scholarship, I tried college again for another year—a state school in New York close enough to him and Ron for frequent visits—but my soul never stopped panting for the chance to sing professionally. My Hog Farm debut had reawakened my dream.

I have plenty of regrets—not finishing college is one of them—but overall, my life has been pretty darn euphoric. Fame is *not* the reason; plenty of demons there. It's my family that has made my heart full.

The sound of our heels clicking against the concrete floor echoes off the walls as Adelaide and I make our way down the long hall. She slips her hand inside mine. *She's so proud of me,* I think as the two of us follow the stage manager.

He holds open the stage door while Adelaide and I move into the darkness. "Watch your step," he says, shining his penlight on the floor to guide our path. We weave through road cases and monitors, stepping over fat cables snaked across the floor. As soon as we reach the left wing of the stage, Adelaide tucks inside. She knows right where to stand.

"Break a leg, Grammy," she whispers as I follow the penlight toward the front.

My band members are already at their instruments. I wave to them before picking up my guitar. Two spotlights cast a blue haze on the lip of the stage. As soon as I step inside the beam, I hear the roar of the audience. Chills race across my flesh. After all these years the applause still takes me by surprise, as does the voice of the announcer. "Ladies and gentlemen, please join me in welcoming Miss. Suzannah. Withers."

I'm sorry Chip Monck couldn't be here. From what I understand, he lives in Australia now and couldn't make it. Stepping up to the microphone, I gaze into the audience. "Hello, Woodstock! Man, I am happy to be here!"

A guy in the audience shouts, "We're happy too, Suzannah!"

I give him a wave. "Thank you! Most of you probably don't know, but I played my first gig right here at Yasgur's dairy farm on the Hog Farm's free stage. It was the first time I'd ever sung in front of a live audience, and I almost wet my pants."

Loud whistles and cheers follow.

"But I gotta say. I wouldn't be here tonight if it weren't for the love and encouragement I received from a man I met right here, fifty years ago." I smile to myself at the remembrance of Leon, our Woodstock weekend, and the blissful year we spent together before I left for California. The cross he gave me dangles from my neck.

"This first song I'm gonna play tonight is very special to me. I got the inspiration for it right here, at this magical place we know as Woodstock. It's called 'If Not for You.'"

The audience goes berserk. Their cheers echo inside of me while I think back to the day I received my record deal. Six long years after I wrote the song in the fall of 1969, it climbed to number six on the Billboard chart. I look back at Bernie, my electric guitar player. Once he gives me the nod, I glance down at my white acoustic Martin guitar and pluck the tender opening.

So much time spent looking for myself
Trying to find out who I am
All that led me here to you
In this moment where we stand
Until now—I've been searching for my truth
Could it be—I have found it here in you?

chorus
With so many still longing for
The wonder of it all
In your eyes I found living proof
In this world so incomplete
And at times—so much to lose
I would have had my doubts
I would have given up
But for you
If not for you

Who would have thought, who could imagine
The time it would not take
To find my miracle, in the shape of you
Just in time, just for my sake
Until now—I've been searching for my truth
Can it be—I have found myself in you?

chorus
With so many still longing for
The wonder of it all
In your eyes I found living proof
When a heart is so broken

Seems there's nothing you can do
But fall apart, lose your way
I should have given up; I would have lost my faith
But for you
If not for you
If not for you, baby
Oh, if not for you

After strumming the last resounding major chord, I peer out into the audience. From one end of the amphitheater to the other, the crowd has risen to their feet. I feel the same sublime joy I felt after singing Beatles songs on the Hog Farm stage fifty years ago. Who would have thought I, Suzannah Jean Withers, would someday have a standing ovation from fifteen thousand people? Fifty years ago, that was little more than a far-fetched dream. But a beautiful boy encouraged me to try.

As happy as it makes me to see all the faces in my crowd, there is only one that matters. And he is in the front row, beaming up at me. His teeth may not be as white as they once were, his full head of dishwater-blond hair is practically gone, but to me he is every bit as beautiful as he was the day I banged his knee with Livy's car door. Every bit as tender, every bit as protective, and even more trustworthy than he was that fateful rainy weekend in 1969.

Some have called it *luck*. Others *fate*. We like to call it *divine intervention*.

After his graduation, Mr. Wright moved with me to California to earn his master of divinity degree and was ordained an Episcopal priest in 1974. He credits me with helping him to discover his true calling. I credit him for helping me to claim mine.

With a palm to my lips, I blow my husband a kiss.

"Woodstock"
by Joni Mitchell

I came upon a child of God
He was walking along the road
And I asked him where are you going
And this he told me
I'm going on down to Yasgur's farm
I'm going to join in a rock 'n' roll band
I'm going to camp out on the land
I'm going to try an' get my soul free

We are stardust
We are golden
And we've got to get ourselves
Back to the garden

Then can I walk beside you
I have come here to lose the smog
And I feel to be a cog in something turning
Well maybe it's the time of year
Or maybe it's the time of man
I don't know who I am
But you know life is for learning

We are stardust
We are golden
And we've got to get ourselves
Back to the garden

By the time we got to Woodstock
We were half a million strong
And everywhere there was song and celebration
And I dreamed I saw the bombers
Riding shotgun in the sky
And they were turning into butterflies
Above our nation

We are stardust
We are golden
And we've got to get ourselves
Back to the garden

Author's Note

Dear reader,

My beloved literary agent, Holly Root, told me that many people wrote their passion projects during COVID-19, regardless of whether the book was in their genre. I was one of those people. With so much time on my hands, I had the perfect opportunity. Or so I thought. Much to my dismay—and frankly, my ignorance—it took much longer than I had expected. Writing historical fiction is not for the faint of heart! I have deep respect for the authors who have made their careers writing historical fiction. They all deserve medals.

In August 2019, while I was watching the TV coverage of the 50th Anniversary of Woodstock, the idea for *Kissing the Sky* bloomed. If I was going to write a book set at Woodstock, I wanted it to be accurate. But that would be a bigger challenge than I had thought. Not only did it require a ton of research, but in many cases, the "personal accounts" were unreliable. It was nearly impossible to figure out the running order of each band and exactly when each announcement took place. There's quite a bit of truth to the saying, "If you remember Woodstock, you weren't really there."

My research included interviews with attendees, musicians, and festival organizers. In addition, I listened to the original recordings, watched all the documentaries, and read everything I could get my hands on. The first person I talked to was Michael Lang, the creator of the festival. We had a lively conversation, and I feel fortunate to have spoken with him before he passed in 2022 at the age of seventy-seven. I also interviewed Michael's Woodstock production assistant, Joyce Mitchell, before she passed away in 2024 at almost ninety-three, my mother's age! She gave me invaluable information about some of the inner workings of the festival, and I found her to be quite a dear lady.

Chip Monck was incredibly generous with his time. He spent hours both on the phone and through email with me, even sharing his personal photographs of the weekend. I don't know about you, but I found his delivery hilarious, especially when speaking to those monkeys who refused to leave the scaffolds. He certainly kept his cool, considering the chaos he encountered that weekend! As for his and the rest of the announcements, each one is taken from the actual recording except for a few obvious fictitious ones. For the sake of the story, some may be a little out of order, but they are all verbatim, which leads me to another wonderful resource, Andy Zax.

Andy is the producer of *Woodstock—Back to the Garden: 50th Anniversary Experience*, an incredible photography book and compilation of every single recording at Woodstock, including the announcements. He was as generous as Chip, sharing crucial information. I wish I had found him sooner. Quite a bit of my early research came from Michael Lang's memoir, *The Road to Woodstock*, and, like most Woodstock accounts, had a few errors in terms of the timing of the performances and the announcements.

The original Woodstock audiotapes had been in storage for thirty-five years at the Atlantic Records facility in New York City but moved in 2005 to a Warner Music facility in North Hollywood. It was there that Andy encountered the tapes on a temporary "new arrivals" shelf. After seeing all the material and realizing that there was much more of it than he'd ever imagined, he was motivated to pursue the project. The head of A&R at Rhino Records was willing to back him, and Andy worked on it until its release in 2019, just in time for the 50th anniversary. Finally, any speculation about the timing of the bands or exactly what was said during each announcement was put to rest. As you have learned, the Woodstock announcements are as iconic as the bands themselves.

I also had the great joy of interviewing Melanie before she died in 2024 at the age of seventy-three. She, too, spent hours on the phone giving me an accurate account of her time on stage in the rain. If you haven't heard her song "Lay Down (Candles in the Rain)," you should download it right now. During her performance, the Woodstockers were encouraged to light candles to create a special atmosphere, thereby inspiring Melanie to later write about it. From what I understand, that night was the impetus for holding up lights at concerts, the tradition that continues today.

I exchanged emails with David Crosby and was planning to fly to California to interview him face-to-face when COVID-19 hit and the world shut down. Sadly, you know the rest of the story from 2023. RIP, David. Your genius will never die.

Another person I interviewed was Rona Elliot, who served as the public relations liaison between the festival organizers and the local community. She too gave me valuable information.

As a child of the sixties and seventies, I fell madly in love with folk and rock music. Even today, I'd rather listen to the music of that era than any other. Besides that, Woodstock had always fascinated me. Although I was too young to attend, I had often wondered what it would have been like to be one in a half a million at Yasgur's dairy farm. I saw the Woodstock movie with my college roommate in NYC in 1977. To say the least, it was quite the eye opener for this once sheltered Southern girl. I couldn't believe people would actually walk around naked, right out in the open, in front of God and everyone! Of course, back then, no one had ever seen a nude person on TV either. Oh, how times have changed.

Suzannah's story came to me while wondering what it would have been like to grow up in an ultraconservative home, fall in love with Paul McCartney—like millions of young girls—and be told you could no longer listen to the Beatles because of John's comment about Jesus.

I wasn't raised Southern Baptist—I was raised Methodist—but my grandmother and my father were.

It is not my intention to call out those who are Southern Baptist, or any denomination, for what they believe. I am a storyteller, and it is my job to imagine. It is my job to wonder and learn about all sorts of things, in this case the ultraconservative families who prohibited rock music during a critical time when rock and roll was a powerful source for social change.

I was eight years old when my mother took my sister and me to see the Beatles in Memphis, and that day started my lifelong love of their music. I'll never forget the high-pitched screams from the teenagers and not being able to hear a single note the lads sang. Nor will I forget the Klansmen outside the Mid-South Coliseum and how terrified I was at the sight of them.

Since the Vietnam War raged on during the time of the festival, I didn't see how I could write a novel set at Woodstock without including a Vietnam subplot. In no way am I condoning desertion. I am simply stating that it happened, quite a lot. According to the US Department of Defense, there were a total of 503,926 Vietnam War desertions between July 1, 1966, and December 31, 1973. This compares with an estimated 50,000 desertions during World War II and 13,790 during the Korean War. The Canadian government estimates somewhere between 100,000 and 120,000 Americans crossed the border between 1965 and 1975: 55,000 as deserters, the rest resisters.

On September 16, 1974, President Gerald Ford, a WWII veteran, issued a conditional amnesty to thousands of Vietnam-era draft evaders and military deserters who would agree to work for up to two years in public service jobs. He was quoted as saying he wanted the nation to move beyond the war, which had cost more than 58,000 Americans their lives and caused great division in our country. A subsequent pardon for draft evaders without requiring them to perform public service was issued by President Carter, but that did not include military deserters.

In today's dollars, the Vietnam War cost the United States an estimated $843.63 billion.

Although I was too young to know any young men who fought in Vietnam, I remember watching in horror the first televised draft lottery in 1969, as random birthdays were pulled out of blue capsules and pinned on a bulletin board. I remember watching the newscasts that broadcast the devastation on the front lines. My husband, whose draft number was 323, did not have to serve. The two of us watched all eighteen hours of Ken Burn's ten-part documentary on Vietnam. Considering the tragedies that Mr. Burns so aptly depicts, it is no surprise that there were so many desertions.

A note on lyric permission. That is quite a to-do! Song titles are not copyrightable, so that's why I simply mention several in the book. I was thrilled to receive permission to quote lyrics from Richie Havens's estate, Country Joe McDonald, Joni Mitchell, Crosby Stills and Nash, and The Hollies.

Since Suzannah becomes a famous singer, I thought she needed her own song. I approached two other famous singers, Michael McDonald, and his wife, Amy Holland McDonald, to help me cowrite and produce an original song for the book. I had worked with Michael as his right-hand person for many years, and he and Amy are dear friends. Once our schedules finally merged, "If Not for You" was written in under two hours, clearly a *divine intervention*. Amy's lead vocal is rich and beautiful, and Michael's background vocal is, as always, distinctive and sublime. Among the instruments you'll hear are Michael's piano and organ, and only he could talk his Doobie Brothers pals into rounding out the rest of the instrumentation. If you haven't already, please consider downloading "If Not for You" on any streaming platform you wish.

Woodstock, as "they" say, shaped a generation. It is my hope that no matter what generation you come from, you may have turned the last page and thought, *I've been to Woodstock.*

With all my heart and soul, I thank you for reading.

Peace & Love,
Lisa Patton

Acknowledgments

As I get older, the days seem to speed by faster than a comet. It's hard to believe I've been working on this book for six years, and it's finally time to thank those who have made *Kissing the Sky* a reality. My biggest fear is that I may leave someone out. If that someone happens to be you, please know it was unintentional. When I do remember, rest assured I'll be balled up in the fetal position.

There are three people that deserve the most gratitude. Putting their first names in alphabetical order seems the only fair way to determine who gets top billing. Since *h* comes before *n* and *n* comes before *s*, Holly, you're first.

It's hard to put into words what my brilliant literary agent means to me. Suffice to say my appreciation is bottomless. Without your belief in my work and the way you Root for me, I'd have never been published in the first place. Giving up is not part of your DNA. You are a warrior; I'm astounded by what you've accomplished in the world of literature since we first met. Landing on Team Root all those years ago now seems miraculous.

My extraordinary editor, Nancy Holmes, comes next. Another fierce warrior, Nancy fights for those she loves and believes in. I'm beyond fortunate to have landed within your visionary orbit. You're not only smart as heck, but you're fun and lively and your taste is sublime. I feel like the luckiest author on earth.

Last, but certainly not least, my wonderful husband, Stuart, rounds out the top three. He is the one in the trenches, watching me laugh, cry, retreat, and sometimes pout about whatever book I'm attempting. He's in the toughest seat of all, but somehow he manages to survive, all the while encouraging me to keep my butt in the chair. Thank you, honey, for believing in my dream, not to mention a business that confounds your innermost being. I love you and am beyond blessed you're mine.

To my superb cover designer, Jarrod Taylor, and art director, Amanda Kain. Can you hear me screaming all the way to Washington state? I love love love my cover. You nailed it! Thank you very much.

Faith Black Ross, you are a beautiful dev editor. You found things I missed completely. You made the book stronger and a much better read. On behalf of myself and all our readers, thank you.

Mindi Machart, Davy Kent, and Brenna Bailey-Davies, your eyes are sharper than a Ginsu knife. The little errors you catch are astonishing. Thank you for polishing my manuscript until it shined.

Jen Bentham and Angela Elson, without your production expertise we would have fallen apart. You were attentive and kind, enduring all my changes. I'm so very grateful for your patience.

Our cool map is designed by Mapping Specialists Limited. Thank you.

My publicists, Kathleen Carter and Rachael Clark from marketing, I'm so thankful you hopped on to help sell and promote this book. Lucky me! And to the Lake Union sales team, merci beaucoup.

Alyssa Maltese at Root Literary, your reaction to my book deal, even after all this time, keeps my heart smiling. Kat Miller at Root Literary, you are another person who deserves my sincere appreciation.

Adriana, Ariel, Kristy, Michael, Fannie & Patti, I am honored and humbled by your words of praise. Thank you from the bottom of my heart for taking time away from your own books to read and tout about mine. Your talent astounds me every time I read one of your NYT bestsellers.

Amy and Mike McDonald, there aren't enough words in the English language to thank you for lending your genius to our song and all the many production hours you've spent perfecting it. If not for you, the song would not exist. It's better than we ever dreamed it could be (Go get 'em, Sister!). Y'all are dear to me, and I'm beyond grateful.

Todd Doughty, thank you for every single solitary thing you did to help me. You are a rare friend and an extraordinary human.

Other extraordinary humans are my author friends who often halt their own workdays to encourage me, guide me, and talk me down off the writer's rugged cliff. You are, without question, the best part of this job. Laura Benedict, Paige Crutcher, Helen Ellis, J.T. Ellison, Fannie Flagg, Patti Callahan Henry, Traci Keel, Joy Jordan Lake, Ariel Lawhon, Laura Lane McNeil, Adriana Trigiani, Marybeth Whalen, and Karen White, I wouldn't want to do this without you.

Chip Monck, all I can say is wow! You jumped in, patiently guiding me through that zany weekend of all rock weekends. I love your humor from 1969, and I love it today. Thank you for sharing your photos and exclusive information. I am honored you trusted me.

Andy Zax, another wow! You are a treasure trove of information. Thank you for brilliantly bringing Woodstock, and all its glory, back to life and sharing your knowledge with me.

To Michael Lang for creating Woodstock and to all the artists who played, thanks for giving me something grand to write about. And to Joni Mitchell for writing a song about it and for all your other songs that dulled the needle on my record player. The same goes for CSN&Y.

Gina Gallo, thank you, Woodstock sister, for sharing your personal account of Three Days of Peace and Music. You'll never know how helpful you were. And how much I adore you.

Anne Marie Norton, thank you for believing in this story and giving me peeks into the '60s I was a little too young to understand. By tirelessly reading this book multiple times over, and listening to me groan, you helped me to not give up. You are a true, faithful friend.

My dear friends Penny Preston and LeAnn Phelan, you also listened to me groan more than anyone deserves to do so. Thank you for loving me through thick and thin. Cary Brown and Elise Crockett, after sixty-two years of friendship, having you with me to celebrate this book deal in Cayman still seems like an impossible dream. Your excitement meant everything to me. Vicki Olson, Debbie Cassetty, and Oyuki Barajas, your enthusiasm and encouragement kept me going. Thank you!

Jennifer Hart Williams, thank you for listening and listening and listening some more. You let me talk about this book ad nauseam and kept your gorgeous smile the whole time.

Thanks, Bernie Chiravalle, for not only my awesome website but for your musical expertise in teaching me about capos and Beatles chords.

Bennie McDuffee, thank you for introducing me to Elva Bertram, who shared her personal Woodstock experience with me. You were both so helpful. You were, too, Lorrie Losapio!

Much appreciation to my early readers who, thank God, didn't give up on me after reading one of my early sh$%#y drafts: Kristy Bee Barrett, Lise Bohannon, Elise Crockett, Todd Doughty, JT Ellison, Emily Kay, Blake Leyers, Amy McDonald, Dylan McDonald, Anne Marie Norton, Rae Ann Parker, Kathy Peabody, Jennifer Pooley and Penny Preston.

My Pilates friends: Chelsea, Cindy, DeDe, Heidi, Julie, Laurie, Laura, Megan, and Molly. Thank you for the laughs and most of all the kind support. You give me strength to carry on.

To all my readers and book clubs and independent bookstores who have supported me throughout my career, I'm grateful beyond words.

To my bonus kids and grandkids: Shannon, Sara B, Sloane, Whitney, Tommy, Andy, Emily, Taylor, Rylan, Levi, Ty, Annie, Quinn, Ella, Judah, Arie, Wendy, Boone & Lars. I love you all.

Michael and Will and Brennen and Henry, your faith in me means everything. I do this for you. Showing you the good that comes from working your butt off and never giving up is one of the legacies I hope to leave you, second only to desiring Godly character. I love you so much it hurts—*often*. ;-)

Above all names, I am most grateful to the Master Storyteller, Jesus—my Helper, my Counselor, my Prince of Peace. I could not have written a single word in this book without You.

Book Club Questions

1. Did you or any of your friends or family members grow up in a household that restricted access to music? If so, did you comply or rebel?
2. The music of the '60s has multigenerational reach. Which bands and/or songs from this time period do you, your parents or grandparents, and your children or grandchildren connect to most?
3. As the Cat Stevens song declares, "The First Cut Is the Deepest." Do you think of your first love in a positive or a negative way?
4. Suzannah's relationship with her domineering father resulted in her low self-esteem and her inability to trust. What other ways can family trauma manifest in a young woman or a young man?
5. Have you ever had a friendship with someone who was able to make you follow him or her no matter the consequence?
6. Have you ever been in a close friendship with someone so attractive and charismatic that it made you feel insecure or insignificant?
7. Were you surprised by Ron's defection? We don't often talk about soldiers who defect or resist, but the numbers tell a different story. Considering the horrors of war, and the way it can impact a soldier's mental health, how do you feel about it?

Do you agree with Ron that some people aren't meant to be soldiers? Do you think the government should ever reinstate the draft?

8. Have you ever been close to a man like Suzannah's father? How did he impact your life?
9. Was your mother strong or weak? Did she let your father make all the decisions, or was she the decision maker?
10. Do you think Suzannah was right to leave home?
11. Did you or someone you know grow up in a home where the threat of going to hell was preached on a regular basis?
12. The use of psychedelic drugs as a form of therapy to combat depression has gotten a lot of attention in the last few years. Is that something you would ever consider for yourself or a loved one?

About the Author

Photo © 2020 Rachel Chiaravalle Schulz

Lisa Patton, the bestselling author of five novels, is a Memphis, Tennessee, native who spent time as a Vermont innkeeper until three subzero winters sent her speeding back down to the South. She has over twenty-five years of experience working in theater, radio, TV, and music, including a decade with Doobie Brother Michael McDonald, who, along with his wife, Amy, helped Lisa cowrite and produce "If Not for You," an original song for *Kissing the Sky*. A graduate of the University of Alabama, Lisa is the proud mother of two sons, eight bonus children, and twelve grandchildren. She and her husband live in the rolling hills of Nashville with their four-legged furry son named Ziggy.

To find links to the original song "If Not for You," please visit Lisa's website at www.lisapatton.com or go to Amazon Music/Amy Holland "If Not for You." Connect with Lisa on Instagram, @lisapattonbooks, and on Facebook, Lisa Patton.author.